THE DOOR INTO
SOMEWHERE . . .

Miles the Magician rose and wrapped his cloak around himself as if the thin robes would protect him from the sailing wind and snow. A moment later, Jonathan watched him hunching out over the snow, bent over, his robes flailing and whipping about him. Snow flew, obscuring the wizard entirely for the space of a long minute. Then he was visible again, waving his right hand before the door as if expostulating the necessity of its opening up.

Slowly, the dark face of the door paled a bit and seemed to shimmer as if a slowly brightening light were being shined on it. Through the transparency that had been the iron door could be seen the blue of a summer sky and the green of vegetation. An amazed cow wandered by beyond the opening, looking back at the wizard with a face full of stupefaction.

"It's time," Twickenham called. "Hurry."

Also by James P. Blaylock
Published by Ballantine Books

THE ELFIN SHIP

THE DISAPPEARING DWARF

James P. Blaylock

A Del Rey Book

BALLANTINE BOOKS • NEW YORK

A Del Rey Book
Published by Ballantine Books

Library of Congress Catalog Card Number: 82-90496

ISBN 0-345-30376-8

Manufactured in the United States of America

First Edition: February 1983

Cover art by Darrell K. Sweet

To Viki

And to Johnny,
without whose wise counsel and splendid example
this book would have been impossible

Contents

And what conclusion dost thou draw, corporal Trim, cried my father, from all these premises?

I infer, an' please your worship, replied Trim, that the radical moisture is nothing in the world but ditch-water—and that the radical heat, of those who can go to the expense of it, is burnt brandy,—the radical heat and moisture of a private man, an' please your honour, is nothing but ditch-water—and a dram of geneva—and give us but enough of it, with a pipe of tobacco, to give us spirits, and drive away the vapours—we know not what it is to fear death.

Laurence Sterne
Tristram Shandy

Chapter 1

The Man of Leisure

It was late May, and the weather was warming up in Twombly Town. The great brass kaleidoscope had been wheeled out from under a shingled awning where, as usual, it had been stored all winter so that it wouldn't turn color and go to bits in the rain. It sat now amid a sea-green clump of moss that had sprouted late the previous year, covering the little bit of ground where Mr. Twickenham's airship had landed. No one could determine the reason for the sprouting of the strange moss, not even Professor Wurzle, but the stuff was covered with a thousand little flowers in a rainbow of pastel colors and was so altogether beautiful that it really didn't much matter where it had come from.

Mayor Bastable had hired an assistant town gardener to oversee the plot. But the weather was so unusually fine, and the sight of the flowers so peaceful and idyllic, that the fellow had fallen asleep in the middle of the moss for three days running, and the Mayor was forced to pay a lad to go out and roust him every half hour or so.

It turned out that the moss, which had come up on its own and would probably go on in much the same way, didn't need a gardener anyway; so Mayor Bastable created a department of agriculture, and the assistant gardener was put to work planting strawberries all up and down the avenues. He'd even planted a big patch behind Jonathan Bing's cheesehouse.

On the twenty-fourth of May, Jonathan was out poking around in the strawberry patch, trying to find enough ripe ones to smash up over ice cream. Jonathan's dog, old Ahab, was out there too, sniffing along the rows. He didn't care much about strawberries. In fact, it's reasonably certain that he liked his ice cream better without anything smashed over the top. There were certain bugs, though, out in the strawberries, that Ahab liked to chase about. So they were both busy there amid the little creeping vines, or at least were trying to be busy. Actually there weren't any more bugs out than there were strawberries, and wouldn't be, likely, for a couple of weeks yet.

Jonathan had done well that past December with his raisin cheeses. He'd made such a good profit selling the things to the dwarfs in Seaside that he was set for a number of months. In fact, the previous January he had considered that he could abandon cheesemaking altogether for nine months out of the year, then make up a big batch of raisin cheeses come fall, sell it downriver, and slide on through spring and summer again. It was an appealing thought—so appealing that he talked himself into giving it a go for a year. He hired a helper, old Beezle's grandson Talbot, who was given to tramping in the woods making fearful noises on a tuba. He did it, he said, to frighten away bears and goblins. Jonathan asked him if it wouldn't be just as simple not to tramp in the woods at all and so not have to bother with the tuba, but Talbot said quite simply that that "wasn't his way."

He had a tremendous aptitude for cheesing, however, and by the first of May was making any number of fine cheeses without any help at all. At that point Jonathan had become a man of leisure, something he had fancied for a long time.

Men of leisure were always appearing in the books of G. Smithers of Brompton Village, Jonathan's favorite author. Every one of them wore a white suit so as to alert casual passersby to his status as a man of leisure; and in G. Smithers' books, such passersby, if they had any decency or intelligence about them, were invariably impressed. So Jonathan bought a white suit and a whangee from Beezle's store and, after about a week, worked up enough courage to go abroad in it. He set out having convinced himself that he cut a moderately fine figure, but halfway to town he ran into his friend Dooly who, quite innocently, remarked that Jonathan, dressed in that suit, was the spitting image of a gibbon ape he'd seen once in a sideshow up in Monmouth. Jonathan decided against going into town. He returned home instead and asked Talbot whether he looked more like a man of leisure or a gibbon ape. Talbot, who had just come in out of the woods with his tuba, said that all things considered it was about a tossup.

The result of all this was that Jonathan had given up both the white suit and the idea of being a man of leisure. He gave the suit to Dooly later that week, and Dooly, having nothing against apes of any nature, wore it when he went off down south to meet old Theophile Escargot, his grandfather. According to Dooly, they were heading down to the tropics—where such a suit would be just the thing— to go off pirating in Escargot's undersea device.

Since then Jonathan had shingled his roof, built new screens for his windows, and fixed the bank of casements along the east side of his house that leaked when it rained. He was thinking of kicking his front door to bits in order to build a new one, but he wasn't desperate enough for that yet. He'd worked his way through half of G. Smithers, having long ago come to the conclusion that reading is perhaps the finest thing in the world to do in one's leisure time. But then it turned out that a man of leisure hadn't any *leisure* time; he just had suitcases full of the same sort of unidentifiable time, and reading for the sake of filling expanses of that sort of time wasn't as satisfying as it might be. So he had put down G. Smithers, called Ahab, and wandered out to the strawberry patch. He considered, after that first month of being a man of leisure, that he might do better to go back to being a full-time cheeser. A man has to have his work, after all—at least that's what the philosophers said. And he'd just about decided to pack up the whole business when Professor Artemis Wurzle, dressed in a striking sort of suspendered hiking garment, came clumping up the path from town in a determined way.

He seemed altogether too determined. It was easy to see that he wasn't just out after spring mushrooms or waterweeds and sticklebacks for his aquaria. Ahab went wagging along the path to meet him, suspecting that the Professor had some nature of treat—a dog biscuit or bit of cheese— in his shirt pocket. The Professor hauled out one of the square biscuits from Beezle's market that had the taste of rye about them and handed it to Ahab, who seemed pleased.

"Hello, Professor," Jonathan said.

"Hello, Jonathan," came the reply. "I've just been down to town. Talked to Beezle. He tells me you've become a man of leisure."

"Until about five minutes ago," Jonathan replied. "But I gave it up. It was too tiring. I couldn't quit and rest, as Dooly would say."

"How about the suit? Beezle says that you bought an amazing suit, and cut a fine figure in it too."

"I kept being mistaken for a gibbon ape," Jonathan said. "White suits don't do me much good, I'm afraid."

"They don't do anyone any good," the Professor explained. "Especially at night. They tend to attract the rays of the moon. Something like osmosis. Set a man mad eventually. I did a treatise on it back in my university days. No white-suited man can stay sane long—not if he goes out after dark."

"Then it's just as well I got rid of it," Jonathan said. "I would have become a mad gibbon ape. A frightening thought. I gave the thing to Dooly, though. He doesn't know anything about this moon madness business."

The Professor thought about that for a moment before coming to the conclusion that moon rays probably wouldn't bother Dooly much anyway. He started to explain something to Jonathan about the scientific principle of saturation points, but it was far too hot there in the sunlight for such lectures. Jonathan suggested they wander over to the house and saturate themselves with iced tea. Ahab bounded off in the wake of young Talbot, who was trudging away in the direction of the forest, carrying his tuba.

All in all, Jonathan's house was fairly cool. There was such a profusion of windows that breezes blew in from every which way. Oak and tulipwood and liquidambar trees grew on all sides and shaded the roof from the sun. The house and its three little out buildings—a smokehouse, cheesehouse, and shop—sat atop a little rise about a quarter mile from town. Mayor Bastable's house was two hundred yards east, and in between was a broad expanse of pasture. To the north, beyond the cheesehouse and smokehouse, was a little garden, partly fenced by a tangle of berry vines that piled up right to the edge of the forest. Beyond that, for as many miles as anyone cared about, were the deep woods, rising up out of the valley toward the misty, distant mountains. On a clear day Jonathan could sit in his living room and see the snow-capped peaks of those mountains miles and miles away.

"Quite a view you've got from here, Jonathan," the Professor commented. He was standing in front of the windows holding a glass of iced tea in his hand.

"It is that."

"Makes a man content." The Professor smiled. "That garden and your big front porch and the valley all spread out around you—it would be hard to leave."

"Impossible." Jonathan remembered the look of determination on the Professor's face and suspected that all of this home and hearth business was leading up to something.

"But as a man of leisure, doing nothing all day but gazing out the windows and standing about in the strawberry patch waiting for the green berries to turn, you run a terrible risk, Jonathan."

Jonathan nodded. "Just what I've been saying. All this free time takes the wind right out of your sails."

"Exactly. What you need is a vacation from it."

So that was it. That explained the Professor's look of determination. He wanted to go off traveling and he aimed to talk Jonathan into going along. "But I just got home," Jonathan stated flatly.

"We've been back six months," the Professor said, "and you've got an air of boredom about you. It hovers around you like a little cloud. They say that once you've tasted the highroad you never lose your craving for it. It's like root beer or brandy or green olives. Traveling is in your blood."

"I'm not sure they are correct," Jonathan answered. "And besides, I've my cheeses to see to."

"Talbot can see to your cheeses."

"Then there's my garden," Jonathan said weakly. "It'll go up in weeds."

"Give it to the Mayor," the Professor suggested. "How many of those zucchinis do you think you can eat anyway? There's not a man alive who can eat zucchini for three days running with a straight face. And I seem to recall, Jonathan, your having said something about going off this spring to visit the Squire. What happened to that idea?"

"I don't know." Jonathan swallowed a last gulp of iced tea. He looked at the little patch of sugar at the bottom of the glass. It *would* actually be fun to see the Squire again, not to mention Bufo and Gump and Stick-a-bush. And it would be nice to travel on holiday rather than on business. "Why doesn't this sugar dissolve like it's supposed to?" he asked the Professor. "You can stir for an hour and there's still sugar on the bottom of the glass."

"It's a matter of chemistry," the Professor replied knowingly. "Very complex affair."

"Is that it?" Jonathan seemed satisfied. "When do you want to leave on this venture?"

"That's the spirit!" Professor Wurzle shouted, pouring himself more tea out of a green glass pitcher. "We leave tomorrow. At sunrise."

"Impossible. I'll need a week," Jonathan replied.

"What for?"

"I've got to square the lad away about the cheeses."

"I had one of his cheeses last week. He doesn't need any squaring away," the Professor stated emphatically. "Just tell him to keep at it while you're gone. You trust him, don't you?"

"Of course," Jonathan said. "He'll do well."

"Then we leave tomorrow."

"I need time to lock up, to stow things away."

The Professor pulled out his pocketwatch, gave it a look, strode over and shut one of the casements, then slid the flip-lock into place. He looked at the pocketwatch again. "Seven seconds," he said. "Multiply that by eight, add ten seconds for the door, and this room's locked up tight. A blind man doesn't need more than five minutes to lock up a house."

Jonathan could see that his rationalizations were crumbling in the face of reason. "How about supplies, Professor?"

"They're loaded. What do you think I've been doing all morning, chatting with Beezle about white suits?"

"Loaded where?" Jonathan asked, convinced, finally, that fate had raised its peculiar head once again.

"Why onto your raft, of course. I took the liberty of picking the lock on the hold. We're ready to push off. In fact, we could leave tonight. There's a full moon. We could sail by moonlight and troll for river squid." ´

"Tomorrow," Jonathan said, "will be soon enough."

The sound of an approaching tuba echoed out of the forest, and away up the path beyond the berry vines Talbot and Ahab could be seen tramping in out of the woods, pursued neither by bears nor goblins. The Professor jumped up and pushed open the screen door. "I'll just inform the lad of our plans, Jonathan. I have all the dates and such written down. Don't worry."

Jonathan sat over another glass of iced tea, looking out the window. G. Smithers lay half finished on the table beside his chair. Just an hour earlier Jonathan had been convinced that he couldn't read another word. Now it seemed to him as if there were nothing in the world he would rather do. And it struck him that he'd be on the Oriel or somewhere off along the river road when the strawberries finally ripened. Talbot and Mayor Bastable would get the lot of them.

But then it was true that he could always take G. Smithers along with him, since he'd have hours of good, lazy reading time ahead of him on the river. It was true too, that if it was strawberries he wanted, the Squire would be just the man to see. In fact, Squire Myrkle probably ate them by the bushel-basket-full, being as large as he was. Furthermore, when he finally returned home from his trip, he'd feel pretty much as he had when he got home from the last —doubly glad to see his little house and his wheels of suspended cheese and all the rest of the things that the Professor had pointed out as making a man content. There was nothing like returning home from travels to make a man content—and, of course, you couldn't return until you'd gone. So there Jonathan was at last—going again. He walked into his bedroom to pack his bag.

Chapter 2

Toads in the Meadow

THERE wasn't any fanfare that next morning on the dock as there had been months before. Jonathan wasn't setting out as any sort of hero, only as a man off on holiday—travel for the sport of it. Most of the people of Twombly Town, in fact, probably thought the idea fairly foolish. It was a rare villager who traveled beyond the City of the Five Monoliths, where the fair was held at the end of each summer, and none of them would consider going even that far if the fair weren't there to attract them.

Jonathan, however, had, as the Professor put it, gotten some of the highroad into his blood. It seemed to him, although he might have been mistaken, that travel lent a sort of romantic air to a person—gave one a set of what Theophile Escargot would call *bona fides*. He could imagine himself barefoot, wearing an old cocked hat, and sitting about on the end of a wharf in the Pirate Isles, drinking rum and talking in a worldly and salty way to a one-eyed man with a parrot on his shoulder. He could see himself blowing through Twombly Town with just the right sort of sunburned wrinkles under his eyes and a pocket full of strange gold coins pillaged from the kings of Oceania.

Part of him, however, suspected that if one were to be a gentleman adventurer or a man of the world he'd best be born to it—that it was some sort of natural talent. If he were to *assume* such a role he'd probably develop a mysterious and unfortunate likeness to a gibbon ape. In truth, his adventures of the past fall hadn't made him feel any different at all; he still woke up in the morning good old Jonathan Bing, the Cheeser. But then, all things considered, he wasn't altogether dissatisfied with such a fate.

He envied the Professor in a mild way, though, bustling around there on the docks that quiet morning, the sun creeping up over the hills to the east. The Professor didn't care a bit for adventures or for becoming anything at all. He was content to be off searching for a peculiar species of river clam or calculating the changes of color in the rainbow ice floes in the Mountains of the Moon. Science was enough for the Professor. More than enough in fact. He never ran out of wonders to investigate.

The new day was already warm. A breeze was blowing down the valley and it felt how Jonathan imagined a trade wind should feel. It had the smell of summer blossoms on it and the musty, weedy smell of the river. There was just enough breeze to blow his hair up out of his eyes and to rustle the leaves on the oaks. The wind would be at their backs on the way downriver—an advantage, certainly, if they were concerned with time. But then that was just about the last thing Jonathan was concerned with, so he determined not to hoist the sail anyway. He and Ahab picked their way along the path that ran through the meadow past the Widow's windmill. It was rough going because through some marvel of nature about a billion little toads had hatched out in the night and were making off across the meadow to determine the lay of the land. Jonathan and Ahab had to look sharp to avoid stepping on any. He paused to scatter a handful over Ahab's back in order to give the critters a lift down to the river. Also he wanted to see the Professor's face at the sight of the toad-laden dog; his mind would be a furor of theses and speculations.

The river wound away around a distant bend, its glassy surface broken only by an occasional little eddy or the swirl of a fish. The shore grasses were jeweled with dew that gleamed in the new sun. It was the sort of day that made Jonathan determined to get up with the sun henceforth, just for the sake of the morning. Such ideas, of course, would evaporate as quickly as the dew on the grass, and the idea of sleeping until noon would be every bit as appealing to him by late evening as the idea of rising early was to him there on the meadow.

He poked along after Ahab and finally clomped out onto the wharf. Just for the fun of it, he checked the trout lines that Talbot had tied along one of the wide joists that supported the dock. It was Talbot's habit to check the lines each morning about seven before settling in to make cheese. There were, invariably, no trout on the lines. Talbot had begun by using lumps of old cheese as bait—not a bad idea at all—but the cheese had fallen so quickly to bits that the hooks went unbaited for about twenty-three hours out of every twenty-four. He had determined, finally, that yellow lumps of rubber would work as well as cheese and found that the rubber could be depended upon to stay on the job and not wander off. The result, however, was pretty much the same. The Professor said that it was likely, at least from the scientific angle, that lumps of yellow rubber affected fish in pretty much the same way that tubas affected bears and goblins, and that Talbot would do well to study the situation a bit more before putting too much faith in rubber cheese.

There were about a half dozen trout, actually, nosing about in the water. They seemed to be gathered around one of the floating rubber cheeses, looking at it as if mystified. As Jonathan watched, one of the trout swam off into the shadows and then came back with two of his friends who, along with the rest of the trout, hovered about, eyeballing the false cheese. The Professor walked over to see what it was that so captivated Jonathan.

"These trout seem to be studying Talbot's rubber cheese," Jonathan said. "I wonder if their concern is scientific or philosophic."

"Almost certainly philosophic," the Professor replied. "They're coming to conclusions about the nature of such a beast as would dangle lumps of rubber beneath a dock."

"They can only conclude, then," Jonathan said, "that we're a race of lunatics. They'll score our significance in terms of dangling rubber cheese. Perhaps we should drop a book down on a string, or dangle some symbol of technology like a compass or a marble or a bar of soap."

"That would just make matters worse. They'd wonder why

we worked up such marvels, then dumped them into the water."

About then, from the green depths of the river, a school of long, rubbery river squid came undulating along, scattering the trout in a half dozen directions. They had great round protruding eyes and a dozen tentacles that trailed along behind. They paused momentarily near the surface, took a look about, then disappeared into the depths, leaving Talbot's rubber cheese dangling forlornly there in the current.

"There must be a whole world of stuff going on down there that we don't know anything about," Jonathan observed. "It would be strange to live in that sort of green and shifting light. Too many shadows for my taste."

"I'm not sure I agree." The Professor walked back across to the raft. "I'm at work on a set of plans for a device much like Escargot's. A subsurface boat. Imagine what you'd see."

The two of them idled along for another half hour, then cast off and angled out into mid-river. Two men in slouch hats, smoking pipes and trailing fishing lines, spun past in a canoe. They disappeared around a distant swerve of the shore. Jonathan watched Twombly Town grow smaller, and he saw, finally, before he too rounded that bend, young Talbot, tuba and all, coming along down the path toward the wharves in order to check his lines. Talbot waved at them from afar, and as the raft swirled away out of sight of the village, one echoing mournful note from the mouth of Talbot's tuba reached them, a sad and distant farewell.

Jonathan was immediately homesick in the warm silence of the morning, not as cheerful and full of expectations as he had hoped to be. The Professor broke the silence by banging the coffee pot about and by clattering together pots of butter and jam. When he cut into a loaf of fresh bread, the smell of coffee and bread seemed to Jonathan to be the smell of life itself. Never one to fly in the face of anything as significant as life, he ripped into a big hunk of bread smeared over with apple butter. Then he tossed back a cup of coffee, the combination of coffee and bread effectively scattering the morose mood he seemed to have slipped into. He decided, in fact, to throw out a line of his own and catch a couple of those trout who had been making mock of Talbot's rubber cheese. By the end of breakfast, Twombly Town might as well have been about a thousand miles behind them, and it seemed to Jonathan as if the future held great undefinable promise.

Along the banks of the river, everything was green and moving. Beavers and water rats brushed through the willows and splashed in the shallows past egrets and herons that stalked along on spindle legs with an eye toward fish. Some miles below town they passed the first of the great stands of oak that ran together finally into deep forests. It seemed to Jonathan that the oaks were at once beautiful and ominous and that they held ageless mythical secrets. He had been told as a boy that on Halloween evening oak trees ran blood rather than sap, and that once every hundred years on that same night incredibly old trees in the depths of the woods performed ancient circle dances before an audience of goblins. It didn't surprise him a bit, in fact, that both elves and goblins lived in the midst of oak woods.

The same trees that had been skeletal and foreboding the previous autumn were clothed now in green, and their great limbs hung out low over the river, shading the still water along the shores. Jonathan lay on his back, barefoot on the deck, watching the intermittent blue sky and green tangle of leaves overhead. He was relatively happy to dawdle along so and smoke his pipe, and he hoped that the trout would ignore his bait for a bit longer. He was struck by the strange thought that it was too bad he hadn't baited his hook with Talbot's rubber cheese so as to guarantee his peace, and it occurred to him that perhaps Talbot wasn't as thick as he seemed. Perhaps he liked the *idea* of fishing more than its generally preferred result. The thought appealed to him; it seemed to take some of the wind out of the trout's sails.

Just when he thought he could go on so all afternoon, the Professor slumped down beside him on the deck with what appeared to be an old blueprint. "Here it is."

Jonathan raised up onto his elbow and peered at the thing. It seemed to be the dusty old floor plan of some multistoried stone edifice, of a castle perhaps. It didn't mean anything at all to him. "Are you going into real estate?" he asked the Professor.

The Professor winked at him. It was a wink full of meaning. "Both of us have been into this piece of real estate already, Jonathan. And if it wasn't for the Squire, we'd likely still be there, two heaps of bones."

Jonathan looked a bit closer at the plans and recognized the great hall on the ground floor with its high trestle ceiling. There was the immense stone chimney and the great windows through which he himself had hurled a wooden bench. It was a drawing of the various levels of the castle on Hightower Ridge, abandoned now by its master, Selznak the Dwarf. Jonathan was immediately suspicious.

The Professor tried to placate him. "I found this drawing at the library in town, of all places. I thought I knew every map and manuscript in there. I was nosing around in Special Collections and there it was, just tossed on the counter in a heap as if someone had brought it in yesterday and had left it there for me. Wonderful luck, really."

"So you were studying architecture then, eh?" Jonathan asked, squinting past his pipe at the Professor.

"A bit. Lately, though, I've been studying the lower levels on this drawing." The Professor paused to grab a handful of shelled almonds out of a cloth bag and toss a couple into his mouth. "Look at these hallways that run off here from the cellar. They must run away into the earth. And look at this notation. *Cavern of Malthius* it says. Then this one, *Cavern of the Trolls.* Isn't that something?"

Jonathan tapped his pipe out into the river and admitted that it was indeed something. The Professor pointed to another bit of faded lettering almost lost in a blur of smeared ink. "To the *d-o—*" the Professor was reading the inscription off letter by letter. "What do you suppose that means?"

"Obviously it used to read, 'to the dog,'" Jonathan said. "Trolls lived in this cavern, a dog lived down here. Probably there was another room for cats and one for pigs and one for curious people like this Malthius chap who showed too much interest in finding out which room was which."

The Professor smiled and shook his head. "It's not dog, Jonathan; there were at least four letters here."

"Dogs then," Jonathan countered. "An even better reason not to go poking around there, as I see it. Last December, after we spent such a fine evening there, you said you had intentions of returning to do a bit of exploration. I have this feeling that's where we're heading right now—into trouble. Into a castle full of trolls and dogs and hobgoblins."

The Professor nodded. "As men of science we have a duty to investigate that tower."

"In just two days," Jonathan said, "I've been a man of leisure and a man of science."

"This notation here," the Professor continued, "hasn't anything to do with dogs. I'm sure of it. It refers to a door, I think."

"A door to where? To the center of the earth?"

The Professor perked up at the idea. "Quite possibly so, Jonathan. There are theories about it being hollow, you know."

"Seems unlikely that a chap could wander into it through a door, though, doesn't it?" Jonathan asked.

"It seems unlikely that toads fly in the Wonderful Isles, or that the elves cast nets in the clouds to gather rain fish."

Jonathan admitted that all that sounded unlikely too, just as the Professor said. "What do you expect to find in the tower, Professor, besides deviltry? Bufo and Gump smashed the Dwarf's laboratories to bits, and Escargot warned them away from the upper story. I think we should heed his warning. He knows more about Hightower Castle than either of us."

"That's true," the Professor replied, idly tossing an almond across the fifty-odd feet of water that separated them from the shore. It *splupped* into the river just as some sort of great fish, moving too quick to identify, leaped out of the water and snatched it up.

"Yoicks!" shouted Jonathan. "I've got to get word of this back to Talbot. It's salted almonds he wants, not lumps of rubber."

"As I was saying," the Professor resumed, "Escargot likely had reasons of his own. He's a fine fellow—don't get me wrong—but his motives seem to be suspect as often as not. Maybe there's something in the upper level he just didn't want us to see."

"Like what?" Jonathan asked.

"Who knows? Some magical device. A treasure maybe."

"Then it isn't too likely that Escargot would have just warned us away from whatever it was and left for the coast. He would have taken it with him."

The Professor shrugged. About then Ahab woke up, his spot of shade beside the cabin having been chased off by the sun. The Professor tossed him an almond, and Ahab chomped it up with a show of great relish, working the thing back and forth between his teeth as if attempting to get just the right sort of hold on it. He seemed so pleased with the nut that the Professor gave him another one. Jonathan and the Professor could hardly sit and eat the things in front of him, so the three of them finished off the little bag between them.

"What do you say, then?" the Professor asked, folding up the wrinkled parchment that he held in his hand.

"You're the captain," Jonathan said. "If you say we put into Hightower Harbor, then I suppose we do. Do you really think there's any treasure there?"

The Professor shrugged. "There could be in a castle like that. There could be treasure anywhere. Sometimes there is."

Jonathan nodded in agreement. That seemed reasonable, at least in the philosophical sense.

Chapter 3

The Shanty in the Swamp

❦

FOR two days they didn't see a soul—no lumber rafts or trade barges passed them; they never caught up with the two slouched-hatted fishermen who had spun past in the canoe that first morning. Once late the first evening, just as the sun disappeared beyond the fringe of forest to the west, they saw what might have been either a bear or a troll in the shadow of a tangled oak; it was swatting at fish in the river. Jonathan wished he had Talbot's tuba just for the sake of seeing whether the instrument would have the effect on the beast that it was rumored to have. He remembered his own run-in with two trolls months before in almost the same spot, and the general amazement of everyone involved—trolls as well as men—at the wild and unlikely behavior of Professor Wurzle's oboe weapon. "Those were the days," Jonathan thought, feeling for all the world as if that marvelous adventure had occurred ages ago, back in his wild youth, perhaps.

Everything was so unutterably peaceful along the river, however, that this time no such adventures befell them. They managed to read like whizbangs and smoke any number of pipes of tobacco. On the second morning the trout began to cooperate and they ate fish for lunch and again for dinner. Then Jonathan came up with the bright idea of stirring a bunch of broken trout meat into their scrambled eggs the next morning. After they finished, the Professor remarked that, for himself, he hoped to never see a trout again. Not on a plate at least. Jonathan felt pretty much the same way.

The shores of the Oriel began to stretch out as they ap-

proached Hightower Village. Broad green stretches of meadow, alive with columbine and lupine and wild iris, seemed
to have pushed the forests away toward the distances. To
the east rose the White Mountains, covered in clouds and
mystery, first visible across a stretch of grassy lowlands,
then disappearing beyond a stand of towering hemlock or
a cluster of mossy alders.

Lilies bloomed in the slack water along the banks, and
among the floating leaves and the tangled roots swam a
company of pond turtles and frogs, clambering up onto lily
pads as big around as a plate, then sliding off again with a
splash into the placid waters. The meadows gave way finally to swamps and fens scattered with the twisted shapes of
long dead trees and occasional stands of alder and cotton-
wood that had managed to find a hillock high enough to
keep their roots out of the surrounding waters.

That section of shore was dark and murky and cheerless,
even on a fine day in the spring. Even the wild flowers that
sprouted here and there in the swamps appeared to
Jonathan to be doleful sorts of things, sad bits of color
cast about in the gloomy stretches of swamp.

The Professor took the long view—saw the whole business through different eyes. There were no end of snakes
and bugs and biological wonders afoot in the swamps, and
at night in the summer, the lowlands burned with the tiny
fires of a million glowworms, a jar full of which would
work as well as any lantern to light a traveler's path. The
Professor's talk of bugs and worms, however, did not do
too much to change Jonathan's attitude. Nor did the craggy
shadows of Hightower Ridge improve it much, for there,
jutting up from the rocky crest, were the granite walls of
Hightower Castle. It was impossible to say where the gray
cut-granite of the tower walls began. It looked as if the
tower had sprouted from the ridge itself and that there had
never been a time that the tower was anything but a partial
ruin. It seemed as ageless as the dim stones of the broken
land roundabout it. To the Professor, the tower was a
mystery; to Jonathan it was more of a curse. His only con-
solation was that its most recent occupant, Selznak the evil
conjuror dwarf, had been chased away upriver. An empty

tower seemed a bit less foreboding than a tower occupied by an evil dwarf—but not much less.

It was relatively early in the morning when they sailed into Hightower Harbor, still fairly quiet and empty. Only a few people had returned since Selznak's disappearance. Jonathan was relieved to see, however, that the windows of the boathouse were no longer boarded up and that some half dozen children were trapping crayfish along the banks. At least the village wasn't wholly deserted as it had been that past winter.

Jonathan and the Professor decided to waste no time poking around town, but to trudge along the path through the swamp immediately and investigate the castle. They agreed to return to the raft before nightfall to avoid sleeping in the tower and upsetting any resident ghosts or demons.

They packed a lunch and set out carrying a rope, a lantern, a torch, and a dozen candles. Each brought along an oaken walking stick, not so much for support along the trail as for warding off goblins or clobbering a possible troll. The trail wound in and out through clumps of moss-hung trees, seeming to take the long way around. Three times they came upon forks and decided on each occasion to follow that fork that steered them in the general direction of the tower. That seemed to work well twice.

Some few minutes after following the third fork, however, they found themselves before an old stilted shanty with plank walls. Weedy mud had at one time plugged the chinks in the walls, but had long since fallen to bits. Little was left to keep the north wind out. A ruined porch with a stile railing slanted across the front, and on it sat a wizened woman who appeared to be so incredibly old that she was more a bag of dust and dry bones than flesh and blood. Her face was lined so deeply that it seemed to Jonathan that she could have profited as much as the walls of the shanty from an application of mud. She sat in the ruins of an armchair staring out through apparently sightless eyes. Jonathan didn't like the look of her by half, nor of a bundle of what appeared to be dried bats that hung over the door. She was dressed in black. Faded lace hung in tatters round her collar and sleeves. A cat sat beneath her chair, idly batting at a long shred of lace that dangled in front of it.

Jonathan and the Professor stood silently for a moment, both of them prepared to tiptoe off back down the path toward the fork where they'd gone astray. Ahab watched the cat, black as a moonless night, but didn't mutter any sort of greeting. He seemed to like the look of it about as much as his master did. The cat wandered out from beneath the chair and hopped up onto the tilting porch railing, staring down placidly at the three of them. The old woman stirred and fingered the lace on her sleeve. She smiled slowly with her mouth, but her eyes didn't move. Jonathan noticed with horror that she hadn't any color in her eyes, that they were the same dead milky gray over all, like the belly of yesterday's fish. It was as if they'd been drained over long years of their color and sight, and the old woman had faded like a lizard on a rock to become part of the general colorless murk of the swamp.

She rose slowly and terribly from the chair, supporting herself on a curiously carved stick, dark with age and use. It looked certain for a moment that she was about to totter very slowly forward onto her face on the porch. She didn't though; she simply continued to stare ahead of her.

The Professor took his hat off even though she couldn't appreciate it. He introduced himself and Jonathan politely. It was Jonathan's idea to make off down the path, but he wasn't about to go alone, and clearly this was just the sort of thing to fascinate the Professor. The old woman didn't respond at all to the Professor's pleasantries. She simply smiled for a moment more, then reached out one withered hand from the midst of the muff of ruined lace, pointed it shakily at the space between Jonathan and the Professor and said eerily, "So you've come."

"Some mistake." Jonathan looked at the Professor, then back at the old woman. "You've got the wrong party. We're out on a picnic actually. On our way to the waterfall for a swim." He motioned to the Professor in a meaningful way. The old woman laughed, or at least tried to, but didn't sound as if her heart were in it, as if she were approving of Jonathan's sense of humor. She curled her finger slowly, inviting them up onto the porch, and, as if suddenly becoming animated, she jerked her head to the left and looked Jonathan full in the face, cackling with sudden brittle laughter.

Jonathan was off down the path with Ahab at his heels. He could hear the Professor pounding along behind. With a shudder of horror he heard the screeching of the cat and cackling of the old woman mixed very clearly with what sounded for all the world like the swishing and crackling of old robes and lace, as if the witch herself were following close on.

They ran all the way to the fork, and Jonathan would have abandoned the path to the tower and continued running all the way back toward the harbor if the Professor hadn't stopped for breath and shouted at Jonathan to do the same.

Bent over, hands on their knees, they both puffed away for the space of a minute. Jonathan listened for the swish of robes or the cackle of laughter, but he couldn't hear a thing above the pounding of his heart and the sound of his breathing. He determined that, old lady or no, he would whack the devil out of her with his stick if she showed up along the path—and that went double for her cat. "That about cooked my goose," Jonathan said after a few moments.

The Professor forced out a bit of a laugh. "She sure put the fear into you."

"Into *me?*" Jonathan mocked. "I'll lay odds you haven't run so fast in forty years."

"You gave me a scare, bolting like that."

"It wasn't me giving anyone a scare. I'm not the sort of chap to give people a scare. You know as well as I do what she is. She was one of the ladies Dooly saw last fall in the moonlight that night, sailing across the sky—she and her cat both probably. If that *was* a cat." Jonathan watched the Professor waving a match in the general direction of his pipe bowl, his fingers shaking like sixty. "Are you trying to light your pipe or the end of your nose?" Jonathan asked.

The two of them burst into a fury of wild laughter, and it was a moment before they'd laughed themselves out and set off down the path once again, both Jonathan and the Professor looking on occasion back over their shoulders.

They agreed several times not to make the same blunder when they came to the same fork on their return.

In another hour they wound up the steep, rocky ridge to the tower. They hurried along in the shadows of the giant hemlocks that grew along the path, and they avoided sunlit stretches. The fact that it was a warm day had little to do with their keeping to the shadows, although both of them insisted that such was the case. The tower simply seemed to have a pall of evil hanging about it—an atmosphere that had risen over countless years out of the ground itself.

All in all, the shadowy tower had an inhospitable look to it that Jonathan didn't like any more there in the light of day than he had at midnight months before. Jonathan began to wish he had brought a jacket even though he knew it was as sunny a day as he would ever see.

"I rather think we're letting the countryside here get the best of us," the Professor observed. "We're expecting some grim thing that we've no cause to expect. This isn't any haunted house, after all."

"It's not?" Jonathan asked. "It must average pretty high as haunted houses go. This whole place seems about as haunted as can be. It feels like the woods are full of goblins."

"Nonsense. It's all your imagination."

"I just don't have your optimism," Jonathan said, as the two of them struck out across the grassy expanse between the forest and the door of the tower. With Ahab following, they scuttled along, both of them hunched over and hurrying as if they sensed they were being watched by something —something in the very air that surrounded the tower.

The door swung heavily in on its hinges, opening to reveal the cobbled floor of the great hallway and the stone fireplace that took up most of the wall perpendicular to the door. There in the fireplace lay a heap of cold ashes, and before it lay the pile of bleached bones used by the terrible Selznak as fuel. On the floor were scattered the strange remnants of their encounter that past fall: the stuffed snake Squire Myrkle had poked into the Dwarf's ear and the gnawed turkey bone that had so overwhelmed the skeleton. There was an empty tankard and a few human rib bones and the bottom half of a skull. Nothing had been altered.

No one had, apparently, been in the tower; the dwarf hadn't returned. The long window opposite the door had a gaping hole. Despite the breeze blowing in through the broken window, a good layer of dust, smeared with the tiny footprints of rats, sat on the sill. Below the sill lay a dozen human bones—the legs, feet and pelvis of the skeleton who had almost found its way out to freedom. Outside in the dirt and weeds lay the rest of him, the skull yellowed and staring up toward the sun overhead.

All of this skeleton business didn't serve to make the interior of the tower any more homey, but it did remind Jonathan that he and his friends had, once before, dealt fairly handily with a similar assortment of horrors. He hefted his stick and supposed to himself that what he had done once, he could do again. Then he recalled his wild flight from the old woman on the porch and decided wisely that vanity, more often than not, turns men into fools.

There was nothing to suggest, then, that the tower was occupied by anything other than the pall of evil that even the winds blowing in through the open window couldn't disperse.

"Where shall we start?" Jonathan asked, looking at his pocketwatch. "There're five floors above and your caverns and cellars and dog rooms below. Where does the treasure lie?"

"I'd say below, despite Escargot's warnings about the upper story." The Professor was unrolling his parchment on the floor. "It's standard practice, according to the authorities, to bury the stuff, not to haul it upstairs."

That seemed reasonable to Jonathan. "It's after noon," he said, shoving his pocketwatch back into his pocket. "We'd better be out of here by four o'clock if we want to make it through the fens before the sun goes down. I want to eat dinner on the raft and not at some pleasant shanty in the swamp."

The Professor nodded. "Agreed. You keep an eye on the time." With that he set out toward the winding stairs that led to both the upper and lower reaches of the castle. The way to the cellar was blocked by a wooden trap door made of heavy oak planks. Attached to it was a chain that angled up into a sort of pulley-crank device. The chain and crank were as rusty as if they'd been out in the rain for a year, and had a look of disuse about them. Jonathan threw his weight into the wooden arm of the crank, but the thing just sat and stared at him. He tapped at it with his stick, and chips of rust flew off, dusting the stone stairs with red bits of iron. The Professor and Jonathan both leaned into it, but with no better result. Then Jonathan whacked it with his staff, raising a spray of rust, but not noticeably loosening the thing.

The Professor pondered for a moment. "We could melt lard all over it," he said, snapping his fingers. "Oil the thing up. If we keep on banging on it with your stick we'll just bend the devil out of it."

"You're right," Jonathan agreed. "When we were here last, the Squire and Bufo found a pantry upstairs. There was a roast turkey there at the time, so Selznak must have done a good bit of cooking. There's sure to be lard around somewhere."

So the two of them, followed by Ahab, climbed back up the stairs to investigate the pantry. They didn't find any lard, but they did find a bottle of whale oil which would do just as nicely and wouldn't have to be heated. They also discovered in a dark, cool hole beneath the floor, racks of bottled ale, laid down long before by Selznak. Jonathan shoved four bottles into his knapsack along with an oil lamp, a jar of oil, and a handful of wooden matches. They discovered a cupboard full of what had once been loaves of bread but which had become little greenish-brown petrified lumps, too thoroughly dried out and reduced even to be of interest to mice. There were jars of pickled mushrooms and eggs and peppers, but several had burst and spewed juices and debris over the rest of the jars. Neither Jonathan nor the Professor had any desire to have a go at the contents of those jars that hadn't burst.

"Selznak seems to have done all right for himself here," Jonathan said, shouldering his pack. "He was a regular gourmet, eating pickled eggs and mushrooms and roasting turkeys. Too bad he had to be such an evil sort. You wouldn't think that anyone who had such an appreciation for food would go about terrorizing people so. Somehow

I can't imagine Selznak eating anything at all. Plates of dirt, maybe, or webs, but not bottled ale and roast turkey."

The Professor nodded. "I know what you mean. He wasn't the sort of person to *like* anything, food included. He must have fought pretty hard against appreciating any of it."

"That's right." Jonathan sighed happily as they once again reached the bottom of the stairs. "If he hadn't, some of the pleasure of eating all this stuff might have leaked out and ruined him."

Jonathan twisted the top from the jar of whale oil and trickled a bit over the moving parts of the crank and pulley. He joggled the crank and poured some more on. Then he leaned out over the door itself and poured a bit along the chain and onto the iron ring that it passed through. He was careful to keep the oil off the handle of the crank itself so that he could get a good grip on the thing. When there was as much oil dribbled on as seemed to be sensible, he capped the jar and put it back into his pack next to his lantern.

The Professor tapped at the crank to loosen it, and the thing moved ahead a quarter of an inch. Then he tapped the other way and moved it back. After a few moments of tapping and jiggling, Jonathan gave it a heave, and the rusty chain dragged and rattled through the ring. The heavy door creaked open, its hinges screaming as if protesting at being awakened. Below was impenetrable darkness. The stairs curved down and away to the left out of sight. A cold blast of musty air blew up the stairwell at them, rushing anxiously out of the darkness toward sunlight and freedom. Jonathan cocked his head and listened, although he didn't give much of a thought to what he was listening for. He had the vague idea that if he heard anything at all he'd trip the catch on the pulley, slam the trap, and leave town. But there was nothing but silence below—not even the scuttling footsteps of rats.

"What are you listening for?" the Professor asked. "The moaning of ghosts?"

"I suppose I am at that," Jonathan said. "And I suppose that's why you're whispering."

The Professor, vaguely surprised to find that he had indeed been whispering, spoke up bluffly. "Hello," he shouted down into the darkness. "It's just me, the taxman! That'll scare the daylights out of them," he said to Jonathan. "Not that there's much daylight down there left to scare."

Jonathan rummaged again in his pack, coming up with the lamp, the torch, and the candles he and the Professor had brought along. "This torch is too smoky," he said. "Let's use the lamp instead and save the torch and the candles."

"Good idea." The Professor twisted the wick up in the lamp as Jonathan lit it. Light stabbed out into the darkness below, but it didn't do much more than make everything else seem that much more black. Ahab peered past Jonathan and the Professor and growled down the stairs. Jonathan had a high regard for Ahab's instincts, and he felt a bit like growling at the darkness below himself, just to let whatever was there know that he carried, as his friend Dooly would have aptly put it, a whackum stick. With the glowing lantern held at arm's length, the three of them descended the stairs that spiralled downward into what turned out to be a surprisingly deep cellar. Jonathan stepped slowly from tread to tread as if the stairs were about to crumble to bits. Actually, however, they were solid as rock and seemed to be hewn out of the ridge itself.

At the base of the stairs was a broad, open chamber with tunnels running away into the earth on three sides—one toward each of the Professor's various caverns, likely. Jonathan clumped down onto the stone floor below the final stair, and the floor, oddly, emitted a hollow thud. Behind them sounded a metallic click and the confused ratchet clatter of a banging cog and a chain rattling through an iron ring. The heavy trap door banged down, the hollow *whump* blowing a gust of air down the dark spiralling stair and into Jonathan's upturned face.

Chapter 4

The Cavern of Malthius

❈

JONATHAN handed the lamp to the Professor and followed him back up to where the trap lay nestled in a niche of stone, entirely blocking the stairwell. Jonathan bent in under it, put his back to it, and pushed, but nothing happened. It was like pushing against the side of a mountain. There were no levers or pulleys or any such thing to manipulate either.

"That was a trap door, all right." Jonathan once again descended the stairs. "The latch was sprung when I stepped off the last stair. People like you and me aren't meant to get out of here, I suppose."

"Nor anyone else," the Professor said.

"Anyone else would have stepped off to the side, maybe, and not sprung the trap."

The Professor scratched his head. "Still, no one would take the chance of being trapped here. Either there's another exit or a device to work the pulley from below. If there's such a device, we'll find it. There are only two physical laws that apply in this case—the law of gravity and Pinwinnie's Push-Pull Theorem."

"Pinwinnie?" Jonathan asked.

"Of course. Why? Do you think that Pinwinnie's Theorem wouldn't answer?"

"Not at all." Jonathan smiled. "I have complete faith in Pinwinnie. Complete faith."

"All right then," the Professor continued, "in the light of scientific knowledge, the workings of this door will be made manifest."

"That's good," Jonathan said. "Because in a few hours the light of this whale oil lamp isn't going to be making anything manifest."

"You've got a point there." The Professor waved the lamp in question out toward the chamber. "Now that you mention it, we'd best be on our way. One of these tunnels leads to an exit, or I'm a codfish. There's too much good air in here to suppose this cellar is enclosed."

"Let's go then," Jonathan urged. Ahab trotted across the floor of the chamber and, wisely, into the mouth of a tunnel that seemed to slope slightly uphill and gave Jonathan the hope that it led out into daylight. They wandered along the passage for twenty yards or so before it leveled off for a hundred yards. The tunnel itself was narrow and high, the roof being out of sight overhead. By stretching out his arms, Jonathan could easily touch both sides. After a bit he began to suspect that the tunnel was sloping very gradually downhill, but it was hard to be sure. The lamp didn't throw enough light for them to get a good look either up or down. Jonathan called a halt, reached into a little pouch that hung on his belt, and hauled out the little ivory ball with the elf runes on it that he kept for good luck. He laid the ball on the floor of the tunnel, and they watched as it tottered forward and began to roll with increasing speed down the dark corridor. Ahab went nosing slowly after it and Jonathan followed, picking the thing up and putting it back into his pouch.

The two of them pondered for a moment. Jonathan was for going back, but the Professor was for going on, pointing out that just because the tunnel was running downhill that didn't mean it would continue to do so. After all, it had started out uphill. Jonathan was pretty sure that the Professor favored going on as much for the sake of scientific pursuit as for finding a way out, but he agreed in the end to follow his lead.

Soon there was no doubt they were descending, and rapidly so. Down some sections they fairly slid along, and although it seemed foolish to Jonathan, the deeper they descended, the more fascinated the Professor became with the idea of seeing what lay at the bottom of the tunnel. It was impossible to say how deep they were. In the faint twilight of the oil lamp everything looked the same from one step to the next. Nothing but the echo of their footsteps on the stone of the tunnel floor reminded them that time was passing—that and the lowering level of oil in the lamp. There was enough left in the jar for them to refill the lamp twice. So, worse come to worst, they could at least light their way back to the cellar above.

They stopped to rest, finally, on a heap of stones, and Jonathan held up the lantern to get a look at the rocky ceiling overhead. The pale rays of light shone on fissured granite, shot through with veins of quartz. Clumps of crystals the size of a man's fingers jutted down here and there, and among them were long spires of amethyst, glowing purple in the lamplight.

"Give me a hand here, Professor." Jonathan heaped several of the larger rocks scattered about into a pile and then clambered up onto them in order to reach the ceiling. He stabbed away at the amethyst crystals with his penknife, nicking the blade in the process, but loosening several wonderful pieces. One, a crystal as long as Jonathan's hand, was marbled with deep swirls of emerald green. He went to work on another, the chip, chip, chip of the blade striking stone echoing off down the tunnel.

In the flickering darkness of the shadows cast on the roof by the jutting crystals, the tiny hairless head of a little beast, something the size of a rat with blind, pink, lidless eyes, peered out at Jonathan from behind the very crystal he chipped at. Another peeked out from behind the first, and two more stared blindly at him a ways farther on. The first dropped suddenly from its niche in the granite ceiling, spread gauzy batwings, and whirred away into the darkness, a long pointed tail trailing coldly across Jonathan's forehead. Jonathan shouted and tumbled backward, scattering rocks and thinking only of saving the fragile lantern he was still holding in his left hand. His right shoulder hit the wall of the tunnel and whale oil spewed out of the lamp, burning droplets igniting a spreading pool of it on the tunnel floor. The tunnel, instantly, was alive with light and with the fleshy whirring of a thousand spidery wings as little blind bat things dropped from the ceiling and screeched their way deeper down the tunnel. Ahab raced about up and down the corridor barking, as Jonathan and the Professor crouched next to the pile of stones, brushing at hairless tails. In a moment the tunnel was both silent and dark, the sloshing oil having extinguished the burning wick in the lamp and the pool on the floor having burned itself out.

Jonathan, rummaging in his bag, found wooden matches and a candle. By the light of the candle, he refilled and lit the oil lamp. He blew the candle out and shoved it back into his pack along with all the amethyst and quartz crystals he had chipped loose. "What were those things, Professor," Jonathan asked. "Bats?"

"Not bats that I've ever seen. I've come across blind cave bats before, but nothing like those critters—nothing with tails. These looked like bats that had gotten mixed up with 'possums. Probably one of Selznak's experiments."

Jonathan grimaced. "I don't care much for Selznak's experiments. In fact, they give me the creeps. Let's get out of here. This tunnel isn't going anywhere but down."

"I believe," the Professor said, "that we're in the tunnel that leads to the door. I *have* to see that door."

"Or dogs. Or pink bats. Or some other horrible thing. I'm about ready to have a look at the door on Hightower Tavern myself." Upon mentioning Hightower Tavern he remembered the four bottles of ale he had in the pocket of his knapsack, but a wet spot on the canvas seemed to promise trouble. Sure enough, two of the bottles had burst in the fall. He pulled chunks of glass out of the sack and dropped them into cracks and crevices in the rock walls. He uncorked the other two bottles, handing one to the Professor, who wasn't at all unhappy to see it.

The ale was sharp and dry, just the thing under the circumstances. Jonathan was in the middle of pointing out that Selznak could have made a fortune as a brewer when he noticed that Ahab was gone. He and the Professor set out down the tunnel at a brisk pace, assuming that if he'd gone back up, they'd find him for certain on their return.

Forty yards along, the tunnel took a sharp turn to the right, then ended at the mouth of a pit that dropped straight as a stone into the depths of the earth. At the brink of the pit, sniffing along, was old Ahab.

"End of the line," Jonathan told the Professor in a relieved sort of tone.

"Not at all," the Professor replied. "Look here." He pointed at what appeared to be iron rungs set into the stone walls of the pit. "And look at this." He ran his hands over long gashes cut into the rock. "This has all been hacked out. Widened, probably."

"So it has." Jonathan wondered whether the Professor was actually considering climbing down an ageless iron ladder into a dark pit a mile beneath the earth. "What sort of lunatic hauled a pick down here to break rocks, do you suppose? It reminds me of those Eastern madmen who carve whole cities into a walrus tusk. Takes them a lifetime."

"No one dragged a pick down here." The Professor ran his hands over the gashes in the rock. "They dragged it *up* here. Look at these marks. They were chopped in from below. Something crawled up out of this pit from below."

"Great," Jonathan said. "Selznak's ancestors, no doubt."

"Well we've got to find out." Whereupon the Professor dropped a stone into the void. It struck after just a couple of seconds, exciting the Professor no end, but alerting Jonathan to the sad fact that he was about to follow the Professor deeper yet into the earth.

"I'll climb to the bottom of this pit," Jonathan agreed, "if the ladder goes that far. But that's it. If the tunned goes on beyond as it has, I won't follow it. We've used almost half our oil, and we're a good two hours farther away from getting out of here than we were in the cellar. In ten minutes we'd better be heading back there."

"Done," the Professor called, swinging a foot into the abyss. Jonathan ordered Ahab to stay put and clambered after the Professor, climbing down slowly with the lantern slung over his arm, its wire handle resting in the crook of his elbow. It was about twenty feet to the bottom of the pit. From there, the tunnel ran on.

"This is it," Jonathan said. "This tunnel could go on for a hundred miles."

"Shine the lantern on ahead," the Professor said, paying no attention to Jonathan's observation. "I think we're here." And when they held the lantern out they could see, vaguely, something that looked like a door—a great, arched iron door sealing off the tunnel. "The door!" the Professor shouted, striding up to it. "I knew there was a door."

There was, however, no handle on the door. Nor was there a keyhole. There was just a great iron slab of a door. No cracks were visible anywhere around the perimeter and no hinges showed along either side. The Professor thumped on it, but his fist striking it didn't make any more of a sound than if he had struck the smooth granite of the tunnel wall.

"Yes, this is the door," the Professor whispered as if fearing that something crouched listening beyond.

Jonathan was struck with the humor of the situation— the Professor's obvious delight at having found an iron slab at the end of a tunnel. He rapped on the door with the end of his stick. "Hello, monsters!" he said, putting his ear to the door. "Hello, monsters!" came an answering echo which made both of them jump and took some of the life out of Jonathan's lark.

"I hear something," the Professor whispered. "Listen!" The two of them held their breath and heard a faint sloshing sound away off in the darkness. Suddenly the glow of the oil lamp seemed feeble and the circle of light around them seemed to shrink. Jonathan shouldered his club like a ball bat, waiting in horrified anticipation for the door to creak open. The sloshing sounded more loudly off to their right in the darkness of what might well be a tunnel parallel to their own. A faint, damp, fetid breath of wind touched their faces and a pale tentacle arced out of the darkness and dropped between them, feeling the ground roundabout as if searching for something. It wasn't difficult to guess what.

Jonathan quelled an urge to slam at the thing with his club as he and the Professor edged back along the wall toward the ladder, both of them watching in horror as a second and then a third tentacle followed the first. A heaving and sloshing sounded from the darkness.

The Professor was up the ladder first, moving wonderfully fast for a man of his age. Jonathan was close behind, just far enough back so as not to be kicked in the face. He felt, just when the Professor reached the summit, a rubbery tentacle brush along his pant leg, tickling his bare leg above his sock.

It seemed to take an hour for the Professor to hoist himself over the rim—enough time anyway for whatever it was below to snake a cold tentacle around Jonathan's calf. Jonathan shouted, nearly losing his hold on the rough iron rung of the ladder. He kicked his leg uselessly, unable to detach the thing which seemed to be feeling about as if trying to determine what manner of prey it was that had stumbled into its lair.

"The lamp!" the Professor shouted.

Ahab barked furiously and capered back and forth before the mouth of the pit.

"Throw the bloody lamp at it!" the Professor yelled. And Jonathan, not waiting for a third invitation, slid the lamp down his arm into his hand and flung it down into the darkness below. There was a flash of burning oil and a weird ululating howl followed by slapping and sloshing and the release of Jonathan's leg. Jonathan hauled himself out like a sprung jack-in-the-box, and, before groping away down the darkness of the corridor, turned with the Professor to watch the thrashing of the thing below. It seemed to be all head with pink, blind protruding eyes like the pink bat things. Its long slash of a mouth twitched and slavered and it slammed itself with mottled blue tentacles in a seeming effort to extinguish the fire which it could feel but couldn't see. Behind it, down the tunnel from where it had come, shone a dozen sets of pale eyes glowing in the firelight. Jonathan and the Professor decided to leave.

When they could no longer hear the thing's cries, they slowed down a bit. Jonathan had taken the lead, banging along like a blind man with his stick in front, and the Professor simply followed along, one hand on Jonathan's shoulder. Ahab didn't seem to need a stick or a hand on anyone's shoulder, and it was the realization of that that made Jonathan hold up finally. They decided against lighting the torch, knowing that they'd need it later, especially given the possibility of their running into more pits of the sort they'd just clambered out of. Candles wouldn't do since the small weak flame would keep going out as they traveled. So instead of lighting anything, Jonathan tied a lead to Ahab's collar, the Professor kept his hand on Jonathan's shoulder, and the two of them followed Ahab back along the passage until they burst out finally into the great cavern below the trap door. There they lit two candles and discussed further plans.

They decided, in the end, to take the tunnel which, on the chart, led to the Cavern of Malthius. Jonathan speculated that whoever Malthius turned out to be, he would likely be better company than the creatures they'd just visited. The decision, as it turned out, was a good one.

The corridor that led to the cavern was relatively short. They had to stop to re-light the candles four times before they reached it, but when they finally stumbled out of the tunnel into the immense, stalactite-hung cavern, they saw an amazing spectacle.

The cavern was broad and deep with an astonishingly high ceiling. The rays of the sun shone through cracks and fissures above, as if filtering through piles of rock. The ceiling was so riddled with holes and cracks that it was a marvel it stayed up at all. There wasn't any need for candles. The most amazing thing though was the furniture stacked roundabout. There were piles and piles of it. Immense wardrobes and long dining tables, gray with dust and dark with age, lined the walls. There were trunks spilling over with clothes and there were any number of old chairs, huge carved chairs with rags of tattered leather dangling from green brass studs.

In the dim shadows of one corner stood a collection of stuffed animals, a sort of taxidermist's wonderland, that looked as if it had stood just so for two hundred years. An elephant with long curving tusks and tufts of wooly hair along his back watched them through green glass eyes. Beside him stood a great long hippo and three crocodiles that had to have been twenty feet from head to tail. There were zebras and antelope and great cats and a weird hollow-eyed buffalo that was almost as big as the elephant. Four white apes stood in a cluster farther back in the darkness. Pushed in among these strange dusty creatures were more chairs and wardrobes and tables and candelabra and such, heaped together in disarray.

The cavern seemed to be the storage room of an ancient natural history museum that doubled as a warehouse for antiquities. Jonathan was briefly troubled by the disquieting thought that all the stuffed beasts were just a hair's breadth from animation, that perhaps when night fell the old lamps and candelabra would begin to glow and the ruined clavichord would begin to tinkle and harp and the apes would sit round the table to a phantom meal while crocodiles lounged on broken divans.

But all that was unlikely. He and the Professor, thinking of treasures, began rummaging in the scattered trunks, finding for the most part nothing but ancient clothing. In the trunks scattered beneath the fissures in the ceiling, the contents had been reduced to a sort of damp black webby business. But those more sheltered from the weather were in far better shape. There were heaps of sequined dresses, of silks and laces and fine waistcoats and top hats. There was a trunk full of costume jewelry, of rhinestones and glass baubles and false pearls that spilled out over the sides of the trunk and flowed away over the floor. All in all, both Jonathan and the Professor were astonished—not so much by the furniture itself or the trunks of ancient clothing or even by the weird assortment of stuffed animals, but by the combination of the lot of it, hidden away there in a cavern in the earth. It was like something out of a book by G. Smithers.

There wasn't any treasure to be found, however. Both of them collected heaps of odd finery before stopping to think that it was unlikely that they would find a way to haul the stuff along with them. The idea of leaving it behind was unthinkable, but it was, in the end, the only idea that made any sense. The Professor discovered several trunks of old costumes, enough to outfit a castle full of people for a masquerade. Among the feathered hats and rubber hands was a patchy sort of ape suit, complete from top to bottom. Jonathan slid the mask over his head but then pulled it off again when bits of hair and paper and rubber and leather fell from it.

"I have to have this," he said to the Professor, who himself had found a great, hollow alligator's head.

"Wear it when we visit Lonny Gosset. It'll knock him into the fourth dimension."

Jonathan smiled. "I was thinking that I could wear it about town. People might mistake me for a man of leisure."

The Professor nodded. "It's possible. Dooly might anyway. Dooly and Beezle. The suit looks a bit like some of the finely tailored garments he sells."

"Does it look much like a real ape's head?" Jonathan asked, turning to have a look at the heads of the four white apes that stood beyond the elephant. But the apes were almost lost in shadow. In fact, the cavern was growing steadily darker as the sun outside dropped beyond the tree-line.

"Do we want to spend the night in here?" the Professor asked.

"No," Jonathan replied decisively, looking about him at the shifting shadows of the somber furniture strung with cobwebs and at the glass eyes of the wild array of stuffed animals. "Do you think we can get out through one of those cracks in the ceiling?"

"A snake might if he were fired out of a cannon," the Professor said. "We've got one more tunnel to explore, though. Let's light the torch and have a go at it. At worst we can make our way back up to the cellar."

Jonathan agreed to the plan. It made little difference if they explored the tunnels at noon or at midnight. He was fairly sure that he'd rather spend the night tramping through the caves in search of a way out rather than trying to sleep. Such an atmosphere as existed beneath the tower would be bound to have a bad effect on dreams.

"Let's bring these two suits," Jonathan suggested. "We'll give them to the Squire."

"Capital idea," the Professor agreed. "They're right up his alley."

Jonathan found a broad expanse of serviceable cloth and laid it out over the stones of the floor, then he piled the ape and alligator costumes onto the center of the cloth and discovered, finally, that the alligator suit lacked a hand. There seemed to be no point at all in carrying along an unusable suit, so the two of them tore into the costumes until they finally found the hand at the very bottom of a sadly deteriorating trunk. Beneath the rubber alligator hand lay a folded trunk lining—an old, yellowed square of parchment patterned with random lines and faded script. A series of elf runes were visible in one corner. The Professor pulled the parchment out of the trunk while Jonathan dug two candles out of his pack. The heap of ape and alligator parts was quickly forgotten.

"This appears to be a map," the Professor observed, pointing out an arrow in the top right below the word "north." The Professor leaned over the parchment and sniffed at it. Then he held a corner over a candle and eye-balled it closely. In the candlelight glowing through the parchment, the ink appeared to be a dark purplish color, and the Professor announced, to Jonathan's surprise, that it was octopus ink.

"This is a pirate map," he said decisively. "There's no mistaking it. Who else uses octopus ink? No one. This is the real thing."

"It's pretty old though," Jonathan said. "This stuff must have been down here for a hundred years."

"This map couldn't have been," the Professor declared. "It wouldn't have lasted any hundred years. Someone hid it here, and I bet I know who it was."

"These candles aren't worth much," observed Jonathan as he shook the melted wax off his hand. "They're half gone already. Let's roll this thing up and get out of here."

The Professor rolled the map tightly and tied it round with strips of cloth. Jonathan gathered the corners of the cloth on the ground and pulled the whole pile into a bundle, tieing off the top with another cloth strip. The Professor shouldered the pack, and Jonathan slung the bundle ponderously over his shoulder. In the last guttering light of the two candles, they left the strange cavern and once more made their way back to the cellar where, without wasting any time, they lit their torch. In the fuming, sputtering light they strode away after Ahab down the third tunnel toward the Cavern of the Trolls.

Chapter 5

Goblins

❈

THE tunnel didn't slope at all, but seemed to run directly along the ridge which rose above the tower. It occurred to Jonathan that if such were the case, they were farther from the surface with each step they took. Soon, however, the tunnel curved around sharply to the left and angled away in a downriver direction. They trudged on for what must have been a mile, the path neither rising nor falling enough to worry about. It narrowed so at one point that they had to crawl along for twenty yards on their hands and knees, covering their trouser legs with red clay. The Professor heartened to find that the floor of the tunnel was no longer rock, and some twenty yards later he discovered the crooked end of a tree root thrusting through the ceiling.

Just ahead of them, the tunnel began to drop away, and the two debated in the flickering torchlight whether to follow it or return to where they had found the tree root and dig their way out. Neither, however, was in a digging mood, so they pushed on, following the twistings of the corridor as it wandered along through the earth. Jonathan realized all of a sudden that he was monstrously tired. The costume on his back seemed to be weighing more by the moment, and he began to consider the wisdom of just putting the suits *on*. But the idea of the two of them tramping through subterranean tunnels dressed as an ape and an alligator seemed a bit on the ludicrous side, so he abandoned it.

The tunnel widened just then into a cavern about half the size of the Cavern of Malthius. The Professor whispered that this must be the Cavern of the Two Trolls. And though they knew that whatever trolls might have inhabited

39

it a century before would have long since moved on, both of them trod along stealthily, squinting into the dark recesses ahead of them. They found themselves, finally, at the opposite end and saw in the distant reaches of the tunnel that stretched out before them a bit of light shining in the darkness. There was no mistaking it. Two hours earlier they would have assumed it was sunlight and popped right along toward it. But Jonathan's pocketwatch said it was almost eight o'clock in the evening. The sun had been dropping swiftly an hour before. The light, moreover, seemed to shrink and grow and dance on the walls of the cave, very much like the light of a flickering campfire—the fire, perhaps, of a pair of trolls or a company of goblins or a band of robbers.

It wouldn't do to make their presence known before discovering what exactly lay ahead, so they smothered the torch. Then, by the light of a single candle, they untied the bundle of costume parts and crawled into the things. Jonathan shoved the expanse of cloth into the backpack and pulled the ape mask over his head. The Professor did the same with the alligator head. Sweating inside the suit, Jonathan shouldered his pack, and the two of them went creeping away down the tunnel toward the fire, Ahab following along behind. The cackle of crazy laughter echoed up the tunnel, and Ahab growled in reply. Then came the ragged piping of a goblin flute and the hollow thud of a copper gong being struck with a stone mallet. From the shadows of the tunnel they watched the party of goblins that sat about the fire roasting fish. One kept shoving fish carcasses into the sprigs of stuff that passed for hair on his neighbor's head. The second goblin, unhappy at having his hair combed with fish carcasses, fetched the prankster a great smack with what appeared to Jonathan to be a river squid, flailing at him until the squid was reduced to parts. Then the two of them fell to poking and punching each other, to the huge delight of their several companions.

"Let's rush at them," Jonathan whispered through his ape mask. The Professor nodded ponderously, and together they rushed howling at the little band of goblins. The two involved in the fish war rolled about on the cave floor, biting and scratching, and obviously assuming that this new howling was simply jolly shouts of approval from their companions. Their fellows, however, left off their cackling at the sight of the approaching ape and alligator now sailing at them out of the darkness. Then the lot of them shrieked and bowled away down an adjacent tunnel. The two warriors rolled into the fire, scattering burning sticks. The one who'd been so free with the fishbones leaped up, his ragged shirt in flames, and dashed off. He was followed close on by his opponent, and their shrieks died away finally in the distance.

Jonathan and the Professor lost no time in shedding the costumes and bundling them up once again in the makeshift bag. Both noticed, almost at once, that a cool, fresh breeze was blowing along the tunnel. Fifty feet farther along they saw the deep blue-purple of the night sky beyond the dark arch of the cave mouth, and they emerged finally into the warm evening, midway up the steep slope of an oak-covered hill.

Some mile or so to the north rose the stone tower atop Hightower Ridge. Below it they could see the pinpoints of light shining through shanty windows in the swamps and the dark line of the Oriel winding slowly along the floor of the valley. Directly below them shone the lights of High-tower Village and, Jonathan was quick to point out, of Hightower Tavern where there were hot meat pies and poached salmon as well as bottles of ale.

Ahab seemed to sense the truth in Jonathan's observation, for he promptly began to pick his way through the chaparral and around the boulders on the moonlit hillside, heading toward the lights of the village. Jonathan and Professor Wurzle followed along, the dark cave mouth disappearing in the shadows of the oaks behind them.

"You know," the Professor said, "perhaps we shouldn't be too hasty here."

"We'd better be," Jonathan replied, "if we want anything to eat. The tavern probably doesn't keep late hours. Besides, I've had my fill of wandering through caves."

The Professor nodded in agreement. "I've had enough of that myself, although it's a pity we didn't have a chance to explore the upper rooms in the tower. Tomorrow's another day, though."

"That's just what I said to myself when that squid had me by the leg," Jonathan answered. "And speaking of tomorrow, I'd like to spend a quiet day on the river, bird-watching perhaps, or hunting clams—something adventurous."

The Professor stopped and sat on a great chunk of smooth granite, producing his notebook and pen from inside his shirt. "What I meant about being hasty," he said, sighting down toward the river over his thumb, "is that we'd be foolish to lose track of the location of the cave mouth. I have the feeling that we didn't begin to really explore those tunnels. I'd like to come back some day with a trade barge and haul that elephant out of there."

"Haul it out how?" Jonathan asked. "Do you plan to cut him up and carry him up the stairs?"

"That's just the point. There's more to that cavern than meets the eye. If that elephant was hauled down there, then there's some sort of grand entrance that we know nothing about. And how about those goblins chasing away down that side tunnel? Where were they going? And the door? We've got to figure out how to open it. There's justification, I think, for a scientific expedition here, and I plan to propose it to the Exploration Society during the fall symposium."

Jonathan nodded his head, relieved that the Professor hadn't suggested that the two of them undertake the expedition by themselves. In a moment the Professor had roughed out a crude map complete with landmark sightings and distance approximations.

A half hour later, dirty and tired, they pushed in through the door of the tavern and slumped down at a table in the corner. A woman in an apron looked askance at the toothy alligator head that poked out through an opening in Jonathan's bundle. The past year, however, had seen such strange times that she took whatever came her way pretty much in stride, or at least seemed to. Jonathan pulled the bundle out of the way and stuffed it under the table, loosing the ape's head in the process. The thing rolled out, bumping against the woman's shoe.

"I see you carry an ape head," the waitress remarked.

"After tonight," Jonathan explained, half truthfully, "I wouldn't go anywhere without it. It's wonderfully useful when a person runs into trouble."

"No doubt." The woman picked the thing up and handed it to Jonathan. "It looks like my late husband, only he wasn't useful for much of anything. What do you want to eat?"

"Roast beef," Jonathan answered promptly, "and a plum pudding."

The waitress gave him a look of re-evaluation—a look that implied that Jonathan also had a great deal in common with her late husband. "We have a cold joint of beef in the larder and a loaf of black bread. And we have a bit of cheese and a tub of pickles. But we don't have any plum pudding."

"We'll have all of that then," the Professor said. "And a pitcher of ale and a plate of milk for the dog here, too." He pointed without looking toward the alligator snout poking out from beneath the table. Ahab had, unknown to the Professor, wandered away and fallen asleep in front of the door, taking advantage of the cool breeze that blew in off the river.

"Anything you say," the waitress nodded slowly. She bent over and patted the peeling nose of the alligator. "Good pup," she said. Then she turned and disappeared into the kitchen.

"She thinks we're crazy," Jonathan said.

"Evidently so. There might be unlooked-for consequences to carrying around these outfits. People don't often enough take the long view."

Jonathan nodded in agreement as through the door came Lonny Gosset, the milliner. "Mr. Gosset!" Jonathan shouted. "By golly!"

Surprised, Gosset sat down at their table and ordered a pint from the waitress. "Well well," Gosset said. "What ho, eh? Chasing devils again are you? Transporting cheeses?"

"Neither. We're on holiday," the Professor explained. "We're on our way toward linkman territory, down beyond the Wood. We're off to see the Squire."

"The Squire is it," said Gosset, who was one of the Squire's most ardent admirers. "Fancy that. On holiday. I haven't been on holiday since I was a lad. I have a shop to see to. Trade's picking up. Everyone needs a straw hat in this heat. I can't make them fast enough."

The three of them sat about discussing the millinery trade, Jonathan and the Professor cutting off hunks of beef and cheese and bread. Ahab joined them almost as soon as the food arrived and drank the milk which the waitress had set down in front of the alligator. Jonathan was itching to have a look at the treasure map as was, probably, the Professor. But instinct told him that it was a dangerous business displaying such items in public. Finally, however, curiosity and anticipation overcame instinct; so, when late in the evening he and the Professor and Gosset were the last customers in the tavern, he suggested to the Professor that they unroll the "papers" they had found in the trunk.

Wurzle untied the rolled parchment and flattened the map onto the cleared table top. Jonathan and Gosset bent over the thing as the Professor traced lines and read sections of faded lettering. The terrain on the map was very obviously along a major river—a river much larger than the Oriel, evidently near the sea. The place names were foreign to all of them—even to the Professor, who had traveled extensively in his time.

Gosset thought that the map was a wonderful thing, but being far-sighted he could make nothing of it. Neither Jonathan nor the Professor bothered to point out the fact that it was a treasure map. They had a high regard for their old friend Lonny Gosset, of course, but that, quite reasonably, was immaterial under the circumstances.

Most puzzling of all the notations on the map was the legend scrawled across the top—merely the word "Balumnia," the name, possibly, of the city along the river or of the country where the river lay. The whole thing was a mystery. The name seemed vaguely familiar to both Jonathan and the Professor, although neither knew why. It seemed to Jonathan that he had seen a reference to Balumnia in a book by Glub Boomp, and the Professor recalled having heard once of a Balumnian toothed whale, although he couldn't remember where or when. Gosset observed that the word meant nothing as far as the millinery trade went. In the end they were little better off than they had been as mapless adventurers and were, in truth, a bit deflated. The very age and appearance of the map, not to mention the wonderful fact of its having been written in octopus ink, seemed to promise chests of pearls and coin and jewels. The three of them sat silent over the sad remains of their dinner, Jonathan and Professor Wurzle feeling oddly cheated, and Lonny Gosset sound asleep and threatening to tumble from his chair. He lurched finally and jerked awake with a wild look in his eye and shouted "Gabardine and wool!" very loudly and pointed at Jonathan. "Wha?" he said, waking up altogether. "Have I been asleep? I suppose I have."

"Quite all right," Jonathan said.

"I've been working all day," Gosset said by way of apology. "I'm making a wizard's cap. If I'd known what was involved in it, I wouldn't have taken the commission. Seems like a lot of foolery to me. And all the time I'm stitching the thing and soaking the materials, there he is, shaking toads at it and chanting this and that and whispering over the thing."

"Who?" Jonathan asked excitedly. "What magician? Does he want a tall hat?"

"Tall? I should say he does. I told him the thing would never stay on, but he said he'd put a spell on it and make it."

"Miles the Magician?" the Professor asked.

"*Meelays*," said Gosset pronouncing the name correctly. "He's the one. Do you know him?"

"Yes," Jonathan answered. "And unless I'm a truffled cod, he's just the man to consult when it comes to unfathomable maps and distant lands."

The Professor nodded and waved at the waitress who was reading a book near the bar.

"Where is this magician?" Jonathan asked Gosset. "Is he staying in town?"

"He's staying in this very inn." Gosset put some coins on the table. The Professor, however, insisted on buying Gosset's ale.

"You haven't a magician upstairs, have you?" the Professor asked the waitress when she brought their change.

The woman rolled her eyes. "You'd be friends of the wizard then," she said, a flat note of finality in her voice. "I should have thought as much. He's up there now, burning herbs in Room Four."

"Perhaps I'll just go up and have a word with him," Jonathan said, hauling out the ape suit. "Good old Miles. He should get a bigger thrill out of this than those goblins did."

The Professor looked like a man who thought it was too late in the evening for larks. The waitress looked as if she knew all along that it would come to such a thing as ape suits. Gosset was asleep again.

Jonathan put on the suit, shook debris out of the mask and pulled it on. Then he took the mask off and turned to the Professor. "What if I burst in with the ape suit on but wearing the alligator head?"

"He'd know something was wrong right away."

"You're probably right," Jonathan said. "We wouldn't want to ruin the effect."

The waitress nodded. "You're not going to kill him are you?" she asked matter-of-factly.

"Kill him!" Jonathan cried, horrified. "We're not crazy."

The waitress nodded again. Jonathan set out up the stairs, laughing inside the ape mask at what Miles' reaction was likely to be. Room Four was easy to find, there being only two numbered rooms on the second floor. Even through his mask Jonathan could hear the sound of chanting through the panel door. The smell of smoking herbs—especially sage, orange blossom, and lilac—came wafting out from underneath. Jonathan knocked twice, hoping he wasn't interrupting anything beyond some harmless meditation.

The chanting stopped abruptly. "Hello," came Miles' piping voice. "Who is it?"

"The maid," Jonathan shouted in what he assumed was a feminine sort of falsetto, wondering what it sounded like filtered through the mask.

"Come in," Miles said. Jonathan obliged him by flinging open the door and, for the profit of those downstairs, mouthing what he thought would be a fair imitation of an ape yell before capering into the room. He intended simply to race in and jig about for a moment, then snatch off the mask and have a good laugh. He hadn't even gotten entirely through the doorway, however, when Miles, who had been sitting cross-legged on the floor, leaped with a shout to his feet. He had the look of a man whose worst fears had come to pass. Confronted by the tufted sight before him, he hunkered down into a spell casting position and waved his hand, shouting fearfully.

Jonathan left off his jigging, realizing that somehow, inexplicably, his ape head was on fire. Before him danced the spell-shouting magician and behind him lay the stairway. He turned and raced for the stairs, pulling at the ape head and shouting for the Professor to fill a pitcher with water. It was the waitress, finally, who doused the flames with a bucket of ale. Miles appeared on the stairway, flabbergasted.

"Professor!" he said. "Fancy meeting you here. Is this your ape?"

"It's me," Jonathan cried, finally able to remove the mask.

"Jonathan Bing! What in the world?" Miles turned to the waitress as if for an explanation.

"They said they were friends of yours. It seemed likely to me."

"It's absolutely the case. We go way back. Six months at least. Why are you dressed so, Jonathan? I didn't recognize you."

"A little joke," Jonathan replied.

"Of course, of course, of course," Miles was nodding enthusiastically.

Jonathan looked at the sad remains of his ape suit. "I caught fire somehow."

"It was my toasting spell that did it, I'm afraid. It was the first thing that came to mind."

Lonny Gosset inspected the ape mask and concluded, to Jonathan's relief, that he could repair it tolerably well. He took it with him when he left for home a few minutes later, promising to meet them all for lunch the following noon.

"So," the Professor said when they'd settled down around the table over an apple pie that the waitress had discovered in the pantry. "What brings you south?"

"Bad business," Miles said gravely, shoveling pie into his mouth.

"Dwarf business?" Jonathan asked fearfully.

"Perhaps. Although I can't for the life of me see how. I hope not, for the Squire's sake."

"The Squire?" Now the Professor was agitated. "What's happened to the Squire? I knew we should have hung that bloody dwarf!"

"It's just as well you didn't try," Miles said. "I was up in the City of the Five Monoliths nosing around most of the winter. I promised Twickenham in a way that I'd keep an eye on Selznak. Of course he was up to no good, but it was pretty common stuff—murder and the like—and it was clear he knew I was there. In April he disappeared. I had it on authority that he was off downriver, so I moseyed along down to the Wood, where I lost track of him. You can't track evil through the Wood. There's too much of it there already. So I took care of a bit of business in Willowwood and started back up to Twombly Town to say hello to the two of you. I was camped along the river when who should come riding up on ponies but Bufo Morinus and Gump Ooze. They'd been advised by Twickenham to seek me out if there was news of the Dwarf. He's a powerfully conceited villain, that Selznak, and capable of going to wild lengths for revenge. Now it might be coincidence and it might not, but Selznak had put in an appearance up in the territory. Two days later the Squire disappeared."

"Disappeared?" Jonathan shouted, finding it difficult to imagine the Squire disappearing.

"Gone. I'm on my way there now, but I have to have my cap repaired first. Your man Gosset is working on it. He's a marvel with caps, they say."

"And ape masks."

"Well," the Professor said, "we're heading your way then." He told Miles of their plans to visit the Squire.

"I've got to warn you," Miles said, "that there's dirtywork afoot. There may be rough weather ahead."

They drank their coffee and finished the pie over the rest of Miles' tale. The Squire, it turned out, had simply disappeared. He had been sitting in his library one moment and the next he was gone—whisked away. It was a mystery and a villainy, Squire Myrkle being, of course, the next in succession to the linkman throne.

Danger or no danger, by the end of the tale they were doubly determined to continue their journey. In fact, they agreed to travel with Miles the following afternoon—just as soon as his magician's cap had been repaired by Lonny Gosset. Jonathan was anxious to be off, and disliked the idea of moping around all day in the still half-deserted village. He was relieved, since immediate travel would squash any possibility of further exploration of the tower. And he was intrigued by the promise of adventure. But most of all, he was anxious to help out the poor Squire who had, almost single-handedly, delivered him and the Professor from the hands of Selznak the Dwarf and his minion, the Beddlington Ape.

They decided to raft downriver to Willowood Station so as to avoid that part of the river road that ran through the fringes of the Goblin Wood. They would leave their raft in Willowood, rent ponies, and be at Myrkle Hall in a week's time at most. If they hurried they could be there sooner. A week sounded like a woefully long time, to be sure, but there wasn't any getting around it. Miles the Magician had sent word into the east to alert the elves of the Squire's disappearance. There was the ghost of a chance that an elfin airship might at that moment be humming along out of the White Mountains toward the territory, an airship that could sail them to Myrkle Hall in a matter of hours. But the chances of such an airship spotting the three of them on the river or along the river road was slim. They would have to put up with being anxious.

The treasure map was forgotten in the excitement of the evening. Late that night, when Miles retired to his room and Jonathan and the Professor left to sleep aboard the raft in the harbor, they remembered the map and decided to show it to Miles in the morning. But before they had gotten halfway down the street to the harbor they had a change of mind. It seemed to both of them that treasure maps, somehow, weren't worth their concern under the circumstances, that the Squire's disappearance rather deflated the importance of treasure and that, given the dangerous nature of their undertakings, they would be wise to roll the map up and ignore it until the Squire was safe. They shook hands on the decision without any regrets.

Chapter 6

Laughter in the Fog

❖

THEY met Gosset at the tavern the following afternoon. He pushed in backward through the door wearing a rejuvenated ape mask and carrying the wizard's obstreperous conical cap. The thing was even taller than Miles' old cap, and it was a wonder of twirling stars and moons and ringed planets. Atop the pointed spire sat a carved ivory head with two faces, a grinning baby face with puffy cheeks on one side, the leering face of a wizened old man on the other. The cap wasn't as heavy as it looked. It seemed somehow to be animated, to want to roll and leap about, and the ivory ball on top spun slowly, seemingly of its own accord, the alternate faces blending into one continuous blur of a face—a face that looked weirdly like Miles the Magician.

"Here we are, then," Miles said, taking the hat from the mystified Gosset. "This is perfect, sir. Together we've made an astonishing cap."

"Astonishing!" Gosset cried. "The thing's alive. Magic, I call it."

"Magic and more." Miles fitted the cap onto the top of his head. The thing settled over his forehead where it seemed to relax visibly, as if it were home at last. Miles rose and took a few creeping steps across the floor, much to the astonishment of those few villagers who sat about nibbling lunches. Then he leaped once or twice in the manner of a ballet dancer, crouched, spun round, flailed his arms about and did, as a sort of encore, a forward flip that led in the end to a chair being kicked over with a bang.

"Here now!" the tavern keeper shouted, coming around

51

the end of the bar carrying a rag. "Look what's happened to the chair here."

"Pardon me," Miles said. "How unfortunate." He set the ivory ball aspin, shouted something that sounded like a ruined birdcall, and pointed at the upturned chair which rose slowly into the air, settling finally on its feet. "There," Miles said.

Two diners leaped up and rushed out of the room; a third buried his face in a newspaper. "Touchy about wizardry in these parts, aren't they?" Miles remarked, sitting down and removing the cap.

"It's not surprising," Jonathan replied. "They've seen more than their share of it recently. It's wonderful the way the cap stays on your head like that, even when you're capering around."

"It's a proper cap now. A good cap knows its owner's head and fits it like a cap of snow on a mountain."

"I should say." Jonathan remembered the cap as it had been six months before, wobbling and falling, and Miles tieing the thing to his chin until he was about to choke.

They bought Gosset a pint of ale and a cottage pie and bid him adieu. It suddenly seemed unjustifiably frivolous to be mooching about over lunch. In half an hour the raft was in midriver, spinning along past Hightower Village. They rigged the sails to take advantage of the north wind, and the raft leaped ahead as if anxious to be off downriver.

Miles set up a little pot of smoking herbs and thumbed through a book of incantations for one that would increase the force of the wind. Whether his new cap heightened the power of the spell or whether Miles was simply a very potent wizard was hard to say, but by late afternoon the wind blew straightaway down the river so prodigiously that the hemlocks and alders along the banks began to whip about and the rigging began to whistle and groan. Miles lit a new batch of herbs and worked feverishly to reduce the spell, but in the end Jonathan was forced to reef the sail to avoid ripping it to bits.

It was dark before the wind died down. Since they had made tremendous progress that day, they agreed to sail on through the night keeping watch in shifts. At around four in the morning they rounded a headland and drifted into the long section of dark water that flowed still and eerie past the great expanse of the Goblin Wood. All of the rafters, Ahab included, sat about on the deck watching the dim line of the forested shores and the shifting moon shadows of the oaks on the river.

Several times they saw the flickering of goblin fires and the glowing faces of jack-o'-lanterns through the trees. The faraway gonging of a copper drum told of a goblin revel somewhere in the heart of the Wood. When the sun rose over the hills in the west and the sky was gray with dawn light, two skeletons, jerking along like marionettes, appeared on the river road. A faint clacking and moaning floated out across the waters as the rafters watched in silent dread. Miles finally shouted a toasting spell at them, but the distance must have been too great, for the things disappeared into the shadows of the woods, as if anxious to avoid the rays of the rising sun.

The sun, of course, was as welcome to the rafters as it was unwelcome to the creatures of the Wood. With a pot of coffee and a morning breeze, they once again set sail and hurried along toward Willowood where, the following afternoon, they left the raft moored to a piling and set out overland on hired ponies.

Their trail ran along the river road for a ways, winding beneath hemlocks and oaks and redwoods. The little-used road was green with spring mosses and oxalis, and it would have been an enjoyable thing altogether to simply meander along studying the toads and newts and collecting wild flowers to press. But there wasn't any time to enjoy the scenery. They rode as hard as they dared all that day and the next, leaving the Oriel behind and climbing into the foothills that rose slowly toward the Elfin Highlands.

The trail seemed to follow the most leisurely, meandering course between the crests of the scattered hills. It didn't seem to Jonathan to be the straightest or quickest course, and he said as much to Miles.

"The straightest course often leads to the crookedest ends," Miles announced cryptically.

They forded any number of little streams and crossed broad meadows of clover and wild grasses, camping in the evening beneath clear, star-laden skies on the tops of hills away from the dampness of the meadows. Late one evening when they were halfway between the river and their destination, they sat around their campfire chatting about possible reasons for the Squire's disappearance. None of them could fathom it. The only evidence that Selznak the Dwarf had had a hand in it was based on his being seen in the territory at around the same time. Although that was certainly suspicious, it was little else beyond that. Jonathan pointed that out, but Miles didn't seem to agree. As the evening wore on, Jonathan began to suspect that somehow Miles was sure Selznak was up to deviltry, that evil forces were stirring in the land, and that their recent routing of the Dwarf from his stronghold on Hightower Ridge had merely caused a temporary calm in a dark and gathering storm.

The night was warm, too warm to warrant a fire really, but they had built one anyway for the sake of cheerfulness and because there was good dry wood lying about. Stars glowed overhead in wild profusion. Jonathan had been told once that elfin galleons sailed among the stars casting long golden seines into the reaches of the heavens to fish for star jewels. He hadn't much believed it at the time, but there, lying beneath the glowing tumble of the Milky Way, it didn't seem half so unlikely. Stranger things had come to pass.

He was just about to doze off, had just slid down into a curious dreamland in which he and Ahab were rowing a little boat along a river through the stars, when the Professor shook him awake. Miles, Jonathan saw, had clambered onto a jumble of boulders and was peering off through the moonlit night toward a nearby stand of willow that sat at the mouth of a little valley where two hills came together along the path to linkman territory.

Jonathan and the Professor joined him, and together they watched wisps of fog curl up from among the willows as if it were leaking out of the earth. The fog swirled about in the otherwise clear night air, drifting slowly along toward them over the meadow. Jonathan could hear Miles mumbling—casting spells probably—beneath his breath. The cloud of fog drifted nearer until, some forty feet from their camp, it seemed to flatten itself against an invisible wall.

The fog whirled and danced for a moment, then set off in a wide circle around their camp, brushing over the tops of the meadow grasses. Jonathan, for just a moment, thought that he could hear the sound of low laughter on the breeze, and the Professor cocked his head just then as if he too heard it. The fog hung about for a moment at the edge of the woods below them, then disappeared into the shadows.

The three of them tramped back down to camp and were astonished to find that the campfire had gone out. It hadn't just burned down, but was cold, as if it had been out for a week. It appeared to have been blown out, blasted, for sticks and ash were scattered all over the bedrolls.

"What the devil?" Jonathan exclaimed. The whole incident seemed inexplicable.

"Whatever it was, it's gone," the Professor observed.

"We hope he is," Miles said.

"He?" Jonathan echoed.

"Who can say?" Miles replied. "I have my suspicions."

Jonathan was beginning to develop suspicions of his own. He lay thinking about them for a bit, but he didn't work things through very far before he was asleep, falling almost at once into the same dream about rowing among the stars. This dream, however, was permeated with an aura of peculiar dread—the sense that he wasn't out rowing for pleasure, but was being watched and pursued by something that was hiding in the purple, misty darkness behind him. The night was full of such dreams. In the morning, the group was off at sunrise, eating as they trotted along.

For two more days there was nothing to signify that they were in linkman territory, for they passed no farms or cottages and saw no other travelers. Five days after setting out from Hightower Village, however, they awoke to the jingling of cow bells and to the sight of a herd of great hippolike cattle clomping down along the meadows below them, pursued by two serious-looking linkmen, both of them smoking long cherrywood pipes.

By noon they had passed through three fairly large villages and were told by a wild-eyed linkman with a broad, grinning face that they were some six miles from Myrkle Hall. They lunched on bread and cheese and a flagon of

wine, passing all of that back and forth to one another as
they rode along. An hour later they swung round a bend
in the road and there before them, perched on a distant
hill, lay Myrkle Hall—a vast, half-timbered lodge that was
a perfect amazement of porticoes and gables and dormers
and turrets surrounded by an expensive park, neatly laid
out with a winding stream that ambled between rocky
pools.

Jonathan could imagine the pyramidal Squire, dressed
in his voluminous, suspendered trousers, eating a jolly
breakfast on the wide veranda that fronted the hall, and
he wondered what sort of villain could have possibly
brought the Squire to harm. The answer, of course, suggested itself almost immediately. It must have suggested itself as well to the others, for there, settled in front of the
hall, was an elfin airship.

Jonathan, the Professor, Miles, and Ahab arrived to find
that a haze of mystery hung over everything. Even the elves
were stupefied. There was a general discussion, in fact,
going on in the dining hall when the three travelers walked
in. Twickenham the elf was there along with his friend
Thrimp. Several linkmen were present: Bufo Morinus,
Gump Ooze, and, of course, the Squire's young friend
Stick-a-bush. Another linkman, a sad-looking chap dressed
as a footman, wildly repeated the story of the Squire's disappearance. He carried on loudly, shouting "Blast me!"
once in a while to dramatize the tale. It was clear to
Jonathan that such elaboration was necessary, for the man's
story was a bit short of detail.

It was a moment before Bufo spotted the three of them
standing in the entry hall. "Mr. Bing!" he shouted. "Professor!" Ahab trotted across to where Bufo stood carving
a roast beef, as happy, it seemed, to see his old friend Bufo
as to see the roast beef.

A wonderful meal was being laid out, and it seemed
about twice as wonderful to the three travelers who had, in
truth, been eating some fairly sorry jerked beef and hard
rolls most of the time along the trail. Aside from the roast,
there was a great steaming pudding and heaps of fried
potatoes. Bowls of spring fruit lay everywhere.

The three travelers had just enough time to shake hands

all around before being hustled into chairs and handed glasses of wine. There were nine of them there at the table, which was so long that it could have easily sat another nine without anyone being cramped for elbow room. At the head of the table stood an immense chair supported by heavy carved legs—a chair clearly intended for someone of great bulk. On the backrest was the Myrkle coat of arms —a roast goose rampant on a ground of heaped grapes and the back view of a fleeing goblin with his pants afire. It was the strangest such device Jonathan could remember, but it fit the Squire admirably, as did the chair. But alas, there it sat, empty, while the rest of them gobbled the Squire's food.

"So, Bufo," Miles began once the meal had gotten underway. "What ho? How stands the investigation?"

"Yes," urged Twickenham, who, along with Thrimp, had just recently arrived. "This gentleman's story sounds like stuff to me, begging your pardon, my man. It sounds crazy." Next to Twickenham's chair sat his own pointed, astronomical cap—a cap not unlike the wizard's but without the ivory head on top and not nearly so tall. The cap, Jonathan decided, was a badge of rank of some nature. The other elves he'd known, including Thrimp, wore pointed hats of varying hues, but without the complex design of stars and moons and planets. It was perhaps an indication of the seriousness of the mysterious doings that both Twickenham and Miles had been sent for.

"We're not sure," Bufo said, waving a hand at the poor footman who, along with the rest of them, was tieing into the roast beef and pudding. "This man's story is peculiar —too peculiar to be a lie, if you ask me. This is the Dwarf's doing, or I'm a blind man."

"When was the Dwarf seen?" Twickenham asked.

"About a week and a half ago," Bufo answered, scooping up a handful of fried potatoes. "He was served at the inn at Glimby Village. He had his hat and cloak and staff. There was no doubt it was him. And he was asking about the Squire."

"Why, do you suppose?" Jonathan asked. "What possible gain could there be in harming the Squire?"

"Or kidnapping him," Bufo added.

"Ransom?" suggested the Professor.

"Selznak doesn't need money," Twickenham said. "Revenge is more in his line. Revenge or . . ." But he didn't finish the sentence. Instead he thrust a forkful of pudding into his mouth as if to plug it up.

"Or what?" Stick-a-bush was horrified.

"Nothing," Twickenham said.

"Let it go," the Professor agreed. "There's no use getting worked up over something like that. What could he do with the Squire anyway?"

"*Do* with him!" Stick-a-bush gasped.

"What the devil is that!" Gump shouted, pointing at the window. Everyone leaped to his feet, and Bufo rushed to the window. There was nothing there, however, but one of the Squire's truffle pigs, rooting in the flower beds.

They sat down again. "Hey!" Stick-a-bush exclaimed. "Where's my roast beef? I had an end cut and now I don't. Now I have this!" He held up a grisly piece of rare beef that looked as if someone had been at it with a pair of hedge clippers and a set of false teeth.

"Devil's work," Gump said. "That must be who I saw at the window. First he got the Squire; then he got your roast beef."

"*You've* got my roast beef!" Stick-a-bush hollered, pointing at Gump's plate.

"And you've got mine!" Gump returned. "Fair's fair."

"Fair!" Stick-a-bush cried. "I'll show you *fair!*" And he hacked Gump's pudding to bits with his fork.

"Gentlemen!" Twickenham shouted. "Come now!"

Jonathan could see that this was going to be a fairly typical linkman convention. "Here, Stick-a-bush," he said. "I've got the other end of the roast. You can have it. I'm not crazy about it anyway. Too much burned fat for my tastes." Jonathan gave Stick-a-bush his end cut and speared a rare slice off the platter. Peace was restored, and Bufo continued. "We don't know anything about motives, but we do know one thing—Selznak stopped at Glimby Village at least an hour after the Squire disappeared. It's fairly certain that he thought the Squire was up at the hall."

"This grows passing strange," said Miles in the manner of a wizard.

"It does that," Bufo agreed. "Even more strange is that the Dwarf was seen two nights later by Alf the gardener. He was poking about in the nasturtiums and, says Alf, looking in at the window. 'I'm looking for my eyeglasses,' he told Alf—a lie, as we know—and he said he was a friend of the Squire's. So Alf said the Squire hadn't been seen for two days, and the Dwarf said it was a lie. But Alf isn't the type to lie, and Selznak could see that. Alf said Selznak set out across the lawn smoking his pipe like fury and never came back."

"So Selznak didn't kidnap the Squire," Miles concluded. "He didn't even know the Squire was gone."

"Or else," the Professor said shrewdly, "he wanted us to believe all that."

Twickenham shook his head. "He doesn't care what we believe. He does what he likes. That'll be the end of him someday too. That swelled head of his."

"Then where did the Squire go?" Jonathan asked, getting back around to the subject.

"He went right through the wall!" shouted the footman, who had been eating feverishly. "Blast me if he didn't. I'm no madman!"

"Of course not," Jonathan insisted.

"Through the wall?" The Professor shoved his spectacles up onto his nose.

"Through the bleedin' wall!" was the answer.

"According to the scientific masters," the Professor said, "such behavior is unlikely."

"Blast me!" cried the man, who was apparently anxious to be blasted. "There he was, was the Squire, a-sittin' in that chair of his in the library. He had that big glass ball of his and was lookin' at it toward the window. He hadn't said nothing for an hour. Hadn't ate no breakfast. I walks in to offer him a piece o' Mrs. Feeny's peach tart. And I sees him—blast me if I don't—I sees him get up and walk through a big door in the wall. Then he was gone, and he ain't been back since."

"Door in the wall?" Miles repeated. "That doesn't sound so mysterious."

"There isn't any door in the wall of the library," Bufo went on. "That's what makes it mysterious."

"Or a lie," said Gump.

"Blast me!" the footman shouted.

"Let's have a look at that library," the Professor suggested, pulling out a businesslike magnifying glass. "There's been some hocus-pocus here or I'm not Artemis Wurzle."

But in the library, as Bufo had promised, there was no door in the wall. There were banks of single casements along two outside walls and stacks and stacks of books along the others. The casement windows were far too small for the Squire to have climbed through. And it was unlikely, all in all, that he would have undertaken such acrobatics anyway.

"Where was this door?" asked the Professor.

"Yonder." The footman pointed toward the shelves of books.

"A secret panel," Jonathan said, seeing in this mystery a certain relation to the novels of G. Smithers. The Professor set about removing books and tapping on the walls. Then he left the room and disappeared down the hall, tapping against the wall from the room beyond. He walked back in a moment later.

"There's no hidden panel," he stated emphatically. "At least not here. The wall isn't wide enough for a passage either."

"There weren't no panel," the footman insisted. "There was a door. A big, iron door. It didn't have no handle—just a big iron door. I saw what I saw. It swung to and the Squire walked through it, quick as you please. And he took his glass ball with him."

"Then where's the door?" Bufo asked, obviously suspicious of the man's unlikely tale.

"It vanished. *Poof!* Blast me if it didn't. It was there; then it weren't. Just like that. Magic, I says. And I still says it."

"Whisky," Gump whispered into Bufo's ear.

"What!" cried the footman.

"Risky, this venture, I said," Gump replied. "Too much magic."

"That's right," the footman said.

"What was this marble?" Jonathan asked, vague suspicions floating in his head.

"It was the one he always carried around," the footman said. "The one he brought back from the wars."

"From the wars?" the Professor asked.

"The one he took from Hightower," put in Gump helpfully. "That was the wars as far as the Squire was concerned."

"The Lumbog globe," Jonathan mumbled. "Then maybe that's what . . ." He was about to say that perhaps the Dwarf had come looking for the Lumbog globe—the magical glass ball that the Squire had taken for a great marble that previous winter at the Tower.

But before he could finish, Miles the Magician cut in, "Balumnia!"

"Of course!" Twickenham exclaimed.

Jonathan and the Professor gave each other a significant look. "Balumnia?" Jonathan repeated in surprise.

"Has to be," Miles insisted, assuming that Jonathan and the Professor had grasped his meaning. "The door, the globe, Selznak—all the pieces fit."

"I don't understand anything," Gump said.

"A door right there in the wall!" the footman repeated, blasting himself up and down.

"Say," said Bufo to the footman. "Run down to Glimby and give a message to the mayor, will you?"

"Well." The footman hesitated. "I don't suppose that's my job."

"There's a fiver in it for you," Bufo added.

"Aye aye, sir! I won't be gone an hour. If I am, you know where I'll be."

"Aye," Gump murmured under his breath, "at the Twisted Pelican."

Jonathan watched over Bufo's shoulder as the linkman wrote a note to the mayor on paper he found in the Squire's library table. "Hark!" he wrote, "the ants go marching, dooby-doo." And he signed it, "A friend."

"What in the world does that mean?" Jonathan asked.

"Nothing," Bufo answered. "Just having him on a bit. Little lark. Do the mayor some good—keep him on his toes."

The footman disappeared with the note, mounting a

horse and riding off down the road in the direction of Glimby Village.

"It strikes me that there's something about all this business that I don't follow," Jonathan said.

"What's that?" Miles asked.

"All of it. All I know is what I heard from Escargot, that this globe somehow lets a person fly around the world. It didn't make much sense to me then, and it still doesn't."

"Well," Miles said, "that's putting it pretty slack. I'd be surprised if that was all Escargot knew about the globe. There seems to be nothing Escargot hasn't dabbled in—especially when it comes to the seven Elfin Marvels. Do you know how the Squire came by the globe?"

"He found it in the Tower, in the pantry actually."

"Where was Escargot?" Miles asked.

"He was there. He didn't take much interest in the thing —just let the Squire have it."

"I was baffled by that very thing," the Professor put in. "I would have bet the *Tomes of Limpus* that it was the globe Escargot was after when he agreed so readily to journey upriver with us. And then he just let the Squire have it. Didn't blink an eye."

"Perhaps Escargot has his code," Jonathan guessed. "He'd steal from Selznak, but he wouldn't steal from the Squire. I think you're selling him short."

"You're all wrong," Twickenham cut in. "Escargot doesn't need the globe as long as he has his undersea device."

Miles nodded slowly. "I had forgotten about the submarine," he said. "That explains it entirely. One doesn't need two keys to the same door."

Now Jonathan was confused. "What does all this mean? What does Escargot's submarine have to do with the Lumbog globe and what do either of them have to do with doors appearing in the wall of the Squire's library?"

Twickenham smiled knowingly. "It has to do with the nature of the Squire's disappearance. He hasn't disappeared exactly, he's merely off traveling in a land he didn't expect to find. And that's the problem, isn't it? The Squire doesn't know where he is—nor how to get back, for that matter. The Squire, as Miles pointed out, has entered the land of Balumnia."

Jonathan and the Professor once again shot each other a significant look. There was no mistaking it. Apparently the Squire and the treasure were both, somehow, in the land of Balumnia. Jonathan was struck with a sudden memory, a memory that rather confused the issue for him.

"I once read a book about this Balumnia," he said. "It must have been twenty years ago. It was a wonderful book by the elf author, Glub Boomp. A fantasy novel."

"Glub Boomp didn't write fantasy novels," Twickenham put in. "He was an historian."

That seemed unlikely to Jonathan, who vaguely remembered stories about amazing lands beneath the sea and horrible dark woods infested by cannibals and goblins and werewolves. The tales hadn't sounded much like history to him, but then he'd only been twelve or so at the time. Still, unlikely or not, here were Twickenham and Miles insisting that the Squire, somehow, was off in the land of Balumnia. And if Balumnia were real enough to hold the Squire, it was a very real world indeed.

"The Lumbog globe," Twickenham said, "has certain powers. To the uninitiated it affords wonderful dreams—much as Escargot had promised. To the knowledgeable it's a key, figuratively speaking, to a Balumnian door."

"A Balumnian door?" The Professor was a bit more skeptical of all this business than was Jonathan.

"Just so," Twickenham continued, warming to his subject. "A door into Balumnia."

"Like a closet door?" the Professor asked, "or a cupboard door? That seems fairly unlikely, doesn't it?" Obviously the Professor wasn't convinced. "Strange sort of a land, isn't it? Fancy walking into it through a door rather than sailing to it on a ship."

"That's possible too," Miles continued. "There's a door beneath the ocean, the western door. It's somewhere out toward the Wonderful Isles, hundreds of fathoms beneath the swells. The islanders thereabouts catch some of the most wonderful beasts: butterfly fish and winged cod and periwinkles the size of your head. There are said to be chambered nautili that live in the passage itself that produce song bubbles—music so wonderful that when the bubbles burst on the surface of the sea, dolphins gather by the thousands and weep."

The Professor sat there open-mouthed, looking as if about half of him suspected that Miles was having him on.

"And that, of course, is why Escargot didn't need the globe," Twickenham explained. "At least he didn't need it enough to steal it from the Squire; not as long as he had his submarine."

"Then we will need a submarine too," Jonathan said. "We've got to find Escargot and borrow his."

"Not so," Miles replied. "The undersea door is, as I said, the western door. In the White Mountains lies the eastern door. In the north, beyond the City of the Five Monoliths, there's another door. The southern door we won't mention."

"And it's just as well," Twickenham added. "Doors are much like people. There are good doors and evil doors— doors that would better remain shut. The Lumbog globe is a floating door, and somehow the Squire stumbled upon its secret."

"Selznak must have been after the globe then," Jonathan reasoned.

"Almost certainly," Twickenham answered. "Two Elvish Wonders were taken from him: the pocketwatch and the globe. The watch was quickly beyond his grasp. The globe, however, was a different matter. We'd be fools, though, to suppose that only his desire for the globe spurred him on. The Squire, I believe, has reason to fear for his life."

"The fog on the heath!" Jonathan cried. "That was him —the Dwarf."

"Of course," Miles said. "He was heading back upriver, toward the southern portal." They told Twickenham of the little fog that had hung about on the meadow along the trail and had, somehow, snuffed their campfire.

"That's just like something he'd do," Twickenham said, "snuff your campfire. He was on the trail of the Squire, all right."

"Then we'd best be off on that trail ourselves," Jonathan suggested. "Poor Squire. He doesn't know where he is or why he's there. He's probably confronted right now by singing squids, and the Dwarf's after him with an eye toward turning him into a winged toad or something."

"Well," said Gump, sticking in his two cents worth, "we don't have to worry about any squids. The Squire would just eat the things. I've seen him eat squid sandwiches that would turn your head. They were marvels. And he wouldn't care if they sang either; he'd eat them anyway. A singing sandwich is right in the Squire's line."

Everyone laughed at the image of Gump's singing sandwich, but they didn't laugh long. There were plans to be made, bags to be packed. It had become something of a race. The only bit of hope lay in the supposition that Selznak, though he might well enter Balumnia ahead of them, would have no more idea of the Squire's whereabouts than they had. Jonathan was beginning to feel like one of the detectives in a G. Smithers novel. He considered the idea of buying a tweed suit and cap and magnifying glass like the Professor's. But then he recalled that emulating a G. Smithers character often brought about undesirable ends, so he gave up the idea.

It was too late in the evening to set out, so they agreed to be underway an hour before dawn the next morning. Jonathan and the Professor decided to forget their plan of abandoning the treasure map. After all, it was an astonishing coincidence that they had a double reason for traveling to Balumnia, and it would be folly not to take advantage of such an opportunity.

After the lot of them had discussed plans for two hours over apple pie and coffee, Jonathan and Professor Wurzle sought Miles out in his room and showed him the map. Miles pronounced the document authentic and agreed with the Professor that it was probably drawn in octopus ink. There was some possibility, however, that the ink of a river squid had been used. The Professor was quite sure that nothing of the sort was the case, although he admitted, finally, that it was tough to be utterly precise, given the age of the map and the similarity between squid and octopus inks. All the "poulpe" inks bore similarities. At least that's what the Professor said. Jonathan assumed that the ink controversy was evidence of the Professor's concern for scientific accuracy, and so didn't pay much attention. Octopus ink and squid ink were all pretty much the same to Jonathan.

"This would be Landsend harbor," Miles observed, pointing at a great dot on the map. "And this is the Tweet River, flowing past it to the sea. A full rigged ship can sail a thousand miles up the Tweet River. A trade barge can sail two thousand if it wanted to. Nobody with any sense would want to, though. You can see the river mouth here on the map. All this gray area, that's the ocean. These dots are the Flappage Islands. Pirate havens, every one. It's a rough port, Landsend. But it's just the place for treasures."

"What's the likelihood we'll travel this far?" Jonathan asked.

"As I see it," Miles said, "it's no more likely that we travel in one direction than in another. We might just as well set out for Landsend. If we get word of the Squire, we can always adjust our course."

"This has some resemblance to the old needle in a haystack business," the Professor remarked about their search for the Squire.

"It has that," Miles replied glumly. "But I have methods, gentlemen, that may avail us."

Jonathan was fairly sure that Miles wasn't talking falsely. Any man, after all, who could set an ape suit afire with a toasting curse was a good man to have along in a pinch. More useful, no doubt, than the ape suit itself.

Chapter 7

On the Trail of the Squire

❧

JONATHAN was already awake next morning when Miles
the Magician came for him and the Professor. In fact,
Jonathan had been awake most of the night, what with the
double excitement. It had always been Jonathan's belief
that it was folly to worry about unfathomables. He held
that as one of his principal philosophies, even if he didn't
always practice it. Since there was nothing to be done for
the Squire, not that night anyway, his thoughts were mostly on treasures. Jonathan didn't care much for wealth—not
half as much, anyway, as for the treasure itself. The two
times he dozed off during the night he had dreams of finding immense caverns of treasures salted away by pirates
for five hundred years.

He was fairly sure that pirates themselves rather felt the
same way. If books could be believed—and it was beginning
to look as if they could—then it seemed as if pirates spent
their lives amassing great chests full of emeralds and gold
for the sole purpose of burying the lot of it away on some
goat-populated desert isle, only to sail back years later and
dig it up and fight over it and make up songs about it and
bury it again, finally, somewhere else. He had never heard
of pirates spending any of it.

It struck Jonathan as a pity to do anything at all with
the treasure. It would be far more worthwhile to leave it
be, to return every few years and find it again, to sort of
climb about in it yelling like a man who has lost his wits
and let the chains of jewels and the gold coins run through
his fingers and heap up on the floor. And there would no
doubt be grim evidence lying around of the horrible his-

67

tory of it—skeletons in cocked hats run through with cut-lasses and set here and there to keep watch. What a shame to move such a treasure—something like tearing apart an old and crumbling building or chopping down an ancient tree.

The Professor didn't exactly see things in the same light when Jonathan discussed it with him the next morning. He told Jonathan that he had too much of the poet in him—was too romantic. There were things that a man could do with such a treasure. Just for historical purposes it should be catalogued; and given the nature of treasures in general, a good bit of it should be spent on historical exploration and study.

All that sounded pretty punk to Jonathan—which is how Theophile Escargot would have put it. But then it didn't much matter there at Myrkle Hall; after all, they had no treasure yet.

The Squire's cook, a dedicated fellow who was very nearly as fat as the Squire, was up before any of them. He had a mind, he said, to go along with them in search of his master, but he couldn't. It was impossible. It wasn't to be thought of. If they would send word, however, of their homecoming, they'd see a bit of a feast. As break-fasts go, however, they saw a bit of a feast right there. Waffles and eggs and ham and ripe oranges and biscuits and honey and just about anything you please was spread out on the big table in the dining hall. The food was gob-bled down faster than it should have been, perhaps, for Twickenham was anxious to be off.

Five of them were bound for Balumnia: Jonathan, the Professor, Miles, Bufo, and Gump. Stick-a-bush elected to stay behind. He assured the rest of the company that he was itching to be "at" the Dwarf, but it was almost time for him to journey to Seaside with the spring produce from the family farm and return with baskets of smoked fish.

Twickenham and Thrimp were anxious to give them a lift in the airship as far as the portal in the White Moun-tains, but they were anxious to go no farther. Clearly, the rest of the company could get on well enough without the two elves who, Twickenham pointed out, had done little that past twenty-four hours but eat up the Squire's food.

So it was settled. The company piled aboard the elfin ship along with a few meager supplies. They decided to carry little along with them, trusting that the country of Balumnia, wherever it lay, would understand the nature of a gold coin.

The airship rose silently skyward. Jonathan watched through the window as the ground below receded. Myrkle Hall looked like a cleverly built toy amid the surrounding green of the meadows. Orchards became visible, laid out in neat rows beside fields of strawberries. Forests crept along over the hills toward the River Oriel, and when the airship was almost level with two white puffy-cheeked clouds, Jonathan could see the river itself off in the distance, a tiny ribbon of a river running away down the valley toward Seaside. Smoke from what must have been Willowood Station rose in the northeast, and beyond that stretched the dark expanse of the Goblin Wood.

They whizzed away east, finally, toward the White Mountains, leaving Myrkle Hall and the orchards of the linkmen far behind. The mountains themselves seemed to grow as the airship ascended and flew into the dawn. Jonathan had heard any number of astonishing stories about the White Mountains, stories about the tribes of mystics who lived in the shelter of high valleys, cut off from the outside by perpetual storms, sharing their caves and huts with snow apes and white tigers. Elves dwelt in the foothills, spinning elf silver and glass into wonderful toys and building fabulous magical machines like Twickenham's airship. Dwarf villages stretched along the mountainsides below the mouths of deep caves. Almost no villages of men could be found, though, either on the slopes of the foothills or at the higher elevations. It was rumored that there was something magical about the White Mountains that drove men mad, as had happened to the mystics.

The airship followed the slow curve of a little green valley up the foothills. The mountains were heavily timbered and ran with creeks and rills and waterfalls that tumbled along, now visible, now hidden beneath the thick woods, finally cascading out of the edge of the forest to flow into a rushing stream, white and green beneath the morning sun, and falling away down the valley. One hill seemed to give rise to another, and where the one humped and leveled for a space, the river slackened and pooled up into little lakes before tumbling over another crest and dashing away again. Along the banks of these lakes were timbered dwellings that sat so placidly among the surrounding meadows and trees that they were no less a part of the landscape than were the rocks and the woods and the river itself.

High in the mountains the river was considerably smaller, but what it lacked in size it made up for in energy as it raced along over the steepening slopes. Twickenham circled once over a cluster of cottages, and a group of elves surged out onto the meadows around them, waving up at the airship in the blue sky. Sheep and cattle wandered about on the hillsides, and it occurred to Jonathan that the whole scene below was what might be called idyllic.

In a few minutes, the cottages and the elves fell away behind, and shortly thereafter the forests became less dense. The trees seemed to be shrinking and growing sparse until finally there were only a few scattered and lonely junipers, twisted by the winds and almost bare of foliage. Then there were no trees at all, only patches of moss and grasses, blown by cold winds and nibbled by occasional elk and reindeer. The stream disappeared abruptly into a crevice in the rocks, reappeared several hundred feet farther up, then disappeared again.

The airship flew through mountain peaks that rose incredibly above, and Jonathan could see the tiny shadow of the ship on the rocks and cliff faces, pursuing them. Patches of snow appeared here and there in among the rocks. The patches spread and grew until there was nothing about them but snow and the sharp pinnacles and broken humps of gray stone. They skimmed over the top of a great ice sheet that shone silver in the sunlight. The ice began to glow as the airship rose still farther, and as they slanted round a tremendous outcropping of rock and ice and into the sharp rays of the sun, prismatic glints of color shone from deep within the ice as if innumerable gemstones were caught and held in the clear depths of the glacier—diamonds and emeralds and sapphires and rubies that scattered a thousand deep rainbows through the ice.

When it seemed as if there could be no more mountains

to rise above, they sailed round a sharp, sawtooth peak and into the shadows of still another tremendous precipice. It began to look as if there was an infinitude of successive mountains, each range higher than the last. But when the airship rose over the top of that last precipice, there, spread out before them for what seemed like—and might well have been—a thousand miles, were no end of distant snowy peaks and shadowy valleys. Whole empires could have grown up and fallen again within that expanse of mountains, completely unknown to the little village of Twombly Town or, for that matter, to any of the villages of the high valley. Mountain peaks had always seemed a mystery to Jonathan, who was one of those people who fancied that some marvel lay not only on the other side, but quite likely among the tops of the mountains themselves. Once he'd crested those mountains in the airship, however, it was the unfathomable valleys that seemed so disquietingly mysterious. Here were a thousand of them, ten thousand. Who could say what creatures roamed their slopes and what manners of men dwelled there? Any sort of marvelous thing might be the case.

Just as Jonathan sat imagining a few of those marvelous things, he saw—or thought he saw—what must have been an immense bird silhouetted against the distant snow. He watched it wing its way up out of a valley, soar for a moment on vast wings, then disappear again into shadow. Jonathan at first supposed he imagined the thing, for it would have had to have been a hundred miles away, but the Professor grabbed his arm and said in a voice that was almost a whisper, "Did you see it?"

"Yes," Jonathan replied, also whispering for no reason he could imagine other than because of the mystery of it. "How big must it have been?"

"As big as this ship," the Professor answered. "Bigger even."

"A dragon?" Jonathan wondered aloud.

The Professor gave him a look that suggested dragons were unlikely outside fables and fairy tales. "It's more likely," Professor Wurzle explained, "that it was some sort of gargantuan prehistoric bird. A tremendous pterodactyl quite possibly."

Both of them watched, hoping the bird would reappear, but nothing else broke the snowy vastness of the barren landscape.

"Look up there." The Professor pointed toward the sky. Jonathan peered through the glass of the porthole window at a sky covered with stars glowing like brilliants in the deep, purple-blue of the heavens. The sun stood out among them as if quite willing to share the sky with its fellows.

"Strange, that." Jonathan wouldn't have thought, all things considered, that there was much possibility of the stars putting in an appearance while the sun shone.

"Altitude explains it," the Professor told him. "It's a matter of the density of the aether."

"Ah," said Jonathan, who was satisfied, actually, just to know that such a wonder existed.

In the distance a bank of clouds lay on the mountains, and it was toward those clouds, dark and billowing and rumbling with occasional thunder, that the airship soared. They seemed to be dropping toward the snowy slopes and were soon enveloped in the gray mist of the clouds. Snow swirled outside the windows and the airship rose and dipped suddenly on the wind before coming to rest on the slope of the mountain.

At first, nothing was visible outside the airship but the swirling snow. Then in occasional moments of calm, Jonathan could see the mottled deep gray black of the granite mountainside and the brilliant white of the snow lying against it. There in the wall of rock was what at first appeared to be the arched mouth of a cave. It was, however, too symmetrical, too clearly outlined to be a natural recess, and Jonathan realized that what they had settled in front of was a door—the eastern door, as Miles had called it, and that through that door lay the land of Balumnia.

Jonathan was struck with the fact that he had only a light jacket and sweater with him—hardly the things for traipsing about glaciers. It seemed a strange place to undertake a search for Squire Myrkle. He had learned, however, that as far as elf doings were concerned, it was best not to assume anything; so that's what he did.

Miles rose and wrapped his cloak around himself as if

the thin robes would protect him from the sailing wind and snow. With his hat smashed down over his forehead, he disappeared forward. A moment later, Jonathan watched him out in the snow, bent over, his robes flailing and whipping about him, the ivory head atop his hat whirling and glowing. Snow flew, obscuring the wizard entirely for the space of a long minute. Then he was visible again, hunched in a weird posture before the door, waving his right hand at it as if expostulating the necessity of its opening up.

Twickenham bustled back with Thrimp and told the rest of the company to ready themselves. The aisle turned into a confusion of knapsacks and jackets and caps and walking sticks, and the confusion was doubled by everyone's wanting to watch the magician perform his gesticulations before the door. Gump put on Bufo's jacket and Bufo got Gump's hat. Then the two of them accused each other of idiocy and made a complicated and inexplicable trade of a variety of garments until they were finally satisfied, all the time rushing to the windows to check Miles' progress.

The thin wizard stood before the door, arms akimbo, his dark robes sailing, the snow swirling about him. Slowly, the dark face of the door paled a bit and seemed to shimmer as if a slowly brightening light were being shined on it. Through the transparency that had been the iron door could be seen the blue of a summer sky and the green of vegetation. An amazed cow wandered by beyond the opening, looking back at the wizard with a face full of stupefaction.

"It's time," Twickenham called. "Hurry." And the four of them filed down the plank and onto the frozen hillside. "Good luck, lads," was the last thing Jonathan heard Twickenham say. His own goodbye was carried off by the wind which was sharp as an icicle. Jonathan's cloth jacket might as well have been a fishnet for all the good it did. But in a matter of seconds the five of them hunched through the portal and clustered around the befuddled cow. Behind them the snow still blew, great flakes sailing through onto the grass of the meadow on which they stood. The opening faded as if the light that had shone on it was being slowly switched off. Twickenham's airship was a long batwinged shadow against the snow, and as they watched, it rose slowly into the sky and disappeared. The wind ceased to howl, the snow ceased to blow, and Jonathan realized that he was standing before an iron door set in the grassy side of a hill. It was summertime once again, and the closest mountains were just barely visible in the hazy blue distances.

They stood in the middle of a pasture, ankle high in clover, the air roundabout heavy with the sweet smell of the round, purple blossoms. A dozen cattle, huge shaggy things that ripped up great tufts of grass, lumbered along, paying them little mind. The opening of the door and the wind and sleet that had blown through for the space of half a minute had momentarily puzzled the beasts. The sudden closing of the door ended their puzzlement. Jonathan admired that sort of placidity, that genial acceptance of inexplicable or impossible events. He'd never been able to take things quite as philosophically as a cow could.

He was doing a pretty good job with the door, though. That it was in some respects an impossibility didn't bother him much; he was developing a cavalier attitude toward such things. What did bother him was the sudden realization that it would likely not be an easy thing to descend from those incredible heights in the White Mountains once they had found the Squire and wanted to return. In fact, he hadn't given the whole issue half the thought it deserved. Besides, he knew, the possibility, the likelihood even, existed that they would never find the Squire.

As the members of the company removed their jackets, packed them away, and trudged down along the cow path through the pasture, he asked Miles about all this. "What will Twickenham do now?"

"He has his work cut out."

"Do we have some sort of rendezvous planned?" Jonathan asked. "How long will he wait before he flies back up to the door to pick us up?"

"I don't believe he'll do anything of the sort. He'll most likely spend a few weeks on the river."

"On the river!" the Professor exclaimed, catching Jonathan's drift. "How in the world are we expected to get out of here? We'll freeze like smelts in the White Mountains."

"We won't go back through the White Mountains," Miles

explained, tramping around the edge of a pond that had lapped over a section of the path. The shallow water was alive with splashing frogs who leaped out of their way.

"Now that makes more sense," the Professor said.

"Not as much as it would seem," Miles went on. "You see, the door won't be here after we find the Squire."

"Where does it go?" Gump asked facetiously, "to the coast?"

"Perhaps," Miles said. "The doors seem to have something to do with the four seasons, although nobody knows just what. We were lucky we made it through when we did. We would have had to wait for the summer solstice and the chance that the Northern portal would appear. It may not, you know."

"It may not!" Jonathan was beginning to worry. "That's pretty thick. I'm not sure we were lucky to have made it through. How in the world will we get out?"

Miles smiled. "We'll find the globe."

"It just occurred to me," Jonathan replied, "that there's the chance the Squire might just pop back through the very door he came through. He might be eating strawberries and cream at Myrkle Hall right now."

"He might," Miles said. "But I don't think so. He'd have to wait a bit, if I understand the working of the Lumbog globe. And even if he is, we still have a bit of work to do. I told you back in Hightower there was more to this than met the eye, that there'd be trouble ahead."

"I suppose you did," Jonathan said, suddenly regretting that he'd complained. He'd never favored moaning about his fate, and here he was being pettish.

The path wound along through an oak woods, then out onto a pasture again, then once more into the woods. The sun's rays slanted through the boughs, stippling the forest floor with light. They passed two cottages almost immediately, then saw none for a good mile. The trail finally joined something more like a road that curved along the bank of a fair-sized river. Late that evening they came upon a small village where they ate supper at a tolerably good inn.

Jonathan had been vaguely surprised all day to see that Balumnian oak trees grew the same sort of acorns as did the oak trees of the Oriel Valley. He half suspected that the people of Balumnia would be otherworldly somehow, that they would walk on their hands or have pig snouts for noses. But it turned out that Balumnians appeared to be pretty much the same as the people he was used to seeing. There was nothing, in fact, very magical about Balumnia at all. It was pretty much like anyplace else.

When they sat down at the inn, Jonathan's first thought had to do with the nature of Balumnian ale. It would be a tragedy if it turned out that ale hadn't even been invented in Balumnia or that what passed as ale was nothing more than swamp water with dirt in it or fermented onions. The ale, however, turned out to be the real thing—Old Hogweed, it was called—and what's more, it was served cold, a pleasant surprise on a warm summer evening.

There was some debate at the table over whether to push on after supper. It was such a pleasant night that they might well walk another five miles and sleep under the stars. It seemed like a good idea to Jonathan who, by then, had come to fancy the prospect of a walking tour. He'd had an uncle who took such tours, armed with a book of poetry and a fishing pole, and the whole notion seemed fairly romantic. Sleeping under the stars on a summer night lent itself to such romance.

Gump and Bufo weren't quite as keen on the idea as was Jonathan, and were quick to point out that they had walked a good ten or twelve miles that afternoon already and that, all things considered, it was a peculiar thing to sleep in the open when there was such a superior inn at hand. Miles didn't much care one way or the other. In the middle of the debate, food arrived and settled the issue. They worked their way through a big steak and mushroom pie and a second pint of ale, then nibbled cheese and strawberries. After dinner, their spirits having been lifted exceedingly by the food, they took the innkeeper's suggestion and had a little snifter of brandy and a cup of coffee. Rescuing the Squire, all in all, was turning out to be a moderately jolly time.

"Well," Miles said, lighting his pipe and sipping at his brandy, "we've five miles to go by the light of the moon, lads. Drink up."

But Gump was asleep in his chair and the Professor, although he appeared to be puffing his pipe, kept jerking awake every moment or so, then nodding off again, his pipe balancing there out of good nature more than anything else. Though Jonathan was awake, the food and the ale and the brandy played on him in such a way that the idea of walking anywhere was laughable. Tomorrow would be full of walking; tonight would be full of sleeping. The thought that their laziness might ruin their chance of finding the Squire never occurred to him; if it had, it's doubtful that it would have done much to clear away the late evening muddle. In truth, the brandy had carried with it a certain optimism. For the first time since he'd known the nature of the Squire's disappearance, Jonathan felt as if the magical land of Balumnia wasn't so big after all—not half so big that it could hope to hide the likes of the Squire. So, all in all, five miles one way or the other was very likely immaterial.

Shortly before ten the company filed upstairs and collapsed onto feather beds where they slept like halibut until well after sunup the next morning.

Chapter 8

The Detectives

❈

A certain pall of doubt rose with the sun and somehow chased away the previous night's glow of optimism. Jonathan allowed himself, only moments after he woke up, to regret not only the miles that the company hadn't traveled the night before, but to consider the long miles they'd have to travel to catch up. He wondered how many miles a party of men and linkmen and a dog *could* travel on foot in one day. At least twenty-five, maybe thirty. That quantity seemed enormous and affected him badly. Then, sitting heaped on the edge of his bed and looking down at Ahab on the floor below, he began to daydream about Twombly Town and his front porch and about the strawberries that would be big and ripe that very day. All of that thinking and wondering and daydreaming began to give him a major case of the pip. But then it struck him, as it often did five minutes after he'd waked up of a morning, that it was foolhardy to think about anything that early—either of the day ahead or of the previous evening. Such thoughts are *bound* to give you the pip. It was probably a physical or chemical law and could be found in one of the Professor's scientific manuals. So Jonathan began to whistle the lively tune to "Up at Pinky Winky's" instead as he pulled on his boots. Ahab opened one eye and stared at him. He had a look about him that seemed to suggest that Jonathan could have chosen to whistle something else, or, perhaps, not to whistle at all. Then it became clear to Ahab that it was a new day and that they were off on an adventure. He stretched once or twice there atop his rug and hurried over to the door. They found the Professor and Bufo in the hallway. Miles and Gump were already downstairs watching the innkeeper cook bacon and eggs.

Miles' hair was plastered down atop his head, he having already been at the pump, and he was smiling into a cup of coffee. Gump winked at Jonathan and Bufo covertly as they shuffled up, eyeing the coffee pot on the stove.

"Lot of travelers pass through here, I don't doubt," Gump began.

"Like birds," the innkeeper replied.

Gump nodded. Jonathan wondered just how the travelers resembled birds. Perhaps in quantity. To Gump it didn't seem to matter. "Get many odd ones?"

The innkeeper stared at him in amazement. "We don't get much of anything else." Then he looked at Miles in his shiny, salmon-colored robe and back at Bufo and Gump who, waist high and with their pointed cloth caps, might easily be construed to be odd. "Lot of odd ones," he repeated. "Batches of 'em."

Gump nodded again. Jonathan could see where the conversation was heading. Gump was quite clearly playing the detective and was trying to draw the innkeeper out, inconspicuously. "Bet you've had some fat ones come through here," Gump went on, squinting and taking a sip of coffee. Jonathan looked at Miles, who seemed to be choking on something, a reaction, no doubt, to Gump's subtlety.

"Fat ones?" repeated the innkeeper who, unfortunately, was round as a tub. "What are you talking about? Don't make light with me, sir!" he said, flourishing his spatula.

"Not a bit," Gump assured the man, strangely surprised at his reaction. "You misunderstand me. We saw a man up the road. Amazing man. Big as a cartwheel. Walked rather like a cartwheel might, too, if it had legs. Sort of a rotating walk, if you follow me. Looked like he'd been heaped into his clothes with a shovel. And he had an amazing head. Pointed, it was, with tremendous cheeks. And you couldn't much make out his legs at all. They had more of the look of tree trunks about them than anything else. He had a trick that he did with loaves of bread. He'd eat a hole in the center and shove one up over each wrist so as to take a bite out of them as he swung his arms when he walked."

The innkeeper served up the bacon and turned to Gump, a look of suspicion in his eye. "And you accuse me of doing business with this tremendous pinhead?"

"He was no pinhead." Gump stoutly defended the Squire. "I just thought maybe he'd come through here. That's all."

"Why didn't you just up and ask him? Loaves of bread over his wrists! What's your game, anyway? Who put you up to this?"

"Put me up?" Gump asked, surprised again.

"Was it Sikorsky?" the innkeeper demanded. "What's he about? Tremendous pinheads indeed! I'll pinhead him. You tell Sikorsky . . ."

"I don't even know Sikorsky," Gump protested. "I was just shooting the breeze. We met this jolly sort of a fat bogger up the road and . . ."

"Up what road?" the innkeeper cut in, getting his own back.

"Why, back aways."

"Last night you said you came down off the meadows," the innkeeper said shrewdly. "Now you want me to believe there's a fat man's convention up there? A pinhead gathering? This smells of Sikorsky. You tell him to keep his filthy plots to himself. Tell him that Layton Snade isn't a man to be trifled with and that he can take his precious fat man and go to the devil with him!" He slammed his palm against the stovetop with a tremendous clang that prompted the appearance of his wife from the back of the inn.

"What's all that banging?" she asked.

"It's Sikorsky," the innkeeper said. "He's sent this lot of roughnecks over with a pack of lies. This one's babbling about fat men. Seems to think we have more than our share!"

"Oh he does, does he!" the woman shouted. The response seemed to Jonathan to be fairly odd, and he suspected that the coherence of the conversation was declining. The innkeeper was working himself up into a rage. He began hacking at the eggs atop the griddle with his spatula, breaking and scattering the things until they didn't look much like eggs any more.

"We'd better report to Sikorsky," Jonathan said, ending

any possibility of straightening things out. He regretted his words almost as soon as he uttered them.

The innkeeper fell to cursing Sikorsky and Gump and pinheads and Jonathan and just about everything else that was handy. The upshot of the incident was that the five of them were given what is commonly called "the bum's rush," and they found themselves trudging along the road without having had a chance at the ill-used bacon and eggs. Jonathan was sorry he'd spoken up. It had cost him a breakfast, and, on reflection, he realized that the innkeeper wasn't at all a bad sort. Neither was this chap Sikorsky, for all he knew. It had been a bad morning altogether.

Bufo was in an absolute rage over the whole episode. "What was the reason for all that blather about meeting a fat man up the road?" he demanded of Gump.

"I was feeling him out," Gump answered weakly. "We've got to find out about the Squire don't we?"

"Why didn't you just bloody well ask him about the Squire, then? Do you suppose the Squire might have been there in a disguise? 'We met this jolly fat sort of a bogger up the road,'" Bufo said, mimicking Gump's high, tinkling voice. "You're a fine detective. Got us pitched out before breakfast!"

Gump started to reply, then began to sulk instead. Miles, however, came to his rescue. "Gump was right. We shouldn't let on that we're after the Squire. The less said the better."

"Howso?" asked Bufo, still mad. "If you want to know where a man is, you'd best up and ask. I've never seen any good come from so much beating about the bush."

"Under other circumstances I'd be inclined to agree. But we'd be safest to lay low for a bit, if you follow me."

"Incognito," the Professor added helpfully.

"Exactly," Miles said. "We fancy ourselves the hounds, gentlemen, but we might be mistaken. Where the Dwarf is concerned we'd best assume nothing and reveal even less."

All of that cheered Gump up some because he took it as approval of his detective methods. It didn't satisfy Bufo much at all; the only thing that could have done that would have been a plate of rashers and eggs. Their situation for the most part confounded Jonathan, who hated to think that even in Balumnia they'd be under the shadow of Selz-nak the Dwarf. He'd rather hoped that if they met up with the Dwarf in their pursuit of the Squire, they'd just tweak his nose and be on their way. Miles, clearly, didn't think anything of the sort.

They bought a basket of fruit, a loaf of bread and a bit of cheese at a farmhouse, and the food pretty much restored them. The river along the road had grown and in places was more than a stone's throw across. They passed several log chutes that ran down out of the steep forested bank opposite, and watched as great logs slid out of the mouths of the chutes and into the river, bobbing away downstream on the current. The ringing of axes echoed down from the hillside, but nothing could be seen of the men who wielded them.

"Do you suppose this is a tributary to a bigger river?" the Professor asked.

"I wouldn't be at all surprised," Miles said.

"It's a big river we're looking for, isn't it?" Jonathan was thinking of the treasure map. "Maybe this one runs down into the one we want. A fellow could hook up a few of those logs and make a bit of a raft. We've done it before. We could float down to the big river."

"What big river?" Bufo asked. "I haven't heard anything about any big river."

"The Tweet River," Jonathan told him. "There's a city on the mouth of the Tweet called Landsend. We rather thought we'd look for the Squire there."

"Did we?" Bufo sounded surprised. "Why?"

"Because of the treasure." Jonathan anticipated Gump's and Bufo's likely response to the news that they had a line on a hoard of pirate treasure.

"Treasure!" Gump shouted.

"That's right," the Professor said.

"We have this map," Jonathan put in. Then he and the Professor let both the linkmen in on the treasure secret.

"So it's share and share alike," the Professor said finally.

"And a share for the Squire," Jonathan added.

"And a share for Ahab!" shouted Gump.

Ahab danced about when he heard his name added to the list of shareholders. Gump found a stick on the road and threw it as hard as he could in front of them. Ahab, not usually much good when it came to stick-chasing, was struck with Gump's enthusiasm and dashed away up the road to where it lay.

But when he got up to the spot, there was no stick to be seen. A cat sat in its place, smack in the center of the road. It was a black cat, black as midnight, and it looked at Ahab as if it didn't much care whether he stopped to chat or went on about his business. It didn't appear to be a friendly cat. Ahab's treasure enthusiasm seemed to melt away, and he trotted back to where Jonathan and the others were coming along. There was something about the cat that Jonathan didn't fancy—something that wasn't quite right. Its eyes, perhaps, looked a bit too human. Then again perhaps they didn't. Perhaps it was a trick of the sunshine. No one spoke as they filed past the creature, nor did they look back until they were fifty yards or so up the road. It was probably a matter of superstition.

Gump was the first to take a quick look over his shoulder, and almost as soon as he did he shouted, "Hey!" He came to an abrupt halt. The others stopped too. An old bent woman stood where the cat had been, watching the five of them while leaning on a stick. It seemed to grow uncommonly chilly all of a sudden, even though the sun still shone as brightly in the cloudless sky. For a moment Jonathan imagined that he heard faint laughter, something like the clatter of falling icicles, drift past him on the breeze.

The Professor scratched his chin. "She must have been in the bushes or something."

"Let's get out of here," Jonathan said, a bit less sure of himself. Gump and Bufo seemed to be of a like mind, and they didn't waste any time setting out anew, along with the Professor. Twenty steps farther they realized that Miles wasn't following, and they stopped and turned around. There stood Miles, watching. A hundred yards down the road was the figure of the old woman, hunching along, shrinking in the distance.

"She moves quicker than you'd think," Jonathan observed when Miles caught up to them.

"Uncommonly so," Miles agreed.

"I hope she stops at the inn," Bufo said. "She's got Sikorsky written all over her."

Gump laughed a little, probably happy that Bufo had relaxed a bit about getting pitched out of the inn. Nobody laughed much though. They walked on in silence for a ways, convincing themselves that old women were a common enough thing to come upon in any land, Balumnia included. It seemed to Jonathan that perhaps they were a bit overcommon.

They trudged along for another hour, purposefully forgetting the old woman and her cat. Jonathan brought up his log-raft idea again and it was discussed fairly thoroughly; however it struck them as they walked along that they lacked rope and tools and that it would be a powerfully wet time fetching those logs out of midriver. Who was to say what lay ahead of them, either on the road or on the river. They might crest the next hill and find themselves looking down on the Tweet River itself. There might be rapids along the river, or waterfalls or locks or just about anything. They might well spend a day building a raft by the riverside as Squire Myrkle tramped along the highroad above them. Anything might happen. The raft idea, then, was abandoned.

By afternoon the road became hilly. They seemed to be climbing much more often than they were descending, and the river to the left fell away into a deep canyon and disappeared from view. From atop one little hill they could see a wide slash a quarter of a mile east that must have been the canyon through which the river ran. The road seemed pretty much to be winding round in a wide arc in that general direction, so the Professor announced that it was likely that they'd meet up with the river once again, and not too much farther along the line. It still seemed reasonable, or at least possible, that the river they followed would flow eventually into the great Tweet River, so they were anxious not to be too far removed from it.

Late in the afternoon they were still wandering through hilly country. Once the road curved along and ran for a ways beside a deep gorge through which their river rushed along, tumbling wildly over stones and making Jonathan thankful that he hadn't insisted on the raft idea. Then the road angled away again, across miles of meadows criss-crossed by indifferently kept stone walls. Stands of oak dotted the meadows and shaded groups of lackadaisical cows. Jonathan kept a sharp eye peeled for shepherds or farmers or fence menders or anyone who might advise them of the whereabouts of the Tweet River. After all, such a river, which was reputed to be so vast, would have to be widely known. So widely known, in fact, that to profess their ignorance of it would make the company immediately suspect. But the droopy-eyed cattle seemed to be taking care of themselves, for between eleven and four o'clock, the company passed no one along the road.

At four, however, as the five of them labored up a par-ticularly steep hill, discussing the likelihood of their finding a tavern in time for supper, they saw someone at the sum-mit, slouching along in a sort of head-bobbing, carefree fashion. The man was obviously on a tramp, for he had a bindle over his shoulder and he wore far too many clothes, given the pleasant weather. He waved at the company almost as soon as he was visible on the road—a wild, windmill wave that went on about three or four rotations more than was necessary. He wore a billed cap turned side-ways on his head and yanked down low over his forehead so that his hair was shoved out away at right angles like the bristles of a sprung broom.

Gump winked at the rest of them and waved two fingers as a sort of high sign.

"Wait a minute!" Bufo warned, realizing that Gump in-tended to undertake the detective role once again. But Gump waved him silent and, in an altogether innocent and nonchalant manner, hailed the approaching stranger who re-sponded by waving wildly at them once again—so wildly that Jonathan feared it was some kind of signal and he looked behind him down the road. But the road was empty; it was just the man's energetic greeting.

Jonathan was dismayed to see that the man's eyes seemed to be whirling like tops. He understood that to be a bad sign.

"Good day, sir!" said Gump enthusiastically.

"Allo, allo, allo!" the tramp replied, grinning as if the very idea of their meeting along the road was tremendously amusing. "Going my way?" he asked, cocking his head to one side and stretching his eyes open incredibly wide.

"What way's that?" Gump asked, seeking, no doubt, to humor the man.

"That-a-way," was the answer, and he held his hand together in such a way that his various thumbs and index fingers managed to point, at once, in four opposite directions. "I go all over!" he said wildly. Then, as soon as Gump started to speak, he shouted, "Do you?" He laughed like a wildman.

Jonathan could see that Bufo was working himself up fairly thoroughly over the whole affair. He seemed to be itching to have a go at being a detective himself. "We're looking for a man," Bufo began, throwing caution to the winds. "A man named Squire Myrkle."

"Mirtle?" asked the tramp.

"Myrkle," Bufo repeated. "A big man. Very big."

"Ah, a large one!" The tramp nodded shrewdly. "A big Myrkle."

"Just so," said Gump, shoving his way back in now that they were getting somewhere. "Big around as a barrel."

"Like this?" the wildman asked, holding his arms in a circle so as to indicate the possible circumference of a barrel.

"Just like that. And about my height. And with a head that comes to something of a point on top."

"Like so!" the man shouted happily, making a point atop his own head with his hands while balancing the stick from the bindle under his chin.

"That's it exactly, and he walked like this." Gump strode somberly about the circle, mimicking the Squire's shuffling pyramid gait, arms hovering in the air and rotating circuitously.

"Like this," the wildman said, laying his bindle on the roadway and following Gump's example.

"That's it!" cried Gump. "That's the Squire to a tee. You've seen him then!"

"Who?" The man continued to creep about in the manner of the Squire.

"Squire Myrkle!" Bufo shouted, heating up. "Have you seen the blasted Squire!"

"Big man?"

"Big as an elemumph!" Bufo shouted, flying into a rage. "Big as a hippogumby!"

"Didn't see him," the poor man said, leaving off his capering.

"Where is the Tweet River, my good fellow?" Miles finally asked in a friendly sort of way.

The man perked up amazingly. "Tweet?"

"That's right," Miles said. "The Tweet River."

"Like a bird?" the man asked, slowly starting to resume a very satisfactory Squire imitation. He swung his arms slowly. Then, birdlike, he flapped for a few moments saying, "Tweet, tweet."

"Blazes!" Bufo shouted.

"We'd better report this to Sikorsky," Jonathan said to the Professor. The conversation, like the one with the innkeeper, had deteriorated, and it had occurred to Jonathan that mention of Sikorsky would put a fitting cap on it. The Professor apparently thought so to, for he laughed and nodded at Jonathan's little lark. The wildman, however, flapping there, ceased abruptly. He either didn't see anything funny in Jonathan's mention of the fabled Sikorsky or else he'd grown suddenly tired of the interrogation. He gathered up his bindle from the roadway, twisted the bill of his cap round to the other side of his head, and ran off down the hill, never looking back.

Chapter 9

The Disappearing Dwarf

❊

Miles scratched his chin. Bufo and Gump were dumbfounded. Jonathan and the Professor were pretty much the same way. "Well I'm a codfish," the Professor said as they stood and watched the fellow make away. "What do you suppose set him off?"

"Sikorsky?" Jonathan asked.

"That seems unlikely, doesn't it?" Miles said. "Unless this Sikorsky is some sort of local baron or governor or some such thing. Perhaps we should use his name a bit more circumspectly."

"Perhaps so," Jonathan agreed. It suddenly occurred to him that a man's name and an ape suit had a good deal in common. Both seemed to have the power of setting people to flight. He was happy, in the light of that realization, that he and the Professor had left their suits at Myrkle Hall. Why bundle the things around Balumnia when the mere mention of Sikorsky's ridiculous name would have an identical effect?

They trudged the last twenty-five yards to the crest of the hill, Bufo and Gump muttering darkly about the impossibility of being even a moderately successful detective in a land such as this. Jonathan had to admit that they had a point, all things considered, and he was on the verge of suggesting that they start searching out a place to eat. They had a bit of cheese left over from their breakfast, but the stuff had been riding in their knapsacks throughout the hot afternoon, and was, by then, sort of soft and oily and had begun to smell like the bubbling pools in the swamps below Hightower.

88

Jonathan was in the act of tossing scraps of the cheese to a group of interested birds when they crested the hill. A cool wind ruffled his hair, a wind saturated with a familiar musty, weedy smell, a river smell. There, below them, winding slowly along the floor of a river valley that must have been twenty-five miles across, he saw a tremendous, slow, and ancient river, a river that made the old Oriel seem like a trout stream. In the still afternoon sun, the surface of the river was placid, and the water looked as still and muddy as a rain puddle in a field. Willows and cottonwoods and great bent pepper trees grew along the banks and out into the water. Downriver about a half mile was the mouth of the stream they'd been following. Clutches of logs had floated out onto the big river and collected in log jams. A half dozen men cavorted about on the logs, tying clusters together. Others worked on shore, winching the clusters in. The blunt cone of the mill incinerator smoked listlessly beyond, white smoke and ash drifting forth and hovering about in the air over the mill, dissipating slowly.

Upriver some quarter mile lay a good-sized village, spread out along the bank and up the slopes of the hills behind it. A dozen docks ran out into the river, docks heaped with crates and nets and lumber. A long open market flanked the road as it ran along the waterfront, and it looked as if about half the village was tramping up and down between the stalls of produce and fish. The village itself was a pleasant confusion of white clapboard houses and picket fences and dirt roads.

Moored at one dock was a great steamship with a wide paddlewheel at the stern. So it was toward that dock that the five of them trudged. They passed along the road a sign that said TWEET RIVER VILLAGE and another sign that pointed downriver and said LANDSEND—125 MILES. That seemed to answer a few pressing questions. They agreed almost at once that they'd try to book passage on the riverboat if it was bound for Landsend. By boat, it wasn't so very far. By foot, however, it was five or six days worth of tiresome walking. Jonathan, in fact, had begun to reevaluate the wisdom of his uncle's walking tours. There seemed to be a vast difference between walking for sport or romance and walking for the purpose of arriving at a destination. The first had a comfortable poke-along spirit to it; the second had the flavor of work. It made it doubly irritating to realize that the destination, finally, was unknown; that it was just possible—quite possible—that no destination existed, or that the destination had been passed and missed yesterday afternoon and that all further wandering would be purposeless and random. And the truth of it was that there was nothing to indicate that they were an inch or an hour closer to finding the Squire there above Tweet River Village than they had been when flying in the airship high in the White Mountains. At least aboard the steamship they'd have the advantage of being borne along; they'd gain some sort of direction, and that appealed, apparently, to all five of them.

They were in luck. The *Jamoca Queen* sailed the following morning for Landsend and wasn't near full of passengers. The captain seemed fairly surprised that the five of them had any interest in making such a voyage; and after leading them to four adjacent cabins on the middle deck, he suggested they spend the night aboard. "She sails at dawn," he advised them, peering at them in a no-nonsense manner, "come what may."

"What do you expect?" Jonathan asked, surprised at the odd statement.

"Nothing," the captain replied. "Don't pay any heed to rumors, lads. Rumors never sank a ship of mine." With that he turned and clumped away toward the bridge, shaking his head.

"What in the world was all that about?" Jonathan asked.

"Who knows," the Professor replied. "I was afraid for a moment that you were going to mention Sikorsky. The captain looks like the type who'd get a bang out of that sort of thing."

"I thought about it," Jonathan said, "but I had the same impression. I didn't want to land us in the river. We'd best go easy around here."

"You're right," Miles agreed, choosing one of the cabins. Bufo and Gump chose another, and Jonathan and the Professor took the third and the fourth.

When they met on deck a half-hour later, the sun was

disappearing upriver. It seemed to be immense, and when it began to sink in the west it fell amazingly quickly, disappearing bit by bit in an orange shimmer beyond the broad river. For the space of a long minute the river water blazed with reflected sunlight, then cooled and dimmed to green as the tiptop crescent of the dipping sun was swallowed up by the horizon.

Night seemed to be falling almost as fast, so the company clattered down the gangplank and headed toward town in search of an inn. They passed the now silent open market where most of the carts and stands were canvassed and shuttered. A few greengrocers were messing with their produce, and two or three tired-looking women towed empty wagons away into the evening. The deserted market had a desolate air to it, made more so by the crying of birds that stalked along, pecking at bits of fruit and fish that littered the roadway. A musty wind rose off the river smelling wet and muddy, and on the wind, cool and gray, was just the first hint of a fog. It promised to be a dark night, and the five travelers were in no mood to tarry there in the deserted street.

A block up, however, out of sight of the river, things were a bit different. Light spilled from open doorways and the streets were full of people idling on the sidewalks and hurrying in and out of taverns and cafés. Piano music and smoke rolled out of one dark café that had a great sign hanging in the window that promised *Best food in town*. The "in town" had been crossed out and beneath it was scribbled the word, "anywhere," and then that too had been lined through. "Best food" seemed, by itself, to pretty much make the point, Jonathan supposed. The anywhere part was superfluous.

On the chance that the sign was at least partly accurate, they crossed toward the café, the Professor pointing out that the music was a bit too loud for comfort and that noise had an adverse affect on digestion. Miles agreed, but Bufo and Gump, claiming to be hungry as hogs, insisted at least on reading the menu.

They weren't halfway across the street, however, when through the smoky doorway tumbled a ragged-looking lumberjack. With a wild shout he sprang to his feet and raged back inside, shouting something about filthy cheats and scum. Bufo and Gump decided that the sign probably was wholly inaccurate anyway, like those signs that advertise home-cooked meals, and they gave the place a wide berth and steered toward a less active tavern a ways up the street.

A tendril of fog overtook them about then, curling up the road on the late evening breeze and followed by wisps of the stuff that obscured the streetlamps and the doorways and muffled the laughter and the music and the noise from the taverns. They stopped before a tavern called, mysteriously, THE OLD SHADES, which promised entertainment along with the food. A ragged but nicely gaudy poster advertising a stage magician was glued to the window. *Zippo, Wizard Extraordinaire* announced the poster, which showed a picture of the extraordinary Zippo shoving curlicue swords through a woman sleeping in a pine box.

Miles was disgusted by the poster and by the very idea of parlor magic, but it was just the sort of thing that Jonathan liked. The more wild and unlikely the poster, in fact, and the cheaper and tawdrier the colors, the more it appealed to him. It was the menu, finally, advertising gumbos and fried river squid and lime-juice oysters on the half shell that persuaded Miles to follow the rest of them inside.

The tables were set up before a stage that was hung with a weirdly woven tapestry of a crumbling palace. Before it lay a long line of tumbled skeletons that had apparently once stood in file like a line of dominoes and had been laid to waste in the same style. Each lay with a look of mixed horror and amazement on its face, staring sightlessly toward a hooded figure outlined in a lit window of the palace before them. The tapestry gave Jonathan the creeps, but he had to admit that it was just the sort of thing to decorate a magic show.

When their food was served, it was just about as marvelous as the scene on the tapestry. Jonathan had a big bowl of dark, steaming gumbo with weird sea creatures—mussels and oysters and grinning shrimp and kelp crab—looking out of it. It reminded him of a boiled tide pool. Miles had a platter of fried baby river squid—rubbery-looking beasts with haunting eyes, all of them swimming in lemon and butter. The Professor sat before a mess of unidentifiable tentacles and ribby-looking items on a bed of rice. Bufo and Gump, giggling and pointing at the various peculiarities, had ordered steak and fried potatoes.

"No surprises in steak and potatoes," Jonathan said, trying, more than anything else, to convince himself that he'd been wise to order the local specialty.

"You can say that again." Bufo said slicing out a big hunk of rare steak. "What's that devil there?" He pointed with his fork at the business end of a sea cucumber that protruded from Jonathan's soup. "Looks like trouble to me."

"Not a bit of it." Jonathan assured him, gamely tying into the thing. "Absolute delight, actually." He washed the morsel down quickly with a swallow of ale. Bufo didn't appear to be convinced.

The houselights dimmed, a piano banged away, and Zippo the magician bent out under the curtain, bowing profusely. He didn't look much like the mustachioed wizard on the poster. Not only was he considerably shorter and fatter, but he didn't have nearly the same air of mystery and dark purpose about him. He wasn't very old, but he wore a bit of a toupee that was parted down the middle and that had been made originally for someone with a head about half the size of Zippo's. Miles was utterly disgusted and shrank into his seat so as to avoid being identified as one of Zippo's peers.

The show itself, all in all, wasn't half-bad. The magician wheeled out a great mechanical fish that was a marvel of glittering scales and glowing glass eyes. From the open mouth of the fish issued a swarm of green butterflies that fluttered about the stage for a bit then out through the door into the foggy evening. After that, shimmering bubbles poured forth, following after the butterflies, and then, peeking through the rush of bubbles, a tiny, winged pig wandered out. Squacking twice, it flapped away between the tables. Jonathan had never seen the like.

Jonathan turned to Miles. "This is the real thing!" Gump and Bufo nodded awed assent. The Professor just *harumphed*.

"This is someone shoving odds and ends through the mouth of a clockwork fish," said Miles. But if he was un-impressed by Zippo's methods, he clearly approved of his results, for he put a finger to his lip and nodded up at the stage.

Zippo was hocus-pocusing about, and the mouth of the fish head was clacking shut and opening again, rhythmical-ly, as if getting set to spew forth some new wonder. A little, marble-sized ball drifted out, floating, rising and fall-ing like a leaf in the wind. It hovered momentarily then rose into the air toward the smoky ceiling, expanding as it did. It grew to the size of an apple, then to the size of a man's head, then bloomed amazingly into an immense paper flower. A shower of golden glitter fell from the mouth of the flower, sparkling like summer rain in the stagelights. The center of the flower was as purple as a midnight sky and was surrounded by a thousand petals of salmon and silver and sea green and luminous turquoise and emerald like an impossible magical rose from the Won-derful Isles or the Kingdom of Oceania.

As everyone *oohed* and *aahed* over the hovering flowers, a hundred more of the little round buds drifted slowly out of the yawning mouth of the fish, drifting on slow currents of air. Jonathan started as one brushed past his nose. An-other, a dud apparently, fell with a plop into the remains of his gumbo and sprouted there among the sea shells and exoskeletons and crab claws of the unlikely soup. In an instant the air was filled with the weird paper blooms. There were bunches of blue lilacs and clusters of tiny violets. Iris as big as plates slowly changed color, fading from deep crimson and blue to pinks and lavenders. Then, one by one, the things deflated slowly, shrinking away to something resembling a moist purple rubber band and fall-ing lifeless on the floor and tables like unhappy little worms. Somehow the tavern, after the collapse of the won-derful air flowers, seemed sad and empty. Jonathan hauled one of the shreds out of his ale glass and looked it over.

"Helium buds," the Professor said. "From the Orient. Very simple, really."

Miles nodded, but again seemed pleased with the effect

of Zippo's latest trick. Jonathan decided to obtain some of the magical buds—a thousand or two so that he could release a handful any time he chose and never run out.

The show didn't amount to so much after that. If Zippo had one fault as a performer it was that he tossed off his best act halfway through the evening with the effect of making the rest of the show seem like something of a decline. He wheeled out the advertised pine box and shoved a variety of colorful swords through it and, seemingly, through the body of a woman reclining in the box—a woman who was either sleeping or dead. Then he pulled a variety of animals out of a bottomless hat and shoved each down his pants. Then he took off his shoe and pulled the same crowd out again, dropping them, one by one, into his shirt and retrieving the beasts with a great show of spirit from an immense coat pocket. From there they disappeared into his ear and were hauled out wearisomely from his mouth. The gag, Jonathan realized, could quite conceivably go on all night, and it began to seem as if it would when a catcall or two from the shadows at the back of the tavern dampened Zippo's enthusiasm. Thereafter, a deck of cards was waved about and shuffled and manipulated, and cards were fished out of the ears of those grinning members of the audience—including Gump—who sat near the stage.

Finally Zippo produced a mortar and pestle and called on the audience to volunteer a pocketwatch. Jonathan, in a sporting mood by then, yanked out his own, recently purchased from Beezle's market, and handed it up to the taciturn Zippo, who slammed it immediately into the mortar and ground it to dust. A spring or two shot out and bounced on the stage as Zippo worked at the contents of the mortar, displaying it to the shouting audience, finally, as a little ruined heap of bent metal and glass bits and twisted cogs. Jonathan took it gracefully. Clearly this was what was known as prestidigitation, finger flummery. Some valueless old broken watch had gone into the mortar and Jonathan's watch was surely up Zippo's sleeve.

Zippo produced a garish handkerchief and waved it over the remains, making spider conjurations at it with his free hand. "Hocus, pocus, mooliocus!" he shouted, and with a flourish of the scarf, revealed the same ground remains that had once been a pocketwatch.

The audience jeered and laughed. Jonathan, still a sport, laughed along with the rest. He noticed, however, that Miles, somehow, didn't see much humor in the gag. Probably, Jonathan thought, because Miles had little taste for such an obvious parlor trick.

Zippo waved the kerchief over the mortar again and effected the same result. Again he waved the scarf and shouted his mumbo jumbo, and again he uncovered a heap of ruined watch. After the third flourish there was less laughter from the audience; not, it seemed, because they feared the loss of Jonathan's timepiece, but because the ground-watch gag was quickly becoming as tiresome as the animals-in-the-hat production.

Jonathan's sporting attitude, in fact, was fading too, and so was Zippo's enthusiastic flourishing. Then, from behind the tapestry, the pine-box woman pranced out on tiptoe waving a loaf of old bread. Zippo paused, cast the crowd a look of mock surprise, and ripped open the loaf, producing, to everyone's compound astonishment, a pocketwatch. Cheers erupted from everyone as Zippo put the watch into a little velvet bag and passed it down to Jonathan.

Zippo bowed this way and that, nodding to Jonathan, who slipped the bag happily into his shirt pocket without bothering to look inside. He didn't, after all, want to call Zippo's skills into question. All in all, the magician seemed to be as amazing as any Jonathan could remember having seen—outside of Miles, of course, who was a genuine wizard.

Zippo disappeared behind the strange tapestry. As the stage lamps dimmed, the tapestry began to glow. The line of fallen skeletons and the eyes of the hooded creature in the castle window were lit like sea foam in moonlight. The audience, including Miles, gasped in surprised horror as the skeletons, one by one, stood upright and jerked along single file into the dark door of the castle, the thing in the window seeming to fade and disappear into the dark night behind it. When the wall lamps in the tavern were turned up and the audience sat squinting in the smoky room, the tapestry showed an empty rock-strewn night landscape with the castle, its windows and doors dark as pitch, sitting in the foreground.

The general amazement, however, soon faded as the sound of clinking glasses and plates filled the air along with shouts for ale and wine. "Well," said Jonathan, turning to the Professor. "That was first rate."

"Indeed," the Professor replied. "Quite a show. I'm astonished by that last trick with the tapestry. The rest of it was nothing. Very nice, mind you. I don't mean that it wasn't very clever and all. But like Miles said, most of it was a matter of shoving odds and ends through the mouth of a mechanical fish."

"Most of it," Miles said. "Let me see your pocketwatch, Jonathan." And Jonathan plucked the little velvet bag out of his shirt pocket and handed the whole works to Miles who dumped the watch out into his hand and looked at it grimly.

"Yours?" he asked, dangling a sad-looking brass watch by a piece of twine.

"No!" Jonathan shouted, grabbing the watch and examining it. The crystal was cracked across and one of the hands was missing altogether. When he wound the stem he could feel what might have been the crunch and scrape of ruined works grinding against one another.

"Sold!" the Professor shouted, slamming his hand onto the table top. Jonathan handed the watch to Bufo and Gump, who were anxious to have a look at it; then he and the Professor, both with the same thought, climbed onto the stage and ducked beneath the tapestry. There was a little chamber beyond the curtain which was empty save for the sword-punctured pine box. A hallway ran off toward the back of the tavern and led to several rear rooms, all of them empty but the last. There a hunched little man mopped morosely at a dirty wooden floor.

"Where's Zippo?" Jonathan asked.

"Gone out."

"The devil he did!" the Professor shouted, who was, in truth, even more worked up than Jonathan. "Where did he go?"

"Don't know." The man slopped a mop full of soapy water onto the floor and swished about in it. "Just ran out after the show. Didn't say why. Said he'd be back tomorrow night."

"Didn't say why!" Professor Wurzle exploded. "Of course he didn't say why! He's cheated this man out of a watch."

The mopping man nodded and went about his business as if the Professor had commented on the weather or blown his nose. "It ain't the first. Zippo's a hand when it comes to a deck of cards, but he ain't much at palming no watch. Mixes things up. Ain't his fault. A man has to have time to learn."

"Well," Jonathan said, pretty much resigned to the loss of his watch, "he got in a good bit of practice on mine tonight."

"Likely stole it." The Professor wasn't quite as philosophic about the whole matter. But then it was fairly clear to both of them that the little mopping man with his bucket of suds couldn't be held responsible for the lost watch one way or another. So they trudged back up the hallway and bent out under the tapestry to where Gump, Bufo, and Miles sat over cups of coffee. Two full cups sat before Jonathan's and the Professor's chairs.

"Let me guess," Miles said. "He was gone. Won't be back until tomorrow afternoon."

"Tomorrow night," Jonathan said.

"Tomorrow morning, more likely," Miles observed. "After the riverboat sails. I saw him drop the wrong watch into the mortar. But I don't think *he* knew it until after he'd beat it to hash. It's a good thing his assistant was on her toes. That fooled me for a bit. It probably wasn't the first time he's made that mistake."

"So we heard from the janitor." Jonathan was looking at the cheap, broken, substituted watch. He shook it next to his ear and heard rattling and swishing inside. With his clasp knife he pried the back off. The watch was half-full of sand. There were no works inside at all, not even a gear.

"It's the sands of time," Gump said as Jonathan poured the contents of the watch case into a little pyramid on the table.

"Pull out the stem," Bufo suggested, not wanting to let Gump outdo him. "You can dangle it from the string and use it as an hourglass."

"That's right," Gump said, "but you could only use it once."

"He could fill it up again." Bufo sounded irritated.

"Through that little hole?" Gump asked.

"No! He'd take the bloody back off!"

"Well, he'd still lose a bunch of the sand. It would be all over his shoe. His hourglass would run shorter and shorter. It wouldn't be worth a dime."

"Maybe he'd find some new sand." Bufo was exasperated. "Scrape a handful out of the Tweet River."

"Wet sand," Gump said. "If he scrapes it out of the Tweet River, it'll be wet. It won't run out and it'll turn the watch green. So there's your precious hourglass. All a wreck!"

Bufo looked as if he were about to pop. Jonathan gave him the watch. "You can have a go at it if you want," he said. "But it might work better as a coin purse or a weight for a fishing line."

Bufo plucked a half-dollar from his pocket and seemed pleased to find that it fit neatly into the watch case. "I'll use it as a secret compartment." Bufo closed the watch case over the fifty-cent piece. "If we're waylaid by highwaymen they'll never think of looking inside a pocketwatch for money. I'll get away with this half-dollar. Put one over on them."

Gump was in a state. "Highwaymen!" he shouted. "Put one over on them! That's about as smart as the hourglass idea. As if the filthy highwaymen won't steal your watch along with your purse."

"Then I'll slam them in the head with it." Bufo whirled the watch around in a quick little circle on the end of its string. "Then I'll hypnotize the boggers like this." And he waved the watch in front of Gump's face, bouncing it twice off the end of his nose.

"Mig-weed, mig-weed, mig-weed!" Gump shouted, purpling and mouthing the words that, more than anything else, would set Bufo awry.

"Gentlemen!" said the Professor, who favored dignity above all else.

Gump and Bufo took his hint and settled down, although for the next ten minutes they sporadically made puffy-cheek faces at each other. Bufo insisted upon dangling the watch in Gump's direction and whispering, "Hocus, pocus, mooli-ocus," in the manner of Zippo the Magician.

It was midnight before they left. There was nothing much to do aboard the riverboat but sleep, so they'd made the most out of their evening at the tavern. Outside the fog was gray and thick. There was almost no breeze, so the fog hung in the air, wet and cool, muting the sounds of the evening. Streetlamps glowed weirdly through the suspended mists. The posts below the lamps were obscured by the fog, and the lamps themselves seemed to be floating there in the still, damp air, casting their pale rays like cloudy little moons. Their footsteps clacked on the cobblestones of the street, and the melancholy tinkling of a piano sounded from behind them, some remnant of an evening's entertainment in what must have been, by then, an almost empty tavern.

A riderless horse clip-clopped past, appearing some few yards ahead in the mists then disappearing as abruptly, the sounds of his hooves striking cobbles receding slowly into the distance.

The five of them stopped for a silent moment on a street-corner to read a faded and peeling street sign just to make certain they were going back along the same streets they'd taken earlier. It seemed to Jonathan to be a lonesome sort of night—romantic enough, all in all, but one that gave him a desolate kind of feeling and reminded him that he was far away from Twombly Town and the High Valley. The silence and the fog seemed to him to be almost the same thing, as if the fog were visible, hovering silence, and it occurred to him that the white and plodding horse that had come and gone in the mists wasn't actually going any-where; was some sort of night shade that wandered up and down the damp avenues pursuing the sound of his own clacking hooves.

He became aware, as he stood there by the street sign for what seemed like a strangely long time, of a distant tap, tap, tapping—of a stick striking pavement or cobble-stones. The tapping grew louder, approaching, and the lot of them stood without speaking beneath the peeling wooden street sign in the diffuse light of the oil lamp, waiting for whatever it was that approached. All else was silence.

The tapping grew in volume, tap, tap, tap, and then changed abruptly to a hollow wooden thudding as whoever it was that was walking there, shrouded in fog, thumped across a section of boardwalk; then there was a moment of silence, then the tap, tap, tap, once again of a walking stick on cobbles. The musty river fog seemed to whirl about them, although there was still no breeze, and Jonathan pulled his cloth jacket tighter and peered into the lamplit fog.

A dark shape grew out of the obscurity and angled across the street before them—a dwarf in a slouch hat and black cape, tapping along with a brass tipped walking staff. His face was hidden in the shadow of his hat, and he smoked a long, strange pipe, the bowl of which glowed through the darkness and emitted clouds and clouds of vapors that rolled about and twisted and seemed to Jonathan to flee away into the air like the shadows of great bats. But there was no smell of tobacco, only of waterweeds and rotting tree roots and of deep rivers rolling toward the sea. Somehow, none of that surprised Jonathan. Anything else, in fact, would have.

The dwarf and his glowing pipe and his clacking staff faded into the darkness and were gone. Jonathan turned toward the Professor but could see from the look on his face that there was little that needed saying. Gump and Bufo looked as if they'd witnessed a hanging. Miles had a particularly grim and calculating look on his face. They set out as one down toward the street that ran along the waterfront, Bufo and Gump first and Jonathan behind. He was torn, as they stepped along, between the urge to glance back over his shoulder and the urge to cut and run, screaming, back to the dock. He had the terrifying sensation that a withered hand was at each moment descending toward his shoulder, and he fancied he could hear the sound of rustling skirts and labored breathing not a foot behind him. He feared turning to look as much as he feared not looking, and although he insisted to himself that it was all a matter of imagination, he knew it was not —that someone, or something, had made up the sixth member of their company.

If, he thought, they could reach the waterfront—if they could turn the corner into the open market, whatever it was, he was sure of it, wouldn't follow. It would evaporate in the mists, vanish like the rest of the shadows in the dim, foggy evening.

As if in a dream, the corner seemed to be receding, growing more distant as they approached it. It was probably a trick of the fog and the oil lamps and the silence and of the whisk and scrape behind him. He turned and cast a look over his shoulder to break the spell. Behind him, rustling along the cobbles in black robes and ragged gray lace was the old woman from the shanty in the swamp, feeling her way along with her hands before her, clutching at the air, filling the space that Jonathan had filled a moment before, staring at him with milky, sightless eyes.

A scream caught in his throat, again as in a dream, and she held out one withered hand and beckoned to him with a skeletal finger, her mouth working soundlessly.

Jonathan shouted. He shouted for all he was worth, understanding, somehow, that noise—loud noise—was the key here. And he was right. She vanished. A wisp of fog rolled across between him and the witch and when it rolled away again she was gone. There was no cat this time. There was nothing at all but the empty, shrouded street.

"What the devil did you do that for!" shouted Gump, who was shaking with fear and crouching there at the corner. Bufo had him by the arm, and Miles had thrown himself against the brick wall of a cannery ready to let fly a toasting spell.

Jonathan held his hand up for silence. At first nothing could be heard, just the splash of something on the river and the sound of a door being slammed away off up the street. But then faintly, very faintly, the sound of hollow, cackling laughter came drifting down toward them, as if it emanated from somewhere overhead in the veiled gray sky. The skin prickled up along the back of Jonathan's neck as the laughing faded and was gone. He wished it was just a matter of waking up from a dream and rolling over, secure in his bed. But this had been no dream—and it was unlikely, all things considered, that he'd sleep enough that night to make it seem like it had been come morning.

Chapter 10

Cap'n Binky's Blend

❈

WHAT awoke him next morning was the slap of water against the hull some few inches from his head. It was a sort of *swish-splash, swish-splash*. Jonathan knew where he was as soon as he awoke—even before he awoke. He'd been having a dream about traveling in a strange land on a mysterious and perhaps haunted riverboat. The dream had been growing increasingly grim. He'd been sitting on the stern watching the silent forest slide by in the twilight when he became slowly aware of a pair of milky-white, opalescent eyes away to his left, against a whitewashed cabin. In his dream he jerked his head around to have a good look at the staring eyes, which filled him with a certain ominous sort of creeping dread, but when he focused on the eyes he could see nothing but the wall of the cabin. As he turned his head away they flickered into focus as do very distant, almost invisible stars.

He tried looking away, but the sense that they were gazing blindly at the back of his head gave him the creeps. He froze, incapable of movement, afraid to turn around and equally afraid not to when Miles the Magician walked up, the head atop his cap whirling wildly. "Turn around and look at it," said Miles simply. "Treat it like a dirty-dog."

"Should I?" Jonathan asked in his dream.

"That's what I'd do." Miles faded away thereafter like a genie. A little waterfall of sparks revolved slowly in the night air for a moment where his head had been.

Jonathan was struck with the idea that he'd been given that advice once before. He couldn't quite remember, however, if it had been good advice or bad. He turned and looked at the cabin wall anyway. As he did he saw, out of the corner of his eye, a vague amorphous staring face just disappearing in the twilit gloom. There was nothing, finally, but a whitewashed cabin wall. Just for purposes of finality, Jonathan stepped across to the wall and ran his hand across it, smearing beads of dew into a long, wet streak. Beyond the wall he could hear the *swish-splash* of water against the hull of the riverboat. There came to him then, in the dream, a feeling of relief, for he realized not only that Miles' advice had been good advice but that he was involved in a dream and that he actually lay below deck, asleep in his cabin, listening half-consciously to the *swish-splash* of water on the hull.

And that's why, when he finally awakened some few seconds after that thought occurred to him in the dream, he knew right where he was. The strange surroundings didn't confuse him a bit. For a moment though as he listened to the splash of water, he was possessed with the idea that it was, in fact, water gurgling down a drain, perhaps in the kitchen overhead. When it went on, *swish-splash, swish-splash*, for a time, he began to think that the cooks aboard must have an inexhaustible supply of fresh water. That led him to the unpleasant thought that perhaps they were cooking with river water, and it reminded him of the old joke about his muddy coffee having been ground this morning. That, of course, reminded him simply of coffee and served to roust him out of bed.

Ahab, oddly, was nowhere about. Jonathan pulled on his trousers and washed up a bit in the bowl and pitcher that lay on a cramped little chest in the corner. The chest and the bunk took up three-quarters of the space in the cabin, and there was just enough left over to allow the door to swing open. Outside it was warm and sultry. The sky was astonishingly blue and the river stretched out for what seemed miles toward the thickly wooded opposite shore. Overhead the sun shone like a great flaming orange. Jonathan reached for his pocketwatch, only to remember that it had been turned into an hourglass by Zippo the Magician the night before. He shaded his eyes and looked up at the sun which stood at about eleven o'clock or so.

"Hello, Bing." The Professor's voice came from behind him.

"Professor," Jonathan said, "it's morning."

"Well it *was* morning at any rate," the Professor observed.

Ahab came trotting around the corner past Professor Wurzle, happy to see Jonathan up and about. He wagged around in a circle for a moment, canting his head this way and that, alert for bugs.

"I let old Ahab out a couple of hours ago. It seemed to be a good idea."

Jonathan assured him that it had been. "I think I need coffee." He and the Professor clumped along forward.

"Come, the captain has a perpetual pot. He was telling me about it this morning. The first load of grounds went in thirteen years ago. Whoever is on watch is responsible for the pot and has to put in fresh grounds and water whenever it's within three inches of the bottom. And you should see the coffee beans—big, oily black things that look as if they'd been roasted for about a month. They smell incredible, like burnt jungle mud or something. It's indescribable."

"So you're telling me that this coffee is thirteen years old?"

"Some of it is," the Professor said. "Fascinating idea, really."

"And it smells like jungle mud, you say?"

"Something on that order, yes." The Professor nodded. "Don't get the wrong idea, though. The flavor is astonishing."

"Does it taste like coffee?"

"A bit," the Professor admitted. "It's been the case, or so the captain tells me, that in an occasional emergency they had to use river water in the brew. The heat, of course, destroys the organismic debris."

"Of course," Jonathan said, his worst fears having come to pass.

They arrived at the galley about then, and sure enough, screwed to a countertop with carriage bolts big enough to club a man senseless with, was an absolute marvel of a coffee pot.

In fact, if Jonathan hadn't been prepared for some such thing, he wouldn't have known entirely *what* the thing was. There were two pots, actually, sitting side by side. Bridging the two at both the top and bottom were coiled lengths of copper tubing. Suspended overhead was a third chamber with yet another set of tubes spiraling down into both the lower pots. A little valve, shaped like the skinny end of an egg, tooted puffs of steam from the top chamber, dark pungent clouds that lazed along toward an open window some few feet away. There was a strange smell in the air, a not altogether unpleasant smell that seemed to promise river water and hashed-up seaweeds and, as the Professor had stated, burnt jungle mud.

Cap'n Binky himself wound the crank of a glass and wood coffee grinder hanging on the wall. From an open keg he scooped a handful of the blackest, oiliest beans Jonathan had ever seen. The captain caught the grounds in a tin pan. He pulled the top from the upper chamber, fished out a strainer full of wet, steamy grounds, threw the batch of them into a slop pail, and dumped the fresh grounds into the strainer, all the time singing to himself and bouncing his head about in a way that suggested either astonishing satisfaction or pleasant lunacy. He sang: "Some likes it hot, haaa! Some likes it cold, ho! Some likes it in the pot, twenty years old!" over and over again, jigging just a bit when he got to the haaa! ho! parts.

Gump, Bufo, and Miles sat round a table in the corner of the galley. Gump made the pinwheel sign around his ear and pointed toward Cap'n Binky when Jonathan nodded to them. Jonathan noted that the three of them all had empty coffee mugs before them and that the Professor was refilling his own from the tap at the base of one of the big pots. Dark swirling liquid burbled out, releasing a fabulous cloud of aromatic steam.

Cap'n Binky rinsed out the pannikin he'd been grinding beans into and hung it on a hook beside the grinder. "Cup?" he asked Jonathan, pointing toward a row of mugs that hung on wooden pegs.

"Of course." Jonathan looked at the Professor to make sure old Wurzle was actually drinking the stuff and not just involving him in some monstrous joke.

The captain handed him a steaming cup. Jonathan hesitated over whether to ask for sugar and cream. It struck him that it would be like asking for ketchup to pour over roast duck à l'orange in a high-toned restaurant. Just the sort of thing that is bound to set the cook wild. Besides, what good could yesterday's cream and sugar do to thirteen-year-old coffee? So Jonathan decided to plunge right in. He slurped up a big gulp of the stuff as Cap'n Binky watched, eyebrows arched.

The Professor had been correct. The stuff was astounding, incredible—like nothing he'd tasted before, and that was saying quite a bit. He was no slouch himself when it came to brewing coffee, and he had, years before, been at Brompton Village at the food fair when Leo MacDermott and his brother had brewed up a pot of the fabled Jamoca Blue. Cap'n Binky's blend, however, held the aces. It was so rich as to be almost creamy, and there were a hundred unidentifiable flavors in it. Just when he'd come to the conclusion that it was almost chocolaty, he couldn't find any chocolate at all. And when it seemed, after the second sip, to resemble one of those dark stouts made with burnt barley, that flavor disappeared too, only to be replaced with the unmistakeable essence of strange spices.

"This is the finest thing I've tasted," Jonathan told the waiting Binky; as he took another sip, the faint promise of weedy river water appeared momentarily. Not in such a way that when he drank it he thought, this tastes like river water, but as a sort of strange, half-lost memory of wide, deep, cool rivers that mingled somewhere deep in his mind with the waters of the sea.

"Second cup?" Cap'n Binky asked.

"Please."

"Don't take a third," the Professor whispered. "At least not until the effects of the first have worn off." He gestured toward a table where a man sat before an empty cup. He had a mystical look in his eye, as if he were contemplating great things, solving unfathomable mysteries. Before him on the table, next to the empty cup, sat a little stuffed beanbag toad, a foolish lumpy grin painted on its face.

The man poked the toad once in the snout. "Are you a

fish?" he asked it, and he waited a moment for an answer. "Are you a fish?" he asked again, giving the thing a poke on the nose.

"Too many cups of coffee," whispered the Professor to Jonathan. "An hour ago he was as sane as you or I. He bought that toad back in Tweet River Village for his daughter. Told us all about it. Somewhere around the fourth cup he went into a trance and began to speak to the toad about the seven mysteries."

"Did it reply?" Jonathan asked.

"Not yet. It hasn't said a word."

Jonathan looked at Cap'n Binky, who shrugged his shoulders as if to indicate that there was nothing surprising about the man's reaction. "Give me another thirteen years and I'll make him fly," the captain said.

Jonathan decided to be careful with the coffee. He didn't care whether the beanbag toad was a fish or not.

"Cap'n Binky is writing a book about coffee secrets," the Professor told him. "It's a marvelous thing, about a million words long. Maybe longer."

The captain pulled out a high stack of manuscript from a cubbyhole beneath the counter. The title page read *Coffee Making as a Fine Art* by Captain Eustacio Binky, and below that was painted a ceramic-looking cup filled with a multi-colored, swirling business that was supposed to be a symbolic pictorial representation of Cap'n Binky's brew. "This is the first volume."

"My land." Jonathan hefted the several hundred pages of laboriously handwritten manuscript. "This must be the inside word."

"The last word," the captain said, winking at them. He shoved the manuscript back into its hidey-hole.

Jonathan and the Professor wandered over to where their three companions sat. The coffee mystic still asked the beanbag toad if it was a fish, and seemed in no wise disappointed in receiving no answer.

"If you ask me," Gump said when Jonathan and the Professor had arranged themselves at the table, "I still think this is a land full of madmen. We haven't met a sane one yet. At least I can't think of any."

Everyone nodded in agreement. It pretty much seemed to be true, after all.

"We're just on a streak," Jonathan assured him. "It goes that way sometimes."

"That's right," Bufo said. "I was on a streak once. I remember one summer when I saw the Squire in six different places on the same day. Seemed like every time I walked out a door he was walking in. And he kept telling me this joke about a man who crossed a mink and an ape. Heck of a coat, he said, but the sleeves were too long. Then he'd bend over and wave his arms around to give the idea of a man dressed in such a coat. After I saw him the third time he didn't bother with most of the joke. He just came past and said, 'sleeves were too long!' Then I saw him again, down in the village it was. He says, 'Much too long,' and shook his head and made the ape arms. Then, that evening, I passed him on the road, I was going up towards Winkums in a little horse cart and he was walking along amongst the greengrocers filching plums and such. 'Squire!' I shouted. The Squire never said a word. He just swung into his imitation of a man in an ape coat. He didn't leave off either. Went right on humping along the road there. Funniest thing I ever saw. It sure knocked the socks off the greengrocers, I can tell you."

"They'd heard the joke?" Jonathan asked.

"No," Bufo said, "I don't suppose they had. It was the Squire creeping up and down the road that set them off. That sort of thing doesn't happen every day. It's a rarity, if you ask me."

"I dare say." The Professor was peering into his coffee cup as if expecting to see something grand in there. The rest of the company had been silenced by Bufo's story. It was fairly clear, though, that Gump was working his brain bones to come up with something that could match it.

"Are you a fish?" the Professor asked of his coffee cup.

The suddenness of it nearly made Jonathan choke. Miles leaped up in horrified surprise. Bufo snatched the Professor's coffee cup away before he had a chance to drink any more. "Pitch water on him!" Gump shouted.

"Wait!" the Professor cried. "It was a little joke! Just a gag. A lark. I know it's not a fish."

"Are you sure?" asked the man who still sat at his table and poked at the beanbag toad. "I could have sworn that *this* was. Every ounce of my being told me that this was a fish. I had to be sure, somehow. I must have sounded like a fool. Did I?"

"Not at all," Miles insisted, always the diplomat.

"I could see that this was no bloody fish. But then again it seemed like it was, like it had to be. Do you follow me?"

"Of course," Miles said. "Of course."

"Good." The man shoved the toad beneath his coat. "I have a reputation to maintain, don't I?"

Gump winked at Bufo across the table. "That's correct. What sort of a reputation is it?"

The man seemed perplexed. "He's still coming out of it," the Professor whispered.

"What do you mean?" the man asked Gump. "How can you know I have a reputation and not know what it is?"

It was a fair question, but Gump was stuck. Bufo, satisfied that Gump's detective work was once again on the verge of going awry, jumped in. "We can see that you are a man of parts, sir."

"Parts is it!" he shouted, working himself up.

Miles leaned across and whispered to Jonathan: "For heaven's sake, don't mention Sikorsky now."

Jonathan shook his head.

"Your clothes," Gump said. "Such a fine suit with those round lapels and all. Very good cut, it seemed to me. You can tell a man by his clothes."

"You appreciate fine suits, do you? Allow me to introduce myself: S. N. M. Quimby, haberdasher. I'm from Landsend. I was up at Tweet River Village on business."

"Glad to meet you," the Professor said heartily. And he introduced the rest of the company one by one.

"Where are you lads from?" Quimby asked. Then without waiting for a reply he said, "I could go for another cup of that coffee."

"Would that be wise?" the Professor asked.

"Maybe not," Quimby replied, reaching into his coat and patting the beanbag toad. "Where did you say you were from?"

"We didn't," Jonathan said.

"Oh, yes. Well I've always said that if a man can recognize a good suit of clothes, he hadn't really got to be *from* anywhere. Do you follow me?"

"Right down the line," Jonathan answered quickly, hoping that Quimby wouldn't press the issue. Actually, the only two place names he could recall from the map were Tweet River Village and Landsend. And he didn't know half enough about either of them to pretend he was *from* there.

"Been haberdashing long?" the Professor asked in order to change the subject.

"Long enough," Quimby said proudly. "I've got a bit of a reputation, actually."

"Do you?" Bufo asked.

"Oh yes," Quimby replied. "If there's any special case, all up and down the Tweet, it's 'send 'em to Quimby.' That's the word around here."

"Special case?" Jonathan asked, envisioning a line of three-armed men filing into Quimby's haberdashery.

"Oh we get a few. I could tell you some stories. A man came in a week ago who was a case. Never seen anything like him. Tremendous fellow. Big around as I don't know what. He came in the door sideways, but it didn't make much difference. Sideways, frontwards, backwards—there wasn't a lick of difference. I saw him coming in off the street and I shouted to my assistant, I says, 'Bring in that extra bolt and about a gross of pins! The Pillar of Hyglea is coming in for a fit-up!' Pillar of Hyglea. That's just what I said to him. And we needed that bolt, too, before we were through. It was a heck of a suit."

Gump and Bufo had lit up like lamps.

"Big man, was he?" Gump asked.

"Didn't I just say so?"

"That's right. So you did. My friend here does the most wonderful imitation of a fat man walking along a road. Not of your average fat man, of course, but of a really major fat man. Show him, Bufo."

Bufo gave Gump a look. "You do it so much better than I."

"Nonsense," Gump said. "Not a bit of it. I've never seen anyone who could put on a really jolly fat man like you."

Bufo gave Gump another meaningful look, but he got up and did a creditable Squire imitation. Once at it, in fact, he seemed to sort of melt right into the part, and he went rotunding away across the floor, throwing in a few of the Squire's odd mannerisms for extra effect.

"My, he's good," Quimby said. "That's just the ticket! I'd swear you knew the man, if that were possible."

"Perhaps we do," Bufo said, leaving off and sitting down once again at the table. "Did he have a habit of making jokes out of things you'd say, things that weren't really funny at all? Like you'd say, for example, 'Looks like rain.' And he'd say something like, 'Rain-brain-piggley-swain,' or some such thing and laugh like crazy. Like that was maybe the funniest thing he'd ever said?"

"That's your man!" Quimby exclaimed enthusiastically. "That's got to be him."

"And his head," Gump said. "Was it pointed a bit on top, so that it didn't much matter whether he was wearing his pointy-cap or not?"

"Exactly. I even made him a new cap, in fact, and discovered the most amazing thing. It didn't make any difference what size I made. They all just rode a bit higher or lower on his head, that's all. Fitting him with a suit was a challenge, but there was nothing to the hat. Come to think of it, the hat he wanted was just like yours." Quimby pointed at Bufo. "And he was just about your height too. Short fellow. Very short. You two come from the same part of the country?"

"Yes," Bufo said.

"No," Gump said.

"That is, we might," said Bufo.

And at the same instant, Gump said, "We used to."

"We might have used to," Bufo added weakly.

Quimby looked as if he was thinking seriously of having another cup of Cap'n Binky's blend. "What do you mean?"

"Well, we don't know if he's the one yet," Bufo said. "He may be anyone. And then again he mayn't. Did he say what his name was?"

"Yes," Quimby said. "Let me think. Brickle. Mickle. Smickle. Something like that. And he was a duke, I believe. Or a potentate of some sort."

"A squire?" Gump asked.

"That's it! A squire," said Quimby.

"Squire Myrkle, was it?" Bufo asked.

"Right again. And do you know what the weird thing was? He had the most amazing little round gold coins. They said 'Linkman' on them, and they had a picture of a crazy looking bogger—might have been this fellow's father—that said 'King Soot' beneath it. They weren't like any coins I've seen. Never heard of any King Soot either. But the coins were gold. There wasn't any doubt about that. And you can't argue with gold, as the saying goes. So you know this Myrkle?"

"Well, yes," Gump said. "He's an old friend of the family. We aren't looking for him or anything."

"Looking for him!" Quimby said. "Don't bite off more than you can chew! He'd be about as hard to find as the hippo at the duck farm."

"I say we're *not* looking for him," Gump said.

"Well I suppose," Quimby said. "If you find him, tell him Quimby the tailor sends his regards. He was a good customer. Finest suit I ever made. He wanted a 'solid gold coat' he said when he came in. But I told him it would weigh about two hundred pounds so he gave up on it. Settled for Marston tweed. You can't buy better tweed."

"Of course not," the Professor said.

Jonathan nodded.

"Well," Quimby said, "I feel better now. Tiptop. I'm going to my cabin and catch forty winks. It was nice to meet you, lads. Very nice indeed. Let me give you my card. When you're in Landsend you might want a new suit of clothes." He gave each of them a copy of his business card. *S. N. M. Quimby, Haberdasher* was printed on it, and below the name was a picture of an animate suit of clothes walking along a road.

"Very impressive card." The Professor tucked his away in his wallet.

Gump and Bufo looked moderately proud. "We gave that lad a soaking, eh?" Gump said.

"That we did," Bufo confirmed. "Played on him like a fiddle. Drew him out."

Gump smiled. "Wrung him out, I call it. He was pudding in our fingers."

"Modeling clay," Bufo said.

"Chunk of soap," Gump added.

"You did meet with a modicum of success," the Professor observed.

"Two modicums," Jonathan finished up. "We know where the Squire was a week ago anyway. And there's one thing we can count on. The Squire's not the sort to be in any hurry. If he was in Landsend a week ago, he's not far from there now."

"You're right about that," said Gump. "We've traveled with the Squire more than once. He sets out at about noon, dawdles along for about a mile and a quarter, stopping along the way for lunch, and then he puts up for the night. That's his way. He's not your man when it's speed you want."

"Good for us," Miles said. "But you're overlooking the possibility that by now he's not traveling alone. He might have bought that suit right off. Selznak may well have caught up to him since."

"That's possible," Gump admitted. "When he disappeared he was wearing his silk pajamas and smoking jacket. He would have found a tailor right off. The Squire's alert to the importance of correct clothes. Always has been. It's the royalty in him. The blood."

"What all this means," Miles said, "is that anything might have happened in the week since. Anything at all."

"It might have," said Jonathan rationally. "And then again it might not have. There's little we can do if it has, beyond sailing down to Landsend and having a look around."

"True enough," Miles said.

"What time is it?' Jonathan asked. "I'm about starved. It must be one o'clock by now."

"Ten past," Miles replied, examining his watch.

"Where's lunch then?" Jonathan asked.

"There's no lunch served on board today," the Professor told him. "The captain was telling me that we're putting in at a village early this afternoon on the south shore. We'll be there for a couple of hours. We can find a tavern."

About then the riverboat began to slow up. A bell clanged. Two sailors in dungarees and striped t-shirts ran past shouting, "Haul on the bowline!" And Cap'n Binky hollered orders from the bridge. Clearly they were putting into the shore.

"Well, I'm for getting off this tub," Jonathan said, standing up. "I'm going to grab some stuff out of my cabin and be the first one down the plank."

"Me too!" Gump shouted.

"And me," said Bufo. "Let's find us an apple pie and some ice cream."

"Now you're talking." The Professor stood up to follow Jonathan and Ahab toward the door.

Miles said that he would stay aboard and have another cup of Cap'n Binky's blend. He was "studying it" he said, but hadn't come to any conclusions yet. He was fairly sure though that there was magic in it, that the process of brewing river-water coffee for thirteen years was bound to bring about a certain degree of enchantment, and that as a wizard, he was duty bound to investigate it.

The Professor said that as a scientist he understood Miles' interest. He would have the same interest, he said, if the effect of the coffee was due to scientific arcana of some sort. But science, he concluded, wouldn't have much to do with a man's mistaking a beanbag toad for a fish, so the whole mystery would have to be left in Miles' hands.

With that everyone except Miles pushed out and hurried to his cabin. The riverboat was moving slowly up a channel within a stone's throw of the deep woods on the southern shore. A sailor hung over the side and dropped a knotted line into the river, shouting soundings up to Cap'n Binky on the bridge. Downriver about a hundred yards was a dismal looking little village with a single long pier thrusting out into the river. A half dozen lazy dogs lay about on the wooden slats of the pier, and two boys in straw hats fished off the end. One of them, as the riverboat drew up, pulled in a whacking great green river perch, a bug-eyed fish with scales the size of a person's thumbnail. Everyone aboard the riverboat cheered for him, including Jonathan, the Professor, Bufo, and Gump, who were, by then, standing about waiting to go ashore.

The boy held the fish aloft on the end of the line. Then he began struggling to remove the hook, but the fish, irritated at its condition, began to wiggle and bounce. Grabbing the thing by its enormous, splayed tail, the boy whacked it a half dozen times against a pier piling and put the whole issue to rest. "I got him!" he shouted to the assembled passengers. "I took the fight right out of him!"

Cap'n Binky tooted the riverboat horn a couple of times to show that the lad had the support of those on board. Then the boat hove in along the dock, the plank whacked down onto the boards, and three sailors dashed off and made the ship fast. Ten minutes later, the four found themselves pushing through a door on which hung a sign reading, remarkably enough, FAMOUS PIES—ICE CREAM.

"This is the place!" Jonathan said, seeing a waiter go past carrying a steaming pie that was about six inches deep. They lunched, finally, on pie and ice cream just like Bufo suggested, all of them having agreed that a more substantial meal could always be gotten later in the day.

Chapter 11

An Infernal Device

❀

THE night came early, and with it came the river fog. Jonathan and the Professor stood at the starboard rail, watching the dark south shore slide past in the dim distances. At first the ragged top of the forest was a black slash against the evening sky, but as the sun fell farther in the west, the sky and the shadowy forest blended into one amorphous darkness and, by seven o'clock, both sky and forest were obscured by the night and by the rising fog. A mournful horn moaned from the bridge every once in a while, and ghostly disembodied voices drifted down on the wet air to where Jonathan and the Professor stood. Now and then there sounded a returning moan as another boat splashed past somewhere out on the river.

A clattering of footsteps came up behind them. Jonathan turned to see the cook, carrying two slop buckets and wearing a striped shirt, advancing toward him. He nodded, drew up to the rail, and pitched the slops into the river. One pail, Jonathan could see, had been filled entirely with wet coffee grounds. The cook set his empty pails on the deck and lit his pipe. He seemed inclined to talk.

"Quite a fog," Jonathan observed.

"Yep," the cook answered. "Comes up most every night. You get used to it after a while. Sort of get to like it. It quiets things down a bit."

"Pretty dangerous, though, isn't it, running in the fog like this?"

"Naw," came the reply. "Water's good and deep all the way out to Landsend. We don't even take soundings from here on in. Everyone knows we use the deep channel, so

118

they stay out of our way. Is that the sort of danger you had in mind?"

The question seemed peculiar, especially in light of the odd babbling that the captain had done when they first came aboard. "That was part of it." Jonathan pulled out his own pipe.

"But it weren't all of it?"

"Not all." The Professor seemed to be catching on. "There were rumors, back at Tweet River Village. The captain seemed pretty lively on the subject. Is any of it true?"

"Hard to say," the cook said, puffing away. "This is a crazy section of river. I wouldn't go ashore now for all of Sikorsky's gold, leastways not on the south shore—north shore ain't so bad. But the south shore . . ." and he shook his head to indicate his attitude toward the south shore. "I've seen things come out of that fog," he said. Then he stopped and shook his head again.

"Things?" Jonathan asked.

"So to speak. I ain't sure what. Sometimes I think it's just shadows; sometimes I think it ain't." The cook tamped the bowl of his pipe, inspected it, and leaned his elbows on the rail, peering out into the foggy night. His speech had given Jonathan a case of the creeps. "That ain't what worries Cap'n Binky though, I don't expect. He don't much care for ghosts as long as he's full of that crazy coffee of his. He's on the watch, is what I think."

"Sikorsky?" Jonathan asked, playing a hunch.

"Aye," the cook said.

Jonathan shot Professor Wurzle a puzzled look and got one in return. "He turns up everywhere, doesn't he?"

"At least," the cook said. "I don't know why Cap'n Binky doesn't just give him the blamed pot. It ain't worth fighting over. Two-*thousand*-year-old coffee ain't worth fighting over."

Now the Professor was really interested. "Sikorsky wants that coffee pretty badly, then?"

"Offered to buy it. There wasn't any amount he wouldn't have paid, or so they say. He was crazy for it. Crazier he got, the more Cap'n Binky wouldn't sell. Sikorsky wanted half of it, but the Captain said that when he brews a cup of coffee he don't cut no corners. It's all or nothing for him. All for him, that is, and nothing for Sikorsky."

"Good for him." Jonathan liked to see that kind of artistic dedication. "Hang Sikorsky."

The cook nodded agreement. "There's them who would like to. Don't think they ain't tried."

The muffled clang of a bell reached them from somewhere out on the water. It sounded as if it were a long ways off or were being rung from beneath the river itself. But just a moment later a trade barge slipped past not thirty feet distant, lamps lit all up and down the deck. They could see the lamps first, materializing out of the fog like the luminous eyes of a deepwater fish. Then the dark shadow of the barge slid past, seemingly empty. In a moment the whole thing had disappeared.

"I ain't so sure though that Sikorsky himself hasn't got a hand in all this here." The cook waved out over the river.

"You mean in this night business from the south shore you were talking about?" Jonathan asked.

"That's right. That's more Sikorsky's style. Horrors and such. He just don't seem to me to be the type to mess around with infernal devices. Not Sikorsky."

"Infernal devices!" Jonathan said. "Is that so?"

The cook looked half-surprised, as if he'd been caught out. "I thought you said you'd heard the rumors."

"We did," Jonathan said. "But I guess we didn't hear half enough."

"Well, it's just been rumors so far. We shouldn't have put in today on the south shore, though. That was a risk. If Sikorsky wasn't just talking through his hat, we could be in real trouble."

"We've got to search the ship then, by golly," the Professor said. "Time's wasting."

The cook shook his head. "Nope. The captain doesn't waste no time. Not where his coffee is concerned. The lads been at it for two hours now. If there's a device, I reckon they'll find it."

The Professor seemed to relax a little at that. "Not much we can do then."

"Not a bit. I'd be on my toes; that's all. We'll put in at

Landsend in the early morning. You're paid up'here till noon, of course, but if I was you, I wouldn't stay on board. I'd get my stuff and go." With that the cook whacked his pipe against the bulwark, scraped the bowl clean into the river, picked up his pails, and walked away.

"Encouraging sort, wasn't he."

"Full of good news," the Professor agreed. "We'd better alert the others. If something goes wrong we'd best have a plan. We'd better agree on a place to meet up again in case we get separated."

"Landsend?"

"That would be best. There must be any number of post offices in a city like that. What do you say about meeting in front of the post office closest to the waterfront. Top of every even-numbered hour?"

"Good enough," said Jonathan, who liked having such plans. They made the future seem a bit more secure.

The two of them stood smoking idly for another ten minutes. There were probably any number of things to talk about, but it seemed, somehow, as if the darkness and fog and the gray river rolling quietly below demanded silence. Jonathan stared down into the water and began to wonder how deep it was and how old such a wide, slow river like that might be. He'd heard that certain species of fish lived forever, that they just grew bigger and bigger and bigger and found deeper caves to inhabit. There was no telling, he supposed, what sorts of creatures crept up out of the ocean to dwell in that ancient river, down there among the water weeds. As he gazed at the dark surface, lost in such thoughts, it began to seem to him that he could see shadows beneath the surface of the water—dark shadows that humped up toward the surface, then faded again in the depths. He thought at first that it was a trick of lamplight, but as he watched and as he thought about it, that seemed to be less and less likely. A long gray shadow appeared very near the surface and seemed to be running along beside them. It wasn't just a patch of darkness, not just a blotch of shoal water or some such thing, but seemed to have shape to it, the angular, undulating shape of a tremendous whale or a finned serpent.

Jonathan turned to ask the Professor if he saw it too. As

he did, he saw a spiney black hump out of the corner of his eye, glistening in the lamplit fog, arch up out of the water briefly and disappear. He looked quickly back at it, but the shadow was gone. There was nothing but gray river rolling below.

"Can you beat that?" Jonathan asked.

Nothing but silence answered him. The Professor was gone, probably to warn the others about the infernal device business and about the possible post office rendezvous. Jonathan squinted back down into the river, trying to separate the fog from the water and the water from the shadows beneath it. It occurred to him that the weird misty silence roundabout him was not really silence at all. It was more the swish of water and the sound of an occasional distant voice and the moaning of the fog horn and certain unidentifiable night sounds that all meshed together into a sort of pervasive blanket of hushed noise that lay over the boat and the water like the fog. He became slowly conscious of the clip-clop, clip-clop of what sounded for all the world like horses' hooves clattering along cobblestones, but when he listened sharp for it, strained to hear it, it faded and was gone. It must, thought Jonathan, have something to do with the steam-generating devices, something very simple and easily explained.

His imagination, he thought, was setting in to play tricks on him. He loaded up his pipe with fresh tobacco and determined to keep a sharp eye out for deviltry. "I wish I had my fishing pole and a handful of salted almonds," he thought to himself. "I'd catch one of these monsters out of the river and pound the daylights out of him, like the lad on the dock did back at the village. Take the fight right out of him." That was Jonathan's way with bugs—detestable bugs, that is, cockroaches, say, or poisonous spiders. They'd always given Jonathan the wee-willies. He'd found, finally, that the best way to deal with them was to fly right in and beat them all to smash. Dead bugs, it seemed, weren't half so bad as live bugs. There was a world of difference between them. He wondered, as he peered once more into the gloom, if the same thing applied to devils out of the sea. It occurred to him, though, that it didn't. He was the sort who liked to imagine that the sea was full of monsters. It was the idea of being in there among them that bothered him. That, of course, was the problem as he leaned there against the rail. The riverboat seemed to be hauling him along into some sort of night land, carrying him into the midst of a land full of horrors.

He heard then what sounded for all the world like the muffled scrape and splash of oars sliding through oarlocks, but again as he listened the sound seemed to fade away. He tried to go back to thinking about hashing up monsters, but when he did, there was the scrape-swish of the oarlocks again and what sounded like urgent whispering—whispering directed somehow at him. He decided to ignore it, and did pretty well, for a few seconds anyway.

Then, dimly, out of the corner of his eye, he caught a glimpse of a dark rowboat, bobbing on the river, drawing toward him where he stood at the rail. He hesitated for a moment before looking up. Things, all in all, seemed to be taking a bad turn. But he was sure it was there, a rowboat with two men in it—two men who seemed to be whispering to him, strange things, things that didn't make any sense.

He looked and the river was empty—no boat and no whispering men. "It's the fog," thought Jonathan. "They were there but were lost in the fog." And sure enough, when he went back to watching the river below, there was the rowboat again, closer now, there in the corner of his eye.

He continued to stare into the water, not really watching for anything, but aware of the approach of the strange boat and of the scraping of the oars in the locks and the whispering, urgent now and almost understandable. One of the two men in the boat, the one pulling at the oars, had his back to Jonathan; the other faced him, grinning oddly. Dark liquid was splashed across his neck and down his shirt, as if he'd been smeared with oil or had suffered some horrible wound. His eyes were unnaturally dark. He didn't really seem to have any eyes at all, just hollow sockets above his cheekbones. His hair was an oily tangle that fell down beside fish-white cheeks. He was whispering. No, that wasn't it. He was gasping for air, and his breath was whistling in and out. The dark smear on his tattered shirt front spread with each breath, and in one horrible instant,

Jonathan realized that his breath was whistling in and out through a bloody rent in his neck.

Jonathan couldn't move. He stood terrified, gazing sightlessly at the water below. Waiting. The rowboat scraped against the hull of the riverboat. The man at the oars reached across, grasped a handful of his companion's hair, and simply pulled his head off in a spray of blood and a *whoosh* of escaping air. Then, as if delivering a bag of groceries, he handed the ragged, staring head up toward where Jonathan stood. The head rushed up at him, grinning. Jonathan leaped back against a cabin wall, swinging wildly at the thing and shouting. But when he expected to strike it into the river, he struck nothing at all. His hand whizzed through air and nothing else. The boat was gone along with its two passengers.

Jonathan stood pressed against the wet, white wall of the cabin. There was nothing at all on the river. Then, faintly, it seemed to him that he could hear the scrape of oarlocks and the faint splash of oars. The sounds seemed to be fading, receding, as if the rowboat, if that's what it was, was making away slowly toward the south shore through the fog. Then, once again, silence.

By then, Jonathan was very sure of two things. First, that he was going to launch out and find some company, preferably the Professor, who was generally far too rational to have anything to do with ghastly visions. Second, that he was going to stop at the bar on the way and see what sort of brandy Cap'n Binky had laid in.

He stepped along down the deck and around into the companionway where he ran into a grim-eyed Miles the Magician, racing along amid his flowing robes and wearing his enormous pointed cap. The ivory head was spinning and spinning. "Something's not right tonight," said Miles.

"You're telling me," Jonathan said. "There's headless men on the river rowing boats."

Miles looked aghast. "Is there?"

"Either that or I'm going loony," Jonathan answered. "So I hope there is."

Miles wiped his forehead with his hand. "Headless men? Rowing boats?" He shook his head. "I knew it was bad," he said, "but I didn't know it was that bad."

"I think it's going to get worse."

"I do too. I've got to get topside. There's some sort of dark enchantment in the fog that's so thick that I can hardly breathe. I *must* work some counterspells. We're in for it either way, though. Sharp's the word. Believe everything you see. Everything is real."

"Good," Jonathan said, "then I'm not going loony. Where's the Professor?"

"Aft, last I knew. Be ready for anything. Do you know about the post office?"

"Yes," Jonathan shouted at Miles as the magician raced off down the companionway.

Miles stopped and turned. "The old woman you saw in Tweet Village, had you seen her before?"

"I think so," Jonathan said. "Yes, I'm sure of it. Several times."

Miles moaned.

"Why?" Jonathan asked.

"I think she's aboard," Miles said. And with that he flung himself out the door and onto the deck, stamping away forward at a run.

Jonathan popped along to a glassed-in room. MID-DECK TAVERN a sign read over the open door. There was no one inside, not even a bartender. Jonathan found a bottle of brandy in a rack and poured himself what might be called a double: one for the headless boater and one for the old eyeless woman who, somehow, had set out to plague him —to plague them all, apparently. Then he started to think about the cook's warning and about Miles' talk of dark enchantment, and he began to suspect that the night was going to be a grim one. Too much brandy, it was true, might make it seem a bit less grim, but then again it might not. It would do little, in either case, to sharpen him up. And sharp, after all, was the word, at least according to Miles. So he took a couple of good sips, just to get something for his money, and set the half-full glass on a shelf behind the bar and put a little paper napkin over it. He hated the idea of an unfinished drink and so vowed that before he went to bed that night, he'd come back and work on it. Then he put a few coins in the change box on the shelf and went back out into the night.

Three sailors swept past in a businesslike way, looking for bombs, no doubt. Cap'n Binky, up on the bridge, hollered orders at them concerning the boiler room. Jonathan was happy, in a way, that the captain was afflicted with this coffee madness; it explained his frantic and thorough efforts at having the ship searched for Sikorsky's infernal device. Damn this Sikorsky anyway, Jonathan thought. Here they'd come any number of miles, wandered through magical doors and tangled themselves up with witches and enchanted dwarfs, and if that wasn't enough, as if they weren't running into enough trouble, along comes Sikorsky with his bombs and demons. It was enough to give a fellow the pip.

Chapter 12

Things from the River

❧

H<small>E</small> didn't find the Professor aft. He found no one at all aft. What he found, actually, was what appeared to be long trailing tendrils of water weeds and a great quantity of river water slopped about the deck, as if someone, or something, had climbed over the bulwark out of the river, covered with stuff. Jonathan looked around furtively, expecting at any moment to see some shambling horror dash out of the shadows. But all was silent. The thought struck him that Sikorsky, or, more likely, one of Sikorsky's cohorts might have climbed aboard intending treachery. But if he had, it was a mystery to Jonathan why he would wriggle about in the river weeds first, especially if he carried with him the rumored infernal device. It was no use being on the lookout and not following up such obvious leads. He could, of course, go up and alert Cap'n Binky and leave the dangerous work to him, but by then the damage might be done.

The trail of water led away around the starboard cabins. Another clump of weeds lay in a pool of lamplight some twenty feet long beside the bulwark. There was nothing simpler, apparently, than following a man clothed in water weeds who'd just hauled himself out of a river, thought Jonathan. Then the idea of a man clothed in water weeds started to play on his imagination. He saw, shoved into rings along the bulwark, a row of marlinspikes, and he recalled how useful such a device had been months past when he and Ahab had tangled with the two trolls. He yanked one of the things out of its ring and hefted it. He wished he had a brickbat instead, something he wouldn't have to get in too close to use. But a marlinspike was certainly better than nothing when a man was facing down monsters—a marlinspike, that is, and a pair of quick feet.

He stooped along detectivelike toward the second scattering of weeds. The river must be absolutely choked with the things for a swimmer to have hauled so many up with him. On beyond the bunch in the lamplight were more wet footprints leading away. Jonathan stopped momentarily over the pile of weeds and mud. Something bothered him about it. Something that he couldn't quite put his finger on. The weeds were lacey looking things and were black and gray and not green and brown like you would suppose. He bent over and touched a bit of the lacey weeds and found, to his horror, that they weren't wet—that they weren't weeds at all. In his hand he held a tattered bit of ancient black cloth, traced along one edge with faded age-grayed lace.

The bits on the deck were the same. They were obviously so. He dropped the cloth as if it were a reptile. How could he have been confounded into believing the stuff was water weeds? And the footprints, he ran his finger across one of them. It wasn't water at all but was fine gray ash, dry as tomb-dust even in the mist that soaked the deck. Bomb or no bomb, Sikorsky or no Sikorsky, he'd had enough of being on the lookout. As he straightened up he caught a glimpse of a pair of eyes, milky eyes, watching him from the darkness of a recessed doorway not three steps away. There was a whispering in the doorway and the faint cackle of something laughing weirdly to itself, at a joke that no one else could hear or wanted to hear. From the shadows of the doorway, a thin, pale, skeletal hand reached out toward him, beckoning to him with a bent finger. Tattered lace hung round the wrist.

Jonathan was off across the deck in a shot. Never trust a marlinspike when you can trust your feet—that was his motto. But the deck seemed to be heaped with things from the river: glistening piles of weeds and muck and fish, as if the riverboat were a dredger, loaded with debris and bound for deep water. His foot hit a pile of slippery weed—trailing tendrils of rubbery, bulbous leaves and stalks and grass. His legs slewed out from under him and he slid shouting across the stuff. From above him sounded an answering shriek, then another. He rolled to his knees, grasped his club, and found that the shriek was coming from the mouth of a steam whistle near the bellowing stacks.

The ship above him was lit like a carnival. Every lamp blazed and smoked in the fog, and the shadows of running men could be seen darting in and out of doorways, shouting orders. There was a cry from somewhere up toward the bow, and the splash of something hitting the river. Another shriek from the steam whistle was followed by a long booming note from the foghorn. Tremendous wild clouds of steam and smoke poured from the stacks, sailing off to join the fog and the confusion. It was as if the smokestacks had run wild. The escaping steam began to acquire a shape to it, to break up and coalesce again. It seemed to Jonathan that great winged shadows sailed out of the stack and swept away into the night above. As he watched, he realized that it wasn't smoke and steam that poured through the stacks; it was bats. Thousands and thousands of black, screeching bats, whirling out in a wild cloud. And below them, bathed in lamplight atop the upper deck, stood Miles the Magician. He was surrounded by a universe of sparks and was chanting, shouting, pounding with his staff, supplicating or cursing. His arms were stretched out before him, gripping his staff and pounding the deck—*boom! boom! boom!*—louder even than the scream of the whirring, shrieking bats.

Jonathan pushed himself to his feet, and as he did, so did a pile of weeds on the deck. He shook his head in disbelief. The thing on the deck shook its head too, droplets of river water and bits of weed spewing off. It slowly began to re-assemble itself, pulling in a bit there, bunching up a bit here, undulating and waving in the fog before him like a nest of eels. As it did so, Jonathan was possessed with the uncanny thought that the animate river weeds were not only taking the shape of a man, but that they were taking *his* shape. Horrified, he took a step backward and slipped once again in the river trash on the deck. He caught himself with his left hand as he fell and leaped back onto his feet. It was running he wanted, but running on the slick deck seemed unlikely. Suddenly a wild idea popped into his head—he should dash down to his cabin and have a look inside, just to see if he was in there asleep. Then it struck him that that was just the sort of thing you think up in dreams. But all the thinking didn't amount to much as the weed thing lurched forward, moaning and rustling at him. Jonathan raised the marlinspike. "Take the fight right out of him," Jonathan thought. "Smack him up." But the weed thing must have had similar thoughts, for it raised one dripping arm aloft as if it too held a club in its hand.

It lurched at him again. In the center of the tangled mass that formed its face was a dark, dripping hole, a mouth that moaned and blubbered. River mud dribbled out one side, disappearing into the thing's weedy body. It lurched again toward Jonathan who backed up a step. He heard his name being called from above, heard the barking of old Ahab and the shouting voices of Gump and Bufo, but he didn't dare look up. He didn't have a chance to, in fact, for the weed thing, with a terrible slobbering moan, fell on him, cold and clammy and wet as the river itself.

He slashed out with the marlinspike in a wild effort to smash the thing to the deck. The club pulped into its body, slurped down into it, buried itself in bladdery weeds. Almost simultaneously the weed thing thrashed at Jonathan, whacking him on the side of the head with a tendriled arm, covering him with muddy debris.

He wrenched the club free and thrashed at it again and again, pushing backward all the time, away from the shuffling thing.. Suddenly he realized that he was nearing the edge of the deck, that he'd find himself in the river in a moment. The river was surely the last place he wanted to be.

Tendrils of weed wrapped around him. He stumbled and threw the marlinspike down. You can't beat waterweeds to death with a club, or so it seemed to Jonathan. He began tearing at it with his hands, pulling away bits of weeds, clumps of grass. River mud poured from the thing's mouth, and Jonathan shoved his hand toward it to shut it off, to keep it out of his face. He grabbed a handful of muddy weeds and tore it away, tore the top of the thing's head off. As he did, the thought struck him that he was fighting a horror that was partly his own invention, that river weeds weren't so very much more formidable than cockroaches. So he set in to pull it to bits. In a matter of seconds the thing collapsed in a heap on the deck, nothing but muck from the river.

He hadn't time to revel much in his victory, for off the starboard side, rowing slowly toward them out of the fog, was a rowboat with two men in it. Acquaintances of his. He stumbled forward and plucked up the marlinspike from among the weeds. He realized that he was wringing wet from a weird and unwelcome combination of river water, fog, and sweat. There was an unnaturally loud scrape and bump as the rowboat pulled alongside. Jonathan decided to ignore it—to leave the headless man for someone else, someone who hadn't been wrestling weeds. Then he had a better idea. A pile of wooden crates loaded with freight lay against the bulwark. He tried to heft one, but it wouldn't budge. Two others were just as heavy, but a fourth one, smaller than the others, wasn't quite as formidable. He pulled it out of the stack and pushed it along the deck.

Six feet or so below him the rowboat bobbed on the river. Its two occupants were still sitting there, in no apparent hurry. Jonathan could hear the whispering breath as it rasped out through the red tear in the eyeless man's throat. He pulled his crate up by one end, balanced it on the rail, heaved the other end into the air, and sent the whole thing crashing down onto the rowboat and its ghastly crew. He heard a tearing of wood and a fearful screaming. A slat tore loose from the side of the rowboat and came spiraling skyward, spinning past where Jonathan stood at the rail above. It reached the top of its arc and fell toward the river, splashing down beside a grinning head that floated on the water. Wild laughter issued from the thing's mouth. The oarsman and the body of the other man were gone and so were the pieces of ruined rowboat. It was as if they had sunk away into the depths of the river. The grisly, laughing head fell away astern as Jonathan watched.

Then, distantly, way off on the dark river, muffled in the fog, came the sound of oars scraping through locks. Two men in a rowboat materialized, rowing unhurriedly toward him. One of them had a gash in his neck.

It occurred to Jonathan that there'd be some tired zombies in the morning, and he wondered as he went after another crate whether Balumnian horrors were allowed to put in for hazardous duty pay. Then he wondered why in the world he was wasting crates. He dropped the one he'd been tugging on and set off down the corridor, off to find old Ahab, who—unless there were ghost dogs aboard—was somewhere forward, barking furiously.

Jonathan was halfway down the companionway when the ubiquitous old woman—knitting, a cat on her lap—appeared before him. She hadn't been there a moment before; he was sure of it. She cackled with laughter and held her knitting out to him as if it were a pair of mucklucks or a hat. What it was was a tangle of unrelated and variously connected knots looking vaguely like a spider's nest. And crawling on it, to Jonathan's horror, were spiders. What had seemed like lumps of yarn were black, bulbous spiders, creeping about on a tangled web.

Jonathan flung the marlinspike in her face at the same instant that he turned and ran. Cackling laughter chased him out onto the weedy deck once more. Above him, Miles still ripped away, pounding and thudding. Lamps glowed, sparks flew, fog swirled, and the night echoed with a cacophony of shouts, screams, laughter, and the thud of the steam engines. Jonathan raced around to port, hoping as he did that the witch would be off terrifying someone else. Down along the bulwark, charging at him, hooting and waving, came Gump and Bufo, legs pounding. Behind them, reaching and clawing the air, stumbled the man with no head. Behind him, barking and leaping, bounded old Ahab, who, not having as much imagination as some, didn't give a rap for heads one way or another. It was impossible to say, though, who was chasing whom. Jonathan felt distinctly tired. He felt, in fact, as if he were in some sort of clockwork funhouse from which there was no exit. It seemed likely that this madness could go on all night, that the river had a large enough supply of renewable horrors in it to wear down any opposition. Miles' counterspells, majestic as they were, didn't seem to be accomplishing much. Miles himself, when Jonathan looked up at him one last time, was interrupting his chanting and pounding with wild swings of his staff, as if he were trying to knock something off the deck.

Jonathan looked about for something to clobber the headless boater with, for Gump and Bufo were almost upon him. He'd wait for them to sail past, then knock the demon over the rail. As he turned to search the deck, he heard the first of three thundering explosions and watched as bits of riverboat sailed skyward on a sheet of flame. He found himself tumbling backward into a heap of coiled ropes. The ship listed to port. Debris rained down around him, and a second explosion bellowed out. He got one last, wild glimpse of Bufo, Gump, Ahab, and the headless man hurtling into the dark river. The third explosion rang out, and the riverboat lurched about, listed farther to port, and swung round sideways on the river. The starboard side loomed over Jonathan's head like a wall and river water swirled up around him.

There was nothing for it but to swim. He'd heard that sinking ships drag swimmers down with them, although he'd had no real experience along those lines so couldn't say for sure. He'd have to ask the Professor when he saw him at Landsend post office. It seemed wise, under the circumstances, to be optimistic.

He swam as strongly as he could about thirty strokes, not breathing, not looking back. When he raised his head for a breath, he saw behind him the bottom of the boat, almost perpendicular to the surface of the water. The great paddlewheel hung upright, half submerged at the stern. In front of Jonathan was fog. He had to trust to providence. He was sure that neither shore was more than a mile distant, so he struck out once again, more slowly now. Soon he was enveloped in mists.

For several minutes he swam. Then, tiring, he pulled up and began to tread water. He yanked his shoes off, tied them together, and looped the laces through his belt. He felt for his pouch at his waist and found that he hadn't lost it. He was happy that he'd decided not to leave it in his cabin with his clothes. His money, under the circumstances, was more important than his clothing.

It began to bother him that he had no idea in what direction he was swimming. At first it hadn't mattered, but now that he was safely away from the boat, it began to. He had no desire to visit the wooded slopes of the south shore. No desire at all. His quandry lasted about thirty seconds. From somewhere in the fog came the familiar sound of splashing, scraping oars, and dimly, behind him in the mists, Jonathan could see the emergence of the fiddlehead of a rowboat, bobbing toward him. There was the vaguest chance that it wasn't the rowboat he knew it would be. He lay low in the water, sculling away with his legs so as to keep just far enough away to be hidden from it. He heard the whispering before he got a clear view of the two occupants. Jonathan paddled deeper into the fog and waited for them to disappear. Then he set out once more, this time in the opposite direction.

When he knew that he'd put a quarter mile between himself and the rowboat, he called out a few times. He whistled and he shouted and, although once he fancied he'd heard a returning whistle, he didn't hear it anymore. There was nothing to do but swim on and rest and swim on.

The water was awfully dark. It may as well have been black tea that Jonathan was swimming through. The surface of the river was oily smooth. There wasn't a breath of wind. The silence was almost complete. There were no steam engines or booming foghorns to add dimension to it —just vast, flat, eerie silence. Jonathan began to listen to the sound of his arms and hands splooshing down into the water. It seemed to him that he could hear the *plip-plop* of each droplet as it landed, could hear the wash of rising water that his arms pulled from the surface.

It occurred to him—not suddenly, but as an idea that sort of rose out of his mind and hovered there—that if he could hear his splashing so clearly, so could anyone else. Or anything else. He paused to tread water and rest for a bit. It seemed to him that he remembered the Professor having said that water magnified sound. But he could be wrong. Perhaps it was vision that it magnified. Perhaps those monsters that had surfaced near the boat had been about half the size they'd appeared. He couldn't remember what the Professor had said—and he was aware, while all this was going through his head, that he didn't *want* to remember it. He didn't want to think about it at all.

Maybe water appeared to shrink things. Maybe the creature he'd seen in the river was even bigger than it had appeared. But that was impossible. He had no idea how big it was. It had simply been a great, glistening black hump, part of some beast as large as the riverboat itself. Larger maybe.

Jonathan rested for a moment, sculling slowly with his arms. The fog was still dense around him. He was happy that he didn't share Dooly's fear of being locked in closets, for he seemed to occupy a little hollow in the impenetrable gray gloom, a little room with a misty ceiling and walls that ended abruptly at the black water.

He began to wonder how far below his feet the weedy river bottom actually lay. The cook had said that the boat ran along the deep channel. But how deep was deep? Thirty or forty feet? A hundred feet? Perhaps a thousand feet? Jonathan began to imagine himself treading water with a thousand feet of cold, shadow-haunted river below. He knew that such imaginings were a very bad idea, but there didn't seem to be much he could do about it. The idea fascinated him, actually, just about as much as it terrified him.

He pulled his hand out of the water to push the hair from his eyes, and he listened to the splash of droplets around him. He wondered whether the things that were lurking beneath him in the deep water could hear those surface noises.

He realized just then, with a lurch of deep dread, that the river wasn't entirely dark after all. Away to his right there was a faint plop of something breaking the surface of the water. Within the widening swirls the river seemed even darker just for a moment, as if the shadow of a cloud had passed over it, as if a massive turtle or a great finned ray had floated there momentarily, then sank away once again into the depths. The mist seemed to lighten around him, and he looked up to see, of all things, the moon, floating there above a break in the swirling fog. The break closed, the fog darkened, and Jonathan told himself that the shadow on the river had been caused by that one moment of moonlight. But moonlight, of course, doesn't cause swirls and ripples. Clearly it was time to be pushing on—no use dangling there in the water like bait.

Just as he pushed forward and drew back his arm for a stroke, he felt something very smooth and slippery slide across the top of his foot. He yanked the foot in, thrashed in the water to face whatever it was that had come up out of the depths, and saw, almost on the surface, the angular black shadow of a great triangular fin, undulating very very slowly, moving away from him, disappearing into the murk.

Jonathan splashed away across the water. He kicked his feet about ten times as hard as was useful or necessary, possessed by about a dozen simultaneous fears. Uppermost was the fear that he had been swimming aimlessly, in circles. That he had found his way back around to the south shore. That the river saw to it that anyone on it at night would find himself cast up there amid dark forests and zombies and goblins. That at any moment he'd feel the slippery touch of some deep-water creature. That the thing, whatever it was, a tremendous bat ray probably, was merely tasting him, and that in a second, as he thrashed his way toward nowhere, he'd see a great shadow surfacing, feel the thing slam into him and carry him away down into the weedy basement of the river. Mixed with all those dark fears was the wild idea that if he ever reached shore, if he made it to Landsend and found the Professor, he'd have old Wurzle invent a rubber cheese suit for him to wear while swimming in the Tweet River. But then it struck him that this would be a waste of time. There wasn't a chance in five million that he'd ever again swim in the Tweet River—this was his last such swim, one way or another.

He forced himself to look straight ahead. If there were any more shadows in the river, he didn't want to know. He was tiring quickly. The rush of fear had sent him along wonderfully well, but the burst had drained him, and his arms were quickly becoming useless. As far as he could tell, he was no closer to shore than he had been. It felt as if his sodden pants weighed about fifty pounds and that his shoes, strung through his belt, were full of sand.

He decided to stop again to rest, to take his chances with the shadows and to get rid of his shoes and kick off his trousers. He'd keep his belt. His jacket he'd pitched away a half hour before. When he pulled himself upright and kicked his feet, he found himself standing in sandy slime. Before him, not twenty feet away, was a muddy bank.

Chapter 13

S. N. M. Quimby, Haberdasher

❋

Jonathan slogged out across the river bottom and up onto the bank that looked far muddier than it actually was. He climbed to the top with little difficulty. The fog began to clear along the shore although it still hung thick out over the river. He saw that the river flowed across from his right to his left as he stood on the muddy bank facing it. So he'd made it. He was on the northern shore. The moon shone clearly through scattered high fog. There was still scarcely any breeze, something Jonathan was thankful for. The cool night air against his wet skin gave him a case of the shivers.

The land roundabout looked hospitable enough. Lights from a handful of farmhouses dotted the distant landscape. It was late, perhaps nearing midnight, but not so late that Jonathan couldn't find some sort of warm spot to spend the night. Pulling on his shoes, he climbed down the embankment to the river road and sloshed along it for a hundred yards or so. Then it occurred to him that he'd be wiser to hike along the top of the embankment, mud or no mud, so as to have a view of both the river and the road. It seemed certain that wreckage from the ruined riverboat would float ashore and that others besides himself would have swum for it.

By and by he began to see bits and pieces of wreckage on the river—planks of wood, a ruined cot from one of the cabins, kitchen debris—all of it bobbing along placidly yards from shore. When he glimpsed the first bit it seemed to Jonathan that he should do something—swim out and salvage it or something. But then he determined, of course, that there would have been no point in it. More than anything else he hoped that Gump or Bufo or the Professor or Miles would come paddling along, them and old Ahab.

He began whistling when he saw the first of the wreckage drift past. He knew that Ahab could hear him whistle from a long way off, and he was certain that if Ahab were within whistling distance, he'd find his master by hook or crook. Jonathan went on whistling at intervals, trudging along toward a farmhouse that fronted the river road some mile or so away. He stopped now and again to survey the river, and once when he did, he realized that a light glowing on the river side of the road hadn't anything to do with the farmhouse as he had thought. Someone had a lamp set up atop the bank to cast light out along a strip of deserted shore. Several big pieces of debris sat in the lamplight. Jonathan hurried along toward it.

When he was almost upon it, a long rowboat pulling for shore appeared on the dark river. Jonathan had lost some of his fondness for rowboats, but this one was something of a welcome sight. In it sat three people, all of them with securely attached heads. One was a man, another a woman, the third was S. N. M. Quimby, Haberdasher, looking colder and wetter by far than Jonathan felt.

Jonathan slid down the bank and stood waiting. The woman rowed in long, powerful strokes, and the boat fairly hummed across the water. The man, bearded and wearing a hat, smoked a pipe and contemplated deeply. Jonathan shouted at them to let them know he was there and reached out for the painter that the man handed toward him. He set his feet, gave the line a yank as the woman hauled one last time on the oars, and the prow slid scrunching up onto shore. He looked about for something to tie it to and found only a large cabinet which, he supposed, would do as well as anything. As he looped the painter around a corner post he realized with a start that the cabinet had come out of the galley, that a few hours before it had been connected to Cap'n Binky's complex coffee machinery. There were the holes through which the carriage bolts had slid to hold the works on—four smooth holes that might have been drilled a week before. There was no indication that the coffee apparatus had been yanked off or blown off or anything else. It had to have been very carefully removed. Jonathan hoped that it had been Cap'n Binky, and not Sikorsky, who had removed it.

"Mr. Quimby," Jonathan said, extending a hand to help the tailor out of the boat. "Watch out for the mud here. It's a bit slick."

Mr. Quimby shook with cold, his teeth clacking together. "Ooh-ooh-ooh," he chattered, nodding faintly to Jonathan. He held his arms out to the side, monkeylike, away from his body, and his hands shook uncontrollably. Jonathan noticed a big bulge on the inside of his coat.

"Your beanbag toad has come through, Mr. Quimby," he said, trying to cheer things up.

"Oog," the haberdasher replied.

The smoking fellow gave him a look, not understanding Jonathan's reference to the toad. "Been swimmin'?" he asked.

"Yes," Jonathan replied truthfully. "Anyone else out there? There were twenty people aboard at least."

"Would we have left 'em if we'd seen 'em?" the woman asked. It was a logical thing to say, but it fell into the sourpuss category. She began hauling on a line that was tied to the stern of the rowboat. A collection of odds and ends was tied along the rope: a wooden chair, a cabin door, two kegs, and any number of other goodies. The line stretched out into the river.

"Unless you want to lend a hand," the man said to Jonathan as he watched the woman haul in the pieces bit by bit, "you might just as well shove."

Jonathan, however, wasn't so easily put off. "Where can a man dry himself out around here?"

Neither of the two answered.

"We'll gladly p-pay," stuttered Quimby, groping in his suit for his wallet.

Jonathan was on the verge of saying that he'd freeze before he'd pay them a cent, but he hesitated for Quimby's sake, and it was just as well that he did.

"Up the road at the farm." The woman nodded vaguely downriver. "There's a barn in back with a wood stove. There's dry wood, matches, barrels of apples in the back, and a couple of kegs of cheese. Put your money on the back porch in the morning when you leave. Something fair. We'll still be out. Chance like this don't come often. Next village is twenty miles down."

"Thanks," Jonathan said.

The man made a sour face at the woman, but he didn't say anything. She told him to shut up. Jonathan grinned at him and winked as he helped Mr. Quimby up the slope. He thought of telling the man Squire Myrkle's joke about the ape coat, just to cheer him up, but decided that it could wait. There was no use pressing his luck. As they slid down toward the river road, the man still stood sucking on his pipe, watching the woman haul in the line.

"M-mean b-b-boggers," Quimby said.

Jonathan agreed. "Warming up some?"

"A b-b-bit. It's not half so cold here as it was out on the T-Tweet. Not half."

It took about five minutes to get to the farm. The house itself was a big, ramshackle, three story affair. It hadn't seen fresh paint in a good twenty years. What had once been white wood was almost as gray as the river rock that made up the foundation. There was a light on the second floor. Jonathan decided to knock on the door in order to explain what he and Quimby were doing nosing about. But after he'd pounded away three times and no one answered, he gave up. They found the barn, just as the woman had said. There was wood and kindling enough for a year. Jonathan dragged up two packing crates, set Mr. Quimby on one to warm up before the stove, and went off to search for food. All of a sudden he felt incredibly hungry.

He pulled four apples from a barrel, then poked around and found a salt-encrusted cheese. He peeked through a door at the rear of the barn which led to a smokehouse hung with hams, one of which had been partly carved where it hung. Jonathan dug his clasp knife out of his pouch and sliced off a few strips, his mouth watering all the while. The scavenger woman hadn't mentioned hams, but that had probably been an oversight. Jonathan threw the ham onto the stovetop, and in a minute or so he and the recovered Quimby tore into the food, eating in silence.

Drier, warm, and full, Jonathan asked finally, "Did you see anyone else on the river?"

"Bodies, do you mean?"

"Preferably not."

"Well no then," Quimby replied. "I'm afraid not. I caught hold of a cabin door and paddled along till I fell off. Then I washed into a snag and held on there for hours. Seemed like hours anyway. Then our friends in the rowboat came along, towing my cabin door. They would have left me on that snag, I think, if I hadn't made such a row. Filthy pirates. Hauled me all over the river collecting trash, me 'most frozen. On the way in, a body came past sprawled across a big plank. It was the cook, I think, although I can't say for sure. He wasn't in good shape, but he wore the same striped shirt. They went through his pockets, pushed him off into the river, and took his plank." Quimby shook his head at the enormity of it. "Dirty boggers," he said.

Jonathan nodded his head, sorry to hear of the cook's fate but relieved that it wasn't one of his companions who had been sprawled across the plank.

"Dirty, filthy, scum-eating vipers," Quimby said, staring at the fire.

"You said it," Jonathan put in.

"Pitiful snipes."

"Let's burn their barn in the morning," Jonathan suggested.

"What!" Quimby cried, aghast.

"Let's teach these people some manners. Show them what happens when they treat the quality so."

Quimby was wide-eyed. He knuckled his brow. "We can't do that. I'm a tailor, a haberdasher. I have my reputation."

"Did you give them a card?" Jonathan asked, squinting at him.

"Yes, in fact, I did."

"Then it's no good." Jonathan sounded disappointed. "We can't burn them out. They know who you are."

"That's what I'm saying," Quimby explained. "Don't even think of it. Put it out of your mind."

"I've forgotten already," Jonathan said. "It was just a passing thought. I can see now that it was no good."

Quimby looked vastly relieved. He yawned. Quimby's

yawning made Jonathan yawn too. He shoved as much wood as he could into the stove and both of them found comfortable patches of straw. Jonathan knew nothing more until sunlight, slanting in through a window, woke him in the morning. He woke Mr. Quimby, filled a sack with the rest of the cheese, a bunch of apples, and more strips of ham. Then the two of them pushed along down the river toward Landsend, leaving a gold coin on the back porch for their hosts.

They passed nothing along the road except scattered farmhouses. For one ten-mile stretch there were forests and moors, wildly green and overgrown. A couple of hay carts passed, headed in the opposite direction. Alone, Jonathan would have made the trek in hours less time. But it was impossible to abandon Quimby, who, unfortunately, was not built for walks of this nature.

He held up well for five miles or so, but at around ten in the morning he began to feel the heat. He wore a fairly heavy tweed suit, very apt, no doubt, for the weather along the coast. Inland, however, it was a bit much. He took his coat off, finally, and carried it over his shoulder.

"Tie it around your waist," Jonathan suggested. The idea seemed to go against the grain, as if Quimby's haberdasher instincts revolted at the idea of putting knots in the sleeves.

"I'll just wear it," Quimby said finally, and he pulled it back on. Jonathan noticed that the river water had had a grievous effect on the coat. It seemed, to say the least, to be cut rather tight. The sleeves hung about halfway down Quimby's forearms. The trousers weren't much better off; however they'd been cut so full in the first place—all pleated and billowy—that they were still loose enough. They were just a foot or so too short, as if Quimby were on his way to dig clams. Under the circumstances it was hard for Jonathan to understand why Quimby was so fearful of ruining the thing.

Soon Quimby began to sweat and to appear powerfully uncomfortable. Jonathan insisted that they rest up, and Quimby agreed. Their rest turned into a forty-minute search for water. They found a good, clean stream back in the woods, but in the process of hunting for it Quimby bent under a ragged tree limb and ripped a big tear along the shoulders of his coat. The tight fit of the thing encouraged the tear, which ran up to the shoulder seam and then sprung the whole back.

"Fits like a champ now," Jonathan said. "Let those sleeves down a bit, and your reputation is secure. Just don't turn around."

Quimby, however, didn't understand Jonathan's tone and thought he was serious. "I've ruined it!" he cried, pulling the coat off.

"Bit of thread . . ." Jonathan began, but there was no placating Quimby. As a haberdasher he knew a ruined coat when he saw one. It was an open book to him. He threw the coat into the bushes.

"Wait," Jonathan said, fishing it back out. "Rip or no rip, it's better than nothing. It might cool off a bit downriver. I'll carry this a ways."

Quimby thanked him, and after he'd sat by the stream for a while without the coat on, he began to look a bit refreshed. It was close to noon before they pushed on. They hadn't gone far, though, before Jonathan realized that Quimby was walking oddly, sort of rolling along on the sides of his shoes. It turned out that the river water had had the same effect on the shoes as it had on the coat and trousers. Quimby took them off, finally, and hobbled along in his stocking feet. The river road was so dotted with stones, however, that within ten minutes it became clear that that wouldn't serve either.

"I had an uncle," Jonathan said, "who used to stretch shoes by filling them up with water and wheat. The wheat would swell up, and puffo: the shoes would fit again."

Quimby gave him a look that seemed to suggest that down in Landsend they did things differently. He tried to pull the shoes back on then, but the task was an impossibility. "Ruined!" Quimby cried.

"Is that so?" Jonathan asked, stopping in the shade of an oak.

"Entirely!" After dashing one of the shoes to the road in disgust, Quimby threw his arm back as if to launch the second one into the forest. Jonathan snatched it out of his hand.

"Watch this," he said, pulling his knife out of his pouch and hacking away at the shoes. "We'll turn these into a pair of sandals." When Jonathan was finished, Quimby looked uncertain, as if the wet wheat idea had become suddenly appealing. But he found that the shoes fit him, or at least came close enough to fitting him to do the job. He and Jonathan started out once again; the afternoon was wearing on.

The last five miles took about as many hours as the first fifteen had taken. They rested as much as they walked, and, as the sun was setting and they were still not in sight of any village, Jonathan swore to himself that this was the last time he'd go hiking with any haberdashers. He realized, of course, that he was being a bit unfair to haberdashers, so he decided instead that he'd never go hiking with haberdashers in shrunken clothing.

It began to look as if they would spend the night in the woods. There was a bit of food left in Jonathan's sack—enough ham and cheese to make him wish there were more, and one shrunken apple. If it came to sleeping by the roadside, they would be both powerfully uncomfortable and hungry. Jonathan's own shoes and clothing had, somehow, been spared the sort of shrinking that Quimby's had suffered, probably because he bought them big in the first place and washed them a couple of times in hot water to shrink them to size before wearing them. He had always had a deep-rooted suspicion of high-toned clothes like Quimby's; they were too delicate. They might as well be made out of paper. If it came to sleeping in the woods or by the side of the road, Quimby would be in poor shape, and that rather bothered Jonathan. It had taken everything Quimby had just to hike the fifteen or eighteen miles from the farmhouse. A night in the open would be his ruin. It would be a matter of Jonathan's staying up all night feeding the fire just to keep warm—feeding the fire and listening to his stomach growl.

A creaking and rattling behind them made both Jonathan and Quimby turn, Quimby no doubt hoping even more than Jonathan that the hay cart which rattled along toward them on the road would give them a lift into the village. Given the number of peculiar people Jonathan had run into since climbing through the door into Balumnia, he half expected to see a mumbling lunatic driving the cart. But that wasn't the case at all.

They didn't even have to shout or wave or plead. The man in the cart simply reined up, tipped his hat, and said, "Going into the village?"

"That's right," Jonathan said. "We thought we'd be there by sundown, but it doesn't seem like we've got much of a chance."

"No chance at all." The driver pulled his hat off and ran his fingers through his hair. "It's six or eight miles more at least. Take you half the night." He grinned at Quimby in his clamdigger trousers and aerated shoes. Quimby had the look of a man who'd given up hope. "Climb aboard," the driver said, jerking a thumb over his shoulder at the heap of hay in the back. There wasn't half enough room on the little seat up front.

Jonathan didn't wait for the man to change his mind. He hoisted himself over the wooden slats of the bed of the cart, doing his best not to dump loose hay all over. Quimby, however, couldn't get aboard. He took a couple of little leaps at the cart, set his foot on a wheel spoke, slipped off, and wound up sitting in the road. The driver very cheerfully climbed down and gave him a boost as Jonathan heaved from above. Quimby burrowed into the hay, thanking them profusely. Within minutes of their creaking away once again, he was sound asleep.

Chapter 14

The Strawberry Baron

❀

THE sky turned red, then gray, then deepened to a twilight blue. Stars began to blink on, first one by one, then in batches. Jonathan wondered whether they were the same stars that shone above Twombly Town. They certainly appeared to be. He liked the idea that Mayor Bastable, right then, might well be looking up at those same stars and thinking about him. There was the Big Dipper and the Seven Sisters, and as the night grew darker the Milky Way became visible, stretching off through the heavens. The familiar stars and the cheerful, round-faced hay cart driver began to cheer him up considerably.

He learned along the way who owned the various local farms, how long they'd lived where they lived, and what they grew. There was one, a farmer named Streff, who was known, according to the driver, as the Strawberry Baron because he had acres and acres and acres of strawberries. Strawberry barges freighted his produce up and down the Tweet, and people five hundred miles up, in Sunnybrae and Ferndale, knew who the Strawberry Baron was.

All that made Jonathan think of his own strawberry crop. Mayor Bastable was probably tieing into a bowl of those strawberries right at that moment. He determined that if they found the Squire—*when* they found the Squire—he'd tell him about the fabulous Strawberry Baron. Squire Myrkle would, no doubt, insist on coming down to meet him and shake his hand. Strawberry Barons were right in the Squire's line.

Jonathan wondered what effect he'd have on the driver

if he mentioned Sikorsky. It might be safe to reveal that he'd been aboard the steamship and that it had been blown up by Sikorsky, but then again it might not be. There was the ghost of a chance, who could say, that the driver was somehow allied with Sikorsky; was one of his minions. But that was unlikely. The driver seemed to be too cheerful, too full of the right impulses. Given the standard reaction to the mention of Sikorsky's name, however, Jonathan decided not to risk bringing him up. If he were alone he would have. The worst that could happen would be that he would put the fear into the driver and find himself walking again. It was Quimby, though, who would suffer from it. And besides, Jonathan determined, he was quite likely leaving Sikorsky country anyway and would be shut of him forever. Good riddance, too!

They passed two farms, by and by, then topped a rise and came in sight of a long lake dotted with islands. The lake stretched away between hills, and the driver told Jonathan that it was called Lowland Lake because it wasn't a lake so much as a big section of lowlands that were fed with overflow from the Tweet River.

Clusters of cottages dotted the grassy shores. Sailing boats and rowboats and canoes were thick beside long docks. The water was dark and silent and dotted on the surface with glints of starlight. The moon was just then climbing in the sky behind them, and the first faint rays of moonlight shone on the near edge of the lake. On a little sandy beach a campfire burned, and next to it a man sat on a wooden chair, fishing.

"Out after catfish," the driver said, nodding toward the lone fisherman. "The light attracts them. There's big catfish in Lowlands Lake. Thirty or forty pounds is nothing. My old man hooked one off Narrow Island—that's the big, long island out there about a half mile—that towed him and his boat clear across the lake. Fed half the village when he finally got it in. He just skinned it and started in selling steaks at twenty cents a pound. There was six weeks wages in that fish, easy. I never been so sick of catfish in my life. I never did like it anyway."

"I'm with you," Jonathan said. "You know what I think it tastes like? White paint, that's what. You know how white paint smells? That's just how catfish tastes. Makes me feel like I'm eating a paint cutlet."

The driver agreed with him. "That's it exactly. Dirty boggers, eating mud and slime all day long. And ugly too."

Not five minutes after they passed the fisherman they reined up in front of a three-story farmhouse, all stone and shingles and big mullioned windows. A sign hung in the yard that read, LOWLANDS INN—BED AND BREAKFAST.

"If you want to put up in the village," the driver said, "this is about it. There's a boarding house two blocks up, but the owner's a grouch who serves boiled potatoes and grass soup for breakfast. I'd steer clear of it. This place is the right sort—good food and drink and feather beds."

Jonathan invited the man in for a glass of ale, but he couldn't be budged. He had a ways to go, he said, before he got home, and he was late already. So Jonathan rousted Quimby out of a sound sleep and helped him down. They watched the haycart as it toppled and creaked its way into the village and the darkness.

"I can hardly move," Quimby said. "I'm stiff as a post. What I need, more than anything in the world, is a hot bath. That and six years sleep."

"I need supper," Jonathan replied. Since the driver's mention of the ale and the food at the inn, the little strips of ham and cheese in his bag had begun to grow less appealing. The shrunken apple, nutritious as it might be, reminded him of a monkey's head. He shared the whole works among a half dozen cats that hung about the front of the inn. The monkey-head apple didn't attract the cats much either, so Jonathan pitched it into an adjoining field. It seemed to him reasonably likely that some animal would wander into it sooner or later—a cow or squirrel or gopher or some beast that, unlike people and cats, held old apples in high esteem.

They pushed in through the doors of the inn and booked two rooms for the night from a lad in enormous spectacles who read a thick book behind a wooden counter. Jonathan cocked his head sideways to read the title on the volume. He had always been compelled to discover what it was that anyone he met was reading. Often he could tell by the look of the cover that the book wouldn't be worth a thing. Usually if the cover were right—dark and old looking with gold or red lettering—the story inside would prove comparable. A proper book cover held great promise as far as he was concerned. This was just the right sort. There was a painting on the front of a great sailing ship, full-rigged, water spraying from the bow waves, and painted sails billowing as the ship slanted past a rocky desert isle. The title read: *Great Days of Piracy in the Flappage Islands.*

The mention of pirates suddenly reminded Jonathan of their treasure map, and with a start the thought struck him that the map had probably gone down with the ship. The Professor hadn't, after all, had it with him when he was on deck that evening. The map would have been in his cabin. Squids were probably poring over it at that moment, down on the river bottom.

Jonathan began to regret the loss of the map. Then it occurred to him that he hadn't stopped to regret the loss of the Professor yet, or of any of the others either. That, of course, wasn't due to any lack of feeling; he was simply convinced that it was bad form to mourn for someone who mightn't be dead yet. The same, he decided, went for treasure maps.

The lad took their money, gave them each a room key, and went back to the Flappage Islands after directing them down a hallway and to their right where they could, he said, get food and drink. The sound of chairs scraping and glasses tinkling met them in the hall. Tobacco smoke rolled out of an open double door about halfway down. There was, quite apparently, a merry crowd at the inn, for Jonathan heard the sound of laughter and of poetry being recited—familiar poetry, in fact, recited by voices he'd heard before. Followed by Quimby, he walked into a big common room set with tables and chairs and with a big fire burning in a wide hearth. A dog barked twice and raced across toward them. It was old Ahab, cutting capers and bounding back and forth. He tore up to Jonathan, tried to stop at his feet but slid into him instead. Then he raced off a few feet, leaped once or twice into the air in the manner of a frog, and raced back at him again.

"Hullo, old Ahab," Jonathan said, scratching him on the head. "This is Mr. S. N. M. Quimby, Haberdasher." Quimby patted Ahab on the head too. No one else in the room paid them any attention. Everyone was busy watching Gump, who stood on a chair near the fireplace, reading poetry from a batch of connected sheets. Bufo sat at a table next to Gump's chair, listening in a satisfied way. That meant, Jonathan knew, that the poem was a collaboration. If it had been Gump's effort entirely, Bufo wouldn't have been half so satisfied. He'd be itching to tell Gump exactly why the poem was ludicrous.

"The pounding of the engines!" Gump shouted. "The smoking of the stacks! The hush of evil curling fog! The shrieking of the bats!" In these last two lines he let his voice drop to a stage whisper and strung the s on bats out about a half mile. Thunderous applause erupted from the dozen or so travelers who sat about the hall, most of it prompted by Bufo, who had leaped to his feet at the close of the poem and clapped wildly. It sounded to Jonathan as if it had been a good poem—lots of activity in it. He wasn't sure he approved of the attempt to rhyme stacks with bats, although that may well have been what one of his old teachers had called half-rhyme. In any case, no one else in the room seemed to object.

Gump looked up from his pages of poetry and saw Jonathan and Quimby standing in the open doorway. "Bing!" Gump cried, and he whacked Bufo on the back of the head. Bufo, of course, shouted "Hey!" himself, and took a poke at Gump, but he was too late. Gump was already clambering down and making off toward Jonathan. Bufo quickly followed after.

Everyone shook hands and slapped about for a moment. Jonathan was afraid that Bufo and Gump would poke fun at Quimby's suit, but they didn't. Bufo started to once or twice—or at least so it seemed to Jonathan—but his sense of diplomacy won out and he kept quiet. He and Gump did a good bit of winking at each other as they walked toward their fireside table, and Gump, nudging Bufo, hiked his trousers up around his calves and looked woeful for a moment. Quimby didn't notice a thing, however, so no harm came of it. Bufo and Gump, Jonathan could see, were in fine form.

Neither one of them had eaten yet either, so they all ordered a big steak and mushroom pie and glasses of ale before they started to talk. Then Jonathan asked the two about Miles and the Professor.

"Haven't seen them," Gump said.

"Hide nor hair," Bufo added. "We were running along toward you there with the most incredible monster after us."

Jonathan nodded. "I met him—the man with no head."

"That's the one," Gump said. "No head. Can you beat that? How in the world could he see where he was going? That's what I asked myself right off. Fancy a man with no head. Who was he anyway?"

"Some demon from the river," Jonathan answered. "The cook told us that the south shore of the river was haunted, that ghosts and such come out of the forest at night. I guess he was right."

Bufo grimaced into his ale glass. "Right as rain. I saw some things last night that would pickle a fish. There was this old woman with white eyes who came past singing— more like croaking actually. We were up on the second deck smoking a pipe and making up a poem called 'Poor Squire Lost'—I'll read it to you in a minute—and here she comes, walking along with a basket in her hands. She stops and gives us a look, and her eyes were just paste."

"Balls of milk," Gump put in.

"It was horrible. Anyway, off comes the lid of the basket, and what's inside? This headless man's head. All bloody and ragged and awful. At least I suppose it was his. It must have been; they couldn't run that same gag off on too many people."

"So she *hands* it to me," Gump cut in.

"What in the world did you do?" Quimby asked, a look of terror on his face.

"I knocked the bloody thing into the river," Gump said. "Right out of her filthy hands."

Bufo gave him a look. "You thrashed about and screamed is what you did. You didn't *mean* to knock anything into the river. I never saw any such dance before.

It was grand. Gump looked like one of those wiggle puppets the elves make. What a sight. There he is, flailing along, and *whump!* he whacks this bloody head into the Tweet."

"That wasn't it at all," Gump, said heating up. "I just slammed it right out of her hand. And talk about wiggle puppets and being scared out of their wits, what did *you* do but shoot off down the deck like a bloody comet, hooting and shouting."

"That was because I saw the headless man coming up from a rowboat," Bufo explained. "Here he was out looking for his head—that's what I figured—and you're pitching it into the drink. Was he going to be mad or what? You don't just treat a man's head so."

"You do if it isn't attached to him!" Gump shouted. "You do if some old marble-eyed lady is waving the thing in your face. The whole mess of them are lucky I didn't get riled. They'd have sung a sorry tune, head or no head."

Bufo screwed up his face and waved his hands briefly in a show of horrified flailing, miming Gump's assault on the witch. Gump didn't see anything funny in it and seemed as if he were about to pop, so Jonathan broke in to cool things off.

"So this fellow chased you down the deck?"

"We were leading him your way," Bufo said. "Setting a trap, you might say. We figured to run him past and you could brain him."

"I was ready to," Jonathan said truthfully. "But then all of a sudden the bombs started going off, and I ended up in a pile of ropes watching the lot of you sail out over the river. I was afraid you'd had it."

Gump nodded. "So were we. There we were, paddling around in the fog. The spook who chased us never came up. Couldn't hold his breath, I suppose, without any nose. Then a big slab of cabin wall floated by, big as a raft nearly, and we all got on board. It was colder than Christmas, I can tell you, but better that than drowning in some haunted river."

The mention of the haunted river made Jonathan remember the shadows and the shapes that had hovered about him in the water that night. "You're right about that," he said. "The Tweet is no place to take a swim."

"So we just floated down the river," Gump continued. "Must have been hours. It didn't seem like we were going very fast, just kind of lazying along. By and by the fog started to break up, and early in the morning all of a sudden we could see the shore, not very far off at all. We tore a couple of planks off our wall, which was pretty beat up anyway, and paddled like sixty until we got there."

"Anyway, you wouldn't believe where we wound up," Bufo said. "We climbed over this embankment and found ourselves in strawberry heaven. Nothing but strawberry vines with berries as big as your fist for about sixty miles around. And coming along the road was this amazing man dressed like a king with a straw hat on and a pink shirt that was all-over ruffles. 'I'm the Strawberry Baron,' he says. 'Who are you?' Not snooty, mind you, but very gentlemanly. So we introduce ourselves . . ."

"And he bows very seriously." Gump wasn't about to let Bufo get away with the whole story. "He asks us if we might be gentlemen off the riverboat. 'We are,' says we. That's exactly it. He knew that, of course, because we were still pretty wet and we'd floated up on a piece of cabin wall. But he was very formal. Took nothing for granted. 'Come along,' he says, and we climbed up into his buggy and went off down the road to his mansion and ate about a quarter of a ton of strawberries and cream."

"And guess who was there," Bufo asked.

"I give," Jonathan said.

"Cap'n Binky, that's who. Him and the Strawberry Baron are pretty thick, it turns out. They're both food wizards in their way. Part of some sort of club."

"What ever became of his coffee?" Jonathan asked, relieved to hear that Cap'n Binky had survived the blast.

"He had it right there with him. The whole works—coffee and pot and everything. Even his book. Not a scratch. It turns out that he was ready for trouble. He'd unbolted the pot, kegged the coffee, and crated the lot of it up and shoved it into a lifeboat. Got away clean. Rescued a few people too, by the way. He didn't just cut out. He said that he would have gone down with the ship except for the coffee. 'Art first and morality to top off on.' That's what he shouted when he pulled away."

"Is he here?" Jonathan asked. "At the inn?"

"No. He stayed on for a bit with the Baron. We set out early on the milk wagon and decided to put up here for the night. We were planning to rendezvous at the post office tomorrow."

Jonathan nodded. "Me too." Then he told them his story: how he met up with Quimby, and about the cook's being dead, and about walking the twenty-some miles downriver and getting a ride on a haycart and passing the lands of the very same Strawberry Baron, who had been so hospitable.

"And something else," Bufo said, pouring the last of the ale into Jonathan's glass. "It looks like rough weather ahead for Sikorsky."

"That's a pleasant thought," Jonathan said. "What sort of rough weather?"

"The Baron's got up a bunch of men, an army, local farmers and villagers and such," Gump put in. "This riverboat business broke the camel's back. They've had enough. There must have been two hundred or so in little tents in the strawberry fields. Cap'n Binky has them hopping. They were all for setting out in boats that morning, but the Baron wouldn't hear of it. Slow and easy, that's the Baron."

By this time Quimby was asleep in his chair, snoring like a bulldog.

"So it's Landsend for us tomorrow, then," Jonathan said. "How far do you suppose it is?"

"Twenty-five miles," Gump replied. "That's what the Baron said anyway."

Jonathan gestured toward the snoring Quimby. "He'll never make it another twenty-five miles. It'll take us a week unless we can hitch a ride somehow."

"We already have," Bufo said. "There's a mail wagon going down tomorrow morning. We talked to the driver. Squared it with him. Plenty of room, he said. We gave him a couple of coins to cement the deal."

"I'll do the same," Jonathan said. "If he can't take all of us, I'll put Quimby aboard and walk down myself."

"What if we saved our poems for tomorrow?" Gump

asked abruptly in a tone that seemed to suggest that Jonathan would be disappointed. "I'm too tired to get into the spirit."

Jonathan swallowed the last of his ale. "The spirit, I suppose, is important?"

"Vital," Bufo confirmed

"I'm too fagged out," Gump said. "We haven't had four hours sleep in two days."

"Of course," said Jonathan. "We've got a long ride ahead tomorrow. Plenty of time for poetry."

And with that they woke Quimby and the lot of them turned in.

Chapter 15

Doctor Chan's Herbs

❖

THERE wasn't any problem the next morning about getting down to Landsend. The mail cart was a long covered wagon, large enough for eight or ten people, or, as the case may be, for any number of big sacks of mail. But there wasn't actually much mail at all. Only one lonely sack and a half dozen boxes were traveling along with them, so the driver was happy to take on more passengers. As it turned out, the wagon didn't get away until almost ten in the morning. It would put them into Landsend rather later in the day than Jonathan had hoped, but that gave the four of them time to do a bit of shopping in town. Quimby bought a new suit and shoes, which he complained about as being cut-rate. But they were better, he admitted, than his cut-up suit and shoes, which he finally gave to the woman who owned the inn. Before the wagon left, she'd dressed her scarecrow in them.

The rest of them bought a few things too—a change of clothes and such, and Jonathan bought a jacket and a knapsack. They packed a lunch just in case they got hungry along the way, and then, sharply at ten o'clock, rattled off down the road. Although the wagon was covered, the back was open, and now and again they could see little bits of the Tweet River running broad and green beyond occasional hills.

At noon they broke into their food, shoving bits of meat, cheese, and bread up to the driver who, since he was dieting, had brought along nothing but a brown rice salad and a tin of Power's Unleavened Snap Crackers. When Bufo offered him a share of their ham and cheese, he pitched the

157

salad into a ditch, which, Bufo happily pointed out, is generally the most sensible way to treat salads.

"So what inspired you to set in writing poetry again?" Jonathan asked.

"Oh," Gump replied, "we never gave it up. We can't. It's in our blood."

"Like an infection," Bufo said.

Gump agreed with him. "That's right. And some things set it off: changes of seasons, for instance, or weather. Poetry is the sort of thing that just comes sailing in."

"Kind of like a bat that gets tangled up in your hair," Bufo put in.

"Or a 'possum," Gump observed, scratching his head, "that sneaks in at night and ravages your shoes."

Bufo nodded. "That's it exactly. As you can see, metaphors like that fly out like popping corn. A poet can't help himself. He's a slave to it."

Jonathan said he understood. Quimby declared he knew a fellow once who was a poet: he wrote inspirational pieces for the local newspaper. Very heartfelt. Bufo didn't look as if he cared much for inspirational pieces.

"What sort of inspirational pieces?" asked Gump, who, like Bufo, had a natural distrust of all other poets. "Do you recall any?"

Quimby thought it over. "Something about pressing on in hard times. You know, the stiff lip and straight back sort of thing. Bearing up. Doing one's duty. Very stirring, really. Touched home."

"I should say," said Bufo. "Sounds like a laugh a minute. But that's not what *we* write. Not by a long nose. Not that there's anything wrong with it, mind you; this poet of yours was likely quite a gem, in his way. I'll look for his book when I get back home." He winked at Gump to alert him to how clever this final comment had been.

"So anyway, you've run up some good ones, eh?" Jonathan asked.

"Some smashers."

Bufo agreed. "It was the explosions that did it. We were sure you and the Professor and Miles were—well, you know . . . That you hadn't made it. Moroseness is what it was that got things going."

"Morosity," Gump said.

"Pardon me?"

"Morosity, I believe it is," Gump repeated. "Not moroseness."

"You're thinking of porosity," Bufo said. "Like your head."

Gump gave him a look. But by then he was charged up with his poetry, so he let the matter drop. Quimby said that Bufo was probably correct anyway, and that his poet friend had spelled it "morosion" once, which seemed quite suitable under the circumstances since it rhymed, to a degree, with "erosion," which was what was happening to this fellow's soul in the poem. Gump and Bufo looked for a moment as if it was happening to their souls too, but then Gump pulled out his sheaf of papers and cleared his throat.

"Poor Squire Lost," he read in a voice of woe, and he set in on a long poem about the Squire's tragic wanderings in faraway Balumnia. The whole thing took about half an hour and seemed to confuse poor Quimby no end—he, of course, having no idea that Balumnia was a faraway magical land. He seemed to think, however, that poems were by their very nature obscure, and that it was the inexplicable bits that were the best parts. Jonathan sometimes felt the same way himself. The poem ended up something like this:

> And so the Squire trudges past,
> In his coat of golden thread
> Weaved by Quimby who also knit
> The massive cap upon his head.
>
> The towns give way to forests.
> Goblins creep through bogs of peat,
> And headless men in rowboats
> Sail atop the Tweet.
>
> He wanders weeping far and wide;
> His rotund form is shrunk away,
> And with him travels Hope and Home,
> Eastward toward the dawning day!

Gump finished and sat very still. It had been a sad poem, even for Quimby—who, by the end of it, had tears in his eyes. He'd never, he insisted, been a part of a poem before. The poems that his friend wrote weren't the sort that had anyone *doing* anything—knitting hats or creeping through peat bogs or shrinking away or any of that sort of business. This was, he said, awfully powerful stuff.

Jonathan liked the poem too. It had the unmistakable stamp of Gump and Bufo on it. "Are you just going to leave him lost there?" he asked them. "Can't you save him? Hoist him out?"

"Reality can't be tampered with," Bufo said. "We're slaves to it. This will only be half a poem until we find the poor Squire."

"An unfinished symphony," Gump observed.

Jonathan could see the logic in it. "I suppose it has to be such. Let's hope you can finish the poem fairly soon."

The two nodded but didn't say anything. Jonathan assumed they were thinking about the Squire. He knew how they felt—that nothing much had been accomplished yet. But then it was true that they had run into Quimby and learned a bit about the Squire's whereabouts. And if, when they got to Landsend, they could find Miles and the Professor, then Jonathan would count them all well off indeed. They wouldn't have long to wait either, for just about then the driver shouted, "About a mile to go, boys," and kicked up the horses' pace a bit, anxious to get into town.

Landsend wasn't quite the sprawling seaport city that Jonathan expected. It wasn't any bigger, in fact, than the city of Seaside on the delta of the Oriel River. And the Tweet, of course, was twenty times the size of the Oriel. Jonathan had assumed that Landsend, then, would be twenty times the size of Seaside, or some such thing. It was impossible for any of them to know much about the city from within their little canvas-covered mail wagon. But Jonathan sat nearest the rear, so he had the best view.

They couldn't see the ocean, but the air was tangy with salt. A coastal mountain range rose behind the city, densely forested above houses that climbed a quarter mile or so up the slopes. The wagon swung around and revealed a broad expanse of river delta thick with fishing boats. Along the shore were mud flats and backwaters tangled with exposed roots and shore grasses, and dotted with pools of standing water shining in the afternoon sun. Long thin piers ran out across them and into the brackish waters of the delta. Small boats were tied to some of the piers; other piers were in disrepair, often simply lines of broken pilings that weren't much good for anything but pelican perches.

The wagon bounced along past boatyards where the skeletons of half-finished sailing ships sat on great trestled structures and where decaying clinker-built hulls lay scattered about, beyond repair, weeds and wild fuchsias and trumpet flower vines growing through and around them.

The backwaters and mud flats and boatyards gave way finally to scattered inns and cottages. There were people everywhere: vendors selling ice cream, lemonade, and fresh fruit; groups of shirtless sailors and idlers lounging in doorways; shoppers clumping down the boardwalks; children dashing about and carrying on. It seemed as if every third or fourth building sported a sidewalk café, the sort in which you could take an hour and a half over your coffee. Even at four o'clock in the afternoon, an hour that Jonathan would have thought either a bit early or a bit late for lounging about in sidewalk cafés, there were few empty tables.

Most of the buildings along the street were built of clapboard and shingle. The road was paved with square gray stones worn by traffic, all cut from some dark granitic rock. Wherever he looked Jonathan could see wild foliage. Hibiscus flowers bloomed everywhere—great red and orange and yellow blooms with petals the size of a man's hand. Purple trumpet flowers and bougainvillaea twined through fences and trellises, and even unkempt yards were a wonder of bright green grass and wild colorful flowers. Landsend was altogether a beautiful sort of place—in a state, thought Jonathan, of colorful and sublime decay.

It was nicely coincidental that the wagon was hauling them straight up to the post office at the top of the hour. Jonathan barely had time to think "What if they aren't here?" and feel the first pangs of dread and worry when they rattled to a stop not six feet from where Professor Wurzle leaned against the post of a gaslamp reading some sort of announcement or advertisement. Jonathan thought furiously of clever things to say to him, something subtle and witty and surprising, but Ahab got in before him. Catching sight of old Wurzle, he barked twice and leaped down onto the road, nearly landing on the Professor's shoes.

"Ahab!" Professor Wurzle shouted. Then he pushed his glasses onto the edge of his nose and peered over them at Jonathan, Bufo, Gump, and Quimby, who issued, one by one, from the rear of the wagon.

Jonathan shook his hand, feeling as if he hadn't seen the Professor for six months. "What ho?"

"Oh," the Professor responded, "not much ho. How about you?"

"Not much ho with us either," Gump announced.

About then, the driver teetered past under the canvas mailbag and a stack of boxes—what Jonathan's father used to call a lazy man's load. They all shouted thanks to him, since the pile of debris precluded his shaking hands.

"Where's Miles?" Jonathan was sure, somehow, that the Professor would know.

"Down the block."

"Is he okay?" Bufo asked.

"Safe and sound. We had a remarkably easy time of it, I must say. Hardly got wet at all." The Professor greeted Quimby, who stood off to the side a bit, not wanting to push in among the old friends. It was as if his arrival at Landsend had restored him, and he was no longer a wretched soul but was once again a haberdasher with a reputation.

Quimby bowed slightly. "I'll be thanking you, Mr. Bing, and you lads too, for looking after me. I'm not much good at tramping abroad, I'm afraid. Haven't got the constitution for it."

"Nonsense," Jonathan said, patting the man on the back. "It was our pleasure. It's rare that we run into such good company."

"That's right," Bufo agreed, and Gump nodded assent.

"Well," Quimby said. "I'll be off now. I'd show you around the shop, but it's a bit late for that. It'll be closed by now, and my keys are in the river. Come round tomorrow, though, and have a good look. Fascinating business, really."

"It couldn't help but be," Jonathan remarked, although the statement puzzled just about everyone there, including Jonathan, who hadn't really given the matter much thought. Then everyone shook hands, and Quimby disappeared up the avenue.

"What's that you have there, Professor?" Gump asked. "That leaflet."

The Professor held the thing up for them to have a look at. On the front of the paper was a pen and ink drawing of the face of Squire Myrkle, his cheeks puffed out as if they were loaded with horse chestnuts, his eyes crinkly, cheerful, and enthusiastically befuddled. Below the picture was written in bold printing: "Have you seen this man?" Below that, in smaller letters, was information about what to do if you *had* seen this man. Above the whole thing was a headline that announced: REWARD!

Jonathan took the handbill from the Professor, fearing some sort of foul play. "Where was this?"

"It wasn't anywhere. Not yet. But in about thirty seconds it will be hanging from that bubinga on the curbside."

"You made these up?"

"Well, not exactly," the Professor told him. "Miles drew them. What we needed were *leads*. That's what the detective would say anyway. And the way to get leads is to seek out people who've seen the Squire. One of them must know the direction he took when he left town."

"*If* he left town, I suppose you mean," Bufo said.

The Professor shook his head. "I don't know. We've been going about to inns all day, and he isn't at any of them. What's more, he hasn't been. There aren't but a couple left, and they're outside of town on the way to the coast road. But we know he was here, at Quimby's shop, and we can bet that he wasn't in any vast hurry, knowing the Squire as we do. So he *must* have stayed with someone. These handbills will smoke him out."

Jonathan remained somewhat dubious. "I hate to wait around for the smoking."

"Where do you propose to go?" Professor Wurzle asked. "North? South?"

"I see what you mean," Jonathan said. "Let's all post these things. How many do you have?"

"Only one left after this. We've been hanging them everywhere. Unless this is a town full of hermits, we'll get a response. So we may just as well settle in and wait for it."

Everybody agreed that such was the case, even though the idea of "settling in" instantly increased Jonathan's feelings of helplessness. The handbill idea, however, decreased his fears a bit; he couldn't see any reason for its not working.

The Professor pulled out his pocketwatch. "We've got to meet Miles in half an hour at the inn."

"I hope we can get a room," Jonathan said. "This town is full of people. Must be any number of travelers passing through."

"Thousands. But that doesn't matter. We booked your rooms this morning. It was Miles' idea that the fates can be manipulated through optimism. That if we reserved rooms for the lot of you, you'd show up to claim them."

"It worked apparently," said Jonathan, who liked the idea well enough.

"It was a fine gesture," the Professor continued. "Typical of Miles. But I'm afraid fate is one of the seven immutables."

Jonathan was about to ask him what the other six immutables were, but he held off for a moment and the importance of the question diminished. He wasn't even sure, in fact, what an immutable of any sort was. It sounded like one of those wiggly little things you see under a microscope. But he knew that was unlikely. The Professor had doubtless been speaking abstractly.

The four of them and Ahab wandered off along the street, passing bustling cafés and dark, cool pubs. The Professor led them around a corner and up a narrow street that angled away toward the sea. Houses lined either side, two or three stories high, and most of them were faced with balconies fenced by wrought-iron grillwork. Flowering vines crept from pots on the balconies up the sides of the buildings and spilled over the railings. Doorways were framed in green and hung round with trumpet flowers; some shuttered windows were almost hidden behind tangles of vegetation. Doors stood open in more than half the houses, and here and there people sat about on the balconies chatting and watching the street. There were cats everywhere, peeking at them from balconies and from behind potted plants. They gathered in little groups on the sidewalk, passing the time of day, then dashed away hither and thither, across streets and up alleys, off on cat business. Ahab had a look of amazement on his face. Jonathan assumed that he was puzzled to learn of the very existence of such a number of cats. He stopped now and again to study them and was himself studied in return. Ahab had, of course, never held any grudge against cats, and he harbored a philosophy that didn't allow for the chasing of anything—not just for the thrill of the chase, anyway. Peaceful coexistence was his motto, and the cats seemed to sense it. Either that or they felt safe, surrounded as they were by cohorts. One way or another, Ahab made friends with any number of the cats and seemed to be growing to like Landsend as much as Jonathan.

They rounded another corner onto a similar street that ran off toward the ocean. An evening onshore breeze blew straight up the middle carrying the tingling smell of salt and tar and cooling things off a bit. At the top of the street stood a collection of dark little shops behind dusty leaded windows. In front of one dangled a sign in oriental letters that read, DR. CHAN'S HERBS. Ceramic and glass pots and vials sat on a counter in the window. Open bags of dried flowers were heaped among them: tiny pale lilacs, minute purple orchids, citrus blossoms, rose petals. There were wooden boxes of withered lizards and glass jars containing coiled, pickled serpents and peculiar funguses. All of it was scattered about and dusty. Clutches of dried bats hung from above amid bunches of drying herbs.

Next to Dr. Chan's was another shop that bore a family resemblance. Before it dangled a sign that read merely, CURIOSITIES. Jonathan wondered how much more curious its wares could be than those of the mysterious Dr. Chan. The window was so gray with dust that they had to press up against the pane to see inside. When they did, they were presented with the sight of a hippopotamus head, mouth agape, staring back out at them. In among its teeth sat a small, satisfied-looking pig with *his* mouth open too. And in the pig's mouth, peering out as if through a window, were the head and shoulders of a mouse. A price tag dangled from one of the hippo's teeth: Two hundred dollars.

Gump was much taken with the object. "I wonder if the two hundred is for the set," he said, "or just for the hippo."

"Probably for the tooth," Bufo said.

"Imagine having the likes of that in your dining room," Gump continued. "How majestic. It reminds me of one of those informative illustrations of the descent of the beasts from the fishes."

"It's not as good a deal as you thought," Bufo said, his face pressed against the window. "The mouse just took off."

Gump squinted in the window again. Just as Bufo had reported, the mouse was gone. But it peeked, suddenly, out of one of the hippo's ears, then ducked back inside and disappeared entirely, after which a second mouse crawled out of the other ear and jumped down to the floor.

"It's a mouse hotel!" Bufo cried. "Two hundred dollars for a mouse hotel! They probably refer to it as Hotel Hippo. That suckling pig is the innkeeper."

"Too bad this place isn't open," Gump said. "I'd talk him down fifty or so and buy that thing. I've always wanted one."

Jonathan pressed on the door, just for fun, as they turned to walk away. It swung open, creaking on its hinges. Everyone stopped and peered in. The shop was dim; no lights burned to brighten it up. It didn't appear at first as if anyone was there, but just then a deep voice from inside boomed: "Are you coming in or not?"

"Of course." Jonathan felt somewhat committed, having shoved open the door. Gump, anxious to have a go at buying the stuffed hippo-pig, was at Jonathan's heels as they entered. The proprietor sat beneath a small window in a far corner, taking advantage of the watery rays of late afternoon sun that slanted through the dust on the window. An enormous book lay open on his lap. In his hand was a magnifying glass. His hair was frazzled, and he wore a dark suit—the same suit, it appeared, that he'd worn for the past month or so. But his tie was neatly knotted and he gave the general impression of being a rumpled intellectual—someone, perhaps, so thoroughly immersed in his studies and investigations that rumpled suits and frazzled hair were pretty much inevitable. Jonathan concluded right away that he was a sort of indoor, ivory tower counterpart to the Professor.

"Are you looking for anything in particular?" the man asked as he adjusted a pair of thick glasses on his nose.

"No," Jonathan said. "Just browsing."

"Actually," Gump interrupted, gazing nonchalantly about him, "I've been thinking of buying a really first-rate hippo head. Something to hang on the wall in the dining room. They're a dime a dozen this time of the year, of course, but good ones, nice fat toothy ones, are rare in any season." Then Gump pretended to notice the head in the window, and with a critical air he wandered over to have a look at it.

Ahab stood with Professor Wurzle before several strange bins along the wall. Each was filled with bones, some loose, some connected. One bin was labeled *Fish,* another *Birds,* another *Mammalia,* and a fourth *Man.* And sure enough, neatly divided between each were the correct sorts of bones. Ahab didn't appear to be sure whether to be attracted to them or disgusted. They seemed far too dusty and dry to be worth chewing; a good stick would have more flavor. They fascinated Jonathan and the Professor though.

Old Wurzle gingerly plucked out a fish skeleton and examined it. Its head was enormous, at least two-thirds the size of the entire body. The fish must have been little more than a swimming head. "Some sort of pompano," the Professor observed, putting it back and rooting among the bones in the next bin. He uncovered a bird skull as long as Jonathan's arm, the grinning mouth of which was dotted with sharp teeth. Beneath it was a cheesecloth bag of hummingbird skulls, about sixty or eighty of them, like a bag of marbles.

"These would be fun to own," Jonathan said, poking around among the tiny skulls.

"For what purpose?" the Professor asked. "I didn't think you had much interest in the scientific arts."

"Well I don't, really. They'd just be good to sort of have, if you see what I mean. Like Gump's hippo head."

Clearly the Professor didn't see anything in it. "I really hope he doesn't succeed in buying that thing."

"I know," Jonathan said. "Imagine trying to lug it about with us. We'd have to arrange to have it stolen."

In the other bins were no end of rib bones and skulls and feet strung together with silver wires. Above the bins on a shelf was a line of little stuffed crocodiles flanked on either side by stacks of dusty old books. Supporting the books were two curious glass jars, jars that both the Professor and Jonathan saw at the same time. Their reactions were identical.

"*Escargot!*" Jonathan exclaimed.

"Has to be. Look at this." And he upended a fallen placard that was meant to be tacked beneath the jars. *Squid Clocks Available,* it read.

"You don't suppose he's round about now, do you?"

The Professor shook his head. "No. I don't. These jars have a year's worth of dust on them."

"If he were just here in his submarine," Jonathan said, "we'd have a way out of this cheap hotel."

"And *if* we find the Squire," the Professor said, "and *if* we interfere with the Dwarf's machinations and survive. Too many ifs, Jonathan. It would be best not to anticipate anything. Wish for the worst and you'll never be disappointed. I read that once in a sea story. It makes sense."

"I suppose so. But that philosophy doesn't appeal to me much. Let's just ask the gentleman about Escargot."

Gump's attempts to coerce the proprietor into cutting the price of the hippo head had, apparently, gone awry. "It can't be done," the man was saying as Jonathan and the Professor joined them. "Not even for four hundred."

"Four hundred!" shouted Bufo, who was rummaging in a sack of shrunken heads. "Gump, you're a lunatic. You haven't *got* four hundred."

"You could loan me a bit."

"Loan you a bit? What are we going to do for food, eat hippo soup? And what about the poor mice who are living in there? Would you take their home away?"

"I can't sell it at any price," the rumpled man stated flatly. "It's promised. I've already taken half the money down. I think I can get my hands on the head of a wilde-beest, though."

Gump brightened. "What's that?"

"An enormous cow."

"Can you put a pig in his mouth? Or a toad maybe?"

The rumpled man nodded. "I think so. It makes for a striking effect, doesn't it?" Everyone agreed that it did. "But it will take a couple of weeks to get the head."

Gump looked crestfallen. "Do I have to leave any money?"

"No, I'll need some such thing to take the place of the hippo anyway. What do you say to my holding it for a month? If you don't show up, I'll sell it."

"Done!" Gump cried enthusiastically. He turned to the Professor. "We can come back through in a few weeks, can't we?"

"Of course," Wurzle said. "Easiest thing in the world."

"He'll be over it by then," Bufo whispered in Jonathan's ear. "He gets taken by this sort of fit, but it passes."

Jonathan nodded. "Tell me, sir . . ." he began.

"Dr. Chan," the man interrupted, extending a hand.

"Ah," the Professor said. "Dr. Chan of the herb emporium next door?"

"The same."

"What do they use those dried lizards for?" Bufo asked, referring to the pots in the window of the herb shop.

"I don't at all know," Dr. Chan answered. "Something foul, I don't doubt. I'm not much interested in herbs, to tell you the truth. I'm a writer." He pushed through and around heaps of curiosities—carven idols and tooth neck-laces and ancient rugs and clothing—to get at a copy of a book. He handed it across to Jonathan who was closest to him. *Tales of the Deep Sea* the title read, by Dr. Phillip Chan.

"Very nice title," said Jonathan as he flipped to the frontispiece, a fine old etching of a ragged ship mired in an oily, weed-choked sea. Kelp tendrils and such curled up over the bowsprit and wound along the anchor. A half-dozen skeletons in tattered clothes bent over the rail, star-ing in horror at something surfacing toward them from the

waters below. "Where can I get a copy of this?" asked
Jonathan, who knew his kind of book when he saw it.

"You can have that copy, if you like," Dr. Chan replied.
"I have any number of them here, crates and crates of
them as a matter of fact."

"I'll buy one too," the Professor said. Jonathan knew
that the Professor was buying it out of kindness, that he
never read anything but scientific and historical texts. Dr.
Chan, clearly, could use the business.

The Professor thumbed through his copy of the book.
"Sell herbs as a hobby, do you?"

"Not actually," Dr. Chan said. "But writing doesn't pay,
you know. There's not enough income in it to keep me in
soup bones. When my wife died ten years back, I was left
with a bit of money. Not much, mind you, but enough to
invest. So one day I ran into a gentleman who sold out-
fitted businesses, and he put me onto the herb shop. All
stocked up and ready to go. Business wasn't bad either,
Landsend being a port town and all. But my clients, it
turned out, didn't have any money. All penniless. Gypsys
and sorcerers and witches and such, not your moneyed
types at all. But they were loaded with things to trade—
shrunken heads and idols and all that crowd. That hippo
cost me no end of dried newts, I can tell you. So one thing
led to another and pretty soon I had enough stuff to open
this curiosity shop."

"More money in curiosities is there?" Jonathan asked.

"Heaps," Dr. Chan said. "I can sell a man a stuffed
crocodile when he wouldn't touch a dried newt. He
wouldn't know what to do with the newt, but he can
always put the crocodile on his mantel or have it turned
into a hat."

"That certainly seems reasonable," the Professor said.
"How about those squid clocks you advertise—where do
they come from?"

"Oh, I haven't any squid clocks. I thought I took that
sign down."

"Were they made by a local clockmaker?" the Professor
continued.

"Not at all. I buy them from an adventuring type who
comes through now and again. He brings me deep ocean

herbs. And fresh, mind you, not old dried weeds that have been sitting on a beach for six weeks. Most of those fish skeletons I got from him too. He has access to the sea."

Jonathan immediately wished that *he* had access to the sea, whatever such a thing was. "This fellow with the squid clocks, he also brought the whale eyeball and the octopus?"

"That's right," Dr. Chan replied.

"His name isn't Theophile Escargot by any chance, is it?"

"That's your man! You know him then?"

"We've met," said the Professor.

"Keep your hands on your wallets, gentlemen," Dr. Chan remonstrated. "I'm not entirely sure where our friend Escargot finds his treasures, but I suspect that as often as not he lets others find them for him, then appropriates what he wants."

The mention of the word treasure reminded Jonathan of the map from the cellar of Highcastle tower, which, in his happiness at finding the Professor and his enthusiasm for the city of Landsend, he'd thoroughly forgotten. All of a sudden he was itching to be out of the curiosity shop and to ask the Professor about it.

"We've already been introduced to Escargot's methods of doing business," the Professor said.

"Yes, we have," Jonathan agreed. "And I'm afraid we're late for our meeting with Miles."

The Professor checked his pocketwatch. "You're right. He'll be wondering what happened to me. He's been worried about this handbill business from the start. He wanted to lay low, but I thought that laying low wasn't doing us too much good."

"No more incognito," Bufo put in.

"Let me see that," Dr. Chan said, pointing to the paper in the Professor's hand. "I've seen this fellow."

"Have you?" asked Jonathan.

"Yes I have," the doctor said. "He was the one who paid for the hippo head. Said he'd be back for it. He said, in fact, that he'd send a man around. Those were his very words."

"How long ago was this?" the Professor asked.

"About a week. No, less than that. Four days ago, in the evening."

"Was he alone?"

"No. No, he wasn't. Look, is this fellow a friend of yours? Is he wanted for some crime?"

"Not at all," the Professor said. Then, after a moment of hesitation he added: "He's off on a walking tour and something's come up at home. We came along to Landsend to find him."

Dr. Chan gave them a look that seemed to question the likelihood of the Squire's being out on a walking tour—as if the Squire wasn't the walking-tour type. "Since you ask, then, he was accompanied by a customer of mine. Another man I do business with. Deals in human bones, actually, and in certain potions and conjurations. Arcana, mostly, that I know nothing about. There's some demand for it though. His name is Sikorsky." And Dr. Chan seemed to give them a careful appraisal right then, as if to see how they'd be affected by the revelation.

"Sikorsky!" Gump shouted.

"Out of the frying pan, into the fire," the Professor said.

It made Jonathan mad to think that this Sikorsky seemed intent on pushing in everywhere. There was simply no denying him: he tormented innkeepers and madmen, extorted magical coffee, blew up riverboats, sold human bones and magical potions, and somehow, for some astonishingly mysterious purpose, befriended poor, homeless Squire Myrkle. There seemed to be no sense to any of it.

Dr. Chan didn't appear to be much in the mood for talk after that, so the four of them followed Ahab into the dusky street and set off for the inn where Miles waited.

Gump shoved his hands into his pockets and looked depressed. "I knew we hadn't seen the last of Sikorsky."

"We actually haven't seen him at all yet," Bufo said.

"I know. But he keeps popping up anyhow. And now he's got the poor Squire. What does he want with the Squire?"

But no one offered an answer to Gump's question. None of it made much sense.

"Professor," Jonathan said, changing the subject, "I don't mean to seem mercenary at a time like this, but what happened to the map when the steamship blew up?"

"It was in the cabin. And if I understand your concern, I'll ease your mind by saying that it's now at the inn, safe as an oyster. And if you ask me, we'd better be after the treasure tomorrow. Things seem to be hotting up."

"That's certainly so," Jonathan agreed. "If someone answers the ad, we'll have to be ready to go."

"Let's get an early start on it," Gump said.

"Sunrise," Bufo suggested.

"Fancy a treasure hunt." Gump sounded eager. "What sort of stuff do we expect to find?"

"Pirate treasure, mostly," the Professor explained. "It's almost certainly a pirate map. Maybe elf pirates, but I can't say for sure. There were elf runes on the map, but that doesn't mean much. Pirates love to dabble in mysteries—all that skull and crossbones and black spot stuff. We'll know tomorrow, one way or another. There's our inn on the corner." The Professor pointed toward a cheerful-looking, half-timbered building of whitewashed stucco and old black wood. Trellises of blooming bougainvillaea covered most of the walls on the lower half. On the second floor, sets of french doors looked out over the street. One pair was pushed open, and in the doorway, sitting in a rattan chair and smoking a long pipe, was Miles the Magician.

Chapter 16

The Treasure Map

❧

THAT evening, there were any number of stories to tell. Jonathan had heard Bufo and Gump's, and they, of course, had heard his, but all of them had to work through it again for the benefit of Miles and the Professor. Jonathan was anxious to hear how the treasure map had come to be saved and how the magician had cast floating spells while standing on the wall of the galley in the upturned *Jamoca Queen*. Either the spells worked or the ship simply didn't feel like sinking, it was impossible to know for sure, but she'd been swept along down river into the night, adrift in the channel. At a point somewhere beyond the Strawberry Baron's lands, the fog had lifted and they'd signaled a salmon fisherman bound for Landsend. The hulk followed them down and finally ran aground on the delta where it would stay until winter storms broke it up and swept it out to sea. The Professor said that by the time Cap'n Binky arrived it would be picked clean by scavengers. But Jonathan pointed out that Cap'n Binky had saved his coffee and manuscript and anyway had probably resigned himself to the loss of the boat, having assumed that it went down in midriver.

The Professor told Miles of their meeting with Dr. Chan and about the Squire having been seen around town with Sikorsky. Miles didn't appear to be half as surprised as the rest of them had been, although it was clear he didn't like the news a bit. When they all wandered off to bed that night, they left Miles alone, smoking his pipe and squinting shrewdly off into space, deep in thought.

In the morning, Jonathan found a note nailed to the

door of his room. Miles, having little interest in treasures, had gone off for the day to do a bit of detective work of his own and to visit the post office to see whether anyone had answered the ads. "Don't wait up for me," the note concluded. So it was quite likely Miles was onto something —something that had been suggested by the Dr. Chan episode.

Jonathan had hoped that Miles would go along with them on the treasure hunt. Wizards, it seemed to him, must have some sort of affinity to treasures and to wonderful things in general. Surely Miles had no end of door-opening spells and such which could quite possibly come in handy. But at six-thirty they left the inn without either Miles or breakfast. They were back at eight.

"Who would draw up a treasure map and leave out half the details?" Jonathan asked, poking morosely with a spoon at a sad bowl of gooey oatmeal. "That makes no sense at all to me."

"Maybe they wanted to throw someone off the scent. Confuse him," Bufo said. "Maybe it was a joke map."

The Professor shook his head. "Then why draw a map at all? If there hadn't been any map, we'd never have come looking for treasure. Spurious maps don't make sense, not in this case. I'm convinced there's a treasure out there anyway, hidden away down one of the streets that doesn't appear on our map. In one of those old deserted canneries, perhaps, near the wharves, or in the cellar of one of the houses in the alleys behind Royal Street. Some of those slate-roofed, turreted mansions have to be two or three hundred years old. Anything at all might be hidden there."

"If we had six months we could dig through them one by one." Bufo slumped in his chair with his chin in his hands. "If there are three north-south streets between Royal and Oak that aren't on the map, and six east-west cross streets . . ."

"And no end of alleys," Gump interrupted.

"And, as you say, no end of alleys, then how many blocks do we have to explore in that one section?"

The Professor ticked off streets on his fingers. "Let's see, that's . . . eighteen square blocks altogether."

"Multiplied by no end of alleys," Jonathan said.

"How do you multiply something by no end?" Gump asked.

Jonathan shrugged. "You'd have to have a lot of zeros."

"More than we have time for," the Professor put in. "It all has to do with the study of infinitudes. Very complex affair."

"We studied those in school," Gump said. "It was fascinating. You take a line and divide it in half. Then you cut it in half again . . ."

"What do you cut in half?" asked Bufo. "Both halves, or just one? Seems pretty sloppy just to cut one half in half and leave the other one half alone. What does it do with itself?"

Gump looked exasperated. "You only need halves of halves for this experiment. So don't interrupt. Then you cut the line in half again, and again and again. Very fascinating study. Fascinating."

Bufo wasn't impressed. "That's all? Sounds like mumbletypeg to me. I knew all about that by the time I was four. The same thing happens when a pie is being sliced up and you don't want to take the last piece. You just keep sawing off little threads of pie until there's only enough left to feed a bird. And by that time the pie is so stale you might as well pitch it out anyway. I know all about that. You say you had to learn that stuff in school?"

"What Gump was referring to," the Professor said helpfully, "was the theory that there would never be an end to the number of times the line could be cut in half. It would become smaller and smaller and smaller, but there would always be half a line left to cut. The mathematicians tell us, of course, that there's precious little difference between half a line and a whole line. A line is a line, in other words."

"And a pie is a pie, I suppose," Bufo said. "There's something tolerably wrong with the whole idea if you ask me. Pretty soon you get down to a piece that isn't worth having."

"It's entirely theoretical," the Professor explained. "All anybody does is talk about it."

Now it was Bufo's turn to look exasperated. "Talk about it! What on earth for? That means, I guess, that this theory won't help us find the treasure. Is that, or is that not, the case?"

The Professor grinned. "Absolutely. It's of no value to us here."

"I knew it," Bufo said. "Leave it to Gump to bring up worthless theories."

Jonathan suspected that Bufo was in a bad mood because the treasure map hadn't panned out. Sitting around over tired oatmeal wasn't helping to lighten things up. "Am I wrong, or does this oatmeal taste like library paste?"

The consensus was that it did.

"Let's go downtown then and look around for a good café. Something on the water where we can watch the boats go by. Maybe we'll run into Miles."

"Maybe we'll find another curiosity shop," Gump said enthusiastically, "and I can find another hippo head."

Jonathan tried to sound excited about the idea. "That could be. Certainly Dr. Chan doesn't have the only such head in town."

"That would be unlikely," the Professor agreed in an attempt to cheer Gump up a bit. "Let's go."

So off they went, the Professor hauling the treasure map along in order to study it out over lunch. As it happened, there was no evidence of further hippo heads in town. They found any number of interesting shops, but the only heads for sale had to do with moose and deer and, in one shop, with an enormous fish. None of these was far enough out of the ordinary to suit Gump. They did, however, find a nice café with a wide awning, which covered a balcony stretching out over the water. They settled into a corner table, prepared to spend the afternoon there.

It had been hot on the street, but in the shade above the water with an ocean breeze drifting across the delta toward them, it was nicely cool. Boats sailed past below, hung with nets and traps. There was just enough wind to push them along and to kick up the surface of the water in little sparkling wavelets. Jonathan felt as if he could sit and stare out over the water forever. It seemed impossible that the broad and placid river that met the sea was the same dark river that had spawned the weed thing that had attacked him on the deck of the steamship.

He watched a particularly large fishing smack, a wonder of strung nets and winches, make its way out toward the ocean. The several fishermen on board were lined up along the starboard bulwark, pointing and gesturing at something off in the water. At first Jonathan couldn't see what it was; the water appeared to be unbroken. But then a glint of sunlight shot off the silver surface of some sort of tube that was cutting along upright through the water toward the docks. He called everyone's attention to the mysterious thing, and the Professor put on his glasses in order to have a better look at it.

"Why, I'm an oyster," he said under his breath, taking his pipe out of his mouth. "A periscope."

"A what?" asked Bufo, who, apparently, hadn't seen anything at all yet. "Is it some sort of shellfish? Like a periwinkle?"

But no one answered his question. Jonathan was on his feet too, understanding why the Professor had reacted so. For coming toward them, a darkening shadow beneath the green waters of the river mouth, was a ship—an undersea device, a submarine—intent, it seemed, upon docking at one of the wharves below the café.

Jonathan knew the possibility existed that there were any number of submarines in the world. Then again, who could say? Maybe submarines were like the other elfin marvels—the Lumbog globe or Escargot's invisible cloak, or a bottomless bag of marbles owned by Squire Myrkle —maybe there was only one. Six months back, the Professor had said that if Escargot's submarine wasn't elfin, then it had been made by the marvel men in the Wonderful Isles. But as far as Jonathan knew, there were no Wonderful Isles in Balumnia. So he had every reason to hope, contrary to the Professor's philosophy of wishing for the worst, that the ship nosing up out of the depths of the Tweet was piloted by none other than Theophile Escargot, noted thief and adventurer. And it certainly was beginning to *look* as if it was his craft.

The tips of a line of what appeared to be arced shark fins sliced up out of the water as if what was surfacing were some sort of finny deep-sea monster. A row of port-hole windows, lit from within and shining like eyes, glowed beneath. Behind them, protruding from the sides of the craft, two great splayed fins made the whole thing look like some close cousin to a frogfish or tidepool sculpin.

Long strands of kelp and weed clung to the pointed nose and fins of the strange ship, and as it humped up out of the depths and settled on the surface, streams of water shot out of ports along the stern, and the lights within the nose of the ship blinked out.

The craft seemed to be made almost entirely out of copper and brass that had become encrusted over the course of time with verdigris. Here and there patches of clean metal glowed in the sunshine. Around the ports and edging the fins atop and along the sides was bright silver, not in the least dulled or tarnished from voyages in the sea. Jonathan suspected that it was probably elf silver or something very much like it.

Almost everyone in the café was standing along the edge of the balcony watching the approach of this wonderful ship. On the docks below, people had given up work and were gawking away, pointing and shouting and speculating.

"It looks as if Dr. Chan is about to renew his supply of squid clocks," the Professor remarked to Jonathan.

Just then one of the shark fins began to turn as if it were being unscrewed from inside. It twisted and twisted then suddenly popped free, falling back on a hinge to reveal an aperture in the ship. A head shoved out and looked around. It belonged to Dooly, grandson of Theophile Escargot. Half of the rest of Dooly followed; he was dressed in, of all things, Jonathan's man-of-leisure suit. He waved at everyone on the dock. Then he waved at everyone on the balcony at the café. Then he shouted a greeting at a man in a dory who pulled past some twenty or thirty feet to starboard. Then, jerking back around as if he'd been poked in the shoulder with a stick, he squinted up again toward the café. He shaded his eyes with his palm, hunched forward, and shouted, "Mr. Bing Cheese!" He waved both hands in the air, jigging about so enthusiastically that he nearly tumbled out of the shark fin hatch and into the water. Ahab, his head shoved through the slats in the little picket fence that ran around the veranda, seemed to recognize Dooly at about the same time, for *he* began to bark and dance and jig around, and came tolerably close to upsetting a table full of coffee cups.

Dooly sank back into the ship. A moment passed and then another head appeared—the grizzled piratical head of Theophile Escargot. His hair and beard hadn't been cut since last winter; that much was certain. His eyes, peering out of an almost hidden face, seemed very fierce indeed. Jonathan had long ago observed that Escargot had the uncanny ability to change the appearance of his eyes. In his current incarnation as a pirate, they seemed to almost burn, giving him the look of a man who should not be trifled with. Years before, when he'd come through Twombly Town selling cookbooks door to door, just the opposite was the case. He had had a sort of obsequious look about him, a humble look, the look of a man who believed above anything else in his cookbooks. Now he looked as if he *ate* cookbooks—all of which probably explained why he was such a success; he was inscrutable.

Escargot pulled off his cocked hat, scratched his curly black hair, and waved up at the lot of them on the balcony. It looked like a tired wave to Jonathan, the wave of a man who'd come into town looking for a spot of fun only to discover unforeseen trouble. If the hatch had slammed shut and the submarine had turned about and sailed back out of the harbor, it wouldn't have surprised Jonathan much— and it would have surprised the Professor even less.

But no such thing happened. Escargot disappeared below, and the submarine idled up to the dock. The *splooshing* of water in the rear ports fell off, and the ship seemed to shudder just a bit as if it had gotten a chill. Both Dooly and Escargot climbed out and tied the ship to the dock with a heavy line. Then they clumped along up toward the café, leaving a little knot of people behind them chattering over the ship.

"Mr. Bing Cheese!" Dooly shouted again as he and Escargot pushed out through the swinging doors onto the veranda. A great deal of helloing and handshaking and chair-scraping followed. It was like old home week.

"You lads ain't here on holiday, I suppose," Escargot remarked, who, of course, was well aware that it was only with the help of the elves that Jonathan and his company were in Balumnia at all.

"You've got it right," Jonathan said. "We were off on holiday originally, but it got cut short. Foul play popped up."

"Oh?" Escargot motioned at a waiter who scuttled past with a tray of plates. "You lads sure have a nose for it. Now me, I try to avoid it. When I pass it on the road, I pretend to be a blind man, and I tap right along past. You boys stop to talk, and that's a bad idea. Very bad."

Professor Wurzle laughed a bit. "Then later on you run into us, and you have a chat. And first thing you know, we're all in the soup together."

"Ye-es," Escargot drew the word out as if admitting to something he'd rather not admit to. "But the lad and I are here on business. I do a bit of trade with some of the local merchants. Squid clocks and whale-eye charms and the like. There's a big market for dried dialulas and sea lemons here. They wear them as ornaments—broaches and such. It's all the rage. I know where there's heaps of them. Two more runs out through the gate and I'm set for a year. Lately there's been some call for singing nautili too, ever since I brought one up about a year ago. But they're rare as anything, and quick too.

"That's the ticket!" Escargot said when the waiter showed up once again with a steak and fries on a plate. The steak was as broad as a hat brim and looked as if it had been cooked for thirty or forty seconds over a lit match. "A man gets sick of fish," Escargot said, carving out a big forkful of the steak and shoving it past his beard and into his mouth. Dooly had ordered half an apple pie.

The Professor tossed one of the Squire advertisements onto the table in front of Escargot, who paused in his chewing and pointed at the drawing with his fork. "Miles du Bois drew that. I can tell by the little dots in the shaded areas and by the look on the Squire's face. Miles always puts that same half smirk on his subjects' faces. Like they were in on some kind of joke. What're you lads doing hanging around with the magician? You're probably in more trouble than you think." He shoved another bite of steak into his mouth and smacked away at it in a self-satisfied way, like a man who was tolerably sure that *he* wasn't in any such trouble. "What's become of the Squire?"

"Selznak is after him," Jonathan said.

"Here?" Escargot asked. "What in the devil is the Squire doing here? Did he come with you?"

"No," the Professor said. "We came after him. He's here because of the blasted Lumbog globe. Why you ever saw fit to give such a thing away to Squire Myrkle, I don't know."

"He found it first." Escargot shrugged. "If it had been me who found it, it would have been another story. But none of that makes a lick of sense anyway."

"Doesn't it?" the Professor asked, squinting at him.

"Not that I can see. How did the Squire get to Balumnia if he didn't come with you?"

"Like the Professor said," Gump put in, "he had the Lumbog globe, the one he found when we were up rescuing you at the tower last winter."

Escargot gave Gump a pained look. "I know which bloody globe. There ain't but one. I'm the one that let him have it, aren't I? Like the Professor said."

"*Let* him have it?" Bufo said. "He just shoved it in his pocket and took off with it as far as I could see. There wasn't anybody going to take it from him. Not from the Squire there wasn't."

Escargot, of course, purpled at the thought of his not being able to steal a glass ball from someone, especially from the Squire. Jonathan could see that. He suspected that, contrary to the Professor's supposition, Escargot actually hadn't any idea about the true nature of the globe. He decided that it was time to cut through all the sideline talk. "Did you know when you gave it to him that it was a Balumnian door?"

Escargot, flying in the face of manners, plucked a chunk of steak out of his mouth that he'd just that moment shoved in. "It was a what?"

"A Balumnian door."

Escargot sat for a moment thinking about it. "No," he said finally, "but that makes some sense now that you mention it. It explains why that filthy Selznak stole it from me fifteen years ago after I got it in trade from a bunjo man.

A Balumnian door," he said, shaking his head. "Damn!" He threw his fork down onto his plate in such a way that Jonathan was fairly sure he was telling the truth. "Where did you say the globe is now?"

Jonathan told him about the Squire's disappearance and of the doings of Selznak the Dwarf and of some of their adventures since arriving in Balumnia.

Escargot seemed awfully interested in the whole affair. His attitude had changed to that of a man who was sympathetic—a man, perhaps, who was willing to make their troubles his own. "And you're bound to find him, then?"

"That's right." Bufo had a look of determination on his face. "We're going to find the Squire and then make Selznak a sorry case, that's what."

"We'll take him down a peg," Gump said.

Escargot shook his head. "Don't be too impatient. There's them that tried to take him somewhere before, and it landed them in a nation of trouble. Where do you figure the Squire is now? You say you got a lead on him here at Landsend?"

"That's right," Jonathan said. "He was seen four days ago in the company of a man named Sikorsky. Have you heard of him?"

"Heard of him!" Escargot cried, looking at Jonathan in surprise. "Of course I've heard of him. Everyone in the café knows who he is. Everyone except you lads."

"And one of these years we'll find out," the Professor said. "Then we'll know too."

"I'll give you some clues," Escargot began. "He's short. Tolerably short. About Gump's size here. He wears a smash hat with a broad brim and carries a stick and has a patch over one eye. And he smokes a pipe that ain't like these pipes you're puffing on here. Not by a sight. Fifteen years ago he stole that filthy globe from me after I stole it from the bunjo man, and *he* stole it anyway from the Light Elves and didn't know what it was. I thought I did. Fancy that. All these years the joke was on me."

"Selznak!" Jonathan shouted, the truth flooding in upon him. "Sikorsky and Selznak are the same person!"

"That's a fact," Escargot said. "If a man lives in two worlds he can have two names. I've used more than one myself. Sometimes it's necessary. Throws the hounds off the scent. Was it Sikorsky who blew up your ship?"

"So we think," Jonathan said. "He was after Cap'n Binky's coffee."

"If he wanted Cap'n Pinky's coffee he'd take it."

"Binky," Gump corrected.

"Excuse me?"

"Binky, it is, not Pinky. Cap'n Binky."

"Oh, yes," Escargot said. "So you figure he wanted that coffee so bad he tried to blow it to bits? That's something. What I think is that he's leading you lads by the nose."

Chapter 17

Piedmont and Pinkum

❈

WE'VE got to tell Miles about this," Bufo said. "We've got to be on our way now that we know what's going on."

"Where to?" the Professor asked. "It doesn't make much difference as far as I can see. We should have figured that all out days ago—the Dwarf in the fog up at Tweet Village, the old woman showing up on the riverboat that night. It was plain as day and none of us saw it. Not even Miles."

"She's here too?" Escargot apparently knew what old woman was being referred to.

"Yes," Jonathan said. "She keeps popping up. But I'm not sure Miles hasn't suspected. He's onto something, that's for sure. He's known more than he's let on all along."

Escargot nodded. "You lads need a hand, Miles or no Miles. I've got a little business to attend to here in town, but it shouldn't take me long. If I could be of any service—"

"Don't go out of your way," the Professor put in, who, Jonathan knew, suspected Escargot's motives. Jonathan, however, was hoping that Escargot would do exactly that, whatever his motives. One Escargot, especially an Escargot with a submarine, seemed to him to be worth a half-dozen of almost anyone else.

"Dooly lad," Escargot said, "run down to the ship, if you will, and pull out those boxes of clocks and that tub of eyeballs. And bring the you-know-what."

Dooly began winking and nodding and carrying on as if he had a twitch in his eye. He made a circle out of the thumb and forefinger of his right hand and gave Escargot the high-sign, winking once again before dashing off.

"What in the world was that business?" Gump asked, puzzled over Dooly's histrionics. Jonathan wondered the same thing. Apparently Dooly was, in his way, being very secretive, and Jonathan knew it was bad form to press the issue.

"Lad must have the shakes," Escargot said in answer to Gump's question.

Most of the early afternoon was taken up going about town with Escargot, lugging his strange wares. They visited Dr. Chan again, this time to deliver a dozen of Escargot's unlikely but oddly accurate squid clocks and no end of floating octopi and eyeballs and ocean herbs and fish skeletons. To hurry matters along, Escargot had Gump and Bufo and Dooly dashing back to the ship for fresh supplies, then meeting up with him at some agreed-upon spot.

After the visit to Dr. Chan's, Jonathan and the Professor excused themselves and set out in search of Miles, who had, as Jonathan suspected, been into the curiosity shop that morning, seriously buying a quantity of potions, herbs, and dried bats, and quizzing the doctor about Sikorsky. The news rather took the hurry out of their finding Miles, since his conversation with Dr. Chan would certainly have alerted him to Sikorsky's identity. But Jonathan and the Professor were both stricken with a new sense of alarm, and since Miles was, in a way, their general, they were anxious for new orders. They both realized, though, as the Professor had first pointed out back at the café, that while a great deal had been revealed, they had little or no more direction as a result of it.

They couldn't find Miles. He'd been to the post office and, according to the clerk, had picked up a number of responses and then had left a note. "Am running errands," it said, "and may not return until tomorrow. Be patient. Squire seen day before yesterday. Be ready to travel tomorrow P.M."

The note satisfied the two of them only because it seemed to imply that Miles was finally making real progress. The news of the Squire having been seen was decidedly good. If he was in town four days ago, and then again two days ago, it was entirely possible, even likely, that he was *still* in town, maybe having a late lunch that very moment at a café on Stickley Street or in a tavern on High Street.

That possibility sent the two of them up and down streets and avenues for another three hours, poking into taverns, showing the handbill around, quizzing people. At about five o'clock they made one last stop at the post office and found nothing.

When they dragged themselves back to the inn a half hour later, Escargot was in high spirits. He'd had a successful day of it and had even managed to give Gump, Bufo, and Dooly a bit of money for their troubles. To celebrate, he bought Jonathan and the Professor a pint of ale. All of them sat down to dinner shortly thereafter, and for the space of ten minutes there was no conversation at all, only the clinking of silverware against plates and an occasional, "Pass the potatoes."

The Professor was the lightest eater of them all, being aware of his weight for health reasons. As soon as he finished, he once again drew out the worthless treasure map as if convinced that they had overlooked something in it, something that would make sense of the muddled and missing street names.

When he held up the map, Dooly choked on a bite of pudding, and Bufo had to whack him on the back a few times. "Is that a map, your honor?" Dooly was very respectful when he talked and had a fine imagination when it came to people's names.

"It pretends to be," the Professor said.

"It looks like one to me," said Dooly, craning over it to get a better look. "I've seen a few such maps, I have. Had it all explained to me. There's two kinds of maps, you see—if I might go into detail, sir—that a person might care to own. The one, you see, is for going about town if you don't know where you are. The other one is for finding treasures." Dooly waited politely for a response.

"That certainly seems accurate," the Professor said.

"This one here, if you'll pardon my carrying on, is a treasure map on account of the X right there." And Dooly pointed a finger at the uninformative X. It seemed as if Escargot had become aware of the conversation for the first time. As he forked up a mouthful of food, he took a look across the table to see what Dooly was chattering about, and in the process stabbed himself in the cheek, losing most of the food onto his shirt.

He looked from the map to Dooly, then from Dooly to the map and back again, scowling more fiercely with each turn of his head and idly smearing at the goop on the front of his shirt with a fork. "Maps is it?" he asked finally, more of Dooly than anyone else. "It's come to this, then?"

Dooly launched into a series of elaborate hand signals. He scratched his ear wildly, pointing over his shoulder toward the stairs with an extended thumb while raising and lowering his eyebrows. Then he winked hugely. Gump and Bufo, as a lark, set in immediately to follow Dooly's example. First Bufo began winking both eyes together, over and over. Then Gump thumbed his nose cheerfully back at Bufo and crossed his eyes. The Professor, looking up from his map in the middle of their histrionics, could make nothing of it at all. Jonathan shrugged at him and shook his head. Escargot, however, nodded suddenly at Dooly and peered across to have a closer look at the Professor's map.

Gump and Bufo continued making faces at each other, wiggling their ears, puffing out their cheeks and flapping their clasped hands around like bats. The innkeeper, coming in to clear away plates, caught Bufo in the act of shoving a finger into each ear, swelling his cheeks, clamping his eyes shut, and hissing through pursed lips as if he were acting the part of an exploding fizz bomb.

"Is your friend all right?" the innkeeper asked as he picked up Gump's plate and silverware.

"No," Gump said. "He's having a fit. The sea air has an effect on his brain pan."

Bufo opened his eyes at the sound of the innkeeper's voice and made a weak pretense at having been merely smoothing down his hair. "Good food, this," he said in a stalwart, knowing tone. "My compliments to the chef. Very superior."

"Thanks," the innkeeper said, giving him a look. "Are you feeling better?"

"Tiptop." Bufo took a deep breath or two and thumped

on his chest. "This fellow here, though, seems to have cast a dollop of gravy onto the front of his shirt." He pointed at Escargot, who by then had gotten round to dabbing at the stain with the corner of a cloth napkin.

"Would you like a bit of soap, sir?" the innkeeper asked.

Escargot stared hard at Bufo, who had begun to lecture Gump about facial muscles. "No," Escargot said slowly, "I'm saving this for lunch tomorrow."

Jonathan was afraid that Escargot wasn't in the mood for larks, and he decided that a quick change of subjects was necessary. It turned out otherwise, however, for Escargot promptly forgot both his shirt and Bufo and turned once again to the Professor. "Have you tried this map out yet?"

"Yes we have. It's worthless."

"There was no treasure?"

"There was no way to find the treasure," Jonathan put in. "The map is only half-complete. They might as well have written a note on a post card: 'Look for a treasure in Landsend.'"

"Is that so?" Escargot asked. "It's none of my business, of course, but just for the sake of curiosity, where did you lads find this map? It wasn't in Balumnia, I'll warrant."

"No," said the Professor, "it wasn't."

"And you've had it for about six months now, waiting for a chance to use it."

"Nope," Jonathan told him, "we haven't had it two weeks, but you're pretty much correct anyway, if I follow your drift. Two weeks ago the Professor and I went back to Hightower Ridge to have a look around. That was before we heard about the Squire. We found this in the cellar. When the Squire disappeared into Balumnia, we had the opportunity to try the map out. But as I said, nothing came of it."

Escargot sat for a moment thinking. "I'm not sure I like all this happenstance. I get suspicious when things fall out in patterns. But maybe I'm foolish. Maybe I'm looking a gift horse in the mouth here."

"A horse?" Dooly asked.

"That's just a saying, lad."

"Oh," Dooly said. "A saying. Of course."

Escargot excused himself and went off up the stairs. When he popped back down, *he* had a map—the seeming twin of the one in front of the Professor. When the maps were laid out side by side, however, they were clearly different. Although they concerned the same area, the configurations of streets weren't the same. Those streets which appeared on Escargot's map were absent on the other. And the alleys and cross streets that hadn't appeared on the map belonging to Jonathan and the Professor were plainly inked in on Escargot's map. It didn't take but a moment to figure it all out. The Professor laid one map atop the other, grasped them along either side, and held the superimposed maps in the air in front of a lamp.

"Partners again." Escargot smiled.

"I should say." The Professor seemed this time to be genuinely happy about tossing in with Escargot. Gump, Bufo, and Dooly began pointing at the map and debating what tools to bring along.

"We'll need shovels," Bufo said.

"And picks!" Gump cried.

"And wheelbarrows!" Dooly shouted. "About ten of 'em. That should do for starters."

Gump snatched a chunk of gristly meat from Jonathan's plate in order to feed it to Ahab before the innkeeper returned to finish clearing the table. He paused, however, and said to Dooly, "Ten of them?"

"Oh, yes," Dooly insisted. "They're in the book."

"But will ten be enough, is what I mean."

Dooly reconsidered. "No. We've got to have an abundance. Two at least just for diamonds. Let me calculate this." Dooly pulled at the fingers of his left hand. "Grandpa," he asked, "how many wheelbarrows of diamonds do you reckon we'll find?"

"Plan on six." Escargot was studying the two maps along with Jonathan and the Professor.

"Six, then. And three for pearls, three for rubies, five for em'ralds, two for jewelry and gold, and a dozen or so for stick candy. What is that, about thirty?"

Bufo nodded. "Pretty close. Stick candy, though. Is that standard?"

"In the book!" Dooly said.

Ahab poked Gump in the side about then and eye-balled the meat that was still dangling from his fingers. Gump dropped it into his open mouth. "What book is this, then?"

"One I found up at Arnold's. *Treasures East and West*, it's called."

"So how do we get all these wheelbarrows across town?" Gump asked.

Dooly thought for a moment. "We'll hire a man. We can do that now that we're rich."

Bufo nodded. "We could. Or we could work them like dog sleds. Advertise for local dogs. A nickel an hour and all the stick candy they can eat." Ahab looked mournfully at him, as if he wasn't keen on the idea, stick candy or otherwise.

"The Squire's got an emerald," Gump said abruptly. "It's big as a head."

Dooly's eyes widened. "What kind of head?"

"Oh," Gump said. "Just a standard head. It's a wonder, though—round like a ball. If you look at someone through it your face just spreads out all over."

Dooly nodded sagely, as if he'd seen a few major emeralds in his day, too. "We'll find some of those to-morrow. Them and rubies. Yes, sir. I seen some treasures myself, you know. Treasures you wouldn't hardly believe."

"I daresay," Gump said. "Have you seen the Squire's marble treasure?"

"No, how many marbles does he have?"

"About a zillion, maybe more. He's got most of them in big glass jars. And he's got a bottomless marble bag from Mr. Blump and the other elves. You saw that."

"You bet!" Dooly cried, no doubt remembering the river of marbles that had flowed endlessly out of the bag onto the lawn before the palace in Seaside. "They were good marbles, too. Not just cat's eyes and such."

"That's right," Gump said. "The Squire had holes dug in his cellars, and he just lets that bag leak marbles into them. If there were a zillion last week, there's two zillion this week. He spends hours down there shoveling them around with a rubber spade. He used to tie the bag off at night and untie it in the morning, but then he calculated how many marbles *weren't* coming out of the bag and he reconsidered. His cellar is just about full."

Dooly was wide-eyed by the end of Gump's story, and it took him some time to come up with something to say besides "Gee whiz," which he said three times. "Me and Grandpa saw some treasures coming through the gate, didn't we, Grandpa?"

"That's so," Escargot said, beginning to look a bit excited himself.

"Through the gate?" Bufo asked.

"Through the door, he means," Escargot explained. "Under the sea. The western door out by the Wonderful Isles. There's things out to sea there that would turn you inside out. A man can't stand too much of it. Drives him wild."

"Yeah," Dooly said, "like those squid-o-pods in the sea shells."

"Nautili?" the Professor asked.

"That's it. Big around as breadbaskets, they are. There's crabs out there that use the empty shells for chests. It's true. We seen them going through sunken ships and the like. They bring back all sorts of gold and jewels, like crows do, and put the stuff in the squid-o-pod shells— the empty ones, of course. There's a place, fathoms and fathoms down, where there's a whole city sunk under the ocean in among sea weeds the size of a forest. And there's sea shell treasures just laying all over with these crabs just coming and going like ants and nothing but dead men to spend it. I couldn't believe my eyebones. Pearls the size of billiard balls just tumbling out. And diamonds! They liked to blind me there in the lights of the ship. All of this on the bottom of the sea—whales and sharks and schools of kelp bass swimmin' past. It was a wonder."

Jonathan realized that his mouth was agape at the end of Dooly's tale. He'd never heard anything like it. The Professor gave him a look that seemed to suggest that perhaps, given Dooly's propensity for telling stretchers, Jonathan's mouth shouldn't be open quite so wide. But Jonathan was quite willing—happy in fact—to believe in the sea shell treasures.

"Can't a person get at these treasures, then?" Jonathan asked.

"Nope," Escargot said. "Too deep. Smash a man to flinders. Pulpify him." Escargot looked over toward the Professor for support.

"That's correct," Professor Wurzle said. "It accounts for the strange shapes of deep-sea fish. Lord Piedmont attributes undersea pressures to the effects of the moon. Pinkum's theory has to do with the weight of the waters. I myself hold with Pinkum, although Lord Piedmont is more colorful."

"Well that settles it, then," Bufo said. "We won't go swimming for any squid-o-pod treasures, not with Pinkum and Lord Piedmont against us."

Conversation slackened about then, and Jonathan began to feel as if he'd walked up and down the road all day. It was nearly nine o'clock, early enough yet to catch eight good hours of sleep and still be up at dawn. The Professor and Escargot followed his example when he excused himself, and the three of them headed up to their rooms, leaving Gump, Bufo, Dooly, and Ahab making excited plans below.

Chapter 18

St. Elmo Square

❋

THE next morning found them once again on the street. Miles hadn't yet returned. Jonathan and the Professor made a pact to be back at the inn by noon and to drag Bufo and Gump along with them, even if it meant abandoning the treasure. Finding the Squire, after all, was their first concern.

But there didn't seem to be much to worry about. The map was nearly as accurate as a map could be, and it led them straightaway into old, narrow, cobbled streets and between ancient houses, all packed in side-by-side and tilting away overhead. They would have appeared to be ruins but for the flowering vines and dangling orchids that sprouted from chinks in the walls and from depressions in crumbling cornices and window ledges. The deterioration clearly wasn't the result of abandonment so much as of age, for most of the houses were occupied, and the streets were swept and clean.

They topped a small hill and cut down a long alley which led them finally to a dead-end bit of unpaved street. A faded sign hung from the plaster wall of a tumbled house directly opposite the mouth of the alley; ST. ELMO SQUARE it read.

In contrast to the streets they'd just come along, St. Elmo Square seemed thoroughly deserted. Windows were broken and gaping, and tattered lace curtains blew silently through them here and there, out into the morning breeze. Stoops had caved in and collapsed from age; slates from crumbling roofs lay broken in the street. A menacing silence hovered thick in the air, as if the square and the buildings that fronted it were not only abandoned, but had been for years and years so that the silence had had time to gather and thicken and deaden and turn to gloom.

Jonathan strained to hear something—anything that would convince him he hadn't gone deaf. It dawned on him with a grim suddenness that there weren't even any cats about, not one. Ahab seemed to sense the same thing, for instead of dashing out to have a look around, he sat still at Jonathan's feet and waited. Everything, in fact, seemed to be waiting.

Jonathan wished that Escargot would come up with some of his bluff talk, or else that Gump and Bufo would see something in the atmosphere to argue about. Instead, shattering the silence like a knock against a window in the night time, came the slamming of a door behind them. Everyone whirled at once. Twenty or thirty yards down the alley they saw the receding figure of a bent old woman, hobbling along on a stick and followed by a very black cat.

Escargot muttered something under his breath, but Jonathan didn't catch it. Reaching the far end of the alley, she turned and stared back at them, a small hunched figure standing with her head tilted slightly to one side, as if she were listening to the wind. Then she vanished. She just blinked away like one of Zippo's playing cards.

"What was the meaning of that?" the Professor asked. "Has she been following us?"

"I don't think so," Escargot answered, still squinting down the alley toward where the old woman had vanished. "I think she was waiting for us."

"Impossible. No one knew about the maps but us."

Escargot shook his head. "So we think. Just like we think we know why we're here."

"In this alley?" Bufo asked. "We're after treasure. And we better find it too, after all this."

"I didn't mean in the alley," Escargot muttered ominously, "but I'm with you about the treasure. We're doing too much standing around. Let's find what we came for and get out of here."

Everyone loosened up a bit at that and set in to examine the maps. The silence that hung so thickly broke apart and was replaced by the sounds of shuffling feet and rustling paper and voices. Gump and Bufo began to argue about how to hold the map—about which way was up. Dooly said that they couldn't go wrong as long as they remembered that north was always straight ahead. It didn't take long, however, to set things right. Little faded boxes on Escargot's map corresponded quite clearly to the houses on the square. An X scrawled through one of those boxes hinted that the treasure, whatever it might be, lay in a half-ruined house not fifty steps distant.

There had once been a front porch on it supported by cut stones. The whole thing had slumped at one end so disastrously, however, that the pillars at either side had canted over until they had fallen into a heap, carrying a little gabled porch roof with them. Old weather-decrepit remnants still hung by twisted nails, but it looked as if one good storm would pull them loose and scatter them among the ruins that lay in the weeds and dirt.

After picking their way across the debris, getting into the house was a snap. There wasn't any door, just one crusty green strap hinge, bent and dangling from the jamb. Rats scurried away out of sight as the group clomped in onto the floorboards. Everything was still and silent, the only movement being a line of floating dust motes that hovered still and lonely in a single ray of sunshine slanting in down the stairwell through a gaping hole in the roof.

"What do you expect?" Escargot asked suddenly, his voice echoing through the still air. "Ghosts?"

The noise made everyone jump, and Escargot laughed his slow, "Har, har, har," piratical laugh, as if wandering into ruined houses under mysterious circumstances were meat and drink to him. He pointed across toward a shut closet door. "Look into that closet there, Dooly lad. I'll have a go at the kitchen. We didn't sail out here from the Isles to stand around and gawk at a bunch of busted-up furniture." With that he kicked the remains of an overturned wooden chair out of his way and strode off. Dooly didn't move. He just stood and looked at the closet as if it were a goblin nest.

Professor Wurzle stepped across, grasped the door handle, and yanked it open with a no-nonsense tug. With a quick creak of squeaking hinge, the door swung to, and a skeleton, yellow and decaying and dressed in tatters, pitched out onto the floor. The Professor leaped back out of the way, surprised to find that he was holding the loose doorknob in his hand. He stared down at the fallen thing for a moment, a look of amazement on his face, then threw the doorknob into its ribcage; brittle bones crackled and spun away. Dooly began to laugh wildly, whooshing and shouting. Bufo kicked the skeleton's skull loose, knocking off a toothy jawbone. The rest of the skull rolled toward the stairs, hung for a moment on the edge, then bounced down into the darkness of the basement.

"Look here!" Gump cried, bending over and pointing. On the floor were a half-dozen scattered glass marbles.

Escargot raced in, supposing, perhaps, that Gump was exclaiming over a discovered bit of treasure. He stopped and looked down at the marbles. "I hope that ain't all of it."

Gump shook his head. "They were in the skeleton's mouth. When Bufo kicked the jawbone loose, they spilled out. I saw them."

"In his mouth!" Professor Wurzle was astonished. "Jonathan, you're the one among us who reads pirate books. Is there any precedent for this?"

Jonathan thought for a moment. "Not that I remember. I seem to recall having read about a pirate captain named Beetle-brow who did some astonishing things with bugs, but nothing about marbles. Unless . . ." Jonathan began.

"Unless what?" the Professor asked.

"Nothing," Jonathan said. "Nothing at all."

Bufo stared at him wide-eyed. "Unless these are the Squire's marbles, you meant to say. He'd have had some with him."

Gump, anticipating him, cried, "But whose mouth were they in?" He looked down at the skeleton in disbelief. "You kicked his head down the stairs!"

Escargot yanked the skeleton up by its shoulder blades and dangled it in front of Gump. The thing was half again Gump's size. "It's not the Squire," Escargot said, casting the skeleton back into the closet. "The Dwarf wouldn't waste the Squire on a prank like this."

The Professor cleared his throat meaningfully.

"Look here." Escargot pulled an old rusty cutlass out of the closet. "This is pirates we're dealing with all right. If they want to put marbles in dead men's mouths, that don't matter to us. Things don't have to work the same way in Balumnia." Escargot tossed the cutlass back into the closet along with its owner. "Dooly," he said, "come along with me. We're going downstairs."

Bufo peered down into the darkness where the skeleton head had disappeared. "Why downstairs and not upstairs?"

But the answer to that was clear enough. The flight of stairs leading to the second floor was about half-gone. Broken treads dangled in the air below the stairway, and right up near the top landing, for the space of six feet, there were no stairs at all. The stairs leading down, on the other hand, were cut from stone, and although heaved up at one point as if from an earthquake, the stones appeared to be solid. So with candles lit, they descended, Escargot first with Dooly clinging to his coat.

The yellow glow of the candlelight played off the walls and over a few pieces of broken furniture, gray with years of dust. Two rats leaped from the back of an old stuffed chair and ran across a wide and tattered rug. Like the several other pieces of furniture, the chair was in a state of advanced ruin: torn, soiled, and broken and with great tufts of yellowy stuffing thrusting through rents. Escargot pushed on the seat, perhaps suspecting that it was stuffed with treasure as well as cotton wool, but nothing resulted from the experiment other than the issuance of a cloud of ancient, tired dust. There were no closets of any sort that might hide gold and jewels. It began to look as if they'd all been played for fools, either that or the treasure was above them some place, in an attic perhaps. But that was highly unlikely, since, as the Professor had pointed out back at Hightower, treasure was almost always buried, not hauled up flights of stairs.

Jonathan bent over and scratched at the packed earth floor. It was hard as rock and would have been almost impossible to pick through. Then suddenly he had an idea and he tugged at a long trestle table with a cobweb-strung candelabra on it, dragging it free of the rug. Escargot and the Professor, both understanding what he was up to, yanked the rug back into a wrinkled heap. Beneath it a trap door was set into a woden frame in the pounded earth.

Handholds had been cut through the wood of the door at each corner, and it was no great thing for the lot of them to tug it out of its depression and drag it aside. Beneath it was a very dark hole.

The Professor filled the webby candelabra with candles and thrust it down into the darkness. Most of the light seemed to flee back out toward them as if it didn't want anything to do with what lay below. Dimly, some six or eight feet beneath them, they could just make out the last couple of rungs of a fallen ladder.

The hole in the ground and the flickering candlelight all reminded Jonathan overmuch of another hole that he had recently been talked into investigating. He had little desire simply to pop down into it and run into some blue, eyeless squid again. But it was getting on to nine o'clock, and they were bound to be back at the inn by noon. And this particular hole hadn't quite the depth and mystery about it that the deep caverns beneath Hightower Castle had. So he said to his friends, "Be ready to pull me out," as he grabbed the lip of wood that the trap door had rested on and swung himself into the hole.

Almost as soon as he began to drop into the darkness, he heard the tearing of rotten wood. The chunk he held onto ripped loose and came away in his hands, falling with him the few feet to the floor below. It seemed to him an awfully long way down.

His right foot cracked through some brittle business when he landed. Whatever it was bit at his leg and stuck to him like a spring-trap. The Professor shoved the candles into the hole again, and Jonathan found that he had a ribcage on his foot like some kind of impossible shoe. Pieces of the rest of the skeleton were tumbled about, and once again a cutlass lay near one of the thing's hands. Nearby was a cocked hat and a torn and mouldering heap of dark cloth that had once been a cuffed jacket. The dim glow of the dozen candles cast a pink and yellow circle up the side of a hill of gleaming rosy coins—heaps and heaps and heaps of them like dunes of sand in a desert.

Jonathan whistled in amazement and took a wide and cumbersome step toward the coins. Then he remembered the skeleton and kicked his right foot in the air to dislodge the ribcage. Behind on the floor lay the rough wooden ladder. He yanked on the end of the thing and tilted it up to where the others waited, then he pulled on the rungs to see if they were stout enough to hold everyone's weight. The condition of the ladder didn't seem to matter much to his companions, for as soon as it touched the edge of the hole, Bufo began to clamber down, and Gump hollered at him for being too slow. Everyone, Ahab included, crowded into the cellar a moment later, gawking at the gold coins and at the heaped treasures that lay beyond. It seemed to Jonathan as if the vault was as large as the room above, and the whole thing was one tumultuous chest of treasure.

Gump and Bufo were immediately knee-deep in coin; odd eight-sided coins, and round gold plate as big as a man's hand. Jonathan could see gold balls with weird elf runes carved into them, and oblong coins with holes in their centers. There were square coins and round coins and coins strung on golden chains, all plundered from distant lands, no doubt, by the pirates of the Flappage Islands.

On beyond the heaps of coins lay oaken chests, some closed, many thrown open to reveal diamonds and emeralds and rubies and huge pearls with rainbow colors aswirl in the candlelight. There were oceans of jewels, of golden rings set with precious stones and necklaces so heavy with gems that no one could possibly have worn them. There were swords with hilts encrusted with sapphires and moonstones and amethysts.

Other trunks overflowed with damasks and silks brocaded with diamonds and emeralds, and laces embroidered with spun gold and beaded with rubies—the riches of a thousand kings and palaces. Dooly wasted no time before climbing into a huge velvet robe and a pair of monstrous boots. Then he found a golden crown which he settled onto his ears before thrusting at imaginary foes about him with a peculiar, wavy scimitar almost as long as himself.

"Avaunt! Avaunt!" he shouted, menacing the heaps of coin.

Everyone cheered to see him in such a wild display. In the space of a few moments, Bufo and Gump were dressed to match in the most outlandish sorts of finery and were *oohing* and *ahing* and clambering about in the treasure. Jonathan plucked up handfuls of precious stones, letting them run through his fingers like liquid fire. He filled his pockets with coins, then emptied them out, filling them again with diamonds. Then he dumped out the diamonds in favor of emeralds, which had always appealed to him more than diamonds anyway. Then, getting into the spirit of the thing, he found a hat, filled it with gems, and up-ended it onto his head, the flashing jewels spilling out over his ears and into his shirt collar.

Escargot approached the whole affair more seriously, methodically filling small chests with jewels. He paid no attention at all to the gold, which, comparatively, was small beer anyway. The Professor was the only one among them who seemed entirely indifferent either to the wild value of the treasure or to the idea of finding it there, heaped up so and in such splendid abundance. Once he'd gotten a glimpse of the round rune coins he had eyes for nothing else. He pointed out to Jonathan that each coin was different from its fellows, and that each was carved with runes very much like those used by the Light Elves in the White Mountains. Jonathan didn't much care where the coins had come from, although he admitted that it was strange to see coins from the White Mountains in the cellar of an ancient house in Balumnia. But that was the sort of thing that fell into Professor Wurzle's line, and Jonathan was content to let him puzzle over it. The Professor went about digging out the heavy little gold balls, squinting at each in turn before putting it into his pocket. Soon his trousers bulged with the things and sagged desperately.

Just about then Ahab, wearing a crown that Dooly had found for him, came sliding past in a rush of coin, dragging half of a jewel-bedecked skeleton by a boney hand. Still prancing with his sword, Dooly spied the grinning skull and the ivory curve of the thing's ribcage, and he gasped and shouted, pulling his velvet robe up over his head after casting his sword onto the pile of coin. At the sound of Dooly's cry, Bufo and Gump gave off their shouting and dancing. The skeleton rattled on the coins. Ahab dropped it and sniffed at it. As he got a good look at the empty eye sockets and the long, gumless teeth, he stepped back a pace with a look of growing distaste. Finally he seemed to come to the conclusion that it wasn't a dog treasure at all, as one might easily have thought, but was something he didn't want any part of. So he left it grinning there with one yellow claw lying across Dooly's fallen sword.

Dooly peeked out through the folds of his cloak, feeling a bit braver. He avoided looking at the skeleton and grinned weakly at Escargot instead.

The Professor pointed out that their candles were burning down. Four of them were nothing but little heaps of soft wax, and several others were guttering and fizzling, threatening to sputter out. None were longer than an inch or so. The thought of being left in the skeleton-inhabited cellar in the darkness sobered everyone somewhat. So following Escargot's example, they heaped treasure into chests small enough to carry and stacked them near the ladder. Jonathan climbed out and helped lift the chests and Ahab to the floor above. Then, one by one, the rest of the company followed, shoving the trap door back into its place finally and yanking the rug back across it.

The Professor pulled out his pocketwatch and had a look at it. "Almost ten-thirty," he said. "We'd better get these chests back to the inn. Miles is due pretty soon."

Escargot was dumbfounded. "To the inn? Not a chance, mate. None of this is going to sit around in any inn. It's going aboard the submarine, and it's going there now. Miles can wait. There's been a change of plans here. If you lads feel inclined, go along without me. Dooly and I can take charge of this treasure. I aim to find a cart and horse and load it all out of here—every last nickel. I don't figure to be through for two days."

The Professor clearly did not like the tone of Escargot's speech. He had the look on his face of a man who'd been right all along. Jonathan didn't like it much either.

Not that he cared a great deal about abandoning the treasure—he could always take a pocket full of emeralds with him if he wished. And when it came down to it, he trusted Escargot not to make off with his share. But Jonathan had rather counted on Escargot's help in rescuing the Squire. He felt just then like a general who hears that his hoped-for reinforcements had quit the army to become farmers. Escargot, however, was adamant. He didn't stand around to argue his case, he just hefted the chest to his shoulder and climbed up the stairs toward daylight. There was nothing to be done but follow him.

"Well," the Professor said, putting his chest down in the room above, "this chest of gold balls is going along with me. It's far too important, historically speaking, to be given over to the first adventurer who wanders past in a submarine."

"I'll give you a receipt," Escargot said, heating up. "We can get it notarized."

Dooly, Gump, and Bufo laid their chests on the floor too, and Bufo, as an afterthought, ran back down the stairs to retrieve the skull that had sailed out of the closet. He puffed up with it a moment later and shoved it into his knapsack. "I thought I'd take this as a trophy," he said, "and put a candle on it when we get home." Gump looked a bit envious for a moment. Then he seemed to remember that he had all of a sudden become an astonishingly wealthy linkman—that he could buy any number of hippo heads which would make Bufo's skull-candle pale in comparison.

Jonathan thought about it all for a moment. Finally, although it bothered him to do it, he sided with Escargot, who most likely couldn't be budged on the issue. "Take my chest along then. We'll leave a message for you at the inn. Maybe you can come along after us."

"I'll be there . . ." began Escargot, but he was interrupted by the Professor, who made a sort of *whooshing* sound and looked put out.

Jonathan shrugged. "He's right. There's nothing else to do with the treasure. We can't possibly carry it about, and if we leave it at the inn it won't be there when we get back—*if* we get back."

After a moment the Professor nodded slowly. "Perhaps so," he said reluctantly. He patted his pockets, which still held a dozen or so gold balls.

On that note of agreement, they once again hefted their chests and followed Ahab out across the ruined front porch and into the street. Escargot talked over his shoulder as they moved off down the road. "If we can get these down the blasted alley to Royal Street, we can rent a horse cart. For that matter we can *buy* a horse cart. Two horse carts. Dooly can drive one and I'll drive the other. We can cover the treasure with that old rug and some of that furniture. Everyone will take us for junk men."

Right at the mouth of the alley, Gump stopped and lowered his chest. "This isn't mine," he said, fingering some tattered leather straps atop it. "This is yours, Bufo. You've got mine."

"I haven't either. I have my own. I put nothing but rings in it. About a million rings, and it's mine. It's for my collection."

"Collection!" Gump cried. "You've gone and swapped chests. You've got my jewels and you've given me your filthy stupid rings that aren't worth a thing. Who wants a million rings? A man hasn't got but two hands."

"He could wear them on his toes," Dooly offered helpfully.

Escargot had stopped ten steps down the alley and was watching the altercation angrily. "Open the bloody things up!" he said, shaking his head. "Not that it matters. They're all heading in the same direction anyway."

The Professor let another little *whoosh* of air out of his mouth as if he read more into Escargot's remark than was visible on the surface. Gump and Bufo were immediately happy, not so much because they could settle the question of what was in Bufo's chest, as because they could have another look at the wonderful treasure. Dooly dropped his chest and tore at the straps on it too—just to make sure.

One by one the lids on the three chests fell back, and as they did a very mysterious thing occurred. The diamonds and the emeralds inside, the rings, gems, and scattered gold coins, seemed to shimmer in the sunlight and ripple like a landscape seen through distant summer heat. Then, bit by bit, they collapsed inward onto themselves, metamorphosing into junk: twisted bits of wire and bent nails, shards of bottle glass, and the bleached skeletons of little peculiar fish. A dead beetle the size of a mouse lay among the scrap in Bufo's chest. The rusty carcass of an old pocketknife, its broken blade shoved into a cork, sat in Gump's. Dooly's chest, which a moment before was filled with rainbow gems, was a mess of iron filings, sand, and the beaten hub of an old buggy wheel twisted through with bent wire coat hangers.

Professor Wurzle reached into his pocket and pulled out two handfuls of gold balls. When he opened his hands in the sunlight, he held a little pile of bottlecaps with dirty cork washers in them. He threw the lot of it disgustedly to the pavement.

"Goblin gold," Escargot said, taking a wild kick at his chest. "Enchantment. Nothing but filthy, goblin-enchanted trash." He fetched the chest another whack, kicking the side in and cascading a fortune in jeweled necklaces and brooches out onto the cobbles—necklaces that shone for a second in the sunlight and then became fish carcasses and cuttlebones.

The Professor picked up a cuttlebone and scraped a white path across it with his thumbnail. "Squids," he said. "River squids. Miles was right. It was squid ink on the maps, not octopus ink."

"Of course it was." Escargot laughed out loud. "And it took us right in."

"I don't quite follow." Jonathan knew nothing more about squid and octopus ink than he had back at Myrkle Hall.

"Pirates would have used octopus ink," the Professor explained. "Goblins don't go out into the ocean. So they make their maps with the ink of river squids to fool people like you and me. It gives them a great deal of amusement, I don't doubt."

"Aye, and another too, whom I won't name," Escargot said, "but who was kind enough to let us onto these maps."

"Us?" the Professor said doubtfully.

"That's right. I found mine at Hightower Castle last

winter while you lads were entertaining Selznak. We've been set up, is what I think."

The Professor shook his head. "I don't believe it for a moment. Not for a moment. He's not that clever. It's altogether impossible."

Jonathan pulled the lid back from his chest, watching the gems within flutter into a heap of trash—dried fish eyes and shining scales that had once covered a great river perch. Scattered across the bottom were handfuls of watch parts: gears, lenses, little nuts and bolts and screws. Nestled in among all of it was a brass pocketwatch—a very familiar looking brass pocketwatch. Reaching in and pulling it out by the fob, Jonathan dangled it in the air. "Zippo was a better magician than we thought."

"Is that yours?" asked Bufo, who still had the little half-dollar watch that Jonathan had given him after the magic show at Tweet River Village.

"The very one." Jonathan was mystified. He wound it up and it began to tick away.

"I'd say this was a bit of good fortune," the Professor said, "but I don't believe it is. In fact, I'm all of a sudden inclined to agree that I've underestimated Selznak all along. All of us have. Even Miles. But then nothing he's done so far has been half as clever as this."

They left the open chests and set out. Clouds were blowing in over the mountains—a summer storm by the look of it—and before they had trudged the length of the alley, lightning zigged across the sky up the coast to the north. Scattered drops of rain began to fall, and Bufo, looking glum and disappointed, muttered something about the indignity of getting soaked after having discovered a joke treasure.

Jonathan didn't feel quite so bad about the whole affair. He assumed that the treasure that still lay in the vault beneath the cellar of the old house would go right on along being a treasure until someone hauled it out into the sunshine. That, of course, made up for a great deal. To top things off, he had gotten his watch back and Escargot, once again, was to be a party to the rescuing of the Squire—and, after all, that was what the whole crowd of them had come to Balumnia to achieve. He almost managed to convince himself that a half-hour of rain might be a pleasant change of pace.

When they stepped out onto Royal Street, Jonathan turned for one last look down the dark alley that stretched away toward St. Elmo Square. He stopped abruptly and clutched the Professor's arm. There amid the scattered and broken chests stood the old woman and her cat, watching them depart through the blur of rain. The black clouds overhead seemed to burst just then, sheets of rain pouring down and obscuring the distant square. Thunder cracked out, rolling and booming like a peal of deep, wild laughter. Then, just as suddenly as it had begun, the rain let off, and the lot of them stood dripping, peering down the long misty alley at nothing at all.

Chapter 19

The Deep Woods

MILES wasn't at the inn. The company sat about, packed and waiting, for two hours. Dooly and Gump and Bufo played cards with Escargot and lost voluminous quantities of jelly beans to him, first at Go Fish, then at Loony Eights, then at Chewn M'Gumm. Escargot kept loaning the jelly beans back out at interest just to keep the game alive, but by two-thirty in the afternoon there were few actual jelly beans left—only a handful of caramel beans that everyone agreed tasted like dirt. All the rest had been eaten, so the winnings were pretty much statistical.

The game was just petering out for lack of finances when the innkeeper came down the stairs rubbing his face and yawning. He had a bleary-eyed, afternoon-nap look about him. "Your wizard was in this morning," he said. "He was in a frightful hurry. Paid up and shoved off, he did."

"You must be mistaken," the Professor insisted. "Shoved off?"

"That's it. Took right off like a dirty shirt. He left a note for you." With that he hurried into his office, then hurried out again with a folded sheet of paper. On it was a brief and cryptic note from Miles: "Squire and Dwarf on coast road this morning. Time is precious. Follow me south. Gross evil afoot. Sikorsky and Selznak one and the same. Look to your wits. Beware Zippo."

"That last bit throws me," Escargot said, reading over the Professor's shoulder. "What is Zippo?"

"Who is Zippo, is the question," Jonathan explained.

"He's the parlor magician who stole my pocketwatch at Tweet River Village."

Escargot nodded. "Youngish sort of fellow, is he? Slimy looking in a way? Nervous? Uses a mechanical fish?"

"That's him," Jonathan said. "You've seen him then?" Escargot nodded again and Jonathan continued. "I suspect that he wasn't the incompetent that we had him pegged for."

"It sounds as if we'll find out." The Professor was hauling his knapsack onto his shoulder and squaring his glasses on his nose. "Let's buy some food and go. We're hours behind."

Escargot suggested that they strike the coast road at a place called the Thirteen Bridges, a mile or two below town. From there the road ran on for close to a hundred miles before it came to another sizeable village. They hadn't quite gotten to the door, however, when the innkeeper said suddenly, "I wouldn't go that way myself." Everyone stopped and looked at him. He shook his head darkly. "Nobody goes south on the coast. Leastways not on foot. Not anymore."

"Not anymore?" Jonathan asked.

"Not for a year or so. Not since that goblin business at the bridges and the horror at Boffin Beach."

They stood blinking at the man, waiting for more information. "Horror?" the Professor asked. "What horror was that?"

The innkeeper gave him a look that implied that the Professor wasn't quite as bright as he appeared to be. "Why *the* horror," he said. "There hasn't been but one. The bloody bones. The Waller party. Hacked to bits. Eaten. Where are you lads from, anyway? There wasn't nothing *but* the horror at Boffin Beach in any of the newspapers for weeks. No, sir. I wouldn't go south on no coast road. Not now, leastways."

Dooly's knapsack dropped out of his hand and clunked to the floor.

The Professor, however, was looking more determined than ever. "Then you'll be happy to hear that your services won't be required on the coast road. We're going down to Boffin Beach and have a bit of a look."

"Let 'em mess with us!" Bufo said stoutly.

"The wimps," Gump put in, clapping a hand onto Dooly's shoulder to pep him up a bit. "They'll sing a sorry tune."

On that note of encouragement, they filed out and down the road to the corner grocery before pursuing their way toward the Thirteen Bridges and the mysterious coast road. After about a quarter of a mile, though, Escargot pulled up short and scratched his head. "I've been thinking that we're going off half-cocked, mates," he said.

The Professor looked as if he thought Escargot was the one who was half-cocked. After an exasperated pause, he shook his head and started off again. But Jonathan had more faith in Escargot. "How so?"

"We could be twenty-five miles down the coast by dark if we were in the submarine, and we could cruise up and down and look for signs."

"And Selznak could be murdering Miles and the Squire in the woods fifteen miles behind us," the Professor said.

Escargot shrugged. "He might be doing his murdering right now. A few of us at least could run far enough ahead to have a look about. We could meet back up at Boffin Beach."

Once again Jonathan stuck up for Escargot. "I'm for it," he said. "Half of us can go along in the submarine and half of us on the coast road. Then if one party falls into Selznak's hands, the other can dash in and rescue them, just like last winter. He won't half expect us to split up. We can't even be sure he knows that the submarine is in Balumnia."

"We saw the old woman at St. Elmo's Square," Escargot said, putting a hole in at least part of Jonathan's argument. "But you're right, lad. Selznak won't look for us to break up. He'll think he has us scared witless, cowering together on the road."

"You know about this Boffin Beach?" the Professor asked.

"I'm a submarine captain," Escargot said. "I have charts, maps. I fish for oysters at Boffin Beach. There's pearl oysters there the size of wagon wheels. I sell them to the elves for beds. There's an old abandoned castle on the bluffs above, but not much else. I don't know anything about any horror. That must have happened while I was out to sea."

"I'll go with Grandpa!" shouted Dooly, who didn't seem to have any desire to travel along the coast road. It was unlikely that he'd run into any "goblin business" under the ocean.

Bufo spoke up about then. "I'm for going along in the submarine, too. They've got the jump on us. It's haste we want now." Gump, for once, agreed with him.

"Then it's settled," Jonathan said. "The Professor and Ahab and I will hike along the coast road and look for the four of you at Boffin Beach. We'll probably run down Miles along the way if we try. He might dawdle a bit and wait for us. He won't want to tackle the Dwarf alone."

There was general agreement on the issue, and everyone shook hands. Once again Jonathan found himself trudging along the road toward the Thirteen Bridges with the Professor on one side of him and Ahab on the other. "It looks as if we're left to our own devices once again," he said.

"Just as well, I think. I'm sorry to lose Gump and Bufo, of course; don't get me wrong. But there's an element of stealth lost when a big crowd goes stumbling down the road. I have a feeling that stealth is what we'll want, just as much as haste. I still don't trust Escargot. He's after that globe, but that's about it. He couldn't care less about the Squire."

"I think you're selling him short," Jonathan said, "although you're right about his wanting the globe. We'll have to wait and see, I suppose."

"We'll see, all right. Let's just not make the mistake of depending on him, that's all. I hope I'm wrong, of course."

Jonathan was sure that Professor Wurzle *did* hope he was wrong. The Professor sometimes fell a bit short when it came to optimism, but Jonathan had rarely known him to be unfair.

In half an hour they rounded a long curving bend in the road that led out of the city and along tidal flats toward the coast. Fishermen's huts stood on stilts here and there above the grasses and stiff low brush of the marshy tidelands, and thin dark canals twisted along toward the sea. Some way below town on a bit of a hill lay a gypsy encampment, smoke from cooking fires curling languidly about a circle of wagons covered with tattered canvas. Not far from the road two dark gypsys were fishing for seabirds with kites. Jonathan was tempted to stand and watch for a bit, as now and again a big gull or heron would swoop down and lunge at the bait dangling at the tail of the bird-shaped kite.

The kites themselves looked nothing like the sea birds they were intended to decoy, and that struck Jonathan as an oversight. But the Professor pointed out that gypsys, being rovers, fished for any of a hundred birds and could hardly be expected to hoist kites enough for all of them. There was a basic bird image, the Professor explained, which pretty much summed up birdness, and it was that with which the gypsys fished.

The idea fascinated Jonathan, especially since the kites were such a wonderful mixture altogether—a sort of hodgepodge of birddom, as if someone had mixed up a duck with a parrot and a snipe and had tossed in a pelican and an ostrich for good measure. The Professor, however, said that the composite bird was nothing next to the composite mammal, which was a wonder to see and was about the size of a house. There had been rumors at the university, said the Professor, that the taxidermist who had been commissioned to make one for the school of biology had run mad after finishing the thing and had had to be taken away in a cart.

"How about human beings?" Jonathan asked. "Is there such a composite for human beings?"

"Yes," the Professor said as they walked along and the fishing gypsys fell away behind them, "but it isn't much to look at. It's pretty much similar to the dummy in the window at Beezle's store."

"The one with the foolish hat and one eye bigger than the other?"

"That's it. Not much to get excited about, not if you compare it to the bird or the mammal."

Jonathan said he'd like to see the composite mammal some day, and the Professor agreed that if they ever got up to the City of the Five Monoliths, they'd pay a visit to the university.

About then they saw the first of the Thirteen Bridges. The road ran out across the tidelands toward deep water —either the Tweet River or the ocean, it was impossible to say which. The bridge was simply a stone arch that spanned forty feet of water and touched down on a long, sandy islet. From there a longer bridge arched out, touched on its own island, and rose once again. So it went for as far as they could see. The rising and the falling of the gray stones looked like nothing so much as the back of a great serpent or dragon humping up out of the ocean. Jonathan counted the bridges he could make out, but somewhere around the tenth, everything faded and dulled into the salty haze of the sea.

They passed no one on the bridges. Boats sailed along below and a few rowboats were moored in the shadows, their occupants lowering crab traps into the water near the massive stone foundations. A galleon stood out to sea about a half-mile, perhaps waiting for the tide, which was low enough to expose a good expanse of muddy bank along each finger of the delta. Here and there people with rolled trousers poked in the sandy mud with clamming forks, unearthing plate-sized clams and tossing them into wooden crates or buckets. But all that went on below the bridges. On top there was no one at all besides Ahab, Jonathan, and the Professor—which was a bit disturbing to Jonathan in light of the innkeeper's warning. The Professor, however, pointed out that if there were no sizeable villages for a hundred miles down the coast, then there would be little reason for traffic on the road. Besides, in midweek it was unlikely that picnickers or idle travelers would be out and about. The weekend would doubtless tell a different story. Jonathan agreed, but mostly because he wanted to agree and not so much because he thought the logic sound.

The sixth bridge was a tremendous span of stones that hung in the air without a thought for gravity. The center of the span was fifty or sixty feet above what must have been the main channel of the Tweet River running deep and dark beneath them. The Professor pointed upriver where a long sand and rock spit formed something of a breakwater a half-mile or so distant. Canted over and three quarters sunk at the end of that breakwater was the hulk of the *Jamoca Queen.*

As each bridge fell away behind them, so did the city of Landsend; by the time they crested the thirteenth, Landsend was itself lost in haze, a sort of shimmering ghost city disappearing in the late afternoon sun. They came out into the ocean breeze atop a sandy hill that fell away steeply toward a rock-dotted strand. Green breakers tumbled along the length of the beach, and the low sun shining beyond them glowed through the pale walls of the waves, turning the sea-green water to a clear pale emerald. All the ocean noises, the crashing and hissing and rushing and the crying of the seabirds, sounded to Jonathan like very wonderful but lonesome music and made him wish for the thousandth time that he lived by the sea so that he could listen to it every day.

But there was no time to stand and gape at the ocean, not if they intended to catch up with Miles. Some quarter of a mile farther along they passed a crossroads that led away east toward the forest. An arrow on a cut-stone marker pointed inland, and below it were the words GROVER—38 MILES. Another arrow pointed north toward Landsend, and another south toward Persimmon Village, some ninety-seven miles distant.

After that the road ran up and down over sandy, grassy hills, the sea crashing on the one side, grasslands running away toward wooded mountains on the other. There was nothing particularly threatening or gloomy about the countryside, nothing that reminded Jonathan of goblins or of the sort of horrors that inhabited the woods along the Tweet River. It was all quite simply deserted.

Soon the sun fell away into the sea, however, and the shadows of the hills and occasional trees grew longer and the ocean grew darker and colder. For another hour they trudged along until finally it was so utterly dark that when the road wandered into a very thick and quiet woods, they could barely make out the trail ahead of them. The distant sound of crashing waves had disappeared, and glimmers of moonlight shone away to their left between the leaves of forest trees. The path farther on was stippled with pale silver that winked on and off as branches overhead blew in the wind. Around them were the biggest trees Jonathan had ever seen, gnarled and twisted and stooped as if they'd seen some heavy weather. Limbs thrust out wildly and mingled together overhead in a tangled ceiling that swayed in the wind, now letting in a thousand shafts of moonlight, then casting deep shadows across the forest floor.

So dense and forbidding were the woods on both sides, that the idea of tossing down the knapsacks and trying to sleep was unthinkable. It was only eight o'clock anyway, according to Jonathan's recovered pocketwatch, and it seemed far more sensible to travel along for another two or three hours, if only to tire themselves out to that point at which they felt positively like shutting their eyes.

So they trudged along by the intermittent light of the moon. Keeping to the path, finally, even when it was lost in deep shadow, was an easy enough thing. Ahab could be depended upon for that. It wound a bit here and there, but it took no sudden turns, and there were no crossroads to confuse the issue. Several times they crossed what might have been game trails, little overgrown paths that led away into the wild depths of the wood, but there seemed to be no reason to investigate them.

Around ten-thirty, Jonathan was starting to feel like getting a bit of sleep. The woods had, if anything, gotten deeper and darker and more musty and ancient. The branches no longer blew overhead; they were quiet and still. Jonathan suspected that the path had been running inland and that the woods were sheltered from the sea breeze by hills. The moon was three-quarters full, sailing higher in the sky amid scattered stars, but only occasionally did threads of moonlight manage to find the forest floor.

They stopped to rest more and more often—every ten minutes or so—and their rest stops grew longer each time, the two of them sitting in a slump and considering tiredly the merits of staying the night in the woods. But each time they did, it seemed to them that a coast road, if it had any sense, would quite likely follow the coast, and that another half-hour or forty-five minutes must surely bring them back around to open, brighter country. So they stood up finally after their rest and plodded wearily along, ignoring the darkness around them and pretending not to hear the rustlings of the night creatures scrabbling in the undergrowth along the path.

Jonathan's mind, without him giving it leave to, kept wandering around to a point where it began thinking of trolls and of bears and of the sorts of shadows that inhabited the Goblin Wood below Hightower. But he knew, of course, that he wasn't in the Goblin Wood. He was in Balumnia, and Balumnia mightn't have any trolls at all, or any bears either for that matter. It had headless men in rowboats instead.

He commanded himself not to think of such things. He made an effort instead to picture the flowers that grew in the elf moss around Twombly Town that spring, and to remember their deep pastel colors that reminded him of painted Easter eggs or of the violets and pinks and deep greens of distant mountains at sunset. But as beautiful as all those thoughts were, hunched trolls and parties of shrunken goblins insisted on creeping in and spoiling things. The forest became gloomier and gloomier, the shadows deeper and more threatening.

He found himself suddenly stumbling into the Professor, who had stopped inexplicably in the middle of the road. "What?" Jonathan asked, even though the Professor as yet hadn't said anything.

"*Shhh!*" the Professor whispered, pointing through the trees toward a flickering light, a fire of some sort, that danced in a clearing a hundred yards or so off the road. A little trail wound away toward it. It was a peculiar sort of fire that leaped and shrank and threw sudden splashes of light into the shadows of the trees beyond it. It seemed to move weirdly about, flaring up here, then dying away, then leaping up again some few yards off to the left or the right or deeper into the trees. It didn't at all seem to be the sort of fire that Jonathan fancied investigating.

But then who could say that it wasn't Miles up to some sort of enchantment, or that it wasn't Selznak himself working mischief over one of his strange fires fueled with dried bones? The Professor stooped and picked something up off the road, then dropped it again, throwing it down as if he'd inadvertently grabbed hold of a dead toad. That wasn't far from the case. On the path lay a dried bat. The Professor was about to kick it into the bushes when Jonathan stopped him by picking the thing up. Through the bat's ears was a bit of string tied in a loop.

"This came from Dr. Chan's," Jonathan said, dangling the bat at arm's length. "Didn't he say that Miles had been in to buy herbs and bats?"

"Yes, he did." The Professor studied it for a moment, then said, "We'll have to take a closer look at that fire."

Jonathan tossed the bat away. He couldn't think of anything else to do with it. If Gump were along he'd work it into some useful object—put a candle on its head or turn it into a door pull. But that sort of thing didn't appeal to Jonathan, not right then. So the two of them crept along the little trail with Ahab between, Jonathan wishing he had an ape suit to hide in, and all of them ready to turn and run at the sound of a broken twig. They were halfway to the fire when they heard a willow flute being played very poorly. There was no melody to it, just an idiot piping followed by low, cackling laughter. They stopped where they were and waited. Whatever sat by the fire was certainly not Miles. Firelight sprang up against the bole of a great tree beyond, throwing across it the shadow of a stooped figure tearing at something with its teeth, a great beef bone, perhaps, or a turkey leg. The sound of slavering and crunching could be heard dimly, and once again the willow pipes started up, this time accompanied by the senseless pounding of a copper gong.

Jonathan realized just then that there were other fires lit in the woods, any number of them, flickering through the darkness. They blinked out, then popped up again, far away like the lights of fireflies, then frightfully close, spawning leaping shadows on the ancient trees.

Without a word the three of them turned and sneaked back out toward the road. Jonathan had the sudden terrible feeling that the road wouldn't be there, that they would wander in the woods all night waiting for the sun to rise, but that the sun would no more brighten the deep shadows than did the threads of broken moonlight. He thought he heard a rustling along the path behind him, the padding of feet and the swishing and brushing of limbs. Then the piping of the willow flute stopped abruptly. It struck him that it was time to run, and he was about to suggest as much to the Professor when he found himself stumbling out onto the coast road, and then dashing off south in the wake of his two companions. The whole short adventure seemed to have given both of them a second wind, and they struck off south, determined to find their way out of the forest if they had to walk until dawn.

Chapter 20

In the High Window

❋

AFTER a half-mile or so, the road widened and the trees thinned, and they trudged out into a clearing bathed in watery moonbeams. In it sat a cottage. It was a very cheerful cottage under the circumstances, its windows lit and its door ajar and the sound of laughter and gaiety tumbling out into the night—not goblin laughter either, but the sounds of people enjoying themselves.

A girl stood in the open doorway watching the road, and when Jonathan and Ahab and the Professor stopped in amazement at the edge of the clearing, she waved and seemed very happy to see them.

Jonathan at first wasn't sure that he was happy to see her, not right then. But it occurred to him that she was very pretty standing there on the porch in the lantern light. Her hair was long and blond, and she had a thin, young figure. Wispy was the only word he could think of right off to describe her as she stood there in a lace dress. She waved at them again. "Come along," she called in a cheerful voice that chased most of Jonathan's suspicions away.

The smell of roast goose wafted out through the open windows, and it was that more than anything else that convinced them to have a look inside. Ahab, however, didn't want to go. He lay down growling, smack in the middle of the road, and wouldn't budge. Jonathan hauled on his collar and reasoned with him but wasn't having any effect. So after a moment he gave up, deciding to come back outside later and entice Ahab in with a bit of roast goose.

Those inside the house were having a good time indeed, laughing and singing and clanking cutlery about and banging plates. The girl on the porch stepped off and took Jonathan's hand. "The wizard said to watch for you," she said, smiling. "He was along earlier but he hurried away again. He said to tell you that things are never as bad as they seem."

That struck Jonathan as being very encouraging indeed —just the sort of thing he'd always insisted upon. His faith in Miles doubled, and he barely gave a thought to the strange fact that the girl's hand was very cold and was dry as dust. For a moment, just as she stepped out into the moonlight, Jonathan had the strange thought that her hair wasn't blond, as it had seemed to be in the lantern light. It seemed momentarily to be gray, like old ashes in a grate, and her face, rather than being pleasantly thin, appeared skeletal just for the slip of an instant. But once again on the porch in the lantern light, she was young and wispy and there was nothing at all to worry about. Whatever he'd seen, the Professor must have missed, for he was rubbing his hands together and gazing at the company within the cottage.

Almost a dozen people were gathered around a long trestle table laden with the most amazing foods: a tremendous roast goose and heaps of mashed potatoes, tubs of butter, and rich smoking gravy. There were puddings, pies, bottles of ale, jars of cranberry sauce, and plates of biscuits. Over the fire in the hearth was a suspended basket heaped with chestnuts that a lad in leather trousers poked at with a silver fork. Everyone's plate was piled with food, and at the head of the table were two empty plates and chairs as if they'd been set there specifically for Jonathan and the Professor. Jonathan could see no reason not to make use of them. It was the only polite thing to do.

So the two of them sat down, and for the first time in hours Jonathan felt as if he could relax a bit. It seemed quite possible that they could induce their hostess to let them spend the night there, and then make a fresh start in the morning.

The cottage itself was cheerful and warm with its timber ceiling and great stone fireplace. Dark oak wainscot circled the plaster walls, and bunches of flowers—lilacs and wild iris and columbine—sat in ceramic vases. Lantern light flooded every corner of the room and spilled out across the polished plank floor, illuminating the faces of the happy revelers.

Jonathan half wondered where they'd all come from, the closest towns being a good long way away, but there would be time enough for questions and tale-telling after he'd dealt with the slices of roast goose that were being forked onto his plate.

All of a sudden he remembered Ahab sitting alone out on the road, and he rose and excused himself and speared a slice of goose with which to convince Ahab to be a sensible dog. But before he got halfway to the open door a gust of wind blew it shut with a wild slam, and a shriek of mad laughter rang out behind him. He found himself caught up in cobweb—cobweb that couldn't have been there a moment before. The lad in the leather trousers was leering at him stupidly, poking with his silver fork at a wire cage full of rats that snapped and popped in the hot fire.

The slice of roast goose, or whatever it actually was, squirmed on the end of the fork in Jonathan's hand, and he threw it with a shout at the cage of rats as he spun round to face the revelers at the table behind him.

Professor Wurzle's chair had tipped over backward onto the floor with him still in it, and two goblins pinched at his arms and cheeks nodding idiotically as two ghouls held the struggling Professor down.

On the table there was no roast goose or pudding or pie. A great tray of broken bloody meat lay there instead: undistinguishable, vile meat that made Jonathan suddenly sick. Goblins stabbed hunks out of it with long knives and grinned up at him, motioning for him to have a go at it first. One of them, the biggest goblin, seemed to be about half melted, as if his face were made of soft tallow. The cottage was full of shrieking and cackling and the smell of dust and age. The lilacs and iris were gone and were replaced with dead weeds and grotesque funguses. Ahab barked and howled beyond the door, and Jonathan was for a second undecided whether to let him in or help the Professor out of his scrape. He hadn't time to think about it much, however, for one of the goblins that had been pinching the Professor's cheek grasped a knife from the table-top and had the look about him of a man considering how to best carve a roast.

Jonathan grabbed the nearest chair and smashed it into the goblin's head. Almost as soon as he did he felt a hot fork spear into his arm. He turned and flailed out at the rat cooker, catching him square on the cheek. His fist skidded across its face, and it was like hitting a lump of clay. Skin and bone gouged away in a spray of black liquid, and the thing, whatever it was, tumbled over, knocking the cage of rats deep into the fire. Goblin laughter shrieked out, and two of the goblins jumped across and pointed and screamed at their companion who lay smoking in the flames, his clothes catching fire and burning with amazing fury.

The Professor was up and out of his chair by then and looking for something to hit. But none of the goblins and ghouls offered him any resistance. Two goblins danced atop the table, stomping and kicking at the bloody feast and slavering and whacking each other with chewed bones. About then, a black cat crawled out from beneath a chair and leaped up onto the tabletop, and Jonathan realized who it was the girl on the porch had reminded him of when she had stepped into the moonlight. He had been a fool not to see it; they had both been fools. Only Ahab had any sense. Then Jonathan noticed that Ahab was no longer barking and growling outside the door and that the lanterns round the walls began growing dimmer and dimmer and that the fire in the hearth was dying and shrinking. Beside it, smiling crookedly, staring through milky eyes, was the old woman of the swamp, of Tweet Village, of St. Elmo Square.

Jonathan was suddenly shoved from behind, shoved toward the door by the Professor, who, in a rage, took a wild swipe with a chair at the witch. The chair broke into kindling wood against the wall, and the witch, her posture unchanged, still smiling vaguely and staring, stood some few feet farther away. Neither Jonathan nor the Professor had any desire to discuss the phenomenon. Jonathan tore the door open, and the two of them stumbled out into the night, shrieks and howls of laughter following close on. The door slammed shut and they were once again on the coast road.

Behind them, all was strangely silent. When they turned and looked back, there was no longer any cabin in the clearing, only bits of stone from an old crumbled foundation and another heap that might once have been a chimney. Beyond there were trees—great, wide trees that grew close together in a line, the shadowy places between them seeming like dark doorways through which, in the far distant shadows, dots of fires glowed, winking and blinking in the night. Ahab was nowhere around.

Jonathan whistled and called. There was little need of secrecy. All the calling and whistling, however, didn't accomplish a thing. Both Jonathan and the Professor knew that they'd find Ahab when they found the Squire and Selznak and Miles. It seemed tolerably certain to Jonathan that they were on the verge of doing just that. They were being toyed with; there could be no doubt. The disappearance of Ahab was more such toying—or at least that's what Jonathan hoped. He started toward the tunnels through the trees, thinking that perhaps Ahab had somehow gone that way. Although the Professor shook his head doubtfully, he went along. But the tunnels themselves led into utter darkness, and no shred of moonlight illuminated the blackness. There was nothing, in fact, to indicate that anything at all lay beyond, except the flickering of distant fires and the faraway piping of willow flutes.

Jonathan whistled tentatively into the trees, then shouted. Again there was no response, no sign of Ahab. It was far more likely, if Ahab had somehow wandered off on his own, that he'd gone farther down the coast road. After twenty minutes of futile searching and whistling, that's just what Jonathan and the Professor did.

Within fifteen minutes they were out of the woods and trekking along a beach in the moonlight. With no trees to break the sea wind, the air had grown more chill, but both Jonathan and the Professor were sure they'd far rather freeze the night away in the open than spend it in the woods hobnobbing with goblins and witches and ghouls.

A fog was blowing in off the ocean, and although through occasional clear patches they could still see the rolling of ghostly breakers and the splashing foam luminous in the thin light of the moon, off to their left the land was almost entirely obscured. It was clearly time to call it a night. They scooped out a good-sized depression in the sand behind several great rocks that blocked most of the wind. Jonathan lay for a moment watching the dark water appear and then disappear in the fog farther down the beach. It occurred to him that a campfire would be nice under the circumstances. Almost as soon as the thought wandered through, he fell away into a deep sleep and began to dream that he had one, but that it was small and cold and needed heaps and heaps of wood.

He kept waking up with cold feet every half-hour or so. When he did, he thought again how nice a fire would be and told himself in no uncertain terms to get up and build one. Then he'd begin to imagine again that he had, but that it was an uncooperative fire that didn't care a bit about keeping anyone warm but fizzled and popped and smoked and languished while he puffed and dropped twigs on it. He began to dream that there were other fires burning roundabout, away off up the beach, fires that danced and crackled until he set out to find them, then snapped away into darkness making him lurch awake to find that he hadn't started a fire at all, not even a smoldering little sad fire, but that his feet were still damp and cold and that it didn't seem to be any closer to morning than it had been a half-hour before.

Twice when he awoke and looked for signs of approaching dawn, he thought for a moment that he saw shapes—shadows in foggy moonlight—moving very purposefully and stealthily along the strand. There seemed to be a moaning on the breeze like wind through the chinks around an ill-hung and drafty door or like the sound of distant ghosts flitting through the night air lamenting their fate. The far-off pounding of copper gongs accompanied the moaning, and once, just for a moment, Jonathan could quite distinctly hear low, chattering laughter as if it too were carried along the wind. It seemed to be emanating from the very fog that hung suspended in the night around them.

Once, shortly before dawn, he awoke sleepily and opened his eyes just for a moment. Above him and off inland beyond the coast road, there shone for a time a light glowing in the mists like a lit window in a high tower. But just when he blinked awake enough to take any real notice of it and to decide to awaken the sleeping Professor, the fog swirled and thickened in the night air and the lights faded and were gone. Again there were shadows around him in the dim night—shadows of things creeping on the sand and the misty vision of a human skeleton jerking along through the dark, clacking like bamboo wind chimes in the thick wet mist, then fading and disappearing into the gray.

Jonathan was hard-pressed finally to say whether he was sleeping or waking at any particular moment. He determined as he lay there, not really trying to sleep but just waiting for the sun, that it made precious little difference anyway, so he resolved to keep his eyes shut and wait. He understood, or so it seemed to him there on the beach, that although he had assumed he'd come to Balumnia in pursuit of the Squire, in actuality he'd simply been waiting—waiting for Selznak to work his evil, to spin his web. Like it or not, he was entangled finally in that web, and his waiting was almost at an end.

Then the sun rose. Or at least the night began to fade into day. With it faded some of his fears, and it began to seem reasonable that he'd done a lot of dreaming during the night—very strange dreaming to be sure, but dreaming nonetheless. It began to seem, in fact, that he'd had enough waiting, that it was time to be off on the hunt.

He rolled over in the cold sand to say as much to the Professor, but the Professor wasn't there. Instead, slumped against the gray, weedy rock, its chin on its chest, was a yellow, ragged-looking skeleton, crumbs of peeled, antique skin hanging here and there from a hollow cheek and an ivory shoulder blade.

Jonathan lurched forward and attempted to scramble to his feet. He shouted for the Professor, since it was the Professor he most wanted to see. But his shout was carried away on the wind and was gone. He found that he *couldn't* scramble to his feet. It was as if he *were* entangled in a web and could thrash about as much as he liked, but that the more he thrashed the less headway he'd make.

On beyond on the rocky beach lay any number of skeletons, slumped in the sand as if they'd been filing along the beach in a line and had been blown over by some great wind, toppled like a line of dominoes. A memory of Zippo the magician and of the foggy night in Tweet River Village flitted through his mind and he thought about the dark magical tapestry before which Zippo had performed. He remembered the lighted windows he'd seen through the mist in the night, windows that hadn't, he was sure, been a part of any dream. He turned slowly and looked inland toward the road. There beyond it, sitting on a rocky hillside above a gray-green meadow, was an old stone castle, a castle shrouded with the same pall of mystery and evil that hung in the atmosphere around the castle on Hightower Ridge. He realized, just then, where the great iron door in the deep cavern beneath Hightower Castle led, what door it was that he'd whacked against with his stick and shouted funny things at. It was quite possible even, given Selznak's powers, that the Dwarf himself had been listening at the other side, smiling and nodding with anticipation.

A light shone in an arched window high in a tower of the castle. A hooded figure stepped in front of the high window, staring out toward the ocean. It seemed to Jonathan that he could see a pair of glowing eyes beneath the hood and that the eyes were looking at him. But he didn't have more than a moment to wonder at it before he was jerked to his feet like a marionette and he found himself marching in a long line of risen skeletons along a rough path that led across the meadow toward the castle. Rocks crunched beneath his feet, and the salt air off the ocean pinged against his cheek. He was reminded of a holy man he'd met once on the road to the fair, who walked with a rock in either shoe. He'd seemed half-crippled by it, but he'd told Jonathan that he did it to remind himself that he was alive. It had seemed pretty loony to Jonathan at the time, but it made a certain sense to him now. He was stricken with the fearful certainty that connections with daylight, with sunshine, with the waking world were far fewer than he had ever imagined, that they were nothing more than the crunch of stones beneath his feet and the taste of salt and seafoam on the wind and the cry of wheeling gulls, and were numbered and falling away with each step that he took toward the dark portal that opened at the base of the tower.

It loomed larger ahead of him. Within, he could see small fires burning, torches, perhaps, hung on the walls. Then he filed in through the open door, down a long stair into the earth and along a dark, musty corridor where he could see nothing and feared that he'd run into the thing clacking along in front of him or feel a bony hand on his shoulder. But when he stepped once again into pale yellow lamplight, there was nothing before him at all, nor was there anything clacking along behind. There was only a little, empty, bat-haunted cavern and the sound of sliding and clanking metal that turned out, when Jonathan spun around, to be iron bars that had banged shut.

All in all, Jonathan felt a vast relief. It seemed quite possible that his imagination had played him false, that there was no immediate reason to fill his shoes with rocks after all. Playing out the scene on the tapestry had, he hoped, been Selznak's idea of a lark. He was relieved too to find that the line of grisly skeletons hadn't all crowded into the cell with him. Where they'd gone, he hadn't any idea. He couldn't even be sure that there had been any skeletons. It was every bit as likely that the Dwarf had spun some magic, made him see things that weren't there. It was certain that Selznak had uncommon powers in Balumnia, powers that exceeded even those he wielded in the High Valley along the Oriel River. Miles, with his dishes of smoking herbs and spark-throwing cap, seemed to be rather weak tea in comparison. Righting fallen chairs and casting wind-increasing spells were all very impressive in their way, but right at that moment, as Jonathan stood alone in his cold cell, such tricks didn't appear to amount to very much. He shrugged and looked around the bare, rocky cavern, then stepped across and rattled the cell bars just on the off-chance that the locking mechanism was old and unreliable. That wasn't the case.

So Jonathan sat down on the dusty, cold floor and waited. One thing was sure: Selznak wasn't about to let him starve to death. He had far too much imagination for that. After an hour or so of sitting in the dim lamp-lit cavern, Jonathan heard the scrape of shoes and saw the flickering light of an approaching torch—a torch, remarkably enough, carried by none other than Zippo the Magician.

Chapter 21

The Weak Link

❊

ZIPPO carried with him a bowl, probably full of gruel, with the end of a spoon sticking out of it and steam rising off the top. The steam alone looked so appetizing to Jonathan that he was ready to eat whatever lay in the bowl even if it *was* gruel, which, Jonathan had read in G. Smithers, was the preferred food of prisoners and orphans. He wasn't sure, however, what gruel was—boiled-down oat husks sprinkled with dirt probably.

"Mr. Zippo!" Jonathan said heartily when Zippo drew up with his bowl. "You're looking pale, sir."

"Zippo," said Zippo. "Just Zippo. No mister. That's not my real name, you see; it's just a stage device. My real name is Leopold Streff."

"Oh, of course," Jonathan said, thinking that somehow Zippo's name sounded familiar. He looked at him closely. The man was fairly young, as Escargot had pointed out, probably in his early thirties. But he was haggard and drawn as if he hadn't slept at all well for a month or two, or as if his conscience was tormenting him. His toupee had disappeared. Zippo shoved the steaming bowl through the bars, and Jonathan took it. Inside was some sort of cooked cereal that looked very edible. Something was sprinkled over the top, but it wasn't dirt. Jonathan determined that it was brown sugar, which, under the circumstances, was an unlooked for but welcome sight.

"So how are you getting on?" Jonathan asked.

Zippo shrugged and shook his head in a way that either meant that he wasn't getting on at all well or that he couldn't talk about it.

Jonathan tried another tack, talking through a mouthful of cereal. "Don't do much performing out here, do you? Doesn't seem to be much of an audience around beyond goblins and skeletons and ghouls and such. I wouldn't think that crowd would go in much for magic."

Zippo looked as if he were about to burst. "Oh they like it well enough," he muttered through his teeth. "They like to spoil it is what. They like to wreck it. Filthy bunch of devils. He made me put on a show for them. A show in the woods. They . . ." he began. "They . . . they ruined it is what. Made fun. They don't *like* anything. Just rip around. They lit my stage on fire."

"What did *he* think about it all?" Jonathan asked. "Laughed, I'd warrant. Am I right?"

But Zippo didn't answer. He looked at Jonathan for a moment, shook his head, put on a taciturn face, and clumped off down the dark corridor, his torch fizzling. Jonathan sat back down and finished his cereal. There was precious little to do but wait. Wait and think about Zippo.

At around noon, he returned with lunch. Jonathan was a bit surprised to find such hospitality and to discover in his lunch sack a pleasant assortment of foods: pickles, cheese, black bread, and a tolerably crisp apple. Then he remembered the contents of the Dwarf's kitchen at Hightower Castle—the bottled ale and pickled vegetables and such. That the Dwarf gave such fare away to his prisoners was probably a matter once again of his toying with them. Selznak saw the whole thing as a lark.

Zippo hung around again without saying much, so Jonathan had another go at him. "Quite a show you put on up at Tweet River Village. The best I've seen. By far. And I've seen a few, I can tell you. Yours held it over them all."

"Do you really think so?" Zippo asked, brightening a bit.

Actually Jonathan did think his show had been pretty good, so saying so hadn't been much of a stretcher. But even if he had exaggerated a bit, absolute truthfulness wasn't really demanded under the circumstances. Seeing Zippo perk up, Jonathan laid it on a bit thicker. "Absolutely," he said. "I've never seen such a hand with a deck of cards. And that mechanical fish was a marvel. Too high-toned for the crowd at the tavern, if you ask me. You could run that fish in front of princes and kings. That's how good it was."

"Well it *was* rather good, wasn't it? Don't think it was his idea either," Zippo continued, "because it wasn't. It was mine. I thought the illusion up years ago. Covered a cow skull with hammered sheet copper when I was fifteen and shot strawberries out of its mouth at my friends. The fish idea came later. The cow head was all right, but it wasn't half mystical enough, if you know what I mean. It was weird, all right, but in an evil sort of way. That wasn't my idea of magic at all. Not a bit."

"Oh?" Jonathan said, taking advantage of Zippo's insistence. "Things change over the years, I suppose." He gave Zippo a look he hoped suggested that evil-looking, copper-covered cow skulls must be right in his line nowadays.

"That's not so," Zippo said, growing even more indignant than Jonathan would have supposed. "That's not it at all. There's circumstances."

"Circumstances?"

But Zippo wouldn't budge. He looked as if he were going to clam up and go away again, so Jonathan changed the subject. "You're right about the fish," he said. "There's nothing more mystical than a fish with golden scales. Unless it's something that floats in the air. The bubbles and butterflies were good, but the flowers were perfect. Enchantment is what it was."

"That's it exactly," Zippo said, cutting in. "Enchantment. Wonder. Marvel. Those are the sorts of things *I'm* after. The card tricks are okay. They *surprise* people, I suppose, but they don't fill them full of wonder, if you follow me. There's minor sorts of magic involved, but there isn't any enchantment."

"That's it entirely." Jonathan once again had to rework his opinion of Zippo. It was seeming more and more odd to him that he would be in league with the Dwarf. He suspected that Zippo's cooperation with Selznak wasn't entirely voluntary or else was a product of his vanity—that without Selznak he'd have no access to magical tapestries or winged pigs or helium buds. "You know who loves that sort of thing?" Jonathan asked. "Squire Myrkle, that's who." He expected Zippo to react somehow, half-figuring that at the mention of the Squire's name he would put on his taciturn face and leave. But that wasn't the case at all. Instead, he started to cry.

It was a very strange sight, Zippo boo-hooing there; it took Jonathan by surprise. "Poor Squire!" Zippo cried.

"What's happened to him!" Jonathan shouted, leaping toward the door as if to grab Zippo and shake him.

"Nothing." Zippo, startled, fell back a step or two. "Nothing, yet." With that, he shook his head sadly and reached into his pocket, pulling out a little leather bag. He untied the thong around the mouth of the bag, upended it over his palm, and poured out a dozen or so marbles. The rainbow swirls of the colored glass threw glints of light in the glow of the torch. "Look at these," Zippo said.

Jonathan took a closer look, supposing that the marbles weren't quite as ordinary as they appeared. They were pretty marbles, to be sure, shot through with ribbons of lavender and emerald and orange, but beyond their beauty as marbles, there was nothing about them that explained Zippo's obvious sense of wonder. "Do you know what these are?" Zippo asked.

"Don't you?"

"Marbles. That's what the Squire called them."

"Did he? He gave you these marbles then?"

"That's right."

"Are these the first marbles you've ever seen?"

"Why yes," Zippo said, seemingly puzzled by the question. Suddenly Jonathan was struck with a strange thought.

"Don't children play with marbles, then, in Balumnia?"

"Where?" Zippo asked, giving Jonathan a strange look.

"Never mind. Why did you say, 'Poor Squire,' when I mentioned him? What's Selznak been up to?"

"Who?" Zippo shoved the marble bag back into his pocket. "I've got to be getting back. He won't like it if I'm away too long. He doesn't entirely trust me. No one does." Zippo sniffled and pulled the torch out of its niche in the wall and started off down the corridor.

"Help me save the Squire," Jonathan called after him. "Save yourself!" But Zippo disappeared. Jonathan sat back down and nibbled his lunch, kicking himself for forgetting that Zippo might well not know that he lived in the land of Balumnia nor that Sikorsky was really Selznak under an assumed name. It was equally likely, of course, that Selznak was really Sikorsky under an assumed name. One way or the other, he'd probably managed to confuse Zippo no end. It was astonishing to discover that there were no marbles in Balumnia, although it really didn't surprise him that Zippo was so taken with them. Jonathan had always thought that marbles, which were, after all, invented by elves, contained some nature of enchantment. It occurred to him that Escargot was missing a bet. He could make a fortune selling marbles in Balumnia and forget about foraging for sea lemons and cephalopods and fish carcasses.

By and by, Jonathan began to grow sleepy. He hadn't slept worth a fig that night, and there was nothing much else to do anyway, so he lay down on the flattest part of the floor he could find and shut his eyes. He discovered after a moment, however, that the floor was lumpier than it had seemed at first, and he wiggled about and curled this way and that and worked at being comfortable for a half-hour before he dozed off.

A noise ruined his nap—a *"psst!"* whispered by someone anxious to wake him. He pushed himself up and saw Zippo standing outside the bars, looking back over his shoulder. He knew that he couldn't have slept more than an hour—not even long enough to feel particularly muddled. So it couldn't be dinner time already. Besides, Zippo hadn't any food with him. He held nothing but his sputtering torch and looked like a man who wanted to talk—like a conspirator, in fact.

"Zippo!" Jonathan called. "What ho?" He decided that he might just as well make a show of being cheerful. Zippo had the look of a man who might spook easily, lose his conspiratorial air and run off in the dark. In fact, he could hardly hold himself still. He thrust his torch from one hand to the other and back again and craned his head about and back and forth, as if he expected someone to come sneaking along the dark corridor after him.

"Dinner time?" Jonathan asked.

"What?" Zippo was taken by surprise. "No, not yet.

I . . ." and he stopped and stood there quaking. "I thought you might want something."

"A pillow would be nice. That and some lemonade. And if you have any G. Smithers novels lying about, bring one of those too."

"*Shhh!*" Zippo hissed. Jonathan shushed and listened for a moment but he heard nothing. "This is no time to be frivolous," Zippo said, peering back over his shoulder once again for good measure. "We're in terrible danger here."

"*We* are?" Jonathan sounded surprised. Then, in a rush of sudden certainty, Jonathan remembered where he'd heard Zippo's name. "You say you used to shoot strawberries out of the mouth of a copper cow?"

"What?" Zippo asked, surprised again at the change of subject. "That's right. Strawberries."

"You must have had plenty of them, eh? Don't they call your father the Strawberry Baron?"

"How do you know about my father?" Zippo asked, startled.

"It's a long story," Jonathan explained. "He was very kind to some friends of mine, and he's keen on having a go at the Dwarf. I'm going to trust you here, because I can see that you've come to your senses. You've got a chance to end all of this foolishness. Your father, along with Cap'n Eustacio Binky, are financing an armed excursion across the Tweet River and south to the coast. Their armies are massing right now. They're not in the mood for quarter, either, I can tell you."

Zippo's eyes became as big around as melons in the torchlight and were filled with a mixture of surprise and joy and fear. Jonathan disliked having to dabble in hearsay, since Zippo so obviously hung on his every word.

"Did he mention me?" Zippo asked, his face full of hope.

"Who?"

"My father. The Strawberry Baron. Did he say anything about me?"

"Of course he did," Jonathan said, warming to his subject. "Of course. He carried on about you. Told a long story about the prodigal son who comes back after wayward years and is welcomed by his father. Very touching, really, the idea of someone coming round in the end."

Once again Zippo was momentarily lost in tears. Jonathan felt awful. For one wild moment he was possessed by the idea of denying it all—of revealing that he knew nothing about the Strawberry Baron but a few snatches of rumor and that it was quite possible that Zippo would be rewarded with a poke in the nose if he went home. But the truth now, he quickly saw, wouldn't serve. It wouldn't solve Zippo's dilemma nor would it get him and the Professor and, he hoped, old Ahab out of their scrape. There would be time later to repair any damage, even if he himself had to hunt up the Strawberry Baron and tell *him* the story of the prodigal son.

Zippo wiped his eyes and seemed to buck up a bit, as if something had lit the fires of dauntlessness within his soul.

"He's taken your friends," Zippo announced suddenly.

"Taken them!" Jonathan cried. "What friends?"

"Why the ones in the undersea boat," Zippo said. "The old wild man and the two elves and the boy with the whirling eyes. Goblins brought them in a half-hour ago. It must have been a savage battle. They were moored right off Boffin Beach, poking around."

"Looking for me," Jonathan said. "How about the wizard? Did he catch the wizard?" Jonathan decided that since he'd invited Zippo to be a turncoat he might just as well trust him.

Zippo didn't know anything about any wizard. The old woman had lied last night in the forest. Miles hadn't left them any message. She knew nothing about Miles. Was afraid of him probably. Miles was at large! A bit of hope surged through Jonathan, but it evaporated again quickly as Zippo's torch, guttering in its niche in the wall, flared up twice like a dying star and winked out. Zippo trembled visibly as if the dead torch were some sort of omen, as if it hadn't actually burned out but had been snuffed out purposefully. Jonathan remembered the scattered campfire and the laughter in the fog that night a week past on the outskirts of linkman territory, and he half expected that the little oil lamp burning behind him would sputter out too. But it didn't. When Zippo saw that there wasn't any immediate danger of being plunged into darkness he settled down again. "They'll be too late," he said, knuckling his brow.

"Who will?" Jonathan was having a difficult time following Zippo's train of thought. Ideas kept derailing, it seemed to him, before they'd had a proper chance to get up a head of steam.

"The armies," Zippo said. "Didn't you just tell me there were armies massing?"

"Yes, that's right," Jonathan responded. "Why do you say they'll be too late? Too late for what?"

"Why, for the siege."

"What siege was that?" Jonathan was more concerned with rescuing his friends than with saving Balumnians from a threatened siege, but he had to be patient.

"Don't you know?" Zippo asked in surprise. "Isn't that why you're here?"

"We're here to rescue the Squire. That's all. And while we're at it, we're taking you along. You aren't fit for this sort of life. It doesn't suit you."

Zippo remained silent for a moment, thinking. "This is tolerably strange," he said finally. "You say you don't know anything about the siege. About the goblins and monsters and ghosts and ghouls and such that have been gathering, or of the shadow that's come over the south coast in the last year."

"Only rumor," Jonathan said. "That and what I saw on the river and in the woods last night."

To Jonathan's surprise, Zippo produced his marble bag again. "You knew what these were."

"That's right. I thought everyone did."

"Do you know whose likeness is on this coin?" Zippo held up a gold piece minted in linkman territory.

"That's King Soot," Jonathan said. "The Squire's father. He's king of the linkmen."

"What's a linkman?"

"Something like an elf," Jonathan said. "Gump and Bufo, who were in the undersea device, are linkmen. Don't you have any of them here?"

"No, nor marbles either. Where did you say you were from?"

"I didn't say," Jonathan said. He could almost see wheels spinning and lightbulbs blinking on behind Zippo's eyes.

"My old master, Nimmo the wizard—I studied under

him for a year before I met the Dwarf—told me once that there was another world," Zippo said slowly. "But it didn't make any sense. He was on his way toward turning into a bird then, and I thought he'd gone spiritual on me. Then when I came here two years later, I saw the Dwarf coming and going through the iron door in the cellar. Do you know about that door?"

"Yes," Jonathan said. "And you're right about it."

"The door disappears," Zippo continued, "for months at a time. I tried to follow him once but I couldn't open it. Spells wouldn't budge it. That's why I thought you knew about the siege. You understand. I began to suspect that you were from someplace else."

"Back up a bit!" Jonathan ordered. "What about the blasted siege? Are you telling me that it isn't a siege against Landsend or Tweet Village or anything?"

"No. I don't much know *what*, but it has something to do with where *you* come from, wherever that is."

Jonathan stood there studying for a moment, and any way he looked at it, from up and down or back and forth, it seemed quite likely that he and the Professor and Escargot had made a ghastly error at Hightower Castle six months previously when they had allowed Selznak the Dwarf to bargain for his life and had let him go. They had assumed that they had foiled his plots, reduced him to a minor villain, taken the wind out of his sails. But they hadn't. Not by a long nose, as Bufo and Gump would say. They'd merely interrupted a broad and elaborate scheme that had gone right on along as soon as Selznak had gained his freedom. If it would have done any good, Jonathan would have kicked himself. But of course that wouldn't answer. He'd have to kick Selznak instead, and the sooner the better.

Then it struck him why Selznak had been so desperate to retrieve the Lumbog globe from the Squire. Kidnapping the Squire had been mere deviltry, but taking the globe had been utter necessity. The globe would become, unless something were done quickly, an open door by which Selznak's creatures could flood into High Valley, probably at first into the dark depths of the Goblin Wood. Sending them through the door in the cellar and, one by one, up the iron ladder wouldn't have served—that much was obvious. Selznak had to have the globe.

Zippo stood outside the cell door watching Jonathan ponder. He seemed very nervous—more so all the time. "Well?" he asked finally.

"That's a good question," Jonathan responded. "How in the world do I get out of here? Can you find a key? You can palm cards and watches well enough. Steal Selznak's keys."

Zippo held a long iron key aloft. "I already have."

Chapter 22

In the Laboratory

❧

Jonathan's heart gave a lunge at the sudden sight of it. "Get me out of here, then. Let's go."

"What will we do?" Zippo asked as he fumbled at the lock with the old key. "We haven't any plan."

"Whenever I have a plan it goes nuts," Jonathan told him. "Let's just move."

The door clicked open, and Jonathan stormed through it. Abruptly he stopped and started back after the lamp that hung on the wall. Then he decided that he didn't altogether want to be a beacon, so instead he pulled the torch out of its mooring, yanked the oily, burned debris off the end of it, and wound up with a two-foot length of heavy wood—just the thing for whacking goblins. Together they set out down the dark corridor and up the stairs, Zippo in front.

"First, we've got to spring my friends," Jonathan said. "Especially the bearded man from the submarine."

"It won't be easy," Zippo replied, creeping along. "They're spread out all over the place."

They reached the top of the stairs. Off to the right lay the doorway through which Jonathan and the skeleton troupe had filed hours before. To the left lay a great hall, open and bright as day. It seemed to Jonathan that he'd come to the end of his sneaking about. There was nothing left but to rush in shouting. It always seemed to come to that. Zippo, however, didn't agree.

"I'll scout it out. Wait here." Zippo stepped into the hall with an air of nonchalance about him. He got about ten feet along when he realized that he was still holding the big iron key in his right hand, the crenelated end of it thrusting through his fingers. He stopped with a gasp, turned, and threw it at Jonathan; the key hit him in the chest, then clanked to the stones below. Jonathan stooped and picked it up, shoving it into his pocket.

Zippo's nonchalant air was dashed entirely. He glanced around him furtively, crouching a bit as if by hunkering down and making himself small he'd be less visible. But there were no shouts of accusation—there was no noise at all. No one was about. Zippo waved his arm like a windmill, and Jonathan, hefting his club, crept out of the shadows. Along with Zippo, he hurried across the hall toward another corridor.

A long stone stairway wound up out of the hall to their right. As they dashed past it, three sharp barks rang out, echoing down the stairwell. Jonathan continued on into the darkness of the next corridor, but there he pulled up short and listened. Once again, he heard barking from upstairs.

"Where's that coming from?" he asked, recognizing Ahab's bark. "Are there cells upstairs?"

"No," Zippo whispered, shaking his head. "All the cells are in the dungeons. There's a laboratory upstairs and a bunch of little cold rooms that haven't anything but ghosts in them. The Dwarf spends half the night wandering through them making conjurations and casting spells."

Jonathan stood thinking for a moment. "A laboratory is it?"

"I'm afraid that's the case."

"Let's have a look at it then," Jonathan said decisively. He turned and headed for the stairs.

"Oh no," Zippo cried. "The Dwarf is sure to be there in the middle of some horrible experiment. He's a vivisectionist. We mustn't go into the laboratory. He'll have no mercy on us!"

Ahab barked again. Jonathan leaped up the stairs two at a time, and Zippo was drawn up after him, both of them winding around and around before emerging onto a landing. Through a dusty window Jonathan had a brief glimpse, as he dashed past, of a distant beach and lines of green, glassy breakers. He became aware just then that his heart was racing along at a gallop and that his breath was *shoosh-*

ing in and out loud enough to alert anyone within earshot that someone had just come dashing up the stairs. Zippo must have been thinking the same thing, for he had pressed both hands over his mouth and was breathing through them in little gasping whistles.

They simmered down a bit as they stood on the landing, but before too many moments had passed Jonathan led on toward a door that stood open a ways. Growling and barking sounded through the door, and for that Jonathan was glad. The noise would help hide the sound of their breathing and their footsteps on the stone floor.

Jonathan hugged the wall and eased along toward the open door. When Ahab was momentarily quiet, Jonathan stopped. He could hear low laughter, the sound of someone chuckling to himself. It seemed to him that the laughter was directed at him and Zippo, that someone, the Dwarf obviously, was watching them sneak along and was about to drop a net over their heads or loose an army of goblins on them. But no goblins appeared. Ahab began growling again and Jonathan crept closer, peering into the laboratory through a crack between the door and the jamb. He was afraid that Ahab would sense his presence and give off his growling, but that didn't happen. Ahab was too busy being angry over having been shoved inside a little cage against the wall.

Ahab's cage was one of many. On either side of him were an opossum and a pig, and above him was the biggest toad Jonathan had ever seen, blinking in a toad's befuddled way. Beneath him were raccoons and badgers and one long-nosed senseless-looking beast that Jonathan couldn't identify—some sort of Balumnian peccary. None of them had half Ahab's spirit.

A long wooden table sat in the center of the room. Above it hung suspended apparatus—coiled devices and tubular complications that led away toward bubbling glass jars steaming and popping along the far wall. Gloomy sunlight filtered in through what must have been a skylight in the roof. Dangling from the ceiling were half a dozen human skeletons in various states of disrepair as if their bones had been systematically removed. On beyond them, against another wall, were immense glass jars filled with a clear greenish fluid. Floating within were bits and pieces of human bodies—hands and feet and internal organs and, in one, a wide-eyed head with black curly hair floating roundabout it. The thing's mouth was open as if it were trying to scream in horror, and it seemed to be looking right at Jonathan through the crack in the door, just as it had looked at him several nights before when it had been thrust up at him by the ghoul rowing the boat through the fog on the Tweet River.

Jonathan realized suddenly that he'd been staring for a long time at the head in the jar. Zippo was tugging on his coat, Ahab was again silent, and Selznak's mocking laughter filled the hallway around them. But still no goblins dashed in; no skeletons lurched out. Instead, as a sort of counterpoint to Selznak's laughter, came a low throaty chuckle—a jolly sort of a laugh, altogether out of place in that room full of horrors. Jonathan peered back in to see Selznak, white-robed and without his familiar hat on, leading poor Squire Myrkle along toward the table in the center of the room.

The Squire had a faraway look in his eye—the look of a man lost in a pleasant dream. If Selznak hadn't been leading him by the wrist, the Squire probably would have simply stopped and stood. He'd clearly been mesmerized and was in a state of passivity. Otherwise he appeared unharmed. He hadn't lost any weight, still looked as if he'd been shoveled into his clothes pyramidally. Jonathan was reminded of Quimby's Pillar of Hyglea and of his calling for an additional bolt of cloth.

Selznak made a grand effort to hoist the Squire onto the table, but nothing came of it. Squire Myrkle stood and looked at him with a dreamy grin. He tried again, pushing on the Squire's shoulders and tugging on his legs, but it was like trying to move a piano. Finally he disappeared from view, leaving the Squire standing there placidly.

Ahab whimpered in his cage, as if he knew that the poor Squire was about to come to harm. Suddenly Jonathan had a fleeting vision of the Squire rowing without a head through the night fog on the Tweet River. He had hefted his cudgel, motioned to Zippo to follow him, and taken one step across the threshold when he heard Selznak's voice.

He stopped, hidden by the door, and edged back out, taking up his vigil. It would be better, doubtless, to lay into the Dwarf once he'd gotten underway on the Squire.

Selznak strode into view waving a half-peeled banana in the Squire's direction. Squire Myrkle took it and munched away at it slowly, sitting down as he did so on the low table. Whereupon Selznak pushed him back, heaved his legs up onto the table, and began fiddling among his instruments, selecting a long curved scalpel and holding it up in the sunlight to have a look at its edge.

The Squire worked his way through the banana and left the peel spread out across his face like a limp squid. Selznak plucked it off and threw it to the floor, then began to probe with his fingers along the Squire's throat. If ever there was a time to rush in shouting and thrashing, this was it.

But Jonathan didn't move. A peculiar voice, just then, issued from somewhere high overhead in the room, a voice that made Selznak look up with a start. It sounded for all the world like someone talking through a speaking trumpet or a long tube, and it said the most peculiar things.

"Stra-a-aw-ber-r-ry pie," came the voice, stretching the words out like a ghost might do if it were setting in to haunt someone. "Choc-o-late fudge! Ro-o-oast goose! Che-e-e-se!" Selznak looked about frantically.

"Who is it!" he shouted. "Who's there! Zippo, if that's you I'll turn you into a scumfish!"

Zippo moaned and clutched Jonathan's elbow. For a moment there was silence. Then, again from overhead came the words "Roly-poly pudding! Peaches and cre-e-e-eam!" Selznak threw his scalpel to the ground and stomped about in a rage, looking up into the ceiling above. Jonathan hunkered down and squinted up into the air, wondering why such things were being uttered and why they sent Selznak into such a rage. He spotted the source of the voice at just about the same time as Selznak did. There, poking out from between iron balusters that supported a railing along an open alcove above, was the open end of a dark cone.

"*Du Bois!*" Selznak shouted, shaking his fist. "You'll pay

for this intrusion. You'll wake up with the head of a duck! I swear it."

But Miles, who was speaking through the end of his conical cap, paid Selznak little heed. "Prime ribs of beef!" he crooned. "Au jus! Yorkshire pudding! Creamed corn and deviled eggs. Hot coffee and cinnamon rolls! Apple pie!" At the mention of apple pie, Squire Myrkle sat up on his table and looked around. Selznak hopped about making a vain effort to stuff cotton into the Squire's ears. "Pay him no mind!" the Dwarf shouted. "I command it! Hocus pocus!" Selznak waved a pocketwatch in front of the Squire's face, frantically trying to put him under again.

Squire Myrkle plucked the pocketwatch from the Dwarf's hand and shoved it away into the pocket of his Quimby coat.

"Veal cutlet!" Miles shouted from above. "Bailey-bob stew! Gumbo! Fried potatoes! Pineapple upside-down cake!"

Selznak gave up his efforts, raced over to a long, apparatus-loaded table, and began working at a vial of white powder. He dipped the head end of a stuffed newt into it, then shaking it to and fro and mumbling, he advanced toward the Squire. Jonathan hadn't any idea what the powder was, but he didn't like the look of it a bit, so he pushed open the door with a slam-bang and jumped into the room yowling and shaking his cudgel.

"Bing!" the Squire cried, heaving himself off his table and standing there woozily looking about him. "The Squire will eat now. The Squire has been promised amazing foods."

Jonathan hadn't any time to discuss food. He dashed across and pulled open Ahab's cage. Free at last, the dog leaped barking toward Selznak whom he very apparently didn't much like. The Dwarf advanced upon him waving the stuffed newt and grinning. Squire Myrkle, catching sight of the plump newt, lumbered that way too, yanking his cap down over his forehead and swinging his arms ponderously.

Jonathan grabbed Ahab by the collar and dragged him back out of the way of the sprinkling dust that hovered in a little cloud before the Dwarf. "Zippo!" Jonathan shouted.

"Zippo!" But Zippo was nowhere about. Jonathan left the Dwarf to the Squire and pulled Ahab out toward the door. He yanked the key out of his pocket, dropped it, scrabbled around for it on the floor, and found it. Then he thrust it into Ahab's mouth, hoping fervently that he wouldn't swallow it. Ahab spit it out and looked at it. "Bring this to the Professor!" Jonathan shouted holding Ahab's nose between his hands and putting the key back into his mouth. "To the Professor!"

Ahab turned and bounded out of the room in a terrible hurry—off, Jonathan hoped, to find Professor Wurzle.

Jonathan turned back toward Selznak and the Squire. Squire Myrkle had wrested the newt from the Dwarf, and he held it by the tail, shaking it in Selznak's direction, laughing all the while. Selznak was making a grand effort to get out his way and to avoid being dusted. It soon became evident why. The Squire suddenly gave off his sprinkling and yawned widely, then slumped to the floor in a heap.

Selznak then turned his attention toward the balcony above, from which the smoke of burning herbs wafted in long, gray searching tendrils. Miles was voicing some sort of chant there, and was peeking over the railing, pointing a conjuring hand in Selznak's direction.

The Dwarf retreated toward his vials and jars and philtres. "Cheeser!" he called, motioning toward Jonathan, who was bent over the heaped Squire. Jonathan looked up at him, but didn't at all like the grin on the Dwarf's face.

"Don't go near him!" Miles shouted from above. "Get away from him!"

Miles gestured wildly with his arm toward the door, knocking two rubbery-looking dried bats off the iron railing and onto the floor below. *"Damn!"* he cried, watching the bats fall. The first, when it hit, burst into flame and lay fizzling there. The second plopped beside it and jellied out into a little pool of black gunk.

"Fire and water!" Selznak cried, rummaging among his devices. "Radical heat and moisture! I'll show you radical heat!" With that he showered Miles with a handful of little balls that burst into flame round the magician's head, one of them landing in his hair. Miles yowled and pulled on his cap as Selznak laughed and pointed at him.

Jonathan wondered for a moment at the antics of the two necromancers, but decided fairly quickly to take Miles' word for it and leave Selznak alone. He hadn't any real desire anyway to have his hair ignited. Instead, he bent over the prostrate Squire, hooked his hands beneath the Squire's shoulders, and heaved, moving him about three-quarters of an inch and very nearly sacrificing his back in the bargain. He heaved again and then again, wishing that Zippo hadn't run out on him. Just as he did, in through the door dashed a wild-eyed Zippo, waving, of all things, the Lumbog globe and shouting, "I've got it! I've got it!"

"Help me with the Squire!" Jonathan didn't care much for the Lumbog globe at the moment. Zippo bent over and tugged on the Squire's arm with his right hand, fumbling the globe with his left.

"Put the bloody thing down," cried Jonathan.

"Don't!" Miles shouted from above.

Zippo looked up to see who in the world it was yelling at him, but what he saw, to his wild dismay, was the leering face of Selznak the Dwarf, whose hand was stretched out toward him. Tattooed on the palm of the Dwarf's hand were three cryptic signs—a pentagram, a star, and a pair of eyes, one of them wide with terror and the other one sly and winking. Zippo looked into Selznak's face, shouted in despair, and flung the globe at him. Then he turned and rushed yowling from the room.

The globe glanced against Selznak's forehead and sent him reeling. If he hadn't been so close, and if the globe hadn't struck him such a sliding blow, the battle would have ended right then.

He staggered into his table of potions, upsetting the jar of white dust into which he had dipped the newt. The jar broke, and a little flurry of powder rose in a cloud. A cage full of birds—sparrows or finches or something—fell beside it and broke open, liberating a score of little birds, which flew out through the dust cloud, got about six or eight feet farther, then began dropping one by one. Some few of them managed to fly almost to the ceiling before plummeting to the stones.

Jonathan, fearful of the drifting cloud that had laid the Squire and the birds low, threw all his effort into dragging his friend toward the door. Squire Myrkle slid inch by inch across the smooth stones until Jonathan could drag him no more.

Selznak had recovered a bit and was shrieking with rage to have discovered that not only had his vial of sleeping powders been dashed to bits, but that the cloud of dust it had become had wafted across and half-hidden the globe where it lay near the table.

Miles was hanging out over the balcony, waving at the globe and shouting spells. The globe seemed to shake and vibrate and to turn once about its circumference, inching toward where Jonathan stood next to the snoring Squire. Selznak shouted spells on his own, and the globe teetered the other way. Then it spun around like a top for a bit, and once again crept toward Jonathan.

Storming across the room and yanking a big leather bellows from its hook on the wall, Selznak began puffing jets of wind at the powder that hung about the globe. Clouds of it whirled and rose, and the stuff thinned and thinned and lost itself, finally, in the air. The globe began to pick up speed and to roll in earnest toward Jonathan, who sprang toward it, only to be slammed on the forehead with the end of the bellows and find himself sitting on the floor. Selznak scooped up the globe and scurried back to his potions.

A trickle of blood ran down across Jonathan's brow and into his eyes. He wiped at it with the sleeve of his coat. When more dripped down he wiped at it again, then pulled his bandana from his pocket and tied it around the cut.

Selznak stood chortling over the globe. It seemed quite likely to Jonathan that the Dwarf would make use of the thing—would open a magical door and step through it and leave the lot of them behind. In fact, he half-hoped that such would be the case. Selznak, apparently, hadn't any such plan. Instead, he set about casting spells at Miles, who himself was busy on the balcony above.

Suddenly a shouting and a tumult in the hallway was followed by a furious barking on the stairs. Gump and Bufo raced in followed by Professor Wurzle and Ahab— all of them bent upon throwing themselves into the fray. There wasn't, however, much of a fray. Selznak was furiously mixing dried leaves and smoking powders and was shouting chants and wailing. Meanwhile Miles dumped shimmering glitter off the balcony, and the stuff floated down around the Dwarf, who began to sneeze uncontrollably. Then, while Jonathan and his companions watched in wonder, the little twirls of hair over each of the Dwarf's ears fell out onto the ground, leaving him as bald as the Lumbog globe. Selznak ran across the room and pulled his hat from its hook, smashing it over his head in a gesture of wild vanity. Bufo laughed out loud to see the Dwarf embarrassed so, and Selznak, in response, threw a handful of fireballs at him, one of which set Bufo's shirt afire. Gump and the Professor raced over and pounded it out.

It was then that Gump caught sight of Zippo's mechanical fish, shoved back into a far corner of the laboratory. "Look!" he shouted, pointing at it. Jonathan wasn't sure what it was that Gump intended, but Bufo apparently hadn't any doubts, for he followed Gump around behind it, and the two of them tugged levers and yanked cranks. The mechanical fish began rocking and whistling and rotating back and forth on its moorings.

A flood of helium buds poured forth—thousands and thousands of them—each one floating toward the ceiling. One by one they began to burst, like popcorn just heating up, and then in a rush of exotic color, dozens, then scores, then hundreds blossomed—giant iris and roses and magnolia blossoms and weird purple antherium the size of buckets. New buds poured from the mouth of the machine. Gump and Bufo were highly satisfied with their achievement, but Miles, swatting at the thickening mass of airborne flowers, wasn't half so thrilled. The flying flowers began to crowd in upon him there on his balcony, and within a minute and a half of the fish having set in, Miles was entirely obscured by the blooms. Jonathan could hear him shouting there, although his shouts were almost drowned out by Selznak's laughter. He couldn't, however, see Miles at all. He couldn't even see the balcony.

Squire Myrkle awoke just then and sat up, shaking the bleariness out of his eyes. He squinted up at the flower-laden ceiling above him—a ceiling that was rapidly dropping toward them as fresh buds bloomed—and he clapped his hands in astonished wonder. He pointed aloft, then

turned to Jonathan. "Vegetation. Very curious vegetation."
He nodded sagely, pursing his lips.

The Professor sprang across, and he himself began
throwing levers and such in an effort to stem the flow of
the buds. The first of the blooms withered even as he did
so, and the air was suddenly alive with the dark little deflated worms, the remnants of the helium flowers. The flow
of fresh buds ceased, either because of the Professor's
efforts or because the device had run out. The last of the
buds popped open as the sky continued to rain withered
bits of debris, perplexing the Squire no end.

Selznak hadn't been idle. Before him on his table
bubbled a small pot into which he dropped odds and ends:
a handful of tiny toads, scraps of his hair that he'd re-
trieved from the floor, and no end of various bird beaks.
The mixture spluttered and boiled and splashed, and just
as Miles fought his way clear of the last hovering buds—
his ivory head sparking and his robes whirling as if caught
up in some mystical cosmic wind—Selznak flung both arms
over his head and let out a terrifying shriek. The bubbling
stuff in the pot arced out and upward, spraying the balcony
on which Miles stood. There was the sound of splitting
rock, and the floor beneath them heaved as if tossed by an
earthquake.

Jonathan sat down hard on the stones and rolled into
the Squire. Zippo's fish toppled over onto Gump, who was
knocked sprawling into the Professor. Above the shout
and clatter came the sound of cracking stone. Miles' balcony, still wreathed in helium blossoms, cracked, then split
asunder, and Miles fell shouting through a tumble of debris
and floating flowers onto the cages of animals below.

Ahab, barking, dashed across toward the odious Selznak,
who whirled to meet him, spraying the room with his little
flaming balls. Ahab yipped and danced back out of the way
while Selznak lifted the cauldron of bubbling cataplasm
from the tabletop and carried it toward the door. The Professor sprang up and went for him, but Selznak menaced
him with the stuff, still boiling and popping and bubbling
up over the side.

Gump moaned a bit about then, having been caught,
finally, by the tumbling fish. He pushed at the thing as it

lay there atop his legs. Professor Wurzle stepped back alongside Jonathan to let Selznak pass, and the Dwarf inched out of the room, threatening them all with the muck in the pot. Once through the door he turned, laughed aloud, and drank several big gulps of the bubbling mixture, thereafter pitching the rest onto the floor and running off down the hall. Squire Myrkle poked at the sorry-looking frogs and bird beaks that had been part of the brew.

"The Squire would like some of this soup," he said, lifting a frog up by a rear leg and peering at it. "Frog gumbo, I believe it is. Is that correct?" When he didn't get an answer from the thing he tossed it back onto the floor and lumbered across to pull the fish from atop Gump.

Professor Wurzle bent over the fallen Miles. "He's alive," he said, listening at his chest.

It struck Jonathan just then that the Professor was far more capable than he when it came to administering first-aid, and that Selznak, after all of Miles' effort, had made off with the globe—the globe that would enable him to loose all his horrors onto the High Valley. So Jonathan without a word grabbed up his club and rushed out into the hallway. By then, of course, there was no sign of the fleeing Selznak; there was only the slamming of a distant door somewhere off down the hall. Jonathan raced along toward it.

Chapter 23

Pursuit

JONATHAN didn't bother with the first three doors he passed. The slam he'd heard had sounded from farther off. After the hall took a perpendicular turning, however, it ended some twenty-five feet farther along at one last door, a door that proved to be unlocked. He didn't just throw it open and pop in. Instead he peeked in at the keyhole first to see if he could make out anything. But nothing was visible. It was almost dark aside from a reddish sort of glow —just a strip of it against the floor across the room—as if light were shining beneath another door. Very slowly he turned the knob, listening to it creak around against the iron plate. The noise sounded to him like the screeching of a parrot, but it probably wasn't that loud—no louder, quite likely, than the drumming of his heart. He heard a faint click as the latch scraped off the striker and the door edged inward, almost as if it were anxious to open and let him in. He crept into the room, hunched over, stepping slowly and softly as if he were walking on new grass. Just when he turned and began to shove the door shut behind him, he felt a cold, wet thing press against his leg.

He leaped forward, flailing with his arms, thinking of snakes and of great, dark fish and of creeping blue squids at the bottom of pits. He very nearly shouted aloud, but didn't. Then he raised his cudgel and whirled around wildly to find himself face to face with old Ahab, who had, it seemed, followed him along the corridor. Ahab stood blinking at him, head cocked to one side and one eye winking as if he were wondering what sort of caper Jonathan was cutting this time.

"*Shh!*" Jonathan whispered, putting his finger to his lips. But of course Ahab hadn't said anything. Jonathan found that he was very glad to see him, not only because he welcomed the company, but because Ahab had a nose for danger as well as a sharp ear. If he could locate the Professor and deliver the key to the cells to him, then it was quite likely that he could find Selznak too. Jonathan wondered at himself for not having asked Ahab along in the first place, and decided that he'd better slow down a bit and think things through.

There wasn't much time to think right then, though, since Selznak probably wasn't standing about, but was hurrying along on some mission of deviltry. So Jonathan shut the door behind him, plunging the empty room into darkness. He stretched his eyes wide just from instinct, as if by yanking his lids back he'd be able to see in the dark. In a moment he could, for although the dim light shining in under the far door illuminated the room only very faintly, there was enough of it so that he hadn't any fear of running into a chair or stepping off into a pit.

The second door was also unlocked. He opened it just a crack and peered through. There was a sizeable room beyond, lit fairly thoroughly. The shadows and lights in the room weren't still, but jumped a bit and danced and traded places as if their source was a dozen or so candles sitting in a draft.

It was entirely possible that Selznak himself was in the room; Jonathan couldn't say. So he threw caution out the window and pushed the door entirely open. Ahab slid past him, sniffing, the fur along his back standing up in a little line. The light was indeed thrown by candles—candles thrust into three candlebras that sat on a heavy bare table along one wall. The base of each, incredibly, was a stuffed goat's head. One had wide, staring eyes as if it had seen something so terrible that it had died frozen in mortal horror. The second's eyes were closed, but not peacefully so—heavy stitches had been sewn through its lids and down into its cheeks. The third goat had no eyes at all; just gaping black sockets. Jonathan could feel their presence in the room, a thick, dusky evil as if the room were a tomb. Why the candles were lit in an otherwise empty room he had no idea, nor did he have any desire to find out. He was halfway across to the far door when he noticed that a pentagram, a copy of the one tattooed on Selznak's palm, was painted on the floor in some dark liquid. His imagination leaped immediately to the conclusion that it was painted in blood, and he suddenly felt weak and sick. He rushed across and threw open the next door, heedless of what lay beyond.

As it happened, nothing did. Just another dark room—a room so utterly dark that he at first considered going back after one of the candles. But the idea of reentering the room with the goat heads was in itself so odious to him that he knew he couldn't. He latched onto Ahab's collar and followed him across the floor, groping along until they encountered the far wall and what felt very much like the wooden panels of yet another door.

It seemed to him that he and Ahab weren't alone in the darkness there—that something else waited in the room, watching him; something that could see him clearly, that could reach out and latch onto his arm with long stiff fingers and stare into his face with little red eyes; some abomination that could only exist in utter darkness. He felt a cold draft on the back of his neck—a clammy cold like the breath of a ghoul—and he heard the sound of rustling off in the corner, the soft *swish-swish-swish* of something stirring, dragging itself, perhaps, across the smooth stone floor.

Jonathan dropped his club and grabbed Ahab's collar with his left hand. With his right he searched for a knob, sliding his fingers up and down the door, pushing at it, compelled by the urge to pound at it, but knowing that whatever lay on the other side would hardly be hospitable enough to let him in. He realized that Ahab was growling, twisting about, looking behind him; then he heard what sounded like the scrape of steel against stone, or perhaps the scratching of long, bent talons. He turned toward the noise, toward the *swish-scrape* that came from the far corner, and saw two glints of light—a pair of glowing eyes watching him. They shut and then opened again—small and close together like the eyes of a pig—and a soft slobbering and sucking noise took the place of the scraping.

Grabbing up his club, Jonathan pounded on the door. He'd much rather discuss pleasantries with Selznak himself than face whatever thing it was that crouched there swishing and slobbering in the corner. He whacked on the door with his club, smashed against it, and each blow echoed out, *boom-boom-boom*, like goblin drums in the deep wood.

Suddenly the door was thrown open. Beyond the doorway, hunched and dusty in the dim light, grinning vacantly at him through sightless eyes, stood the old witch, dressed in her gray lace and ancient black robes. She gestured at him, curling her finger, inviting him into the room just as she had invited him onto her porch at the shanty in the swamp weeks before. And still there was a swishing and slobbering behind him, closer now—something dragging toward him, painfully slowly, but with an evil and insatiable determination. He needed time to think, but his mind was a muddle of terror and indecision.

Ahab's, however, wasn't. He leaped ahead toward the old woman, teeth bared, snarling; he was a dog that had come to the end of his rope—would brook no more nonsense. Instantly, in the blink of an eye, the old woman was gone. Ahab rushed right through the spot where she'd been, sliding to a stop. The sound of cackling laughter filled the room behind Jonathan, and he whirled with an upraised club, ready to pound something into jelly. There, heaped on the stones in the middle of the room, just barely visible in the dim light that shone through the door, lay the ragged, decayed remnant of a human being. Tatters of black cloth and lace partially covered it. One bony arm thrust out and scrabbled at the floor, long, broken nails making the scratching sound Jonathan had heard in the dark. A face, little more than a skull, stared up at him, and its mouth worked and slobbered as if it were trying to speak, to implore his aid, to whisper a secret.

Jonathan couldn't tear his eyes from the detestable thing. He watched as it wavered and shimmered for a moment, as had the goblin jewels in the treasure chests. As he watched it metamorphosed into the girl from the house in the woods, curled up as if asleep on the floor. Then, after the space of half a minute, it shimmered and faded and was gone altogether. Nothing was left but the echoing ring of dry laughter that hung in the air like dust.

Ahab looked up at Jonathan as if expecting an explanation. Jonathan didn't have one. Once again he'd gone out on the hunt and found that it was himself who was pursued. The idea of chasing Selznak appeared suddenly ludicrous to him, and he made up his mind to retrace his steps and find the Professor and the rest. Then they'd search for Escargot, if he hadn't already been released, and together they'd find the Dwarf and deal with him. The idea was appealing. He'd storm back through the room with the pentagram and reduce the goats heads to powder. He was determined. He stepped across, his club over his shoulder, and found that the door had been locked. He twisted and kicked it but nothing happened. He had no choice, finally, but to go on.

In the room where the witch had stood was a row of long windows with a view of the dark forest beyond. Dusty, cobwebby furniture sat about as if it had been waiting for a hundred years or so for someone to come along and make use of it. One wall was ornately paneled with old, wormy, dark wood. At the far end an enormous stuffed chair stood beside a bookcase filled with dark, ancient books. One lay open on a low table beneath a gas lamp. Jonathan felt the base of the lamp and jerked his hand back in surprise at the heat. It must have been burning even while he and Ahab searched in the dark room for a door.

There didn't seem to be any time for hesitation. The Dwarf might well just be slinking away, perhaps having looked up some grim, arcane bit of evil magic. Jonathan pulled the door open and found another hallway, a short corridor that ended at a window twenty feet or so farther on. Two iron-studded doors fronted it on the left. It had to have been through one of these doors that the Dwarf had fled. The latch on the first door turned easily, and Jonathan pushed into a room that at first seemed entirely bare. But as light from the corridor filtered in and chased off some of the gloom, he could see that although the room was indeed bare of furniture, it wasn't bare in any other sense. The stone walls, windowless on all sides, were intricately carved. Strange runes and symbols covered the walls: peculiar twisted faces, sweeping oak trees out of which sailed great flights of bats and which half hid a thousand grinning goblins, numberless indistinguishable carvings muted in shadow.

Jonathan had to satisfy himself that there were no other exits. He intended only to have a quick look about then leave, off to investigate the second room. He found, however, that doing so wasn't quite as easy as that. The carvings seemed somehow to contain countless mysteries. As he stared at them, his eyes picking out first one then another and then another of their secrets, he felt as if he were staring into a prodigiously deep and very clear tide-pool, a pool that ran off into the depths of the sea—that *was* the sea—and that hid great mysteries among waving eel grass and scuttling crabs and slowly creeping snails. He felt as if he were tumbling forward into a dream chasm, spinning away into the heart of that mystery, engulfed by it.

Then he felt a tugging on his leg, and there was old Ahab, not half as concerned with mysteries as was Jonathan and wanting nothing more than to be off. Jonathan saw, as he turned to leave, a pair of eyes carved dead center in the wall opposite the door, staring at him—the same sort of eyes, strangely, that had been tattooed onto Selznak's hand. They seemed more than mere carvings, as if they were watching him, studying him. When one of the eyes winked slowly, then sprang open again, Jonathan dashed out into the hallway, Ahab at his heels. He was possessed by the certainty, or the hope at least, that he'd stood about in the weird room too long and that his eyes, befuddled by the carvings, had begun to play tricks on him.

He hadn't any real desire to explore the final room, both because he suspected that it too would be filled with strange magic and because Selznak had undoubtedly entered it. Jonathan knew that he must have come by then to the rear of the castle. There could be no more rooms, no other hallways. Surely Selznak was behind the very door he found himself reaching for.

He raised his club, set his feet, threw open the last door, and was confronted with an empty room, a room which, like the last, had no second door. It was a high, domed room with a single great window in the top of the dome. Pointing out through the glass was a tremendous brass telescope. The walls all around were painted with moons and ringed planets and great twirling washes of stars. There was nothing strange or evil here—no winking faces or rotting heads, and no Selznak the Dwarf, either. Jonathan shut the door and walked back down the hall into the room with the books and the warm gas lamp. It struck him as impossible that the witch had been thumbing through books in Selznak's library. He hadn't any idea how witches passed their time, but he knew, somehow, that it wasn't in casual reading. It must have been the Dwarf who had lit the lamp. If he hadn't gone along to either of the far rooms, nor had returned the way he'd come, then he'd either gone out the window or exited through a door Jonathan couldn't see, a hidden door.

Selznak had never struck Jonathan as the sort who climbed in and out of windows. He never bothered with stealth, was too conceited for it. "Where's the Dwarf?" Jonathan whispered to Ahab, understanding, of course, that Ahab mightn't understand a word of it. "Find Selznak!" he whispered.

Along with the sniffing Ahab, he went poking about at the old wormy panels that covered the wall next to the bookcase. He pushed on each and felt along edges for latches or buttons. He rapped here and there, supposing that he might hear some telltale hollow plunking. But nothing came of it.

Ahab seemed far more interested in the bookcase. He stood before it growling a bit, like a dog debating with himself over which book he wanted to read next. Jonathan joined him, knowing that while Ahab seemed to have a natural affinity for books and had even gone as far as to have eaten the covers off a few in his younger days, he'd never been known to read any. His interest couldn't be intellectual.

Jonathan tugged on one wall of the case, but it seemed altogether solid. Then he pushed and pulled and opened the leaded doors. The books inside were very neatly ordered. In fact, the case was packed with them, the only gap being just wide enough to take the book that lay open on the table. As he looked at the gap and pondered, an idea popped into his head. He picked up the book and slid it back into its niche. There was the snapping sound of a latch releasing, the faint groaning of a spring, and the entire bookcase swung out on recessed hinges, nearly knocking Jonathan on the nose. He and Ahab slid through, and the bookcase swung shut with a click.

They found themselves in a small dim corridor, about as wide as the bookcase. It led off into the darkness behind the rooms they'd been exploring. Jonathan set out after Ahab, groping for a ways down the dark tunnel. Thirty or forty steps along he came to a stairway, illuminated by light that shone through a vent of sorts in the wall of an adjacent room. He followed the stairs up and around and along another corridor, hurrying after Ahab and finding no other doors to interrupt his pursuit of the Dwarf.

His steps echoed faintly off the stones, but that was something that couldn't be avoided unless he took his shoes off and sneaked along in his stocking feet. Somehow that didn't appeal to him. He was almost to a second stairway when he heard voices through a vent: a low demanding voice and another, higher and pleading.

"I saw you steal it and run off," the low voice said. "Don't deny it. Do you want more of this?"

The high voice stuttered and gasped. "No, no! I took it. I admit I took it. I wanted to give it to, to what's-his-name. The one with the dog."

"You're a liar!" the low voice growled, and there followed another hoot of pain. "You're one of Selznak's filthy cohorts. A magician! Hah! A juggler is more like it. A circus clown. A geek. An entertainer of goblins and idiots!"

Jonathan realized with a start that the high voice belonged to poor Zippo, who was being tormented by someone who very badly wanted the globe. A third voice piped in about then, farther off than the first two. "Are you still in there, Grandpa?" it said.

"That's right," the low voice said cheerfully. "Mr. Zippo and I are doing business. You just hold on. Mr. Zippo is a powerfully slow talker, but I'm speeding him along a bit now." It was Escargot doing the speeding, bartering with Zippo for the globe.

"My father will cook your goose!" Zippo warned. "When he finds out you're here, he'll roast you over a fire. He's on his way now with an army!"

"An army! Your father wears pink shirts," Escargot said ungraciously. "He doesn't care a bit about you. And even if he did, so what? Stealing that barge of strawberries from him was like snatching his hat. I would have sent my grandson to do it but I don't want him involved in such triflings. I, however, haven't any scruples left."

Zippo shouted once, as if his arm had been twisted. "I haven't got it! Sikorsky has it. Selznak. Whatever his name is. He took it from me. I swear it!"

There was silence for a moment. Then Escargot exploded. "Damn!" A door slammed and footsteps died away. Jonathan winced once, thinking about poor Zippo. It was too bad that Escargot assumed Zippo to be Selznak's minion. It was hardly a fair world, it seemed to Jonathan. He hurried up the stairs toward what must have been the upper recesses of the tower. The stairs wound around and around tiresomely and ended abruptly on a bit of a landing and at another bookcase, identical to the one below— containing, in fact, what might easily have been the same books. Above the rows of books light shone through the slats of another vent, and along with the light came the sounds of far-off shouts and what sounded strangely like the clanging of steel on steel, of swordplay, possibly. Mixed in among it all was a low monotonous chanting and the smell of burning camphor and bay leaves.

Chapter 24

On the Meadow

❧

JONATHAN pushed a row of books to the rear of a shelf and climbed up, testing his weight for a moment before clambering farther. Atop the third shelf he was able to peer through the grillwork of the vent into the room beyond.

It was a circular room, the room of a tower, with two great windows in it that Jonathan assumed faced the sea. The only thing he could see through them, however, was a patch of blue sky and the tail end of cloud fluff somewhere off over the ocean. In front of the windows, looking down onto the meadows below, stood Selznak the Dwarf. On a rickety table beside him smoked a pottery jar full of leaves. The Dwarf chanted over the jar, waving a hand at it and swirling smoke from the mouth of the jar up into the air in little wavy clouds.

Next to the jar sat the Lumbog globe, catching the rays of afternoon sun through the window. The globe glowed in a dozen colors, seeming to race with light one moment, then fade and darken the next, almost as if it were slowly breathing there atop the table, waiting for Selznak to make use of it.

A sudden trumpet blast echoed in from beyond the windows along with the sound of clattering hooves, then another trumpet blast and shouts. Almost at the same moment as the second sounding of the trumpet came a furious pounding on the oaken door of the circular room. Selznak didn't seem to pay it any mind, he simply chanted a bit louder over the herbs as he pounded two or three times on the stone floor with his staff, scattering sparks at each thump.

The smoke from the jar swirled thicker and spun slowly toward the ceiling, seeming to coagulate and compress. The shape of shoulders formed and then the rough semblance of a head, a head with wide empty eyes and an open mouth. Then the smoke undulated and dispersed, and Selznak dusted the jar with powders and struck the floor and chanted a bit louder. Again the smoke billowed. For a brief moment a wind blew through the room, ruffling Jonathan's hair through the vents—a hot wind like the wind off a desert. Selznak's robes swirled and danced, and he shaded his eyes with his free hand. The smoke hovered above its jar, unaffected by the wind, and it swirled and grew dense. The face apeared again, hooded, its eyes glowing this time like embers in a burned-down fire. Its mouth worked spasmodically, and it looked around itself as if anxious to be freed from its smoky bonds.

Just then a smashing against the door made it shudder on its hinges. Then came another smashing—the sound of someone thudding against the oak with a battering ram. The face in the smoke paled, then reappeared.

A shout outside the door—the Professor's voice. "Again!" he shouted. "Here by the latch!" Then there was another tremendous slam. Chips of stone flew off the wall and the door shuddered and seemed to push in just a bit.

Selznak picked the globe up from the table, dusting the jar one last time with his powders. He held the globe up in the rays of the sun and stared into it, gathering his robes about him and pushing his hat down over the top of his head.

Jonathan leaped from the bookcase—nearly squashing Ahab, who stood waiting below—and began yanking out books. He couldn't remember if the removed book in the case below had been on the fourth or the fifth shelf, so he pulled books as fast as he could, casting them behind him onto the stones.

The sound of the pounding against the door continued, and Jonathan could hear the slow splintering of wood. He hadn't any idea what sort of creature it was that Selznak was conjuring, but he was quite certain it was something that the Professor and whoever else was breaking through the door wouldn't want to see. He was also certain that the demon was about all they *would* see, as Selznak would be long gone by then from the land of Balumnia.

He jerked another book out and heard the click and screech of the latching mechanism. The bookcase turned slowly in on its hinge, and Jonathan stood ready to leap through the widening gap. Ahab had the same idea. He'd been cheated of the witch an hour before, and so he stood poised there, growling at the growing line of light, determined not to be cheated again.

Ahab dashed through, Jonathan squeezing along behind and expecting to be whacked in the head with Selznak's staff or turned to paste by a demon. Selznak shouted. Ahab barked. The door shivered under another blow and smashed in another inch before jamming to a stop. Jonathan leaped at Selznak, and the two of them went over in a heap of flailing arms and legs. Ahab raced around, alternately biting at the Dwarf and leaping at the smoky demon. Jonathan heard the crack of the Lumbog globe as it hit the floor and rolled. Selznak pushed at him and fought and kicked and then pulled his hat over Jonathan's face.

A sudden crash behind them was not the door being broken open, but rather the wooden table hitting the floor. The pottery jar shattered, spewing burning leaves onto Jonathan's leg. The hot wind he'd felt through the grate whirled like a dust devil, and a thick, acrid stench filled the room, then just as quickly was gone. Jonathan yanked away the hat, lunged across and grabbed the globe from Selznak's clutching hand, and pitched it through the window in a shower of breaking glass.

Just then the door crashed open, and in rushed the Professor and Escargot followed by Dooly, Gump, Bufo, and the Squire. Bufo shouted, "Get him, Squire!" Squire Myrkle piled on top of the spluttering Selznak and sat on his chest, leering into his face. He pulled the Dwarf's stuffed newt from his coat and waved it at him. "Lizard, wizard, pickle-gizzard," he chanted, and squeezed on the newt, puffing a little cloud of white powder into the Dwarf's face, sending him into a paroxysm of wild rage.

Escargot shook Jonathan by the shoulder. "Where is it?"

he asked, half under his breath as if not wanting the Professor to hear. Jonathan nodded toward the window where twisted and broken lead hung with shards of glass. Escargot dashed from the room towing Dooly along behind. Selznak slept peacefully on the floor, looking for all the world as if he'd put his face in a flour bin.

Trumpets blew again outside, prompting everyone to rush over to the window. A battle raged below. Goblins raced back and forth, pursued, Jonathan guessed, by the troops of Cap'n Binky and the Strawberry Baron. And there, sure enough, mounted on a white horse and wearing an enormous cocked hat with a pink plume in it, sat the Baron in his ruffled shirt, shouting and pointing and spurring off into the trees after a little party of goblins.

"I'm hungry," the Squire announced ponderously, squinting out the window at the fray. "We'll eat something."

"Good idea," Bufo said. "What shall we have?"

The Squire held the stuffed newt up and gave it a look. "This isn't a cheese?" he asked in a voice filled with the hope that Bufo would disagree.

"No," Bufo confirmed. "It's not a cheese. We'll find a cheese."

But the Squire turned the newt in his hand as if suspecting that from another angle, from beneath perhaps, it might turn out to be a cheese after all.

Selznak stirred on the floor, so the Squire wandered over to him and squeezed the newt into his face again, perching the thing thereafter across his nose and forehead.

"That's the Strawberry Baron," Gump reported, nodding down toward where the Baron had reappeared on his horse.

"Zippo's father," Jonathan told him.

The Professor gave him an astonished look. "No?" he said.

"For a fact. Zippo told me so himself."

The Squire seemed skeptical. "That man is a strawberry?"

Bufo pulled the Squire away from the window. "No, he's not," Bufo explained. "He owns all the strawberries in this part of the world. Tons and tons of them."

"Is that enough?" the Squire asked.

"Why," Bufo said, "I suppose it is. I don't really know. It mightn't be. Let's find the kitchen."

With that Bufo and the Squire and Gump and, of course, Ahab, who was alerted to the significance of kitchens, went off down the stairs. Below, the battle was running down. Half the men stood about with no goblins at all to chase. Escargot and Dooly appeared, waving at several soldiers nearby and acting altogether nonchalant, as if they'd just dealt fairly handily with a few goblins themselves. Escargot went poking through the weeds, looking up toward the window a couple of times in order to figure out where the globe was likely to have landed. He stooped after a moment, picked it up, gave the two of them above in the window the high sign, and strolled off down the path toward the sea.

Dooly hesitated for a moment, said something to Escargot, and pointed back up toward the window. But Escargot didn't wait; he just hurried on, and Dooly, looking once or twice behind him, stepped along lively to keep up.

"How is Miles?" Jonathan asked abruptly.

"Not well," the Professor replied. "He'll live, but he won't be traveling much for a bit. Not for a good bit. What's Escargot up to here? He hasn't got to run off with the globe. None of us want it."

"He's more concerned with the Strawberry Baron, I suppose. Something having to do with stealing a barge of strawberries. I overheard Zippo mention it."

"He's taking off, then!" the Professor yelled. "He's off without us. Scoundrel!"

The Strawberry Baron by then had dismounted and was walking back and forth before a crowd of captured goblins, whacking his riding crop into the palm of his hand, shouting at them. He seemed to see Escargot's receding form at just about the same time that the Professor began hollering at him through the broken window. The Baron pointed at Escargot, asked something of a man beside him, pointed again, and, with one hand smashing down the hat atop his head, went running off down the rocky meadow in pursuit, calling orders over his shoulder.

"Your horse!" the Professor shouted. "Ride after them!"

Then he turned to Jonathan. "The man's a fool. He'll never catch them."

"Likely not," Jonathan agreed, secretly hoping for that very thing. "Let's go down to see them off."

On the way downstairs they ran into Gump, Bufo, and the Squire, who had, quite clearly, found the kitchen. "Have a look at Miles," the Professor told Bufo as he and Jonathan trotted past. They dashed out across the meadow and down toward the beach. Before they were halfway there, however, they could see that the chase had ended. The Strawberry Baron and four of his soldiers stood atop the rocks watching Escargot and Dooly paddle away through a small swell in the direction of the submarine some hundred yards off shore. Since no other boats offered themselves, there could be no further pursuit.

In the space of a few minutes, the two clambered aboard the submarine, set the canoe adrift, and disappeared into the hold. Whirring and splashing noises reached Jonathan and the Professor as they stood near the others, watching lights blink on behind the portholes and water *sploosh* out from various apertures along the side. The undersea device shuddered once, let out a sigh like a teakettle might that had a broken whistle, and sank beneath the swell.

"Who are *you*, then?" the Strawberry Baron asked suddenly in a voice that made it clear he'd stand no foolery. "Friends of this thief?"

The Professor laughed out loud. "No," he said, "we're not. I am Artemis Wurzle and this is Jonathan Bing. We're acquaintances, in fact, of Cap'n Binky, and we've subdued the dwarf you know as Sikorsky. He's in the tower there, yonder, doused with a sleeping potion."

The Strawberry Baron sent his four companions away at a run toward the tower.

"If you please, sir," Jonathan said very diplomatically, "I'd like to say a few words on behalf of your son."

The Baron tossed his head theatrically, flouncing the pink ruffles along his shirtfront. "I have no son," he said. "My son is lost to me."

Jonathan wasn't about to be impressed by his theatricality, and was tempted to tell him so. But for Zippo's sake he went on politely. "That's just the point. If it weren't for

Zippo, for your son, that is, we—none of us—would be alive. It was your son who set us free."

The Strawberry Baron looked askance at him. "He's a rascal, sir. A brigand. A seeker after fame."

"He was young," Jonathan said. "He quite simply made some mistakes. You don't know this Dwarf. He held your son in thrall. He had great power, could make people do as he pleased. It was Leopold, in the end, who subdued him. Shook sleeping powders in his face. And he tried to capture Escargot too. They fought, sir, but the old man and his grandson locked Leopold into a room and fled."

"Is this true?" the Baron asked.

"Why would I lie about such things?" Jonathan said, knowing full well why he'd lie about such things. It seemed to him that given his past conversations with Zippo, another lie or two could go a long way toward making things right. Jonathan put on his own theatrical face, a face filled to overflowing with seriousness and sympathy. "Have you heard, sir," he said to the Strawberry Baron, "the story of the prodigal son?"

"What son?" the Baron asked impatiently. "Polliwog? I don't care about his son. I care about my own. Where is he, do you say?"

"In the castle," Jonathan replied, and he and the Professor headed back toward Selznak's castle in the wake of the Strawberry Baron. Trumpet blasts sounded from deep in the woods, the sound of Cap'n Binky's forces on the hunt, routing out goblins, chasing down ghouls. "They'd best be out of the woods by nightfall," the Professor said to Jonathan as they hurried along.

Cap'n Binky must have had pretty much the same idea, for within a couple of hours there were no more trumpet blasts. The soldiers set up camp on the meadow, on orders from the Strawberry Baron not to enter the castle. They raided Selznak's larder first, however, and cooked up a tremendous meal under the watchful eye of the Squire, who insisted upon sampling everything to see if it were poisoned or spoiled. None of it was.

Zippo and his father were soon reunited, and during the evening Jonathan coached Zippo about his alleged heroics. The following morning they broke camp and trekked away up the coast road, Selznak trussed up and stuffed into a sack in the back of a cart. At the crossroads, Cap'n Binky, the Strawberry Baron, Zippo, and their troops turned away inland, upriver toward the town of Grover where they'd cross the river on the ferry. They gave Jonathan and his company three ponies and a sledge on which to haul Miles. The Professor concluded that Miles had broken a leg in the fall, as well as getting knocked about a good bit. He could do little but lie on the sledge and rest.

So in midafternoon that day, the party tramped wearily along. Jonathan tried to buck himself up by reminding himself that the lot of them had quite succeeded in their plans. Selznak was overcome, was to be hung, in fact, at Grover. Squire Myrkle was saved, and was, as far as Jonathan could see, none the worse for wear. There he sat, atop one of the three ponies, having a go at two loaves of bread he'd already chewed holes in and shoved up over either wrist. At intervals he'd pluck chunks off and scatter them on the road in order to feed a collection of birds that followed them along, waiting for that very occurrence. Bufo and Gump were busily and secretly making up an ending for their poem, now that the Squire wasn't lost any more. All in all then, Jonathan thought, he should be thanking his lucky stars, as it were. But he didn't feel at all like doing so. He felt like sitting down in a slump with his head in his hands. He liked the city of Landsend well enough, but he didn't half like the idea of sitting about there waiting to leave. More than anything he wanted to be home, or at least to be back in his own familiar world. But the world of Twombly Town and the High Valley was farther away than ever, now that Escargot had flown and Miles was in no shape to travel. By the time Miles was well—in the six or eight weeks it would take for his leg to mend—who could say where the closest portal would be? They might well have to sail a thousand miles up the Tweet or across the ocean to find it. He wondered if Ahab could understand their plight. It didn't seem so. He stuck fairly close to the bird troupe so as to get his share of the Squire's leavings. Somewhere, however, Jonathan concluded, there was still a part of Ahab that missed walking in the woods with Talbot and missed chasing bugs out among the strawberry vines.

The Professor didn't share Jonathan's maudlin humor. "Abandoned us, did he!"

"Well," Jonathan said, still not wanting to think ill of Escargot, "he feared for his life. He hadn't any choice in the matter."

"*Choice!* I'll tell you about choice." The Professor shook a finger in Jonathan's direction to illustrate his discussion of choice. "He *could* have chosen to leave us the globe, couldn't he? We'd be out of here by now if he had. *He* didn't need the globe, not to leave Balumnia anyway. He wanted it so that he could go thieving back and forth; that's it in a nut. Greed is what we're talking about here. He sold us out, that's what. And if it weren't for us, he'd have no bloody globe. He'd have half a useless treasure map and he'd still be a seaweed merchant."

Jonathan protested a bit, but the Professor's assessment, sadly, seemed to be pretty much the case. That bothered him almost as much as their not being able to find a way out of Balumnia.

It was just about dinner time when the company found itself winding round the long bend that led to the foot of the last, or perhaps the first, of the Thirteen Bridges. Gump and Bufo announced that they'd completed their poem, that the unfinished symphony had found a final movement. "Poor Squire Found," recited Gump in ponderous tones, "by Bufo Morinus and Gump Ooze of the territory, poor homeless wretches, cast away on Balumnian shores!"

The Squire clapped wildly at Gump's introduction, pulverizing the remains of the loaves of bread that still encircled his wrists. The bird crowd went wild, sailing in and out and making off with enormous crusty chunks. "Do Ashbless now!" the Squire shouted, clearly under the impression that Gump's recital of the title had constituted the poem itself. "Do Ashbless! The one about the layer cake. The Squire wishes to hear the poem about the layer cake!"

"It wasn't a layer cake," Bufo said a bit crossly. "It was about a loaf of bread. Bread and starvation. Ashbless doesn't write about layer cakes."

"Nor do we," Gump added.

But the Squire wasn't so easily put off. "Bread!" he cried, remembering. "Someone's been at mine." He took a long look at his breadless wrists, wondering how they'd come to be in such a barren state. "Could you give me the loan of a layer cake, my good fellow?" he asked Jonathan, turning around in his saddle and nodding.

Jonathan held his palms out to his side and shrugged. "I haven't got one, Squire. But the next layer cake I run across will be yours."

The Squire blinked at him for a moment. "Why will you run across the Squire's layer cake? It'll ruin it." He shook his head sadly, thinking of his ruined cake.

"Squire," Bufo said. "There *is* no layer cake. Tonight we'll have one though. A cake twenty feet high!"

The Squire looked at Bufo in amazement. "That's impossible," he said. "But I have a hippo head on call in town. We'll eat it."

"Good," Bufo said.

"About the hippo head," said Gump slowly to the Squire. "What would you say to a good wildebeest head instead?"

"Say to it?" the Squire asked. "What did it say to me? What kind of a beast?"

Bufo shouted at the two of them to shut up, then himself recited once again, "Poor Squire Found!" in a loud voice. He launched immediately into the final stanzas of the poem that he and Gump had begun several days before and which had ended with the Squire aimlessly trudging through Balumnia.

> "Until at last the Squire comes
> Tramping into Boffin Bay
> And there he finds the frowning Dwarf,
> Necromancer, wild dismay!

> "But when they grasp the jolly Squire
> Terror strikes the region wide
> They cry, 'the Squire, the Squire is come!'
> And flee away on every side.

> "For who dare touch his copious form,
> His arm is withered at the root.

> *Goblins, ghouls all howling flee*
> *And every tree does sprout with fruit.*
>
> *"Then as he eats and drinks he grows*
> *Stouter and stouter every day.*
> *His friends all weeping find him thus;*
> *Their salty tears they wipe away.*
>
> *"And so they ride in glory there,*
> *By the sea, along the road.*
> *The Squire found, they journey home,*
> *And all is done as I have told!"*

Everyone cheered frightfully at that. The heroic sound of it even pulled Jonathan out of his slump.

"A masterpiece!" hailed the Professor.

"Shouldn't that last line read, 'all is done as *we* have told'?" asked Gump.

The Squire began thundering out applause right then, however, interrupting Gump's complaining. "Every tree sprouts with cake!" he sang, then paused and turned to Bufo. "What went next?" Bufo seemed to have a hard time answering. "All the land did sprout with cake!" the Squire continued, caught up in the spirit of poetry, "and the Squire ate and ate and ate!"

Bufo and Gump looked at each other sadly. But the Squire was the Squire, after all, and it *was* his poem. So the two linkmen seemed to agree silently that he could pretty much do anything with it he liked, and the company tramped across the bridges toward Landsend, not nearly so thoroughly dismayed as they had been a mile back.

The clammers and the crabbers were out again, setting traps and mucking along the mud flats. It hadn't been much more than forty-eight hours since Jonathan and the Professor had passed them two mornings since, but to Jonathan it seemed like weeks. The phenomenon reminded him that it quite likely *would* be weeks before he saw his home again. Months maybe. The effects of the poem began to wear away bit by bit. The galleon still stood out to sea, and seemed to Jonathan to embody the spirit of movement, of being homeward bound. That made him very sad because he knew that all the sailing ships in Balumnia wouldn't do the lot of them a bit of good.

They crested the longest bridge and trudged down the far side. Jonathan heard a shout from below, from one of the clamdiggers perhaps. Then there was an answering shout and a man farther up the shore suddenly cast down his clamming fork and went running in the direction of the sea, disappearing under the bridge.

The Squire trotted his horse over to the edge, bent out over the parapet and waved. The rest of the company followed him, curious at his waving and at the shouting of the people under the bridge. What they saw was Theophile Escargot shoved up through the hatch of the bobbing submarine, waving back at the Squire.

"Need a lift?" he shouted at them, then laughed slowly, "Har, har har," relishing his gag.

There was a wild dash for the foot of the bridge, Miles bouncing and grimacing on his sledge. Escargot seemed to be in something of a hurry. He relaxed a bit when the Professor told him that the Strawberry Baron had turned inland on the road to Grover, but he didn't relax much. He was obviously more fearful of the Baron than he'd let on to Zippo.

Sliding Miles down the hatch was tricky, but not impossible, and in the space of ten minutes they'd given their ponies to the flabbergasted clammers and had boarded the submarine and cranked down the hatch.

It all happened so quickly that Jonathan found himself, almost by surprise, sitting on a leather cushion before a porthole with Ahab curled up beside him, the two of them on their way, in effect, to Twombly Town.

Outside the porthole the sea went silently about its business. A great fish, almost as long as the submarine, loomed up out of the depths and glided by, peering in, wondering at them. Trailing seaweeds grew from the rocks below and rose toward the surface that lay like an undulating sheet of glass on the water above. Jonathan watched in wonder as a great red kelp snail worked his way slowly across a brown leaf not three feet from him, off, perhaps, to visit a friend. The water swirled and bubbled outside, and lights blinked on around the nine weary travelers. The submarine heaved forward and fell away into the deep, passing out of the mouth of the Tweet river, angling down through sunlit grottoes of towering kelp and schools of silvery fish toward the western door, the land of chambered nautili and sea shell treasures.

Epilogue

❈

I N the end it *was* weeks before Jonathan saw Twombly Town again, what with the voyage out of Balumnia and the journey across the sea from the Wonderful Isles. The submarine stopped at Seaside where Miles the Magician was entrusted to a stout little doctor with a red beard, and then bubbled its way as far up the Oriel River as Escargot dared take it. There Dooly and his grandfather parted company with Jonathan, Professor Wurzle, Ahab, and the linkmen and sailed away to resume their pirating. The rest of the company set out on dwarf ponies, and in a matter of four days found themselves once again at Myrkle Hall where the Squire's cook, as he had promised, made them up a bit of a feast. They ate around the clock, it seemed to Jonathan, for two days until none of them except the Squire could bear the thought of another peach pie or roly-poly pudding. During what little time they spent away from the table, Jonathan poked around through the Squire's marble treasure—uncountable marbles, oceans of them, that overran the cellars beneath Myrkle Hall. He filled a leather marble bag with the little orbs of rainbow glass to bring back as a present for Talbot.

Finally they set out, carrying their bundled ape and alligator suits, bound for home. They trotted into Willowood in just short of a week and in the first days of summer sailed away up the Oriel on Jonathan's raft, keeping to the far shore as they glided past the Goblin Wood, intending to stay as far away from adventure as they could.

Hightower Castle stood lonesome and rocky on the ridge above the fens. As they slid past on the river a mile or two away, Jonathan was struck with the sudden irrational idea that the high valley, somehow, hadn't seen the last of Selznak the Dwarf, that the pale smoke of enchanted fires would someday tumble up out of that stone tower once again. But that was foolishness. He was sure of it. The Professor said it was anyway. What *he* was worried about were the creatures that still lurked in the caverns there. It was even possible that in the weeks since the two of them had wandered through those caverns, Selznak had let a few more in through the door. But Jonathan, more out of general tiredness than anything else, was contradictory. He said that he, for one, was willing to let the monsters go on about their business. They were blind, after all, and they lived at the bottom of a pit. He couldn't imagine blue squids climbing one by one up little iron ladders. As for any other monsters having been let loose, that didn't seem at all likely. During most of the time they had spent in Balumnia, Selznak was out somewhere in the countryside. He hadn't reached his castle at Boffin Beach but a day or so ahead of them, hardly time enough to herd monsters from one land to another.

By the time they'd debated the issue there on the river, Hightower Castle had fallen steadily behind. And as it shrank in the distance it seemed to grow less threatening until finally it faded and vanished from both sight and mind.

Their journey ended in early morning when they rounded the last long curve of shore, and paddled into the harbor at Twombly Town, surprising Talbot, of all people, who was out checking trout lines. All the lines were empty except one, which had an old canvas shoe covered in water weeds hanging from it. Talbot threw the shoe back in, assuring Jonathan and the Professor that crayfish would use it as a house. Then he plunked his rubber cheeses back into the shady water beneath the dock.

The Professor set off through town toward his laboratory as Jonathan, Ahab, and Talbot struck out across the meadow for home. Talbot hadn't had any trouble with the cheesing, he said. Nothing to it. A cheese is a cheese, after all. But Jonathan, by then, didn't entirely agree with him. In fact he was itching to be back at it—to have a go at a couple of cheese ideas—cheeses that involved sage and oranges and brandy; he wasn't quite sure in what proportions yet. He knew though that he hadn't much desire to return to being a man of leisure. It struck him, in fact, that it's not so bad at all having work to do if you know you don't *have* to do it. Anyway he could go back to being a man of leisure whenever he wanted—say every other Wednesday—just to keep his hand in. And the same was true, in a sense, of being an adventurer. He'd found both occupations very nice in their way, but as he watched Ahab trotting on ahead toward the strawberry patch, off to see what his bugs had been up to, he was fairly sure that unlike cheesing, such occupations were easily worn-out.

ABOUT THE AUTHOR

Jim Blaylock lives in California with his wife Vicki and their two sons John and Daniel. He graduated from California State University at Fullerton with an M.A. in English. Now he writes and teaches and builds a perpetual room addition atop his house. Although he cannot claim to have worked for the CIA, to have depth tested submarines, won amateur chess tournaments, or mastered the martial arts, he was briefly envied along certain sections of the Southern California coast for owning simultaneously three octopi, two Columbian horned frogs, a pipa pipa, and one regretable Nylarlathotep. Beyond that he was a charter member of the Blake Society.

His first published novel was *The Elfin Ship.*